The Witch of Rose Cottage

The Ravenwood Trilogy Book II

Lora Deeprose

This is a work of fiction. Names, characters, places, and incidents are products of the author's imagination or are used fictitiously and are not to be construed as real. Any resemblance to actual events, locations, organizations, or persons, living or dead, is entirely coincidental.

World Castle Publishing, LLC
Pensacola, Florida

Copyright © Lora Deeprose
Paperback ISBN: 9781629896731
eBook ISBN: 9781629896748
First Edition World Castle Publishing, LLC, April 24, 2017
http://www.worldcastlepublishing.com

Licensing Notes

Cover: Select-O-Grafix
Editor: Maxine Bringenberg

DEDICATION:

For Bear, you are forever in my heart.

Thanks:

My thanks go out to my publisher, Karen Fuller, and the ever patient and talented editor, Maxine Bringenberg, for allowing me to continue with Lizzie's journey of discovery.

Much gratitude and appreciation to my sisters, Amy, Lisa and Tanya for their love and understanding throughout the years. And a very special thank you to my oldest sister, Cari, for her ongoing support both emotional and financial that has enabled me to pursue my curious life as a writer.

CHAPTER ONE

"Hello, you," Lizzie said as she slipped inside the abandoned stone cottage. She crept into the small foyer, her heartbeat thudding in her ears.

When she let go of the door it swung back on its own accord, blocking out the midday sun. Rusty hinges squealed in protest, stopping the door before it closed completely, leaving a small ribbon of lemon sunshine to play over the wide plank floor. Dust motes swirled in the band of remaining light.

Lizzie stood for a moment, her hand seeking out the gemstone cross she wore at her throat. Her fingers pressed against the familiar shape until the cold blue stone warmed under her fingertips.

She had dreamed of this place for months, except in her dreams she had never made it past the front door. Although the recurring dream had robbed her of her sleep and nearly her sanity, Lizzie had believed the dream was a vision leading her not to the cottage, but to the general location. A place she could face the demon hunting her while keeping the people she loved safe.

The dream had been right. She had flown across the country to the remote Kootenays, where she had destroyed the demon and wounded the warlock who controlled it. But never, not even in her secret heart, had it occurred to her that Rose Cottage could be real.

Lizzie stood just inside the doorway, afraid to breathe in case the cottage proved to be a creation of her overtaxed mind. Then all she would be left with would be the grief that constantly threatened to consume her.

She may have triumphed over the demon, but in the process she'd lost everything; her husband, her business, and her home. But it was the loss of her two friends and members of the Order of the Triple Goddess, Gideon and Madison, that completely hollowed her out. Only the elder of the order, Vivienne, had stood by her.

A faint blue light rolled across Lizzie's arms, the sizzle of electricity disturbing the quiet cottage. She flung her arms out, palms facing down, and closed her eyes. Taking a deep breath, she pushed her energy down into the earth, where it dissipated harmlessly. She remained standing with her eyes closed until the ache of sorrow, if not completely gone, was at least reduced to a dull throbbing in her chest.

"Sorry," she said to the empty air. "You and I have been waiting for each other for a long time, and this is not the proper way to say hello."

Focusing her thoughts on the house, she sent her energy out in gentle invisible waves until it touched the plastered walls, being careful not to extend her powers more than a few feet from her body.

Reaching out, she glided her fingers over the uneven plaster rendered over the stone walls, the undulating texture worn smooth with age. She sensed the house's reply as the slightest change in air pressure, as if the cottage had been holding its breath waiting for her, and upon her arrival, it relaxed into itself.

She found a light switch along the wall, but when she flipped it on nothing happened. But her eyes had already adjusted to the dimness, and she could make out the general layout of the space. The small foyer opened up into a well-proportioned room divided into a living room at the front and kitchen to the back. The living room was empty except for a large stone fireplace dominating the north wall.

There were two mullioned windows on the west wall of the living room, and two smaller ones opposite along the kitchen wall. Years of grime covered the rippled glass panes, filling the house with a watery light.

The only pieces of furniture in the cottage were a rocking chair snugged up to a cast iron stove on the wall dividing the kitchen from the rest of the house, and a small pine table standing in the middle of the kitchen floor. Lizzie made her way over to the table, her feet stirring up years of dust. It tickled her nose and she let out three violent sneezes that echoed off the bare walls.

A single candlestick sat on the middle of the table's worn surface, only a stub of candle remaining in the tarnished brass holder. She picked up the candlestick, comforted by the solid weight of it in her hand, the metal cold against her palm. She glanced around the wood stove and fireplace, but she couldn't find any matches.

She knew she could summon the fire element from the air and have the candle glowing within seconds. So much easier than rummaging around in the gloom for matches, but she wouldn't consider casting even such a basic spell. Any summoning or casting would leave her signature in the ether, like a homing beacon that anyone using magick, white or black, could trace back to her.

Although the order was confident that it was just a matter of time before they captured the warlock who wanted her dead, and that he wasn't in any shape to even attempt to find her, let alone use magick against her, she wasn't going to take any frivolous chances. Not when she had fought so hard to keep her loved ones safe. And not when she was standing in the cottage that felt like a promise coming true.

Sensing her surroundings with her energy wasn't risky. It was only when she used her magick to summon the blue-white orbs that could render a man unconscious or worse that she opened herself up to attracting unwanted attention.

Squaring her shoulders, she hunted through the kitchen cupboards and drawers. They were empty except for a sprinkling of ancient food crumbs, a few plastic spoons, and a collection of dead bug carcasses.

She'd been rummaging around in the cottage long enough that her eyes had adjusted to the gloom, and although she would have preferred the comforting glow of the candle to illuminate her way, she'd have to continue her exploration without it.

Before moving through the rest of the cottage, she turned in a circle to properly take in condition of the home. The house had to be at least a hundred years old, but someone had occupied it in the more recent past, as evidenced by the avocado green phone mounted on the wall and the white globes hanging from the kitchen ceiling. A bank of lower cabinets and drawers ran along the wall underneath the windows, with the sink placed in the center. Their plain painted fronts were yellowed with age and their hinges caked in rust. A section of the wall to the left of the window had lost some of its rendering, exposing the grey stone beneath.

She picked up the phone and wasn't surprised to find the line dead. Turning her back to the phone, she made her way to the kitchen window.

Leaning over the large apron-front sink she peered out the window, but the glass was so dirty she couldn't get a clear look at the back of the property. Using the sleeve of her coat, she rubbed at the greasy dust on the glass, but she only succeeded in smearing the grime making it harder to see out. She got the impression of a small yard overgrown with weeds, and spring wildflowers surrounded by a wall of trees.

Before leaving the kitchen, she tried the faucet and was rewarded by knocking pipes and the squeal of air through the open line. She spun the tap closed.

To the right of the kitchen was a mudroom housing a washer, dryer, and a fridge. A long wooden pole leaned against the wall beside the dryer. She was fairly certain by the design of the kitchen what decade the house had last been inhabited, but the brownish gold color of the fridge was a dead giveaway.

Possessing the wisdom not to open a fridge that had been unplugged for an undetermined length of time, she turned her attention to the narrow hall. The windowless corridor was so dark it took her a moment to see that the hallway was empty except for a threadbare carpet running down its length.

The exterior of the cottage had boasted a row of windows on the second floor, so Lizzie knew there was a space above her, just no apparent way to access it. She squinted up at the ceiling, but without the aid of a light she couldn't make out if there was an opening above that would give access to the second story.

Only two rooms led off the hall. The door to her immediate right, closest to the kitchen, revealed a small bathroom. After a cursory glance at the claw foot tub and small sink, she headed towards the last door at the end of the hall.

Half way there, Lizzie walked through a cold spot. The sensation only lasted for the brief seconds it took for her to walk through it, but it was strong enough for her to break out in goose bumps and register a feeling of desolation so strong she cried out in surprise.

She turned back to face the area she'd just stepped through, her heart thumping. She was curious as to what had caused such a sensation, but she had no desire to feel the numbing despair again, especially without the comfort of a flashlight or candle.

Gathering her courage, she tiptoed towards the spot. There

was no longer a coldness, but she knew she was in the right place from the way the hairs on the back of her neck stood up. Taking a deep breath let her energy spool out into the gloom. She felt nothing but the cottage's own distinct and homey energy.

She closed her eyes and furled out her energy just a little further. She picked up a glimmer of something, more of a faint pulse but no emotions. As hard as she tried, she couldn't pinpoint whether it was coming from above or below where she stood.

A migraine gathered behind her eyes. Although physically healed from what the demon had done to her, her ability to use her energy hadn't quite returned to normal. Reluctantly, she pulled in her aura and sank against the wall as a wave of nausea washed over her.

Up until finding the cold spot in the hall, Lizzie had only felt a deep peace emanating from the cottage. In the months of dreaming of Rose Cottage, it had become hers. The sight of it sitting abandoned strengthened her conviction it had been waiting for her, that it would be a safe and comforting home where she could start her new life.

Finding an energy in the house strong enough to emit such sadness was disconcerting.

Her migraine intensified despite returning her energy to its normal state, the sharp pain pounding behind her eyes. Pushing her powers so soon after her injuries wasn't the smartest thing to do. She could hear Gideon's gentle scolding not to tax herself. If he were with her, he would have put a gentle hand on her brow, and using his own skills taken away her migraine and guided her to withdraw her energy to a safe distance. But he wasn't here. By his own choice he had abandoned her. She wasn't sure what was worse; how hurt she felt by his continued silence or how much she still missed him.

Backing away from the strange area, she carefully made her way to the door at the end of the corridor. The floor rose up slightly and she stumbled over the threshold and into a room washed in sunlight. Shielding her face with her hand, she blinked, waiting for her eyes to adjust to the brightness.

When she lowered her hand a spacious bedroom greeted her, complete with a stone fireplace mirroring the one in the living room in both shape and size. The previous owner had installed french doors on the wall facing the backyard, flooding the room with sunshine despite the filthy condition of the glass. Unlike the horrible light fixtures and Formica countertops in the kitchen, she approved of this change to the original floor plan.

Lizzie wrestled with the french doors, finally wrenching one side open, bringing a rush of crisp April air into the stuffy room. Stepping out onto the back veranda, she took a deep breath of cleansing air. Her headache eased slightly, but as she stepped off the porch, her legs wobbled and bright pinpricks of light danced before her eyes.

She hung onto the porch railing until the stars disappeared from her vision and she could continue on through the yard. Looking back at the house, it was clear by the clapboard siding on the mudroom that the space had been a later addition to the carefully laid stone of the original walls of the cottage. It jutted out from the middle of the house, cutting the back veranda in two, creating private covered decks off the master bedroom and the kitchen.

She stood in a small overgrown clearing that ended a few hundred yards from the house, where the forest took over. A three-sided shed stood to the right of the house. Lizzie guessed it was probably used to store wood.

She wandered around the side of the house following the faint remains of a well-worn footpath, then past another wooden structure, this one having four walls and a door. It wasn't much larger than the woodshed.

She was already feeling more herself; her legs solidly

underneath her, her vision clear by the time the path led her through a small meadow ending near the front of the property at an enclosed garden.

When she'd first arrived she hadn't noticed the garden plot, as the approach to the cottage was lined with pine and cedar trees completely blocking the view of the meadow and garden.

Although no loving hand had tilled the soil in some time, it was clear by the large raised symmetrical beds that this was once a vegetable garden. Native plants she didn't recognize had already sprouted and taken over where once rows of lettuce, carrots, and potatoes would have grown. Remnants of wire tomato cages and a wooden A-frame trellis for growing peas or beans had been left to rust and rot. The familiar four-square layout of the beds reminded her of the walled garden of her childhood home in the cloistered convent.

Swinging the wooden gate open, she ambled along the weed infested pathways. Her feet sunk into the ground, still soggy with the spring melt, leaving footprints in her wake that filled with small puddles of water seeping up through the saturated ground. Out in this little patch of garden the air smelled curiously of dill...tangy, fresh, and green.

Growing up tending the convent's gardens and her years of working in her flower shop had made her familiar with a variety of plants and flowers. But as she scanned the beds, looking for any small shoots of dill, not only could she not spot the common herb, she was also surprised that she didn't recognize the assorted native plants poking their heads up through the sodden muck.

With a contented sigh, she stretched her arms up to the sky. Before coming out here she had been confined to a hotel room for her own protection. She didn't resent Vivienne or the order for insisting on the arrangement, but for almost three months she had been without fresh air, flowers, or sunshine. She was almost giddy with the prospect of owning the cottage, of creating a home for herself in such a wild green place. To spend the day digging in the soil of this sad little garden, to bring it back to life and to feel the warmth of the sun on her shoulders as she dug her fingers into the coolness of the soil, filled her with a sweet, clear, resonating joy.

She was tempted to open herself up again to feel the energy in the land, but she'd learned her lesson during her exploration of the house. She was alone in the middle of nowhere with no cell service, and no one knew where she was. She had taken some huge risks over the last few days; given away almost all her possessions and wealth, stolen off without telling anyone to face the evil that had been threatening her and the people she had come to care deeply about. Now that her ordeal was over and Vivienne, Gideon, and Madison were safe, she wasn't about to start living on the edge just for the fun of it.

It was in her nature to be cautious. She'd been so careful with her life and her business. She had tried to make it work with her late husband, to overlook his drinking, his heavy hand, his inability to keep a job. She'd tried so hard to keep it all together, to keep the bad things from happening, to pretend she was normal. But the bad things had found her anyway.

Cautious. The word made her laugh aloud, startling a squirrel in a nearby tree. He scolded her for her outburst. Just this afternoon, when she recognized the road she was driving on as the exact one from her dreams, she hadn't shown much caution racing over the speed limit on a narrow mountain road. Nor did she show any sense when, after discovering the gates to the property were padlocked, she'd scaled the stone wall to gain entry, heedless of the thought of who she might encounter on the other side. Perhaps the last few months had changed her more than she realized.

After all she had been through, the one thing she knew for sure was to trust her intuition. And every fiber of her being told her this place was where she needed to be, and that the cottage had been waiting for her to take her rightful place behind its walls.

She thought of the cottage as hers already, but in truth she was trespassing. Yes, she had found an old for sale sign lying among the leaf-strewn ground when she'd jumped down into the property, and the cottage was clearly abandoned. But she had no idea if the place was still on the market or how much it would cost, or if she could even afford to buy it having given most of her belongings away before coming out here.

"I'll be back soon, I promise," she said, latching the garden gate behind her and circling around to the driveway.

Halfway down the tree-lined drive the sharp crack of a snapping twig made her wheel around to face the sound. Raising her hands, she prepared to throw a ball of energy at her attacker. A branch swayed to her right and she shifted position, bending her knees as a deer broke through the curtain of trees. It stopped short when it saw her, its liquid brown eyes wide with fear. The deer bounded off in the other direction, crashing through the trees as fast as it could go. She lowered her trembling hands, withdrawing her energy.

She thought she had overcome her fear, but she'd misjudged her state of mind. More than ever she longed to make a life here in the quiet solitude of the forest. She obviously needed some time to regain a sense of peace, and she knew the cottage would help her heal.

Taking her time scaling the wall, she placed her feet carefully on the stones and then eased herself up and over the rough surface, so as not to repeat her early spill when she climbed over it the first time.

She landed solidly on her feet on the other side. Back in her rental car, she maneuvered it around the narrow dirt road and headed back towards the village, intent on dropping by the realty office advertised on the sign she'd found.

A staccato drumming of a woodpecker on the hollow wood of a dead tree echoed through the lonely forest as she drove away.

CHAPTER TWO

"I didn't expect to hear from you so soon. How was the broom-maker's shop?"

"I found it, Vivienne. Rose Cottage, it really exists."

"How astonishing. Was it near the broom fellow's place?"

"No, I never made it to his studio. I got lost heading out there, and when I stopped the car to turn around, I recognized the bridge from my dreams. I knew exactly where I was going and I found the cottage. I wanted to call you as soon as I found it, but there's no cell service out there."

"What's it like?"

"It's a sweet little place. Although, it's not in the same condition as we experienced in the *In Between* or in my dreams. It looks like it's been abandoned for at least a decade, if not two. Nothing a little TLC won't fix."

"I can feel how much you love it already. I can sense the house too…it wants you to love it back to life."

The first time Lizzie had met Vivienne wasn't in person, but on another plane of existence called the *In Between*. Vivienne had risked her life to bring Lizzie back after Lizzie's spirit slipped over to the other side.

Since their experience in the *In Between* they had shared a unique emotional bond that went beyond mere friendship. They could feel each other's emotional state and even read each other's thoughts, although both refrained from doing so.

"I can't wait for you to see it. But, I'm getting a little ahead of myself. I'm not even sure it's up for sale, and if it is how much it's on the market for."

"The fact that you found it abandoned seems like a good sign."

"I agree. I'm actually sitting outside the realty office as we speak. I'll let you know what I find out."

"Sounds good."

Lizzie hung up with a promise to call Vivienne as soon as she knew more details.

The realty office was near the end of Broadway, the main and only business street in the small village. Like the other buildings on the block, it was painted a cheery color, the clapboard siding on the squat little building sporting a vibrant apple green coat of paint. Detail sheets listing properties for sale were taped to the large plate glass windows. A cursory glance revealed Rose Cottage was not among the listings.

Before stepping inside the office, Lizzie paused to look down the street. It was a sunny Friday afternoon, but the sidewalks were all but empty. She had gleaned from the few merchants she had come across when she first arrived in the village that it was a tourist town dependent on summer vacationers seeking distractions such as fishing, hiking, camping, and heli-skiing in the winter.

Spring meant the village was in between the two money-making seasons, but even still, the town seemed deserted. The only place showing any liveliness was the coffee shop a half a block down, but even there the trickle of customers seemed feeble to her eyes. Her little flower shop in Toronto could boast more business on her quietest day in her slowest month.

A pang of regret bubbled to the surface as she pushed on the door to the realty office. She missed her thriving little shop.

Watching it burn to the ground had pushed her over the edge and brought her into contact with the Order of the Triple Goddess.

Her life had circled around from finding a family inside the order to being alone again. Perhaps finding the cottage was a chance to start something new, to begin again in a place that didn't know her or what she was capable of. To leave the past and the pain that resided there behind her.

A fresh start. Yes, this was what it felt like to her. She may have found herself alone again, but this time it felt different.

With a growing sense of resolve, she entered the office intent on buying her cottage.

CHAPTER THREE

Inside the office, a young woman sat at a high counter flipping through a fashion magazine. The small interior was tidy, but it looked like it had been a long time since anyone had updated the wooden counter or the battered metal desk and filing cabinets.

The young woman looked up from her magazine, a pleasant smile warming the features of her plain face. Her chestnut hair was pulled back into a ponytail; her bangs, cut in a severe line across her forehead, highlighted her large doe-like eyes rimmed in too much black eyeliner.

They exchanged pleasantries and introductions. The young woman was called Bernadette.

"But everyone calls me Birdie," she said, sliding the fashion magazine under the counter. "Were you looking for a summer rental or properties for purchase?"

"For purchase, I think," Lizzie replied, fingering the buttons on her coat.

"Just let me get some particulars so we can narrow down what's available." Birdie grabbed a note pad and pen. "Are you and your husband looking for an investment or vacation property?

"No, no, I'm not married," Lizzie stammered. Birdie's assumption took her by surprise and she'd blurted out her answer without thinking. She was about to correct her statement, to tell this stranger she had indeed been married but was now a widow. Would it matter to Birdie that Ian had been abusive, immature, and a thief? Would she care if she heard he'd died in a horrible traffic accident a mere three months ago?

Lizzie opened her mouth to tell the truth, but the young woman continued on as if Lizzie's marital status was of no big importance.

"Something in town perhaps? We have some lovely lakefront condos available."

"Actually, there is a specific place I'm inquiring about. I came across a cottage about thirty minutes south of town just off the highway on Quail Hollow Road. There was a 'For Sale' sign on the property, but from the looks of things no one has lived there for a while. I was just wondering if it is still on the market."

"Oh, you must mean Grey House." Birdie put down her pen.

"Grey House?"

"That's what we call it around here. Because of the color of the stones.

"You know it then?"

"Yeah, everyone knows about Grey House. It's kinda rare to find a stone building out here. People tend to build log cabins or timber-frames because they're cheaper and easier to build."

"So, is it still on the market?"

"Are you sure there isn't something else you wanted to look at? The condos I mentioned are move-in ready, and you don't have to do any upkeep, just enjoy the scenery. Or maybe you'd be interested in a new listing that just came in for a spectacular post-and-beam with an amazing view of Saddle Mountain."

"No, the only property I'm interested in is Grey House." She'd almost called it Rose Cottage. Grey house didn't suit the cottage at all. "So is it for sale?" Lizzie asked, gripping the edge of the counter.

"I suppose it is. It's just that it has been empty for as long as I can remember. Let me just check." Birdie slid a large binder across the counter and began flipping through it, the only sound in the office the flutter of paper. "Well, it's not in here. Could the sale sign be from another agency? There's a couple of realtors in Castlegar and Nelson who sometimes take listings for this area."

"No, the sign definitely said Barton Realty. It looked like it had been there awhile though, and it was lying on the ground."

"Mmm. If the sign's ours, we have to have the listing somewhere or it was pulled off the market. Either way, I should have the paperwork that would tell me." She blew an exasperated breath, ruffling her bangs.

"It may be abandoned, but I noticed the chain and padlock on the front gate looked brand new, so surely, even if it's not currently for sale, there must be someone I can talk to about it."

"Sorry, I've only been here a week. I mean, I'm qualified. I got my realtor's license last month, but I haven't had time to familiarize myself with all our listings."

"Is there someone else I could speak with, maybe another realtor?"

"There's just me and the owner. He's out of town right now, and I don't expect him back for another week."

"I suppose I could wait until your boss gets back."

"No, no. I can figure this out. Just let me think," she said, tapping a pen absently on her front tooth. "If our hard-copy is missing from the binder and it's still an active listing, it might be in the MLS database." She glanced over at the clunky computer monitor on the desk. "I have to fire up the computer and then get on the Internet. We only have dial-up so it could take a while. Did you want to go for coffee or something? I'll call you if I find anything."

Lizzie gave Birdie her cell number and the name of the cabin she was staying in at the resort before leaving the young realtor to continue her search.

Lizzie had no idea what to do with herself while she waited for Birdie's call. She wasn't hungry and she wasn't tired. Nervous energy bubbled inside her. She had found the cottage of her dreams. It had been waiting for her, and all she needed was to make it legally hers. Even this small delay was driving her nuts. What she wanted to do was drive back to Rose Cottage, but then Birdie wouldn't be able to reach her on her cell.

She thought about calling Vivienne back and asking the order to help. Over the short time she'd been taken under the care and protection of the order, Vivienne had offered on a couple of occasions to aid with legal and financial matters Lizzie faced with the death of her husband and the destruction of her flower shop. Both times Lizzie had declined, but this time she was tempted to ask Vivienne for her help. The order had a vast network of people, resources, and money. She had no doubt they could have this resolved in minutes.

She started to pull out her cell from her purse when she sighed and dropped it back in. She needed to get a hold of herself. Rose Cottage had been waiting for her for a long time...it wouldn't kill her if she had to wait just a few more hours. The order had better uses for its resources than helping her buy a house. There were hundreds of women who needed the order's protection and a safe place to turn to.

Less than a week ago she'd thought she would be sacrificing her life when she faced off with the demon, and now not only had she succeeded, she had the rest of her life to start over again. The one thing she had an abundance of was time. She had no business to run or friends who needed her, except Vivienne, and she really didn't need Lizzie.

She turned away from the realty office and followed a side street down to the waterfront. Wandering towards the marina, she noted a few pleasure crafts moored at the docks. The rest of the slips were occupied by fishing boats and a small tugboat. There was only one soul on the dock, an elderly man, his shoulders stooped with age. He was unloading a rod and tackle from his boat. She turned away from the marina and walked down to the shore just as he heaved a large cooler onto the dock.

At the water's edge, a brisk wind caressed the dark water rippling the surface. The sky was cloudless and the sun sparkled off the water, creating dazzling points of light on its rough surface.

Pulling her collar up against the wind and shoving her hands into her pockets, she trudged through the wet sand. Her fingers curled around the leather medicine bundle she carried in her coat pocket. Stroking the soft deerskin of the pouch, she felt the objects inside shift under her probing fingers. The medicine pouch was a gift from Gideon. He'd made it especially for her.

She wondered where he was. She wondered if he was still on suspension and working in the order's archives, or if he'd gone back to guarding another woman with magickal talents. She'd once been his charge. He had saved her life more than once and she'd come to rely on him, not just as her guardian but as her friend. More than a friend. And now he was gone. All because he'd kissed her. Kissed her and was caught breaking his sacred vow not to be intimately involved with a charge.

Vivienne had told her she suspected her son had done so to ensure he would no longer be a guardian, a job he never really wanted to do in the first place. Vivienne's words had hurt, hurt because Lizzie suspected they were true. Gideon hadn't contacted her since then, reinforcing Vivienne's suspicions. Lizzie wasn't sure which hurt most, missing him or feeling used.

She was pulled out of her thoughts of Gideon when the sandy beach ended abruptly at a rocky outcrop jutting into the water. The large jagged rocks were impassible. She had walked the length of the beach without noticing the beauty of her surroundings or the distance she'd traveled.

Her nose was running and her ears stinging from the cold

despite her upturned collar. Electing to walk back to her car along the main street and away from the wind that whipped across the choppy water, she backtracked a few yards to the concrete steps leading up to a public promenade. She was out of breath by the time she climbed the steep steps to the small grassy boulevard separating the sidewalk from the houses that enjoyed a view of the lake.

The walk, fresh air, and sunshine did little to alleviate her somber spirits. If anything, she felt more out of sorts. She wanted nothing more than to go back to Rose Cottage and start making it her own. To scrub away the dirt on the windows and let the sunshine flood into the snug rooms of the cottage.

Even after such a quick survey of the house she knew bringing it back to life would take a great deal of work and money. She had one ruby left from her inheritance. Surely once she'd exchanged it for cash, it would be enough to bring the cottage back to life the way she envisioned it, and she'd still have a tidy sum left over. The idea appealed to her enormously. Her thoughts and energy could be totally and completely immersed in such a daunting project. No time to dwell on the past if her time was taken up with the cottage.

Hurrying along the promenade, she took the first side street back onto the shops of Barton's high street. As she passed the shops, she noticed quite a few were closed and dark, the hours posted on the doors indicating they were closed until the beginning of the tourist season, still a month away. The few stores that were opened seemed to close on Mondays and Sundays, and none seemed to stay open past six in the evening. It was like stepping back in time.

Her years living in Toronto had her used to a bustling metropolitan city, open for business twenty-four seven. Maybe not being able to shop whenever one took a notion wasn't such a bad idea. The village, on first impression, did seem to be a sleepy sort of place. Perhaps it came to life a little more when the tourists descended upon it.

It took less than ten minutes to make her way back along Broadway to the realty office and her car. She thought to check in with Birdie before she left for the resort, just to see how the search was going, but when she pushed on the office door, it wouldn't budge. Puzzled, she looked up and noticed a hand written sign taped to the door.

Be back in a while, it said in a looping flowery script.

"Back in a while? How long is a while?" she muttered under her breath.

She was overcome with the urge to stomp her feet and howl in frustration right there on the street. Not that anyone would notice a thirty-five-year-old woman throwing a temper tantrum, because the street was deserted. She could feel her self-control slipping. The blue, stone cross she wore around her neck throbbed with power as the charm placed on it attempted to contain Lizzie's own magick.

Unclenching her fists, she forced herself to calm down. Destroying the realty office in a blast of blue light would not help her possess the cottage any sooner. Dialing down her powers, she channeled them into the ground beneath her feet.

She was about to climb into her car when she noticed the new and used bookstore next to the realty office was open for business. When she'd first passed by it, the interior of the store was so dark she'd mistakenly thought it was closed, but a small sign in the corner of the window announced that it was indeed open.

The one thing she couldn't live without was books. Sister Collette, the nun who had raised Lizzie, had instilled in her a love of the written word. Books were her constant companions, her solace, and right now, she needed to be soothed.

When she'd rushed across the country, arriving in the

Kootenay's to do battle with the demon, she took only what she needed for the confrontation. So for the first time in her life, she didn't have any books in her possession. She needed clothes too, but they weren't nearly as important as having books around her again.

The store had looked dark and closed up from the street, and inside it wasn't much brighter. Floor to ceiling bookshelves were crammed with used paperbacks. She'd always loved the smell of old books, but the store didn't have that glorious perfume she'd become accustomed to. Instead, the air smelled damp and dirty, like someone's unused basement.

There was no one at the front counter, so she followed the handwritten signs posted on the ends of the shelves until she found the section she was looking for. The few lights in the ceiling did nothing to push back the gloom. She had to put her nose up to the creased and worn book spines to make out the titles.

She knew she shouldn't get her hopes up, but she was disappointed all the same when she saw the meager selection of titles to choose from. Sliding a copy of *Pride and Prejudice* off the shelf, she ruffled the pages with her thumb, releasing a powdery sour smell. Nothing could replace the sheer beauty of the first edition Jane Austens she had once owned. The fire had destroyed them all. They had been all she had of her birth mother. One of the few touchstones to a woman she never knew.

She scooped up the only other available titles by Ms. Austen, *Northanger Abbey* and *Persuasions*, before heading down the aisle to look for the section on gardening.

As she rounded the corner of the romance section, a woman appeared out of nowhere. Lizzie let out a yelp of surprise, scattering her books on the dirty grey carpeting.

The woman harrumphed and took a step back as if Lizzie had spilled a bucket of swill instead of a few cheap paperbacks, and she was in danger of getting it on her scuffed brown shoes.

Lizzie quickly retrieved her purchases, but not before getting a whiff of dirty feet coming off the carpet. "Sorry," she stammered. "The sign said you're open, but if you're not I can come back later."

"No, no, the sign says we're open, that means we're open. And there's nothing I can do about it." The woman's dentures clicked as she spoke. "Are you done?" she barked.

"Yes," Lizzie said, unnerved by the woman's off-putting manner. The woman started to walk away.

I'm a demon slayer and I'm being intimidated by a grumpy old woman?

"Actually, no, I'm not. I was wondering if you had a book on native plants." She straightened up so that she towered over the squat woman.

"Over there next to the books on baseball." She pointed over to a stack of books near the display window.

Lizzie took her time looking over the two slim volumes she had to choose from. She could feel the woman's beady eyes boring into her back, but she refused to be rushed. Choosing the book that had color photos and detailed descriptions for each plant, she slowly walked to the front of the store and placed her four books on the wooden counter.

Silently the woman rang up her purchases, but when Lizzie handed over her debit card the salesclerk sneered at it.

"We only take cash." The clacking of her dentures punctuated her words.

Lizzie rummaged through her wallet and produced just enough cash to cover her purchases. As soon as the clerk handed over her receipt and change, Lizzie scooped up her books and made a beeline for the door.

Five days ago when she had arrived in Barton, her initial impression of the village had been a positive one. Granted, she'd only visited a handful of stores, but everyone had been pleasant if a little reserved. The women in the bookstore left her feeling annoyed, and Birdie, although friendly enough, had yet to be of any help to her.

Her frustration slipped another notch closer to anger when she saw the note still taped to the realty office. She tried the door anyway. It was still locked.

She could call up the elements as easy as breathing, possessed magick that could overpower a man twice her size, and had the skill to outwit a demon, but she possessed no special talent to make Rose Cottage hers right now.

As infuriating as it was to admit defeat, she got into her car, and after a quick stop at the grocery store to pick up a few staples to restock her kitchenette, she headed back to her cabin at the Halcyon Resort.

She was driving past the library, her mind bumping up against her aggravation with Birdie, when she spotted a phone booth on the corner of the street. There was nothing special about it—a completely ordinary blue and white phone booth with the Telus logo splashed across the side—but when she saw it, she was overtaken with a near manic urge to make a call. She didn't want to use her cell phone. She didn't want the caller to see her name in the call display and have the choice of letting it go to voicemail.

Without checking her rearview mirror or signaling, she swerved her car over to the curb, eliciting an angry honk from the driver behind her who had appeared out of nowhere. The driver gave her a one-finger salute before gunning his engine down the open street. Lizzie glared at his taillights as he disappeared down the road, then snatched her purse from the passenger seat and rushed to the phone booth.

The booth was such an old fixture that there was no slot to insert a phone card or credit card, and Lizzie had to rummage around in her purse for change. She pressed the receiver to her ear, the handset sticky with grime, as she punched in the number from memory with a shaky hand. The line rang once, just long enough for her to wonder what the hell she was doing.

"Lizzie?" Gideon's voice held a hint of irritation or surprise, Lizzie wasn't sure which. The fact that he knew it was her calling made her heart pound so painfully she clutched at her chest.

She sucked in her breath and slammed down the receiver. She pawed at the folding door but it wouldn't open. Panic rose in her throat and she could taste bile. In a flurry of frantic movements she pounded on the door, then pulled and pushed until the door folded back, releasing her as she stumbled wide-eyed onto the street and back to the safety of her car.

CHAPTER FOUR

In what plane of existence did she think calling Gideon would be a good idea? He wasn't her guardian anymore. By his own choice, he wasn't *her* anything anymore. And how naïve could she have been thinking that using a payphone would mean Gideon wouldn't know it was her calling? The order had at their disposal all sorts of high tech gadgets, and used them as often as they did magick.

Perhaps she'd suffered more than just physical injuries during her fight with the demon. How else could she explain such a boneheaded move on her part? She wasn't sure what was worse, her deep gut twisting embarrassment, or the hurt at hearing the flatness in Gideon's voice when he spoke her name.

She knew she hadn't made up what had taken place between them. She hadn't imagined the passion in his kiss and the desire she'd seen in his eyes. It was Gideon who'd been the first to cross the line between being her guardian and something more. He was the one who had broken *her* heart, abandoned her.

She drove blindly, blinking back tears burning her eyes. The highway was as deserted as the town, which was just as well because, in her growing anger, she heedlessly careened around the sharp corners, ignoring the narrow shoulders and sheer drops as she raced towards the resort.

All morning she'd fought back the edginess tightening her

shoulders and churning her stomach. She'd tried to blame her anger on Birdie's inability to find the listing, and on the crotchety sales woman in the bookstore, but they had nothing to do with her foul mood.

She was angry with Gideon. And she was pissed off at Madison too, now that she'd thought about it. She'd given Madison a job at the flower shop when she was nowhere near qualified, kept her on, and trained her. During the whole ordeal with the warlock, when Lizzie'd been kept in the hotel, the threat of the demon looming over her, she'd thought Madison was her friend. But she'd been wrong. She'd saved Madison's life, and instead of gratitude, Madison, too, had banished Lizzie from her life.

Her energy crackled along her body, the cross at her neck growing uncomfortably warm against her skin as the charm placed on it struggled to contain her powers.

She'd gone through hell, alone. She'd battled a demon, rid the order of imminent danger. But did Gideon or Madison even care? Neither one had tried to contact her to see if she was all right.

She gripped the steering wheel as she whipped around another sharp curve in the road, her knuckles white with rage.

Vivienne had taught Lizzie how to channel her energy during stressful situations so as not to cause harm to those around her, and to feel the emotions without becoming lost in them. But the dark part of herself wanted to let the rage build until it exploded out of her like shrapnel. She had no doubt the force of releasing her amped up power would engulf her car in a fiery explosion. What would it matter? The only person in danger would be herself.

Skin-prickling electricity filled the interior of the car as she felt a strange excitement at the thought of following through with it. As her rage-fueled magick began to build, the image of

Rose Cottage flashed before her; her cottage, her safe little place in the woods.

Swerving the car towards the shoulder of the road, she slammed on the brakes and threw the car into park. She missed colliding with the sheer rock wall that rose up from the edge of the road by mere inches.

Throwing her head back, she howled as she forced her energy down through her body and into the surrounding mountain. The car shuddered from the surge of energy before her power dissipated.

Her breath escaped in ragged gasps as she leaned her forehead on the steering wheel. She had a right to be mad at Gideon and Madison. And dammit, she had a right to be happy. And she would be.

She didn't need either of them. She would have her little stone cottage as soon as Birdie found the listing, and she would create a new life for herself...without Gideon or Madison. She didn't need them. She didn't need anyone.

With the back of her hand she wiped her tear-stained face, then put the car into drive and turned on her signal light. Weary from her spent emotions, she carefully shoulder checked before pulling back onto the highway.

For the rest of the drive she steered her thoughts away from darker places and focused on making mental lists. They included all the things that needed to be done to restore Rose Cottage into a livable home; an electrician to check the wiring; a plumber; the walls needed repair and replastering; the hideous light fixtures in the kitchen had to go; the phone needed to be hooked up; and the heat had to be turned on. She hadn't noticed a furnace in her walkthrough of the cottage. She wasn't even sure if the place was heated.

The lists kept growing. It would probably take her months to reveal the beauty of Rose Cottage. And she craved something as big as restoring the cottage to take her mind away from the things she'd lost.

She was so engrossed with what needed to be done to her new home, her earlier thoughts pushed safely away for the time being, she was surprised to find herself pulling up to the resort. She parked her car in the guest parking lot and quickly zipped in to the main hotel lobby to see if there were any messages for her. There weren't.

Instead of walking to her cabin, she opted to have the bellboy drive her up in the golf cart the hotel used to shuttle the guests staying in the cabins. Bone weary from her tirade in the car, her headache still lurking behind her eyes, she didn't feel like schlepping her grocery bags the uphill distance to her rental cabin.

As soon as she stepped inside her cabin she checked for messages, even though the message button on her phone wasn't flashing. Birdie still hadn't called. She blew out a sigh and glanced around.

The chambermaid had been through while Lizzie had been out; her bed was made and the fireplace had been cleaned of ashes and fresh kindling put in its place. She peered into the bathroom. Clean white towels replaced the ones she'd ruined with her own blood.

Only three days ago Lizzie had awoken in the forest not far from the cabin, weak and bloodied from her battle with the demon, soaked to the skin from the morning rain. With their extraordinary link, Vivienne had managed to reach out to her and helped her back to the safety of her cabin. Lizzie used the fluffy white towels to clean the deep gashes on her palm caused when the fluorite crystals she had been holding exploded into flesh cutting shards.

Flexing her fingers, she examined her palms. Only the faintest traces of scar tissue remained, crisscrossing her palms like the whisper of cobwebs. She padded over to the bathroom mirror, pushing her face as close as she could to the gleaming surface. Pulling her lower eyelids down, she peered at the whites. This morning they had been a sickly yellow, but even that had been an improvement to the blood that had colored them red and washed her vision in a blurred pink veil. Now they were white and healthy looking.

She may not know who her parents were, but they had gifted her with the ability to heal freakishly fast. Yes, she needed to fall into a comma-like sleep for three days for her healing to occur, and she awakened hungry enough to eat a horse, but it was a small price to pay in exchange for being able to bounce back from injuries that normally would involve a stay at the hospital.

Backing out of the bathroom, she retrieved the grocery bags from just inside the front door where she had dumped them. She slowly and meticulously unpacked her food, put the kettle on for tea, and placed her newly purchased books on the nightstand. That only ate up few minutes of her time, and still the phone hadn't rung.

She slipped the untraceable cell phone, given to her by the order, into its charger, then wandered aimlessly around the small cabin. It was chilly, and she contemplated starting a fire when there was a sharp tap on the window next to the fireplace.

"I was wondering if you'd come back," she said, heading over to the window and flinging open the sash, grateful for the welcome distraction.

A large raven hopped inside, ruffled its feathers, and cocked his head at Lizzie. The sleek black bird had shown up earlier that morning after Lizzie had awoken from her injuries. He had joined her in a breakfast of peanut butter on toast just hours before her discovery of Rose Cottage.

She had no way of knowing for sure, but she felt he was also one of the many ravens that had gathered in the forest as she prepared to face the demon. They had stayed, watching sentinel over her until the ordeal was over and she'd managed to get back to the safety of her resort cabin.

The kettle whistled, startling the raven. He spread his wings and cawed in agitation.

"Calm down, it's just the water for my tea," she said, taking the kettle off the stove. "I can't help but notice this is the second time you've showed up when there's food to be had. How does a nice butter tart sound?"

She took the raven's throaty chortle as a yes and busied herself with making her tea, placing two butter tarts she'd just bought on a small plate. She arranged their refreshments on the kitchen table, and before she could take a seat, the raven flew across the room on powerful wings and landed gracefully on the back of one of the chairs. Sliding the plate closer to the raven, she plucked a tart for herself, leaving the other for the bird.

Hopping down off the back of the chair, the raven waddled over to the plate, and with stern concentration made quick work of the dessert, scattering flakes of pastry all over the table.

Lizzie chuckled and took a delicate nibble of her own tart. The raven, finished with his meal, sidled over to her steaming mug and cocked his head to peer inside the cup.

"No you don't, that's mine." She slid her mug out of the raven's reach and got up to fill a small cereal bowl with water from the sink. "Here, try this," she said, placing the bowl directly in front of him.

She sat back down and sipped her tea as the raven dipped his beak in the water, sliding it across the surface then tilting his head back. His throat bobbed as he swallowed.

"If you and I are going to continue sharing meals together we should be properly introduced. I'm Lizzie Benett," she said, placing her hand on her chest.

The raven stopped drinking and turned its head so one of its black shiny eyes stared at her. A drop of water trembled on the tip of its beak.

"And what shall I call you? Poe?" The raven stared. "Okay, I agree...too obvious. William? No, you don't look like a William or Bill." Lizzie took a sip of tea as the two of them continued to contemplate each other. "Alistair? Finley? Duncan? How about Quinn."

The phone rang, startling them both. The raven flew off the table in a flurry of wings to the safety of the top of the fridge, knocking over the bowl of water and drenching her lap in the process.

Lizzie pushed back from the table, scrambling to get the phone and ignoring her now soaked jeans.

"Hello?"

"Hi, is this Lizzie Benett?" asked a young female voice.

"Yes, yes Birdie. What have you found out about Rose...Grey House?" Lizzie heart pounded like a kettle drum.

"Sorry it took me so long. I couldn't find it listed on the computer, so I decided to check our dead files. We store them in a vault in the basement. Well, we call it a vault, but it's just a creepy old room you can only access from the outside through the old coal delivery doors. It took me ages. That place is full of cobwebs and dust, but I found the file down there. Someone must have misfiled it."

Lizzie bit her lip to stop herself from screaming at Birdie to get to the point.

"Anyway, turns out the bank owns the house now. The last owner bought it back in...." Lizzie heard Birdie shuffling through papers. "Back in the seventies. Lived there until the recession in the eighties, when he stopped making payments and just walked away from the place. Then the bank foreclosed on the property and took it over."

"So does that mean it's still for sale?"

"Yeah, but I don't know the list price, because by the time I found the file the bank in Revelstoke was closed for the day, and they won't be open until Monday. I'll call them first thing Monday."

"Can we put an offer in as soon as we hear from the bank?"

"Didn't you want to look inside the cottage first? I don't have any showings booked for tomorrow, and it would be silly to buy a place without looking at it first."

"Yes, yes of course." She couldn't admit to Birdie she'd already been inside, and despite the sad condition of the cottage, there was no question in her mind that she wanted it.

"Does ten tomorrow work for you?"

"Yes, I'll see you at the cottage tomorrow then." All of her earlier frustration and nerves evaporated, and with a pleasant buzz of anticipation she set to work mopping up the water on the floor, humming a tune as she cleaned. The raven watched her from his vantage point on the top of the fridge.

CHAPTER FIVE

Lizzie arrived at the cottage before Birdie on purpose. She needed to see the place again by herself, even if it was just a glimpse through the wrought iron gates. She wanted to be certain the feeling of coming home that had been so strong yesterday was real, and not just a combination of relief and excitement at discovering that Rose Cottage existed outside the dream plane.

As she gripped the bars of the gate, flakes of yellowed paint fluttered to the wet ground. Pressing her cheek against the cold metal, she glimpsed the faint impression she'd left in the leafy debris just inside the stone wall when she'd fallen yesterday. Near where she'd landed on her backside, she could just make out the corner of the realty sign that had been hidden underneath the decaying leaves. The sign that had led her to Birdie's office.

Glancing up the sandy drive, she realized that the feeling was still there. The sense of coming home made her throat tighten. Growing up she'd felt safe with Sister Collette in the confines of the Abbey, but she'd never felt anything like this pull, like a siren's call to the land, to the decrepit little cottage hidden behind the trees. A bubble of laughter threatened to escape her lips.

That morning Lizzie had woken up to grey skies, and as she stood waiting outside the gates of Rose Cottage, a heavy mist descended from the mountain behind the property. It rolled down the mountainside, brushing the treetops as it moved down through the property. It languidly rolled down the packed-sand driveway and through the gates, engulfing Lizzie in a white shroud. The air within the mist was saturated with moisture, and as it passed Lizzie, she was left with droplets clinging to her hair and eyelashes. Even with the gray sky threatening rain, the damp weather couldn't dent Lizzie's mood.

At the sound of tires crunching on gravel, Lizzie stepped away from the gates, rattling the thick chain securing the gate as she let go.

Birdie parked her car on the shoulder behind Lizzie's rental, and as Lizzie walked over to greet her, a stab of worry prickled at the base of her skull. She hoped Birdie had brought a key for the padlock. If she didn't, Lizzie would suggest scaling the wall. She wanted a proper tour of the house and property, and she wasn't going to wait one more day.

"Good morning," Birdie said as she stepped out of her car. She was wearing a heavy plaid jacket over a tight black skirt that barely covered her thighs, and a pair of black Wellies with red rubber soles.

"Morning." Lizzie smiled at the curious fashion statement Birdie made, and wondered if her bare legs were cold in the chill air.

"I've got great news. My father's cousin is married to a woman whose youngest daughter works for the bank in Revelstoke. I had my dad make a few calls yesterday, and turns out she was still working late so she pulled up the computer file on Grey House and emailed it to me."

Lizzie gave her a quizzical look.

"I know, I know, it's not strictly on the up-and-up, but I found out what the bank wants for the house. Wait a sec." Birdie ducked her head back into the car and pulled out a slim manila file from the passenger seat. She was about to place the file folder on the hood of her car, but hesitated when she saw the droplets of mist beading the surface.

Lizzie reached out to snatch the folder from Birdie, but stopped herself short. She took in a deep breath and said, "So what's the list price?"

Birdie opened the file, balancing it precariously in one hand while she flipped through the papers, until she found the one she wanted. "The bank wants $359,000. That includes the house, the twenty acres it sits on, and several outbuildings." She snapped the file closed. "I know it's a bit pricey for this area, but it's sitting on quite a bit of prime land, and is fed by an exceptional gravity fed water source from the mountain right behind the property." Her hands bunched the folder, threatening to bend it out of shape.

"Twenty acres?" The size of the property was a surprise, but it was the price Birdie had quoted that captured her attention. Back in Ontario, a house of equivalent age and construction would go for over double the price, not including the land. She would have more than enough money to buy the house, undertake the renovations the cottage so desperately needed, and have a little left over. Lizzie wanted to grab Birdie by the shoulders and dance around. Rose Cottage could be…no, it *would* be hers just as she'd dreamed it would be.

"Did you still want to see the place? I completely understand if you wanted to go back to the office and look for something better priced," Birdie said, continuing to crush the manila folder in her nervous hands.

"Yes, of course I do."

"You do?" Birdie asked, almost dropping the mangled file on the wet road.

"Yes, I'd love to see the house and everything else that's on the land; that is, if you managed to get a key to the padlock."

"Oh, the lock. That is a curious thing. When I emailed my dad's cousin's daughter, she emailed me back saying there's no record of the bank securing the property and they don't have a key to the gate. But not to worry."

She stuffed the mangled folder in the oversized purse she carried, scurried to the trunk of her car, then pulled out a rather lethal looking pair of bolt cutters almost as tall as she was.

"This should do the trick," she said, expertly positioning the blades between the arm of the lock, and with a strength belying her tiny frame snapped the lock cleanly through. It fell with a dull thud onto the road.

While Birdie ran back to her car to deposit the bolt cutters, Lizzie slipped the chain from around the gate, letting it puddle on the ground, the chink of metal on metal filling the quiet morning. She pushed on the gate and it swung open on silent hinges, leaving flakes of paint clinging to her palm. She absently brushed her hand on her pant leg as another band of mist rolled down the drive and through the gates. For the brief moment as it caressed her face and hands, she felt the softest breath of warmth pass through her.

"Hello, again," she whispered. "I told you'd I'd be back."

"Did you want to drive up to the house?" Birdie asked, joining her inside the gate.

"No, I'd rather walk up if that's okay with you," she replied, already heading up the drive, leaving Birdie standing at the gates. The wet sand shifted under her feet.

"Sure, no problem." Birdie scrambled to catch up with Lizzie, retrieving the scrunched folder from her purse. She immediately began reviewing the pages within.

Lizzie ignored Birdie as she prattled on about the legal description of the land, information about the hydro line, and something called a gravity fed water system. All she wanted to do was run up the drive and go back inside the cottage.

As they rounded the driveway and the trees on either side fell away to reveal the cottage, Lizzie smiled.

"Oh, it's in worse shape than I remember." Birdie snapped

her mouth closed. "But nothing that a little TLC won't remedy," she added hastily.

"You've seen the place before?" Lizzie asked as she mounted the porch steps. She ducked to avoid the tangled canes of a climbing rose draped over the porch posts and zinc gutters. Water from the misty air beaded the soft green leaves and fat buds. One small pink rose bloomed, filling the surrounding air with its delicate ephemeral scent.

"Just once when I was much younger. All the kids in the village did it. At Halloween, you know."

Lizzie turned to look at Birdie, who was still standing in the driveway.

"As a dare. To see who would be brave enough to touch the handle on the door. Just silly kid stuff." Birdie was crushing the manila folder again.

"But why would the village children come all the way out here on a dare? Is it haunted?" Lizzie meant it as a joke, but by the look of panic on Birdie's face, she realized she'd hit on the truth.

Birdie looked down at her feet, her shoulders slumped. "I suppose you have a right to know the history of the place, and I wasn't trying to keep it from you." She looked up at Lizzie. "Oh hell, I was trying to keep it from you, but it's just a tall tale. You seem so keen on buying the place, and if you do, it will be my first sale." Birdie looked at her pleadingly.

"Not only your first sale, but a house your boss hasn't been able to sell. That would be quite a coup for your first run out the gate," Lizzie said from her position on the porch.

"I know as a realtor I'm supposed to disclose everything about the house's history. But because people think it's haunted, no one in town would think about buying it. And add to that its current state of disrepair, not even outsiders looking for a cheap vacation home would want it." Birdie's voice rose several octaves as she nervously danced in place in the driveway.

"So Grey House is haunted? By whom?"

"A witch." Birdie's nervous hands finally tore the manila folder in half. The sound of the paper ripping startled Birdie and she took a half step back from the house, staring at the two halves she now held in her hands.

Lizzie chuckled.

The house was owned by a witch. How fitting she should find out her dream house was once owned by a person very much like herself. In another time and place, she and all the women like her that the order protected would have been labeled as such. If anything, the information about the original owner made her want the house even more.

"You're not mad at me?" Birdie squeaked, stuffing the two halves of the folder into her shoulder bag.

"No. In fact, I have a confession to make as well. I snuck onto the property yesterday and went through the house."

"Yeah, I figured as much," she said.

It was Lizzie's turn to be discomposed. "How did you know?"

"I spotted our realty sign on the ground when we first came through the gates. The only way you could have read the sign was if you'd been on this side of the wall."

"You're right, but I didn't break into the cottage…it was unlocked when I tried the door. So you see, we both haven't been completely honest. And if you don't mention my trespass, I won't mention to anyone, including your boss, that you weren't forthcoming about the house's reputation."

At the mention of not telling her boss, Birdie relaxed and finally joined Lizzie on the porch.

"Why don't you give me the official tour?" Lizzie turned the handle on the door and was surprised to find the door wouldn't budge. "It's locked. I swear it wasn't yesterday." She tried the door again but it remained firm in its frame.

"Here, try this. My office still had the keys locked in our safe," Birdie said, retrieving an ancient looking skeleton key from the depths of her purse. "Maybe the door locked when you closed it."

"Yes, that's probably what happened." Lizzie took the key from her and slipped it into the keyhole. She gave it a hearty twist and was rewarded by the sound of the stiff lock sliding open. Lizzie pushed on the door, causing the stale air to waft out around them. Without hesitation, she walked over the threshold and into her beloved cottage for the second time.

CHAPTER SIX

Lizzie turned to ask Birdie more about the witch, but she discovered she was alone inside the cottage. She poked her head back out the door to find the young realtor still standing on the porch.

"Are you coming?"

Birdie nodded, and with reluctant steps entered the small foyer. Inside it was darker than when Lizzie had viewed it the day before, as the overcast sky didn't provide enough ambient light to filter through the dirty windows. She kicked herself for not thinking to bring a flashlight.

She was about to ask Birdie if she had one in her car when she heard a click behind her and a strong beam of light illuminated a broad swath in front of them.

"Oh, it's not as creepy as I thought it would be," Birdie said, holding a heavy black Maglite in front of her. She swept the flashlight beam to take in the rest of the space. "I'd pictured it looking different."

"You mean, sinister and spooky and full of cobwebs." Lizzie stepped further into the main part of the house, brushing at her hair as she stepped through a spider web hanging down from one of the darkened ceiling beams. "Okay, maybe the cobweb thing is accurate, but nothing a little cleaning won't fix. I thought you said you came out here when you were younger."

"Yeah, I did with a group of my girlfriends, but we chickened out and never made it past the first step of the porch. Besides, the dare is just to touch the door handle."

The two women wandered over to the kitchen table following the beam of Birdie's flashlight.

"Mmm," Birdie said, placing her shoulder bag on the kitchen table. "I know you've already been through the house, but I guess I should tell you the features. It's a good thing I pretty much memorized the detail sheet," she smiled sheepishly, glancing down at her handbag.

It wasn't the details of the stone and mortar of the place Lizzie wanted to know more about, but the witch who had lived there and why she was now supposedly haunting the place. She reined in her urge to ask the questions as she remembered how reluctant Birdie had been to come inside, and the last thing she wanted to do was scare her off.

Clasping her hands in front of herself, she smiled, "I'm listening."

Birdie cleared her throat and looked at a spot just to the left of Lizzie's shoulder. "As close as anyone can guess, Grey House was built sometime in the eighteen hundreds and is a solid stone construction using locally quarried stone. It's got 1,100 square feet, a story and a half with one bedroom and one bath, and includes two fieldstone fireplaces. It was probably upgraded sometime in the nineteen-seventies to include indoor plumbing, electrical, the woodstove, and the construction of the three-season porch off the kitchen."

"Why install the woodstove if there was probably an electric range here at one time, judging from the empty space in the kitchen that has an electrical outlet for a stove? Plus, there is the fireplace."

"Power outages," Birdie replied, her tone suggesting to Lizzie she should have known such basic things.

"So does the power go out a lot out here?"

"Not so much nowadays. But back then it would have, especially during heavy winds and winter storms. But you don't have to worry about that now…BC Hydro's really good at maintaining the lines. Now then, where was I?"

Birdie played the flashlight beam over to the fireplace and then the stove before pointing it to the kitchen cupboards. Birdie quickly swung the light away from the large patch of missing plaster. "Uhm, the floors are original wide plank fir. It would cost a fortune to install something like that today. Did I mention the water comes from a gravity fed system?"

"Yes, you did. But when I was here yesterday I tried the tap but it didn't work."

"Oh, the bank probably had someone come out ages ago to turn off the water and drain the pipes so they wouldn't freeze in the winter. You might want to think about installing a heat tape on the pipes as there is no central heating. And you need to call BC Hydro to get the power turned back on. The fireplaces and the woodstove should be enough to heat the house comfortably, but I guess you could install electric baseboard heaters if you didn't want to fuss with hauling in firewood. Oh, and you should have a chimney sweep clean and inspect the fireplace flues and the cook stove to make sure they are still in good working order. There's probably a few bird's or squirrel's nests up there. That is if you end up buying it."

"I still plan on making an offer, and I appreciate any suggestions on what I need to do to get the place in livable order. You mentioned the cottage has an upstairs. I assume there is a trapdoor or something, but it was too dark to see anything yesterday."

"Let's go look."

Lizzie followed Birdie down the dark pokey hall watching the realtor closely. Birdie didn't react to the spot on the floor where she herself had sensed the strange mix of emotions. Even with her energy pulled in close, Lizzie could still feel the slightest vibration coming from that point in the hall.

"See this?" Birdie shone the flashlight up at the ceiling, revealing a metal slot on its otherwise flat surface of a trapdoor. "That's where the stairs are. There should be a pole with a hook on it somewhere." She played the light around the empty hall.

"Oh, I think I saw it yesterday in the mudroom. The three-season porch, I think you called it."

Birdie disappeared to locate the pole, leaving Lizzie alone in the dark. The hair on the back of her neck stood up and she took a step farther away from the cold spot on the floor. She was just about to join Birdie in the hunt for the pole when the light from Birdie's torch lit up the hall.

"Here it is," she said, brandishing the pole in front of her. "This contraption wouldn't have been original to the house; there would have been a simple ladder propped up into the opening. The stairs are on a hinge and unfold when you open the door. Like this." She handed Lizzie the flashlight and inserted the hook end of the pole into the slot in the trapdoor. With one fluid movement she yanked the door open, dropping the accordioned ladder-like stairs a few feet below the ceiling. Going up on her tiptoes, she grabbed the lowest rung on the ladder and swung the contraption completely open.

"Isn't that ingenious?" Lizzie said, approaching the stairs and aiming the flashlight up into the dark hole in the ceiling. A faint perfume of dried herbs caught in her nose. "Do you think it's safe to go up?"

Birdie shook the stair with both hands and it didn't so much as move. "The treads look solid, the hinges holding. I think we'll be fine." As she spoke, Birdie backed away from the stairs to allow Lizzie to go up first.

Placing one hand on the rung of the ladder just above her

head to steady herself, Lizzie shone the light ahead of her as she climbed. She wasn't afraid, only curious to see what other delights the cottage had to reveal. A railing surrounded three sides of the trapdoor opening, and as Lizzie poked her head into the space above, she used the railing to pull herself up as she stepped off the ladder and into the loft.

The lingering smell of dried herbs and spices embraced her as she took a few steps away from the ladder to make room for Birdie, who scrambled up the ladder to stand as close as she could to Lizzie without physically touching her.

Lizzie panned the powerful beam of the flashlight around the room. The first thing she saw was the stone flue from the fireplace in the master bedroom below. It took up most of the west wall of the loft. The longer walls of the loft were punctuated with a row of windows placed low on the short walls, to accommodate the sharply sloping ceiling. In the space that was roughly the size of the kitchen and living room below stood a large canopy bed, its headboard centered in front of the fireplace chimney from the living room. The canopy of the bed just cleared the ceiling by a few inches, and a heavy woven carpet was pinned under the bed's massive legs.

"Wow, now that's a bed," Birdie said. Together the women walked over to inspect it. Although the bed itself was smaller than current standards, the solid frame and intricately carved posts added to its overall dimensions. All that remained of the fabric canopy were strips of tattered and moth eaten cloth of an indeterminate color, drooping sadly over the wooden ribs of the canopy frame. The lumpy mattress was covered in blue and white ticking stained yellow in several places, and sagged dangerously in the middle.

Lizzie ran her hand over one of the posts, the wood smooth and silky beneath her fingers. "How do you suppose they got this up here? There's no way this could fit up the small opening for the stairs."

"My guess is that it was constructed in pieces, each section brought up here, and the final assembly was done in place. Hand me the flashlight."

Lizzie obliged, handing over the flashlight to Birdie, who was already on her hands and knees pulling and pushing the musty mattress out of the way of the frame. A dank smell rose up, momentarily obliterating the more pleasant lingering aroma of herbs and spices.

"Phew, this mattress is moldy. I don't even want to think about how many mice are using this as their home," Birdie said.

Despite her position next to the offensive mattress, Birdie remained where she was, shining the light over the corners of the frame where the footboard met with the rails. "This is incredible! Look at these joints...they're mortis and tenon. Not a screw or nail in sight." She sat back on her haunches, looking admiringly at the bed. "This has to date back to the house. No wonder it's still here. You'd have to break it into pieces to move it out. Thank God the previous owners didn't have the audacity to destroy such a beautiful piece of craftsmanship."

"You seem to know your way around antiques."

"My aunt owns an antique store in Nelson. She hired me for a couple of summers so I could earn my tuition for my realtor's certification. I'm no expert, but I know enough to see this bed for what it is."

A soft rustling in the eaves behind them had Birdie springing to her feet. She swung the flashlight in the direction of the sound, at the same time jumping over to Lizzie's side, almost knocking her over in the process.

"What was that?" Birdie's shaking hand made the light bob and weave erratically along the eaves. Lizzie only had time to catch a quick impression of a small brown shape before it launched itself towards them. The air near Lizzie's head stirred and something caressed her cheek as it passed by.

Birdie shrieked and dropped the flashlight, and was about to bolt down the ladder when Lizzie reached out and grabbed her firmly by the shoulders.

"It's okay, there's nothing to be frightened about. We just scared a bird that was roosting in the eaves." When Lizzie let go of Birdie to retrieve the flashlight, Birdie grabbed a handful of the back of Lizzie's jacket. With the flashlight in hand and Birdie clinging to her, she pointed it to the top of the bed.

Perched on the canopy's frame was the smallest owl Lizzie had ever seen. It swiveled it dish-shaped head towards them, its claws clicking on the wood as it sidled out of the path of the light. Before it moved back into the shadows, Lizzie had enough time to register the owl had dark eyes.

"See, nothing to be afraid of. It's probably more scared of us."

Birdie let go of Lizzie's jacket but stayed close to her.

"I don't really like birds," she said, moving to stand behind Lizzie. "They kinda freak me out, especially owls, because they don't make any sound when they fly."

"But your nickname is Birdie?"

"Actually, it's my fear of birds that made the kids at school start calling me Birdie in the first place, and the name stuck. I've given up trying to get them to call me anything else."

"Just let me open a window so it can escape, and then we can go back downstairs."

"I don't think it's going to leave. I bet it's been living up here."

"No I don't think so." Lizzie shone the flashlight across the floor. "See, there are only a few bird droppings. If it had been living up here, the floor would be littered with them and we would have smelled it when we came up. The air just smells of dried herbs and dust. More than likely it came in through a hole in the roof and found itself trapped."

She walked over to one of the windows. Birdie followed,

keeping Lizzie between her and the owl. Bending down low to avoid banging her head on the steeply sloped ceiling, Lizzie handed the light to Birdie while she worked on opening the window. The window latch was stiff, but with some not so gentle effort on Lizzie's part, she managed to open the window wide enough to allow the tiny owl an escape route.

With that done, they made their way back downstairs; this time Birdie led the way.

"I'll head back upstairs before we leave and secure the window," Lizzie said as she watched Birdie fold up the stairs and with a firm push with the pole secure the trap door. "That was a beautiful little owl, but I've never seen one with dark eyes before."

"Dark eyes. It's got to be a barred owl, although it must be a fledging because it was awfully small. An adult barred is almost as big as a great horned. I think you might be right about it getting stuck up there; those owls prefer to nest in natural tree cavities, or sometimes they take over abandoned nests."

"For someone who says they hate birds, you seem to know a lot about them."

"It's always better to know your enemies," she said with a wink, her good humor returning now they were back downstairs and away from the owl.

Lizzie led the way into the final room on the tour, the master bedroom. Knowing the threshold was higher from her first visit, she made sure not to stumble over it and was just about to mention it to Birdie when Birdie tripped up the rise in the floor.

"Ouch," she said, hopping on one foot.

"Are you okay?"

"Fine," she said, looking back towards the doorway.

"I noticed that when I came through the first time. And the floor here feels and sounds different when you walk on it."

Birdie played the flashlight across the threshold, walked the perimeter of the room, then examined the stones on the fireplace.

She mumbled excitedly under her breath, then looked up at Lizzie, her eyes gleaming with excitement. "I'll be right back," she said, not waiting for Lizzie's reply as she raced back through the house. "I knew it, I knew it," she said, returning just moments later. Instead of sharing what she'd found with Lizzie, she stomped on the floors, nodding her head approvingly, and marched over to the french doors and flung them open, examining the frame.

"What is it?" Lizzie asked.

Birdie ignored her and started inspecting the ceiling, stopping at the far end of the room opposite the fireplace.

Lizzie could see what had caught Birdie's attention. The plaster work in the far portion of the ceiling didn't match with the rest of the room, as if it had been done by an inexpert hand, and seem to sit a little lower than the rest of the ceiling.

Birdie lowered the flashlight and faced Lizzie with a proud smile.

"Don't you think it's a bit odd that the bed was placed up in the loft if they had this bedroom down here?"

"I hadn't really thought about it. So if it wasn't used as a bedroom, what was it used for?"

"Oh, it was a bedroom of sorts, but what slept here didn't need a bed, or just a bed of straw at the most."

"Spill it. Remember, you're here to show me the details of the house, not drive me crazy."

"You are right about the floor sounding odd. If you look at the planks, they aren't the same as the ones in the rest of the house. Same type of wood and almost as wide, which would have cost a pretty penny even thirty or so years ago, but they're newer. Also, it's obvious the flooring in here is new by what's not there," she said, answering Lizzie's questioning look. "The patina, the dings and dents from years of wear."

"Okay, so the floor has been replaced over the old one, and

that explains why the floor is higher in here. What does that mean, and why are you so excited?"

"The questions are, why was the floor replaced, and what's underneath this one? Those are the important clues. The original floor is more than likely stone or brick. Then you add the fact the fireplace is also a new addition. Again, whoever did the work did a superb job at matching the one in the living room, but like the floor the stones are too pristine and the point work in the mortar is more refined than the original fireplace in the other room."

"I'm sorry, I'm still not getting it."

"This whole room has been renovated. The windows and the french doors are newer than the rest of the ones in the house, although the opening is original. But the clincher is this," she said, pointing to the uneven patch in the ceiling. "I bet my realtor's license that if I went back upstairs and checked, there would be evidence the loft was divided into two rooms. But I'm not going up there with the owl still lurking around."

"Now that you've pointed out all these things I agree with you about the room, but what was it used for before they renovated it into a bedroom?"

"A barn," Birdie said, a look of triumph on her face.

"In the house?"

Birdie nodded her head.

"You're telling me that when the house was first built they kept their livestock in the same building where they ate and slept?" Lizzie circled the room, trying to imagine the light airy bedroom as what is was originally used for.

"Yup, that's exactly what I'm saying. Where the french doors are would have been the barn doors, and I suspect that underneath the porch we'd find a stone ramp for the cows to get in and out easily. There probably weren't any windows in here at all, and that dip in the ceiling is where the hay chute would have been. I'll check later, but upstairs where the new stone chimney is now would have been the hayloft door. That's why the loft would have been walled up, to store hay, and the other half of the room was where the owners would have slept."

"But that's disgusting. Livestock in the same house as people?"

"No, it's not gross at all…in fact, it was all about practicality. You're here in the spring, but this area is in a snow belt. Can you imagine trying to get to your barn in the dark in the middle of a snowstorm? People have frozen to death mere feet from their homes because they couldn't see where they were going. This way, in the winter your cows are easily accessible no matter the weather…easier to milk them and feed them. In the summer, they would have been allowed to graze and stay outside all day."

"The owner lived with her cows. That sounds so unhygienic." Lizzie wrinkled her nose at the thought.

"It's not like they were allowed to wander around the whole house. There was a door separating the barn from the living quarters.

"I guess it makes sense if the winters are as brutal as you say. I just never thought about what it would be like out here in the winter."

"Oh geez, does this mean I just blew the sale? I'm always talking too much." A look of panic spread across her face. "My mom is right; my big mouth always gets me in trouble." Birdie's eyes glistened with tears.

Lizzie put her hand on her shoulder. "Don't worry, you didn't blow anything. In fact, I'd rather you told me what I'm getting myself into so I'm prepared. I'm still buying the cottage, but perhaps I should invest in some outdoor lights and a snow blower."

"Really?" Birdie asked, blinking back the tears still threatening to spill down her cheeks.

"Really. Now, you seem to know everything about this place,

so tell me all you know about the legend of the witch that lived here."

"I don't know anything about that," she said, backing out of the room.

"It's too late now, you've already told me she lived here. Now tell me how she died."

"You know, it's all a fable to keep us kids away from using the place as a party hangout. There's no truth to it."

"Either way, I want to know the story."

As they were talking, they had made their way back into the hallway. Birdie stopped just a few feet into the narrow corridor and turned to face her.

"The story, as I heard it, was that she lived out here by herself, so it makes even more sense why she kept her cows and probably a horse in the cottage. If you needed a love potion or wanted to hex your neighbor, she was the one to see. And of course she had to be consorting with the devil out here in the woods. Why else would a single woman live alone so far away from other people?"

Why else indeed, thought Lizzie.

"Which was bad enough, but they basically left her alone until one year an epidemic hit during the harshest winter ever seen in these parts, killing the young, the old, and the infirm. Then the following summer, a forest fire swept through the valley destroying orchards, farms, and even several houses just inside the village. By that point, the villagers needed something or someone to vent their frustration and anger on. And it didn't take long to blame her for all their misery."

"What did they do to her? Burn her at the stake? Stone her to death?"

"No," Birdie whispered. "They locked her down in her own root cellar until she starved to death."

"How horrid."

Birdie nodded. "It probably took the poor women several

weeks or more to die. Now, because of how she was treated, she haunts this house waiting for someone from the village to dare to cross her threshold, and if they do she locks them down in the root cellar to share the same fate she did."

"Has anyone?"

"What?"

"Been lured to their death by the ghost?"

"No, not that I know of, and I would have heard something. It's hard to keep secrets in this village. Besides, the story isn't true."

"So where is this root cellar?"

"I'm not sure. Usually they're located in the kitchen or the pantry, which is now the bathroom. But I didn't see any trapdoors in the floor of either room, so maybe the house doesn't have one. Or if it ever did, the last owner could have filled it in." Birdie glanced down at the carpet runner lining the hallway.

"Of course," Lizzie said under her breath. She all but ran to the other end of the hallway, got down on her knees, and began rolling the carpet runner up, exposing the battered plank floor.

The door to the root cellar was right where Lizzie had felt the cold spot. A flat wrought iron ring was inset into the trapdoor. Crouching in front of the root cellar, she could feel the energy like a slow drumbeat coming up from the floorboards.

Lizzie grasped the ring and gave it a hearty pull, but the trapdoor wouldn't budge. As she heaved on the metal ring, Birdie took a few steps back until she was standing in the threshold of the bedroom door, plunging Lizzie into the darkness.

"I don't think that's such a good idea. It would just be a dark hole full of spiders and bugs."

Lizzie grunted with effort as she hauled on the ring with all her strength. "Looks like you're going to get your way. I can't seem to get it open."

Birdie crept down the hall towards Lizzie, bringing the light with her. She stopped to peer down at the trapdoor. "It's been nailed shut. Look around the edges, you can see where the nail heads are." She played the beam of the flashlight around the perimeter of the trapdoor.

"Why would anyone nail it shut?"

"I have no idea," Birdie replied, taking a step away from the cellar.

"Maybe to keep the witch from trapping hapless souls down there with her?" Lizzie teased.

"No, more than likely the bank did it so they wouldn't get sued if someone checking out the place accidently fell into the cellar," Birdie said, her words coming out so forcefully it startled Lizzie.

Quietly Lizzie unrolled the carpet, smoothing out a few ripples in the fabric. "I don't suppose you have a crowbar in that magic purse of yours?" she asked, standing back up.

"No, you're out of luck," Birdie said, the relief evident in her voice.

"So what's next?"

"Why don't we take a walk around the property? I can show you the barn, the septic field, and the outbuildings."

Before they headed outside, Lizzie used the pole to lower the attic ladder and scooted upstairs to check on the owl. Birdie stayed down below in the hall.

Using the flashlight, Lizzie scanned every inch of the eaves and double-checked the bed, but the owl was gone. Satisfied it had found its way back outside, she secured the window before joining Birdie for the rest of the tour.

When they stepped out on the front porch fat drops had just begun to patter on the slate roof tiles. Lizzie locked the front door and slipped the skeleton key into her coat pocket.

"If we want to take a look at the barn we should probably hustle. These spring showers can turn into a downpour like

58

that," Birdie said, snapping her fingers. She had retrieved her handbag from the kitchen and was now rummaging through its generous interior. "I think I've got us covered as long as the rain stays light," she said, brandishing two tote-sized umbrellas.

"Are you sure you don't have a crowbar somewhere in that bag?" Lizzie chuckled.

"Even if I did, I wouldn't tell you. I've just about exhausted my bravery quotient for one day," Birdie said, unfurling the umbrellas with a shake of her hands.

Lora Deeprose

CHAPTER SEVEN

Brandishing the umbrellas with both hands, Birdie hit the buttons on the handles. They shot forward and popped open at the same time, the sound like rifle shots in the quiet morning.

Birdie handed one to Lizzie then relieved Lizzie of the flashlight, returning it to the depths of her shoulder bag before stepping off the porch. Lizzie followed, breathing deeply as the rain released the smell of cedar into the air.

"Now, according to the detail sheet the barn should be in the southwest corner of the property," Birdie said, turning left as they walked past the house.

They found the road leading to the barn just to one side of the driveway. Only the ghost of two tracks remained, the weeds and grass reclaiming what was theirs. The path led through the small clearing around the house and headed towards a screen of white pine. Lizzie followed Birdie, trying to avoid the puddles already forming in the uneven ground, her thoughts still on the poor woman who was said to haunt her house.

"What was her name?" Lizzie raised her voice to be heard over the plop of raindrops falling in earnest as they walked past the pine trees.

"Who?" Birdie stopped as they came upon the barn. It was built in a classic style with a gabled roof, large sliding doors, and a hayloft. The siding was board-and-batten, the wooden planks faded a silvery grey.

"The witch, what was her name?" Lizzie asked again,

stopping to stand as close to Birdie as their umbrellas would allow.

"I don't know. We always just referred to her as the Witch of Grey House. Besides, she probably never existed. The story is more than likely just that, a story." Birdie left Lizzie's side and approached the doors to the barn.

"I don't think it is." Lizzie scrambled through the mud to catch up to Birdie, who was looking thoughtfully at the door. "Yes, the villagers could have embellished the story, but there really was a woman who lived alone in that cottage. I'm guessing she was an herbalist or midwife. Couldn't you smell the herbs that once hung from the rafters in the loft?"

"No, it just smelled old and closed up. This is really important to you." Birdie pulled her gaze away from the barn and look at Lizzie through the falling rain.

"Yes, I want to know the history of the house and who's memories I'll be living with. Please, if you know something tell me."

"I've told you everything I know. You have to believe me, there is nothing more to the story, and that's really all it is, just a story." She turned back to face the barn.

Lizzie caught the look that flashed over Birdie's face before she turned her head. She recognized what, for the briefest of moments, had creased Birdie's forehead and made her eyes go wide. She was hiding something, something that scared her.

Lizzie dropped the subject, unsure if she wanted to discover something about her beautiful little cottage she didn't really want to know.

"Seems our Good Samaritan has been here too," Birdie said, fingering a shiny padlock looped through the large sliding door. She stepped away from the barn and sloshed through the rain to the side of the barn. Birdie's rubber boots made slurping sounds as she walked, the ground quickly turning into a muddy bog.

"The side door is locked too," Birdie said, returning a few moments later. "I'll have to go back to the car and get the bolt cutters." She had to shout to be heard over the staccato drumming of the rain on the barn's metal roof.

Lizzie shook her head. "Don't bother. I can look at it later. I'm buying the property for the cottage, not the barn. Let's head back to the house before we get soaked through."

By the time they were standing on the front porch, Lizzie's pant legs were soaked from the knee down and her sodden shoes were caked in a greasy clay. She shivered from the cold even with her heavy coat. Shaking the water off her umbrella, she leaned it against the porch railing and dug out the key for the cottage from her coat pocket.

As soon as she stepped over the threshold, she again felt the sweet comfort of coming home. She didn't think she'd ever tire of the feeling. The thick, stone walls muffled the sound of the rain, and despite the dark interior and lack of heat the house exuded a coziness and comfort from the elements even in its neglected state.

Lizzie could envision a crackling fire in the hearth and herself curled up on an overstuffed sofa, sipping coffee and reading one of her favorite Jane Austen novels. Or perhaps she would settle into the rocking chair by the wood stove while a hearty soup bubbled gently in a cast iron pot.

As Lizzie stood in the middle of the room daydreaming of the possibilities, Birdie had dug out her flashlight, casting a bright glow that pulled Lizzie back to the present.

"Did you want to head back to the office and write up the offer?"

"Do you have the necessary papers with you?" From all that she'd seen this morning about Birdie, she had no doubt the young realtor had come prepared.

"As a matter of fact I do, but wouldn't you rather go someplace a bit warmer? If you want, we could do the paperwork at the coffee shop over a nice hot cup of coffee and maybe something to eat."

"I know it seems unusual, but humor me. I'd rather write up the deal here."

Birdie shrugged. Placing the flashlight on the kitchen table, she then dug through her shoulder bag. She pulled out a hard plastic document holder and continued searching her bag. "Could you shine the flashlight over here? I can't find my pen."

Lizzie obliged.

"Are you sure you want to go through with this?" Birdie asked, finally pulling out a pen and opening the folder of papers.

"I'm not afraid of ghosts."

"There are no such things as ghosts," Birdie said a little too quickly. "No, I was thinking about you being out here all by yourself. It's such a remote location...your closest neighbor is over five miles away. The house has running water, electricity, and phone, but there's no TV or Internet. And you can't even get satellite TV because mountains block the signal. There's not much to do out here. Won't you be lonely?"

Lizzie thought about her late husband and the fifteen years she'd lived with him. Fifteen lonely, painful years. Funny how one could live with another person and feel isolated and disconnected.

"No, I don't think I will," she said with a smile. "Besides, I'm rather looking forward to having some solitude. As for being bored, after looking at the state of this place and the garden, there's more than enough to keep me busy for a long while."

"Well, I have to give you credit. I probably shouldn't say this because, as you know, this sale could make my career, but you are either very brave or completely crazy to choose to live out here."

"I think I may be a little of both," she chuckled.

"Well, shall we get you this house, then?"

"Yes," she replied as they filled out the offer to purchase.

The rain was still coming down in sheets when they stepped back out onto the porch. A few rose petals from the single early rose were strewn on the floorboards of the porch, battered loose by the rain. After locking up, Lizzie handed the key to Birdie.

"No, you keep it. I don't anticipate any problems with the sale. Especially because you're paying the asking price and it's a cash sale. Within a week or two this place will legally be yours. Just don't tell anyone I let you keep the key."

Lizzie curled her fingers around the heavy metal of the key. *Rose Cottage is mine*, she thought. She could hardly wait to tell Vivienne her good news.

CHAPTER EIGHT

Lizzie drove her used pick-up truck through the open gates of Rose Cottage, around the circular drive, and parked in front of her cottage. She'd bought the dark blue truck in Revelstoke after the house purchase had gone through. It wasn't fancy but the heater worked, the brakes were in good shape, and she didn't mind the few dings along the driver's side or the small dent in the bumper. More importantly, it had four-wheel drive, which Birdie had mentioned was a must if Lizzie had any hopes of getting in and out of her driveway in the winter months.

She half hoped the handyman, Audley Jones, would already be at the cottage, but hers was the only vehicle in sight. Instead, she was greeted by a mountain of firewood dumped near the front of the house. As Lizzie threw the truck into park, she let out a frustrated groan. She'd asked the guy who delivered firewood to leave the load at the back of the house near the woodshed to make her job of stacking it easier. Now she'd have to haul all six cords of it around to the woodshed herself.

After less than a week and several faxes back and forth between her lawyer and the bank, Lizzie now was the legal owner of Lot 17, Kootenay District, Plan 1186, 3797 Quail Hollow Road. What Lizzie hadn't realized was dealing with the bank and the lawyers would turn out to be the easy part.

At least Birdie hadn't disappointed her. The day the sale was final, the young realtor had given her the name of a contracting service that could perform most of the work, as well as the phone numbers for the chimney sweep, BC Hydro, the phone company, who to order her wood from, and the local man that serviced septic systems.

Even armed with Birdie's lists and legally owning the place, it had taken two weeks just to get the power turned on. But not from a lack of trying on her part; getting the people she'd hired to show up on time had become an act of futility.

She had mentioned her frustration to the proprietor of the hardware store when she went in to purchase some supplies. He chuckled as he explained to her the people of Barton ran their lives by something the locals referred to as Kootenay time. He went on to explain that when she made an appointment for a Tuesday, it was best to ask what month the Tuesday was in that they planned on showing up. And if the appointment was set for one o'clock, that meant the service person would show up anywhere between one and three or not at all. It would have been funny if she hadn't experienced the truth of his words herself.

From what she'd pieced together, the varied excuses the workmen offered when they finally showed up had to do with whether the fish were biting, whether the weather was too wet or too warm, or if there had been a two-for-one special at the local pub the night before.

The only things keeping her from pulling out her hair in frustration at whoever hadn't shown up yet again was her frequent talks over the phone with Vivienne, and her almost daily visits with Quinn, the raven. She never told Vivienne about her aborted phone call to Gideon. Instead Quinn had heard her sorrows and the whispers of her secret heart as he perched at her dinner table nibbling at the food she'd placed before him.

Vivienne still planned to come out for a visit, but her latest attempt at pinning down a date was scuttled by urgent business. Business that should have concerned Lizzie as it pertained to tracking down the warlock who had sent the demon to kill her.

She'd destroyed the demon, and from all accounts from the seers she'd managed to inflict severe injuries on the warlock, and had given the order a clear idea of where he was located. Yes, she should have been worried when Vivienne told her the warlock was on the move and the order had yet to capture him, but now that she had Rose Cottage she felt nothing could harm her. And she determined to pour all of her attention into restoring the only place she had ever felt truly at home.

Despite the delays, Lizzie had managed to have the septic system looked over, the old fridge and musty mattress from the loft removed, and the chimneys inspected and cleaned. Audley had come over the day before and turned on the water and bled the pipes, so now the cottage had all the basics she needed to move in permanently.

The man from the phone company was supposed to arrive in the afternoon to hook up her phone, but from her experience with Kootenay time, she didn't hold much stock he'd actually show up when he said he would.

As she hopped out of the truck, she couldn't help but smile at the improvements to her little cottage. The shutters sported a new coat of glossy black paint, and they now hung straight and true. Audley had fixed the hole in the roof and replaced any missing or cracked tiles with new slate ones. The door had been repainted to the cheery blue it had been in her dreams, and had been planed down so now it opened smoothly.

Lizzie herself had painted the porch floor a soft dove grey, and the ceiling of the overhang the same pale blue as the door. She'd even managed to squeeze in a few afternoons weeding the flowerbeds and pruning the climbing roses around the foundation of the stone house.

Lizzie jiggled her keys in her hand as she surveyed the changes to the outside of her cottage. There were only three keys on the keychain; one for the truck, a shiny silver one for the newly installed back door lockset, and the darkly tarnished skeleton key for the front.

When she'd had the new lock installed in the back door she couldn't bring herself to replace the one for the front. The heavy skeleton key was more to her than just a key. The very first owner of the cottage had used the exact same one. Lizzie wondered, when the woman of long ago used the key to open the door, did she feel the same sense of welcome, of coming home, as Lizzie did every time she stepped over the threshold? This link with the witch of Grey House, to this other woman who chose to live by herself, was important to her far beyond her ability to explain it.

Unlocking the front door of the cottage, Lizzie stood in the foyer for a moment to enjoy the feeling of her new home before heading back outside to begin the process of moving in. She lugged in her suitcase, which was the only thing she'd brought with her from Toronto, and headed back out to carry in boxes and bags of her most recent purchases. They included cleaning supplies, an inflatable camping bed, two folding chairs, a cooler filled with ice, beverages, and a few perishable food items, sacks of food, fresh linens and towels, and several boxes full of second-hand plates, bowls, cups and cutlery she'd picked up from the charity shop on High Street.

She'd also purchased a new fridge, a mattress, and box springs, but those items wouldn't be delivered to her cottage for another few days. She could have bought more new furniture, but she wanted to fill the house with things that had their own history, that had been cherished and worn in by years of service. In the meantime, she would temporarily be using an inflatable bed and camping chairs to add to the table and rocking chair she had inherited with the sale of the house.

Although she was the only human within miles, she wasn't alone as she trooped back and forth from her truck to the cottage. It was a beautiful late April morning and the air was filled with bird song. Thrushes competed with robins to see whose voice was more sweet and enticing. Chickadees twittered from low branches, and dark-eyed juncos hopped around the undergrowth emitting their funny little pops and squeaks. She heard the helicopter buzz and rapid-fire vocalization of a hummingbird before she caught a brilliant flash of fire out of the corner of her eye as the bronze feathers on its tiny breast caught the sun. The ever present squirrels nattered and chirred when Lizzie walked near the trees they were hanging out in.

She was home and she was happy. She'd thought such contentment was beyond her ability to have or even create in her former life. And she'd never imagined she would feel this serenity even while her shoulders ached from hauling a truckload of supplies and sweat trickled between her shoulder blades in the growing warmth of the sun.

Audley still hadn't shown by the time she'd stacked her supplies in a neat pile in the empty living room, but she wasn't surprised or annoyed. Unlike some of the service men, Audley at least showed up for each of their appointments, even if he usually ran a good forty-five minutes late and arrived with a distinct skunk-like aroma clinging to his clothes.

Lizzie chuckled to herself as she filled a cleaning bucket at the sink. She must be adjusting to living out here if she was starting to embrace Kootenay time and overlooking her handy man's penchant for pot smoking.

As the bucket filled with hot water, she dug out a bottle of all-purpose cleaner and added a generous capful to the water. It pleased her to see the water flowing clear from the tap. This was her place, her tap, and her water that flowed into the bucket. She'd never owned her own home before, and she'd underestimated the sense of security she felt. The apartment she'd shared with her late husband was owned by her mother-in-law, and before that she'd lived with Sister Collette at the priory.

When the bucket was full of hot soapy water she snagged a few cleaning rags and headed to the master bedroom. After flinging open the french doors to let in the fresh air, she began scrubbing the years of grime off the windows in earnest. After cleaning the bedroom, inflating the camping bed, and making it up with fresh linens, she put the black tail feather from Quinn in an old Mason jar and placed it carefully on a cardboard box she was using as a nightstand.

With the bedroom set up, she moved on to the kitchen. From her supplies she dug out a bottle of stove blackening and set to work reviving the wood stove.

Lizzie was so engrossed in the task and up to her elbows in blacking that she had no idea how much time had passed when she heard the sound of Audley's van pulling up the drive. The ear-splitting rumble of an engine that desperately needed a new muffler had become the familiar herald of his arrival.

Setting her polishing rag and tin of blacking aside, she made her way to the front porch just in time to see a sleek silver truck pull up next to Audley's battered cube van. The truck flashed silver fire as the sun winked off the chrome adorning every possible surface. Even the hubcaps were spotless and shiny.

Upon exiting the van, Audley scrambled over to the truck before the occupant could open the driver's door, fumbling with the handle and finally getting it open. Whoever owned the truck commanded a servile devotion from her handyman, and caused him to move faster than she thought possible. She had become accustomed to Audley's slow shuffling gait and plodding movements as he went about his work, and the slightly vacant stare he wore as frequently as the grungy plaid work shirt he always showed up in. The change in Audley startled Lizzie.

It wasn't until the two men made their way around the vehicles that Lizzie got her first good look at her visitor. Although he moved slowly, using the assistance of a cane, and his right arm was strapped across his chest in a sling, he exuded an aura of power and strength. Where Audley was rope-thin and small in stature, the other man was broad shouldered and over six feet tall.

Lizzie was so used to seeing the men of Barton dressed in stained jeans and T-shirts, sporting scruffy beards and weather beaten faces, that the man's well-groomed appearance seemed out of place. He was dressed in pressed chinos and a fresh periwinkle blue cotton dress shirt. On his feet were the requisite steel-toed work boots, but his were pristine, not even a scuffmark marring the smooth leather. He wore his blond hair short and neatly styled, and his clean-shaven face highlighted his sharp jaw and strong chin. The remnants of a black eye and a scar along his forehead did nothing to blight his good looks.

"Morning Audley," Lizzie said, stepping off the porch and wiping her blackened hands on a clean rag while she sized up the newcomer. Although he was handsome, Lizzie felt her ire rise as his gaze wandered from her face to her chest. She crossed her arms and narrowed her eyes. A flash of surprise clouded his eyes before he looked back up into her face.

"Morn'in, Ms. Benett. This here's my boss, Mr. Ryan."

"Call me Jon," he said, switching his cane to the hand in the sling, extending his healthy left arm towards her.

"I'd shake your hand, but I think you'd come out the worse for wear," she said, holding up her blackened hands in explanation, keeping her tone cool.

"It's good to see the new owner of Grey House isn't afraid to get her hands dirty," Jon said, using his cane as he stepped closer to Lizzie.

"Not at all, but I'm afraid I've gotten more blackening on myself than the woodstove," she said, wiping at the ink-dark stains in vain. "I'm more used to digging in the dirt than restoring a house, but I'm finding it surprisingly gratifying."

Lora Deeprose

She looked up at him. His soft grey eyes reminded Lizzie of the mists that danced through the woods on rainy days. She felt herself sinking into the depth of his gaze, her earlier irritation dissolving.

"I see the firewood got delivered," Audley said, shuffling between Jon and Lizzie.

Lizzie blinked at Audley, trying to find her voice. "Yes, not quite where I'd specified, but at least I can cook and heat the house now, which is good seeing as I'm moving in today." Lizzie took a step away from Jon.

"I'm sure Audley won't mind hauling it into the woodshed. Right Audley?" Jon said.

"I'll get right on it, Mr. Ryan." Audley scrambled over to the mountain of wood and began filling his arms.

While Audley struggled with the firewood, Jon reached into the front pocket of his chinos. "Audley, use my truck, it'll be faster," Jon said, throwing the keys in Audley's general direction.

Audley had to drop the firewood he was holding to snatch the keys from the air. The logs clattered to the ground, barely missing his toes. "Right, boss."

"And use the tarp in the back so that you don't scratch the truck bed." Jon's tone was lighthearted, but Lizzie detected just a hint of unnecessary aggression. "I hope you don't mind me dropping by unannounced, but I wanted to check on how the work was progressing," Jon said to Lizzie.

"Not at all."

"Normally I would've been out here on day one of the job, but as you can see I've been indisposed lately," he said, gesturing with his cane.

"Yes, Audley mentioned you'd been in an accident. And I'm glad to see you're on the mend. Did you want to come in and see what's been done so far?"

"As long as I'm not pulling you away from anything."

72

"No. I've just spent most of the morning cleaning years of dust and cobwebs, and it wouldn't take much convincing for me to take a break. I've got some iced tea in a cooler if you want some."

"I could use a cold drink. It's surprisingly warm out for early spring."

Lizzie led the way up the porch as Jon followed at a brisk pace despite his cane. She held the door open, and as he stepped past her into the cottage, she felt her body tingle in response to his nearness. He smelled of something exotic and spicy, and below the expensive aftershave the unmistakable scent of a man.

She was normally reserved around strangers and even more so if they were men, but her reaction to Jon left her breathless and a bit shaken. Shaking her head, she followed Jon into the dimness of the cottage.

Chapter Nine

She gave Jon a wide berth as she made a beeline for the kitchen sink. While she scrubbed at the stove blacking on her hands she clamped down on her energy, but it didn't seem to help. She could still feel his presence filling up the space and wrapping around her like a warm blanket.

After thoroughly drying her hands, she took her time folding the kitchen towel and placing it over the back of one of the camping chairs in the hope her wildly beating heart would slow down. Taking the long way around the table, she retrieved two iced teas from the cooler in the corner of the living room.

Jon ambled over to the kitchen table, leaning his cane on the arm of one of the camping chairs. He slowly scanned the kitchen, his eyes narrowing as he took in the sad state it now stood in.

"This kitchen needs to be completely gutted. The cabinets have seen better days, and those seventies light fixtures have got to go," he said, looking up at the ceiling.

Lizzie chuckled. "I see we are in complete agreement on that score," she said, handing him a glass bottle of iced tea.

As he reached for the bottle, his fingertips brushed against hers. A jolt of electricity raced up her arm as their hands touched, and she pulled her hand back in alarm. Lizzie imagined she heard the sizzle as the air crackled before the glass bottle slipped to the floor between them, exploding in a spray of glass and amber liquid.

Jon's eyes widened, his good hand still outstretched to

receive the bottle.

"I'm so sorry, that was clumsy of me," she blurted out.

"Here, let me help," he replied.

They both bent down at the same moment, cracking their heads together. Lizzie clutched her forehead. Jon, unstable on his feet without his cane, stumbled back and fell in an ungraceful sprawl into the camping chair, wincing as his bad arm banged against the edge of the table.

"Oh my God, are you okay?" Lizzie scrambled to his side, being careful not to touch him, her throbbing forehead momentarily forgotten. "Your arm, are you hurt?"

He smiled up at her, and his soft grey eyes held a hint of amusement. "My arm's fine, but I'm a bit embarrassed at my lack of grace. I've been through much worse recently, and it will take a lot more than knocking my head with a beautiful woman to put me back in the hospital."

Lizzie felt the heat rush up her neck, burning her cheeks, but she couldn't pull her eyes away from his. It was Jon who finally lowered his eyes, breaking contact, but quickly looked up again, worry clouding his face.

"Lizzie, you're bleeding."

She looked down at herself but couldn't see anything wrong.

"Your arm." He stood up quickly.

She held up her forearm, her eyes focusing on the thin line of blood snaking its way across her skin. She was no longer in her sweet little cottage but standing in her old kitchen apartment, the ceiling lights shattered at her feet, staring at the door her enraged husband had just slammed in her face. It was the last time she'd seen Ian alive.

"You need to sit down." Jon guided her with his good hand towards the other chair. "You've gone a bit pasty."

Before she knew it she was sitting down and Jon was hovering above her. Her head swam and her vision greyed around the edges. She blinked at him, trying to get her vision to clear.

Straightening up, Jon retrieved his cane and walked over to the sink, his cane making hollow thumps on the floorboards. Producing a white handkerchief from his pants' pocket, he ran a corner of it under the tap before making his way back to Lizzie.

She'd almost regained her composure by the time he stood in front of her, but she was finding it difficult to catch her breath.

"Now, hold up your arm so I can see it," he said, his voice low and soothing.

The rational, cautious part of her seemed to have temporarily separated from her, as she had no intention of letting Jon touch her again. Yet as she opened her mouth to put him off she saw her arm hovering in the air between them.

Using the wet corner of his handkerchief, he gently dabbed at the cut along her skin. She braced herself for another jolt of energy but it never came. Instead, a pleasant warmth spread over her, like the sensation of stepping into a nice bath. Lizzie pursed her lips together to stop a contented sigh that wanted to escape.

As he worked at washing away the blood, Lizzie's eyes wandered to his muscled forearm tanned a toasted brown, the blond hairs on his arms making it look like he was dusted in gold.

"There, that should do the trick. I thought it was deeper than it is. Sure bled a lot for just a scratch." Jon folded over the damp corner of the handkerchief, now stained pink from Lizzie's blood, and slipped it back into his pants' pocket.

Lizzie slowly pulled her eyes away from watching his movements and focused on the cut on her arm. It had been deeper just a few minutes ago, but by the time Jon had finished administering to her, her fast healing ability had reduced the laceration to a mere scratch.

She looked up at him and her eyes locked on his again. She felt a gentle tug that made her lean towards him as if she was being softly pushed from behind. The dull rhythmic thud of firewood being thrown into the back of Jon's truck could be heard in the silence of the cottage.

"Who are you?" he whispered.

Lizzie's eyes widened as she heard him speak the exact words running through her own mind. "I beg your pardon," Lizzie said, lowering her arm and covering it protectively with her other one. Instantly the cocooning warmth surrounding her was gone.

Jon took a step back and regarded her with a crooked smile. "That didn't come out right. Maybe the knock to my head loosened a few brain cells. What I meant was, where did you come from? The Kootenay's is a pretty sparsely populated area and I know everyone hereabouts, so I know you're not from around here."

"Oh, I moved from down East," she said. Recovering herself, she stood up and moved away from him. She picked up the broom and dustpan that was leaning up against the wall and began sweeping up the broken glass from around the table with broad swiping strokes.

Jon stood back, leaning on his cane and watching as she worked. "So what would make you move clear across the country to this backwater hamlet, of all places? Or should I ask who?"

She was back to being irritated with him. Ignoring the question, she dumped the dustpan full of sticky glass shards into the dustbin and set about wiping up the floor.

Rinsing out the rag and draping it across the faucet, she straightened her shoulders and turned to him. "You know what they say about assuming things." She raised an eyebrow when his only response was to chuckle.

She stomped over to the cooler and pulled out another cold drink for Jon, even though she wanted to throw it at him rather than play the good hostess.

"Forgive me, I don't mean to annoy you, but you have to face the fact you moved to a village of less than two thousand people, most of whom are related to each other. You're not just an outsider but a single woman. That makes you a curiosity."

"Because I'm an unmarried woman...seriously?"

"Not just because you are a woman, but because you moved out to Grey House, of all places, on your own. That is bound to raise speculation. I'm just doing my duty to the village to get all the gossip I can gather and report back."

"Well, sorry to disappoint the villagers, but there's nothing to tell." Unscrewing the lid on the iced tea, she handed Jon his drink, being careful not to touch him this time. "I simply wanted a change of scenery. City living had become too big and noisy. I was out here on a vacation and happened across this place. It had everything I was looking for, and so here I am. No great mystery," she said coolly, removing the lid off her own drink. There was no way she was going to tell anyone the real story, and Jon with his cavalier attitude ticked her off so much she wasn't even going to share that she was widowed. "As far as my single status goes, that's really no one's business."

"Oh, but it is. There aren't many available women living out here, and your arrival has caused quite a stir. I wouldn't be surprised if you find a few young men at your doorstep wanting to take you out to the next spaghetti dinner at the church. That is if you like men; if you don't...well, that's going to cause even more excitement and gossip." He raised the iced tea to his lips, and in three deep swallows had half the bottle finished.

"Well, if the fine people of Barton want to waste their time talking about me I can't stop them, but there is really nothing to tell. And I'm not looking for a husband and I'm not gay. I just want to live in peace and quiet." She put down her barely touched drink.

"Just give it some time, and when the novelty of a new person in town wears off, they'll leave you alone," he said, carefully placing his empty bottle on the table. "I can see that I've upset you and I apologize. I've been told I can be a bit blunt at times."

He reached out and placed his hand on her shoulder. "Forgive me?"

She nodded, startled and relieved that his touch didn't bring about another zap of electricity.

"Now, how about you show me the rest of the house?" He trailed his hand down her arm, his fingers barely touching her skin. He'd ruffled her feathers with his assumptions and nosey questions, but his touch elicited the complete opposite reaction in her. She didn't want to show him the rest of the house...she just wanted him gone.

"Sure," she said, stepping around him and down the hall. "Unlike the kitchen, which I agree with you needs a complete overhaul, I'm not going to touch the bathroom other than give it a good cleaning. Audley checked the plumbing and everything is in working order. And I like the charm of the claw foot tub and the porcelain sink with the two faucets for hot and cold," she said, as they both peered into the tiny room.

"I completely agree. This reno probably dates back to the late seventies, but at least whoever put in the bathroom was smart enough not to put in a robin's egg blue tub." Jon's voice had taken on a professional tone, which Lizzie far preferred to his earlier demeanor.

She showed him the back porch and he spent a great deal of time inspecting the small space, thumping the walls with the handle of his cane.

"This room could do with some proper insulation. If you're going to use it as a laundry room like it's set up for, the last thing you want is for the pipes to freeze in the winter."

Lizzie agreed to add it to the list of things for Audley to do, and as she led Jon down the hall, he stopped abruptly.

"What do we have here?" he asked, prodding the floor with the end of his cane. "The floor sounds different, hollow."

"There's a trapdoor under the carpet runner. It leads to the root cellar."

Jon didn't display any strange physical reaction to the area he was standing on, not that she expected him to. Other than the first time through, she herself hadn't felt anything either. Even when she had Audley pry open the door, and with a flashlight in hand peered down into the dark hole in the earth, she'd sensed nothing. Not even a slight vibration.

"Have you been down there?" he asked.

"I didn't go all the way down, but I took a quick look."

"Did you find anything?"

"No witch's bones, if that's what you're asking. And her ghost didn't try to push me down the ladder either." She grinned at him when he looked surprised.

"So you know about the witch of Grey House. And you still bought the place."

"Yes, the house needed me and I wasn't about to be scared off by a ghost story. I'm curious, how far did you get?"

"I beg your pardon?"

"The dare. Did you manage to touch the door handle, or were you brave enough to step inside?"

"Only if you count this visit. I've never been on the property before this. I didn't grow up here."

"Oh, so you're an outsider too."

"Yes and no. I'm from the States, but I have relatives here and my family vacationed here in the summers when I was very young. I didn't decide to settle down here until five years ago, and opened my construction and reno business. Like you, I needed a change of scenery and a slower pace of life. And I've found both out here."

She nodded as an awkward silence settled between them. Not wanting the moment to endure any longer, Lizzie searched for something to say. Until she figured out who Jon was and why she felt so mixed up around him, she decided to stick to a safe topic.

"There is so much about this cottage that I find endearing, but I think this is probably the neatest thing about the design." Grabbing the pole she'd left in the corner of the hall, she expertly looped the hooked end into the ring in the trap door in the ceiling and unfurled the hinged stairs from the attic.

"How clever," Jon said, ambling forward to peer up into the loft. "Too bad I can't manage the stairs in my current condition. I'd love to see the space up there and check on Audley's re-roofing job."

"Perhaps when you've mended you can come back and I'll show you." She blushed when she realized that came out more as a come on than she'd intended. "I mean, if you're interested." She winced when she realized that sounded even worse.

"Yes, I am interested." He pinned her with a look that seemed a little feral to Lizzie. When he took a step closer, she busied herself with the pole, pushing the staircase back up on its hinges and closing the trapdoor with more force than was necessary.

"Ms. Benett?" Audley's voice flooded her with relief.

"We're back here," she called out, stepping forward to meet Audley as he turned the corner to the hall.

"Ms. Benett, there's a guy from the phone company wanting to speak wit'cha. I told him to wait outside."

"Thank you, Audley. I'd better go see him." She turned to Jon. "If you'll excuse me."

"By all means. I've taken up too much of your time as it is. Perhaps you can show me the rest of the house another time."

She was going to point out that the only room left was the master bedroom, but thought better of it. A comment like that with Audley within hearing range was sure to get the tongues wagging in the village.

"I need to get going anyway…there's a few projects I need to check in on. Audley, have you finished stacking the wood?"

"Almost done, Mr. Ryan."

"Well, hadn't you better get out there and finish it?"

"Yes, yes right on it." Audley shuffled out of the hallway and back outside at twice his normal speed.

Jon turned to Lizzie as they followed Audley to the front door. "He's a good worker, but he needs direction and a firm hand or he wastes time."

Audley may move a little slowly, but she'd never had to keep on him to get the work done. Jon's comment made her feel the need to defend her handyman. "Well, I have no complaints. He's done a fine job."

"Maybe it's your feminine charms working their magic on him."

She was suddenly tired and wanted Jon to leave. She may be inexplicably drawn to him, but he irritated her. She ignored his flirting and swung open the door.

"Please come in," she said to the grey-uniformed man standing on the porch. He was in his mid-fifties, with salt and pepper hair and kind blue eyes. His phone company uniform looked freshly ironed, and he wore a utility belt around his trim waist that bristled with a collection of strange little tools and a large orange phone receiver used to check the lines.

"Good afternoon. I'm Rick with Telus Communications, and I have a work order to install a phone line and two handsets for a Ms. Benett," he said, glancing down at the metal clipboard in his hand.

"Where's Murray? Doesn't he usually handle the service calls for out here?" Jon asked.

The older man looked up from his clipboard. "Yes, but he's on vacation and I'm covering his area until he gets back. I normally work out of Castlegar." Turning to Lizzie he added, "You're Ms. Benett?"

"Yes, come in, Rick. I've been expecting you."

"The first thing I need to do is run a line for the bedroom phone. If you could show me where that is I can get started."

"Head down the hall to the right of the kitchen. It's the door at the end."

Rick retrieved a box containing phone cable from the front porch and disappeared down the hall, his utility belt jingling as he went.

"Well, Jon, it was nice meeting you, but I have a few things I need to do before the day gets away from me. Not the least of which is to finish blacking the stove," she said, making an excuse not to linger with him.

"Sure thing. But before I go, I was just thinking, if you're serious about gutting the kitchen, I could draw up a few designs that would suit the cottage. I was thinking something that's unfitted would be more in line with the feel of this place. I've done a few kitchen renos in my time, and I could find you the best deals on cabinets and such."

She wasn't sure if she ever wanted to cross paths with Jon again, but instead she heard herself say, "Sure, I'd like that."

"Okay. Well give me a call when you're ready. Here's my card."

She carefully plucked the card from his fingertips, avoiding any accidental contact, and glanced down at it. The card was navy with embossed gold lettering proclaiming Ryan Construction and Renovations, with his cell number listed below. It was ostentatious and not at all to her taste, but even from the little time she'd spent with Jon, it definitely suited his personality.

"I will, and thanks for coming by," she said, shutting the door before he even got down the porch stairs. She wasn't quite sure what she felt about Jon Ryan except that she was glad he was gone and she had her cottage to herself again. Well, almost to herself. She turned on her heels to find the phone guy, but before she even made it down the hall, she heard his footsteps coming closer.

"Ms. Benett?"

"Please call me Lizzie."

"Lizzie, would you mind showing me where exactly you'd like the phone jack placed?"

She didn't hesitate to follow him. Nothing intense or unsettling emanated from his energy. After showing him where she wanted the phone jack she left him to his work. She headed back to the kitchen and set about finishing her earlier job of blacking the stove. Working methodically, she applied the thick polish with a rag, burnishing the cast iron surface with slow meticulous circles. The work calmed her nerves.

She purposefully pushed away the niggling thoughts about Jon that kept bubbling to the surface. She couldn't deny her instant and disconcerting attraction to him or the strange reaction upon touching him. His presence threw her off, made her feel a familiar recognition she couldn't explain, while at the same time the tingling of danger that made the hair on the back of her neck stand up.

Rick returned to the kitchen just as Lizzie was putting her supplies under the kitchen sink.

"I'm all done in there, I just need to check the line in the kitchen and install your new phone sets, then I'll be out of your hair," he said as he moved to the phone on the kitchen wall, his utility belt musically punctuating his movements. As he lifted the receiver to his ear his shirtsleeve slipped down, exposing a few centimeters of skin on his inner wrist and a sliver of blue ink tattooed there.

Lizzie inhaled sharply.

"Your line's dead," he said. "Mice most likely ate through the wires somewhere between here and the junction box. Happens a lot out here. Won't take but a minute to fix."

Lizzie nodded dumbly as he slipped out the back door.

She couldn't be sure what she'd seen, for it had only been for the briefest of seconds, but her instincts told her she was right. If anyone else but Lizzie had seen his wrist they wouldn't have seen a tattoo. It was one of the quirks of her abilities...certain magickal charms had no effect on her.

If she'd had a chance to see the whole tattoo, it would have shown the three phases of the moon, inked in a distinctive indigo dye. A tattoo that marked him as a member of the order.

She hadn't kept where she was a secret from Vivienne, but she'd been clear that she didn't want anything to do with the order. Discovering the phone repairman belonged to her recent past shot hot anger through her veins. She couldn't imagine Vivienne would go behind her back like this.

She tried to convince herself it was just a coincidence, but she remembered Jon asking where the regular repairman was. What were the odds that the man called in to cover the regular guy from the phone company belonged to the organization that had taken her under its protection because of her magickal powers? No, she knew the truth...even though she'd refused to have a new guardian and no longer wanted anything to do with the organization, something was up.

The screen door to the back porch slapped against its frame as Rick returned. "I was right. The line in the junction box was chewed clean through." He lifted the receiver on the kitchen phone.

From where she was standing, she could hear the constant high-pitched hum of a dial tone.

"You're in good working order. Now I'll just go get your new phones and you're good to go."

She followed him back to the bedroom as he plugged in the new phone and showed her how to access her voicemail, the whole time paying close attention to his left arm, but try as she might she couldn't get another look at the tattoo on his wrist.

85

She was itching to call Vivienne to ask why she'd sent Rick to check up on her, and why she'd done it in such a sneaky manner, but she would have to wait until she was in town to use her secure cell phone to make the call.

She couldn't imagine anyone out in the Kootenay's would have even heard of the order, much less want to cause harm to its members, but she would never invite even the slimmest possibility of someone tracing her call to her friend even if she was currently ticked off at her. She'd just have to wait until she was in town to give Vivienne a piece of her mind.

Back in the kitchen, she waited as Rick installed the second phone on the wall then gathered up his tools.

"If you could just sign here," he said, handing her his clipboard and a pen.

She scribbled her signature and handed him the paperwork back.

"Before I forget, here's your new phone number," he said, handing her a small card.

She didn't even look at the card, just walked Rick to the door. She had no intention of venting her ire at Rick, but before she closed the door on him she couldn't resist a quick shot.

"Thanks for your work today, Rick," she said with cool politeness. "Please make sure to tell Vivienne I said hi."

"I will, but you could tell her yourself," he said just as the phone in the kitchen rang. She turned towards the shrill sound of the phone, her mouth open in shock.

"Have a good day, Lizzie."

She whipped her head around, but Rick had already shut the door behind him.

She stomped over to the phone. "Hello Vivienne."

CHAPTER TEN

Grabbing only her key and a brand-new padlock, Lizzie stormed out of her cottage. She locked the front door, but even the comforting ritual of using the worn metal key to secure her home did nothing to dispel her dark mood.

Out in the golden glow of the late afternoon sunshine she stomped down the driveway, past Audley's van and down to the gate. She saw no signs of the handyman himself. The woodpile was moved and she speculated that, with his duty done and his boss off-site, Audley had taken a long deserved break. He may have a few quirks, but over the past weeks she had begun to trust the odd little man. She'd even given him a key to the back door, giving him strict instructions to lock up after himself if she wasn't around. He'd taken the key but had told her that no one locked their doors in the country. Lizzie had insisted, and the few times she'd left Audley to head into town, she'd come back to find he'd done what she'd asked, her little cottage locked up tight.

It was just as well she didn't have to talk to him...she was in no mood to see anyone. Her anger surged through her in waves that she constantly channeled down into the ground.

She wasn't pissed off with Vivienne anymore. It had taken the better part of their conversation before Lizzie had calmed down enough to hear her friend's explanation and subsequent apology. Vivienne had meant the surprise installation of a secured land line as a house warming present of sorts. It meant they could talk whenever they wanted and Vivienne could reach her, at a moment's notice, in the unlikely chance the warlock managed to find Lizzie again.

Yes, she'd forgiven Vivienne for not giving her the heads up about the phone. That wasn't what now drove her out of her cottage and away from finishing her work. It was her friend, Madison, who had her wrapped in a tumult of emotions.

She needed a brisk walk and fresh air to sort out her feelings that had her heart knocking painfully in her chest and her throat tightening with a sorrow too deep to name. Vivienne had told her that Madison was out of the hospital and back at the motherhouse in Toronto. Lizzie's young friend had fully recovered from her extensive physical injuries with the help of the healers, but she refused any offer of seeing a therapist to deal with the abuse she had suffered at the hands of her boyfriend. The boyfriend Lizzie had put in a coma when she used her magick to stop the last most brutal attack.

That was worrisome in itself, but when Lizzie finally summoned up the courage to ask if Madison had wanted to see her, Vivienne told her the words she didn't want to hear. Even with Vivienne's most diplomatic skills, she couldn't soften the blow of the truth. Lizzie had hoped Madison's refusal to see her was just temporary due to her frail physical condition. She'd really believed, in time, Madison would see that Lizzie had saved her, and that she loved her deeply. But that wasn't the case.

Lizzie had longed for a sense of family, and in the short three months she'd been protected and surrounded by Gideon, Vivienne, and Madison she felt she'd found one; a protective tribe that understood and welcomed her as part of the group. She'd been terribly wrong.

When she hung up the phone she tried to concentrate on washing down the kitchen cupboards, but her bitterness leeched out her earlier enthusiasm for getting the cottage in order. She was too hurt by Madison's rejection to be of any use to herself.

She swung through the gate, and turning left down Quail Hollow Road, she marched down the gravel road determined to outpace her temper. She was headed to her postbox just a ten-minute walk from her cottage. When she had stopped by the post office to arrange mail delivery, the post-mistress had informed her she needed to purchase a padlock and secure it on her assigned box before her delivery would begin.

By the time she'd reached the green metal boxes positioned at the crossroads, her mood had shifted to one of resignation. It seemed to her that her life wasn't meant to include a family; her past was evidence of that. If she wanted to find even a small sense of contentment in her life, she had to let go of her need to belong.

Wasn't that why fate had pulled her to her cottage in the middle of nowhere? She should count her blessings and be grateful that she still had Vivienne in her life and her snug little cottage to keep her safe.

She found her postbox and secured the new lock on the outside. A smile of amusement turned the corners of her mouth, despite her dark mood. She now understood why the postmistress was emphatic that Lizzie needed a proper lock before delivery of her mail would commence.

The three-by-five foot green metal box only contained four compartments, and other than the new lock Lizzie just attached, there was only one other in place, so old and rusted it looked like it would never open. The other two boxes where secured with sticks threaded through the metal hasp on each compartment door.

She turned to head for home when a loud thud followed by a horrible cry shattered the peaceful afternoon. She stood rooted to the spot, listening, but there was nothing but silence; even the birds had stopped singing. The unnatural quiet was worse than the scream she'd heard. Icy fear trickled down her spine.

She ran down the road away from her cottage and towards

the direction of the cry. Her sneakers slipped on the loose gravel road. Lungs burning, she picked up her speed.

She'd only covered a few hundred yards before the sound of a fast approaching vehicle made her stumble with uncertainty. It roared towards her on the narrow road. Following her instincts, she jumped into the ditch just as a white sedan blasted past her, pelting her with gravel churned up by its back tires. It was going so fast she only had time to register the rust spots mottling the driver's side and the blur of spinning tires before it disappeared in a cloud of dust.

Scrambling out of the ditch, she ran with all her might, anger propelling her faster than her earlier fear. Spotting the injured animal lying in the middle of the road, she slowed her pace down to a trot. She wasn't sure what she was looking at. The animal lay on its side, its broad muscular back facing her. It looked like a bear, but it was covered in thick shaggy white fur with three buff colored splotches near its back end.

Cautiously she circled around it. Sensing her movement, the animal swiveled its massive square head to look at her. Large brown eyes locked on to hers, the pupils large and dilated. She saw pain in their depths, and a plea for help she couldn't ignore.

As she approached the animal eye's followed her movements, its jowls puffing out as it struggled to breathe. She scanned down his body, getting her first good look at the dog's injuries, although she still wasn't completely certain what she was looking at was a dog.

Exhausted from the effort of holding up its head, the dog dropped it down on the gravel road with a horrible thud. A deep sigh, sounding more human than animal, escaped its black rubbery lips.

Lizzie swallowed hard when she saw the gaping wounds on both its back legs and the dark stains soaked into the road underneath. She fell to her knees in front of the animal, gravel biting painfully through the fabric of her jeans. Choking on the bile rising in her throat, she forced her panicked mind to slow down and focus on helping the dog.

She widened her gaze, allowing her perception to go beyond her normal vision. Instantly colors appeared around the dog, pulsing and swirling, close to its thick white fur.

Zeroing in on his hindquarters, the knowledge of his injuries popped into her mind. He—for she knew the dog was male, the information floating in through her connection to his energy— had two broken legs, the right one in two places, the left just above the anklebone. The left hip had been completely sheared off. The gaping wounds running from his groin all the way down both legs were coated with dirt and gravel, the result of being dragged under the car across the road's rough surface.

No internal injuries.

Relief washed over her, but she knew she had to act fast. He wasn't bleeding internally, but if she didn't get his energy stabilized, the shock could kill him before she got him to a vet. She had no idea if the village even had a vet. Then there was the question of how she was going to transport him there once she figured out where it was. She'd have to leave him to get her truck and hope he survived until she could get back. She hoped Audley was still at the cottage. She'd need his help to lift the giant dog into the truck bed.

Distracted by her thoughts, she let her energy slip too deeply into the dog's field. For a brief moment, her legs where encased in white-hot fire. The throbbing heat of pain snaking up through her left hip made her cry out as her heart fluttered and waves of nausea cramped her stomach. Worse than the physical pain were the tortured howls echoing through her mind.

Scrambling to withdraw her energy to a safe distance, she gulped air, willing herself not to pass out. Sweat trickled down her brow and stung her eyes. She had to do something to help the dog, but she had no idea how to use her gifts.

She thought back to how she'd released the elementals from protecting her without being taught how to do it. Vivienne had explained she'd somehow accessed the information from her ancestors. This knowledge she carried in her DNA.

She held the thought of helping the injured dog, and she almost shouted in relief when her ears filled with the buzzing that signaled she'd opened up the right portal to the information. And then she knew…she knew exactly what to do.

She raised her hands skyward. With a silent prayer, she connected with the universal life force and pulled down the strong pulsing light into herself. Then she turned her attention to the earth below and breathed in the strong heartbeat of the Great Mother. Drawing up the steady grounding current, she let it mingle with the luminescent starlight of the galaxies that now surged within her.

Her brief dance with the dog's pain was forgotten as the power of all life thrummed within her. She allowed the two healing energies to build up inside her until she couldn't contain them any longer.

"It's going to be okay, big fella. I'm going to help you," she said, in a soft soothing voice.

The dog's chest heaved as he let out a rumbling sigh, which she took as consent to continue.

Steadying her hands just a few inches above his ruined hindquarters, she released the healing energy. It coursed out of her palms and into the dog in a steady stream of violet light. Within seconds she saw his aura brighten as the healing light continued to work its magick. She kept her hands steady as she watched his breathing become deeper, his chest rising slow and steady. She wasn't alarmed when his eyelids fluttered once then slowly closed. Through their connected energy, she could feel his heart rate slowing down but getting stronger, and his aura continued to brighten and expand upwards from his prone form. The dog was no longer suffering shock nor was he weakening towards death...he had simply gone to sleep.

Lizzie legs were numb from kneeling so long, but she stayed motionless as the violet light continued to pour out from her palms. Just a few more minutes and then she'd be free to run back home to get her truck. She didn't want to leave the dog but she saw no other way. She may have been able to strengthen and stabilize him, but it was beyond her capabilities to heal broken and shattered bones.

As she let the final surge of violet energy filter through her hands, she sensed someone behind her. Definitely female and powerful, although there was no malevolence fanning out through whoever possessed such a strong life force.

"I was wondering how long I'd have to wait before you felt me near," came a melodious voice. "Not long at all, as it turns out. You have quite a gift."

With a rustle of skirts the woman knelt down next to Lizzie, the smell of sundried hay and lavender announcing her presence before she shifted her large frame into Lizzie's peripheral vision.

"When you didn't hear my truck pull up I didn't call out to you for fear of startling you. And that wouldn't have been good for you or the dog. Or me if you'd accidently turned that power in my direction," the woman chuckled softly.

Lizzie turned her head to look at the woman kneeling next to her. She was surprised to discover the voice that sounded like the dance of a soft breeze belonged to a woman so ancient she reminded Lizzie of one of the gnarled hemlock trees growing at Rose Cottage. Her round suntanned face was deeply etched with a crisscrossing network of wrinkles, and her pure white hair was pulled back from her face in a long braid that hung down her back. Her eyes were a brilliant green with no hint of the cloudiness of age, which Lizzie found disconcerting. Those bright sparkling eyes didn't match the face in which they belonged.

The woman reached out a speckled hand, the skin paper thin, and placed it gently on the sleeping dog's head.

"You've done an excellent job with this beautiful boy. I think it's safe to move him now."

Lizzie couldn't find her voice so she nodded instead, and turned her attention back to the energy still flowing from her hands. She sent her gratitude to the universe and to the earth as she slowly withdrew her connection to their energy. Then with a deep slow breath, she pulled in her own life force, but kept a thin thread attached to the dog so she could monitor how he was doing.

"Now, let's see about getting this fellow to Dr. Laurie." The old woman sprang up gracefully, her age and bulk not seeming to impede her in the least. "I think I have a tarp tucked behind the driver's seat that we can fashion into a stretcher of sorts."

The musical tinkle of bells accompanied the old woman as she strode towards her vehicle and rummaged around in the cab.

With slow painful movements Lizzie eased her hip onto the ground, and using her hands she pulled her sleeping legs out from under her.

"Here's the ticket. I knew I'd stashed this thing in here for a reason." The old woman held up a large square of folded canvas. She gave the door to her truck a hip shot and it slammed shut with a heavy clunk, the sound of bells punctuating the woman's movements.

Lizzie pushed herself onto her hands and knees as the blood rushed down her legs, making them prickle and throb.

"Wait a second child, and I'll give you a hand up." More sounds of bells shivering with each step the woman took.

On all fours, Lizzie saw the swish of the purple cotton of the woman's voluminous skirt, and tanned feet clad in apple green rubber sandals. She wore several anklets strung with tiny silver bells around her thick left ankle.

Tucking the tarp under her arm, she offered her other to Lizzie, who gratefully accepted it.

"Upsy-daisy." The woman gripped Lizzie's hand firmly, and with an effortless pull yanked Lizzie up onto her unsteady feet. Lizzie wasn't tall, but she towered over the old woman.

"Thank you." Lizzie uttered her first words since the woman had arrived.

"Just hold still a minute to make sure you've got your legs firmly underneath you. We don't want you toppling onto our poor injured friend here." The woman held firm to Lizzie, her green eyes gleaming with amusement.

When Lizzie felt steady enough, she helped the old woman unfold the tarp, wafting a faintly musty smell of old canvas into the air. They laid it down close to the dog's back. She saw what the old woman intended to do, but she had no idea how they were going to manage it.

"Any suggestions on how to get him safely on the tarp without hurting him anymore?" Lizzie gazed down at the furry giant. He still appeared to be sleeping. "Or how to lift him into the flatbed of your truck?"

"What a silly question to ask. Or maybe you're new to your powers." The woman peered at her, then her lips parted into a wide smile. Her wrinkles deepened around her eyes and mouth, her smile revealing surprisingly white teeth. "Yes, like a shiny new penny you are."

Lizzie mouth dropped open.

"Child, close your mouth or you'll catch flies." The woman chuckled when Lizzie snapped her mouth shut in response.

With the jingle of bells the old lady sashayed over to stand near the dog's head. "Just a simple spell is needed, nothing too complicated."

Lizzie shook her head, trying to focus on the strange little woman before her. "I don't know what to do. I think it would be better if I went home and got my handyman to help carry the dog."

"Pfft," the woman replied, flapping her hand dismissively. "If you can perform a healing like you just did, then a small spell like the one we need will be a cake walk for you."

"I don't think—"

"Then don't. Time's wasting, and our boy here needs to get to a doctor. Go stand by his back end, if you please."

And with that said, the old woman raised her hand and began the incantation.

CHAPTER ELEVEN

Lizzie sat on the thinly cushioned bench in the vet clinic's waiting room, the old woman perched beside her. She ran her fingers through her windblown hair to smooth out the tangles.

She'd elected to stay in the back of the truck bed with the dog on the ride into town. The spell the woman had cast enabled them to float the dog onto the tarp and then smoothly transfer him into the back of the truck. The dog had slept soundly through the process, and didn't even stir when Lizzie settled down next to him, gently placing his head in her lap. The whole way there she stroked his head, murmuring soothing words. She avoided looking at his ruined back end.

An hour had passed since the vet and her assistant, using a stretcher, had carried the dog into the clinic. They had rushed him straight into the x-ray room, leaving Lizzie and the old woman with the receptionist to fill out the necessary forms. Lizzie gave her name and phone number as the contact person, but neither the old woman nor she could offer any information about the dog itself. In the blank space for the dog's name, she saw the receptionist jot down the word *unknown*.

Lizzie shifted on the uncomfortable bench and glanced at the clock on the wall. It was past dinnertime, and the receptionist had long since packed up her things and gone home for the evening, locking the door behind her.

Images from her past overlapped in her mind…flashes of sitting in the hospital emergency room with Madison as they waited for the doctor attending her husband to come to them with the news of his passing. There were other images, of a time before then when in her loneliness and despair she had done something rash.

A warm dry hand on hers brought her back to the present. "There, there child. No need to dwell on the past. Those times don't exist anymore. That kind of pain needs to be put to rest."

Springing up from her place on the bench, breaking contact with the old woman's comforting gesture, Lizzie paced the small waiting room, her eyes focused on the worn out pink linoleum.

The tight circles of her pacing made her dizzy. She'd stopped to read the labels on the cans of dog food lined up neatly on a plywood shelf near the reception desk when the door to the back room of the clinic opened and out stepped the vet, a worried look furrowing her rather masculine brows. She wore a large white lab coat over her tall frame, and it billowed as she walked towards them.

A sudden urge to sit down had Lizzie scrambling back to the safety of the bench and the comforting presence of the old woman.

"That bear of a dog has a strong will to survive, but he's pretty busted up," the vet said, pushing her round wire-framed glasses up the bridge of her thin nose. "If you'll come with me, I'll show you on the x-rays."

They followed her into the small exam room and stood silently as she slotted several films into the light box and began explaining the extent of his injuries. He had suffered everything Lizzie had sensed when she first connected to his energy, right down to the sheared hip joint.

"I'll do my best to patch him up, but that's only the first hurdle. If he gets through the surgery and doesn't suffer any infections, he's still going to need at least three months to heal and recuperate. If everything goes well he should regain the use of his legs, but with that hip he's most certainly going to have a limp."

Lizzie stole a quick glance at the old woman and was surprised to see her nodding calmly, a small smile playing across her lips.

"The surgery isn't cheap, and then there's the pain meds and antibiotics he'll need," the vet continued. "He isn't wearing a collar and he doesn't have a tattoo or a microchip, so by all accounts he's just a stray. Do you really want to put that kind of money into a dog you don't even own? You wouldn't be considered irresponsible if you just want to put him down."

"No," Lizzie said. "Do the surgery. Do whatever it takes," she blurted out before the old woman could speak. "I'll pay for his surgery and whatever else he needs after that. Just please don't put him down."

Dr. Laurie looked over at the old woman as if waiting for her approval. The old woman gave a slight nod of her head.

"Well, because you're a friend of Grandma Faye's I can give you a discount, but you're still looking at a minimum of a couple of thousand dollars, and that's not including the meds."

"Just fix him."

"All right then," Dr. Laurie said, rubbing her hands together as if to warm them. "The operation is going to take several hours, so I suggest you go home. I call you in the morning and let you know how he's doing."

Lizzie had every intention of staying until the dog was in recovery, but before she could say as much Grandma Faye took her gently by the arm and guided her out of the exam room. As she firmly pushed Lizzie through the door, she called out over her shoulder, "That will be just fine, Dr. Laurie. That dog couldn't be in more capable hands."

She wanted to argue with Grandma Faye, but the look in the old woman's eyes made her reconsider. There was a steeliness there, right below the kindness, which made Lizzie swallow her words.

It wasn't until they were back in the truck headed down the highway for home that Lizzie realized how late it had gotten. The sun had dipped below the ridge of mountains, the peach colored sky already fading into lavender, although true twilight was still a couple of hours away.

"He didn't even slow down," Lizzie said. "I was standing at the mailboxes when I heard the horrible sound. It was only a few seconds after I heard the dog scream before the car sped past and almost ran me over. He was going so fast all I had time to do was jump out of the way." Lizzie pressed her lips together and blinked hard. "It wasn't an accident," she whispered.

"No, it doesn't sound like it," Grandma Faye said in a calm steady voice.

"But why? Why would anyone deliberately run down an innocent animal and leave it to die?"

"Evil doesn't need a reason any more than kindness does. It is in the act of doing either good or bad that the power exists, and not always in the motivation behind it."

Lizzie was too tired to follow the old woman's logic. To her, doing something cruel made no sense, no sense at all. She rubbed her gritty eyes with the heels of her hands, then dropped them heavily on her lap. All she wanted was a cold glass of water and a soak in a hot bath.

"Will he be okay?"

"Now, I can't be a hundred percent certain on the design fate has in store for that dog, but I feel pretty confident between the healing you gave him and Dr. Laurie's expert hands, our boy will come out just fine."

She knew they were just words, that Grandma Faye couldn't guarantee a positive outcome for the dog, but she found them reassuring all the same.

"Thank you for stopping to help. If you hadn't come by when you did I don't know what I would have done."

"You're welcome, but it wasn't chance that brought me to you. I was out feeding my chickens when I felt your magick. Hit me like a ton of bricks. I startled the flock when I cried out, and it just about knocked me on my bottom."

"About that. What we did back on the road, I'd like to keep that part between you and me. I moved out here so I could have some anonymity."

Grandma Faye kept her eyes on the road as she spoke. "Not to worry, your secret is safe with me, child. And I would appreciate the same consideration. The villagers know me as Grandma Faye, the dotty old woman who sells her eggs and homemade bread at the farmers' market, and I'd like to keep it that way."

"Consider it done." Lizzie relaxed, knowing her new life and the solitude she craved was still safe.

"Some things that exist in the world are better left in the shrouds of mystery, especially when it comes to the inhabitants of Barton. Even without meeting you, the villagers are already speculating about you. The less they know about the truth the better."

"What are they saying?" Lizzie forced herself to sound calm, but she could feel her heart fluttering in her throat.

"Oh, the usual and the not so usual." Grandma Faye slowed the truck down as two deer appeared at the side of the road. Stopping the truck on the empty highway, she nodded at the deer as if in acknowledgement, and waited as they carefully crossed the two-lane blacktop before she proceeded.

"Now what was I saying?"

"The villagers. The gossip they're spreading about me."

"Ah yes, let's see. Some are saying you are an eccentric millionaire from down East and you plan on buying up the whole village and using it for your own amusement, like Marie

Antoinette when she built that rustic hamlet and went about dressed like a milkmaid."

"What? Well, at least they got where I'm from right."

"I liked that one, it at least showed some creativity. The rest of the rumors are pretty run-of-the-mill. You are living out in the middle of nowhere because you are escaping a bad marriage or a lesbian affair, depending on who you talk to. Some say that you are just another city slicker who wants to try her hand at being a back-to-lander, and then there's the perennial favorite, seeing as you *are* a single woman and you bought Grey House no less, that you are a witch come to curse the village and practice your black magick."

"Oh God," Lizzie moaned. "What am I going to do?"

"Do? Nothing, my dear. If you ran around telling people about yourself, it wouldn't change a thing. In fact, you'd just give them more grist for the mill. You need to understand nothing much happens out here, and gossiping about a new arrival is the villagers preferred sport, next to fishing and drinking. In time, they'll get bored with you or someone in the village will cause a stir and become the new target for a while."

They rode in silence as Lizzie digested the old woman's advice. Hearing what people were saying about her brought the anger that seemed to be constantly simmering just under the surface rising to the top, but she refused to allow herself to feel it…she wouldn't give the prying villagers the satisfaction.

"You seem to have the residents of Barton pegged. Were you born here?

"No, but it's been over thirty years, so I'm only now considered part of the village and no longer an outsider."

Lizzie looked out the window at the lake, its water dark and brooding as sunset gave way to the deeper hues of nightfall. It looked menacing without the sun to sparkle off its surface, a black cold entity not unlike the one she'd vanquished in the forest not far from here.

She didn't know if it was the stress of the last few hours or Grandma Faye's depressing revelation that the village wouldn't open its arms to Lizzie in the foreseeable future that made her see a menacing vista, when really all it was, was a cold mountain lake at dusk.

Turning her attention back to Grandma Faye, she said, "I know from my past experiences I'm not the only one who has certain…talents, but I find it remarkable that it turns out there's another like me living just down the road."

"Life can be that way, full of surprises we didn't see coming."

Grandma Faye turned off the highway, and following Lizzie's directions, drove down Quail Hollow and rolled to a stop in front of the white gates of Rose Cottage. Lizzie got out and opened the gate, then climbed back into the cab as Grandma Faye insisted on dropping her off at her front door. She parked just behind Lizzie's truck. Audley's van was gone, which didn't surprise Lizzie since it was long past his quitting time.

Lizzie wanted to ask Grandma Faye what she knew of the first owner of Rose Cottage to find out what she thought of the legend, but looking up at her cottage she just wanted to peel off her dirty clothes and feel the heat of a hot bubble bath on her skin. She knew the polite thing would be to invite her neighbor in, but she was just too tired to follow convention and her mind was too preoccupied with the furry brute now being operated on. She hoped Grandma Faye's faith in the vet wasn't misplaced.

From the porch steps she waved goodbye until Grandma Faye's battered truck slipped through the trees lining the driveway and disappeared out of Lizzie's sight line. Reaching into the front pocket of her jeans, she dug out her key and unlocked the front door.

With a weary sigh she stepped into her cottage, shutting the door behind her. Even though the day had brought heat, the thick walls of the cottage had kept the inside cool, and with the setting sun, Lizzie felt a definite chill inside her home. The hair on her arms rose and she shivered.

Before he'd left for the day, Audley had laid kindling in the fireplace hearth and filled the woodbin next to the woodstove. If she weren't so tired, she would have lit a fire in the stone hearth in her bedroom to warm it before she crashed for the night. Instead, she stood at the sink filling a glass from the tap, already anticipating stripping off her soiled clothes and sinking into a bath.

She gulped down the ice-cold water, her empty stomach cramping from the intense cold. As she greedily drank, she sent a quick prayer to the goddess to watch over the bear of a dog.

Bear.

She couldn't think of a more fitting name for the oversized shaggy creature. She'd never had a dog as a companion before, and she looked forward with a ridiculous sense of joyful anticipation to opening her home to him.

Swallowing the last mouthful of water, she heard the squeak of rubber-soled shoes on the wood floor behind her. She turned towards the sound, alarm prickling her scalp, but her reaction was slowed by her exhaustion. She realized she was in danger a half-a-second too late.

CHAPTER TWELVE

The woman crouched on her haunches staring at Lizzie, a strange light shining from behind her. It danced and swayed, growing brighter then shrinking back to an eerie glow, only to intensify again. Lizzie glanced around the earthen room trying to make out the source of the strange luminosity, but could find nothing in the empty space but the woman opposite her.

As the soft glow brightened again, it illuminated the woman's dark green dress puddled on the tamped earth floor hiding her feet. The dress was made of a course fabric, the hem dirty and frayed. Strands of dark hair peeked out from underneath a white cotton cap cradling the woman's head. The woman remained motionless, revealing nothing in her dark unblinking eyes.

Lizzie tried to ask the woman for help but she couldn't speak. She needed to get out of this place. She wasn't supposed to be here. Without her voice to plead for help, she reached out her hand in supplication. But instead of helping the woman vanished, taking the light with her, plunging Lizzie into darkness.

CHAPTER THIRTEEN

The smells of damp earth and decay filled Lizzie's nostrils and clogged her throat. She gagged and tried to sit up, but sharp glinting razors of pain sliced through the back of her head, forcing her to remain lying on her side.

She took a shallow breath to avoid inhaling the cloying aroma of rotting vegetation. The darkness pressed in on her. Placing her fingertips lightly on her eyelids, she blinked to make sure her eyes were open, so thick was the darkness she found herself in.

She groped around in front of her, feeling only the gritty surface of hard-packed dirt under her fingers. Something skittered across her hand. She yelped, pulling her arm back sharply.

Remaining in a fetal position, she hugged her knees to her chest, shivering from the cold seeping up through the ground. Only when she focused on slowing down her breathing did she manage to push the edges of her panic down a few degrees.

Where was she?

She pressed her memory for a possible explanation, but her thoughts were disjointed. She remembered a round, wrinkled face of a kind old woman. A tinkle of silver bells.

The woman had helped her with something. No, not something, an animal. An injured animal. Yes, a dog. She'd come across a dog that had been hurt and lying in the middle of the road. Grandma Faye. Remembering the old woman's name seemed to unlock the rest of the events.

She remembered the dog she'd named Bear, the trip to the

vet, and the subsequent ride home with Grandma Faye. She recalled feeling tired and thirsty. So thirsty. She had wanted to soak in a hot bath, but had detoured to the kitchen to get a glass of water. That's where her memory abruptly ended. The rest was darkness, and then waking up to more darkness in the shivering cold space she now occupied.

No, that wasn't quite true. There was something in her kitchen. She tried to tease the recollection forward, but all she could summon up was a sickly-sweet smell. Even now, with the loamy perfume saturating the air, she could still taste a gag-inducing sweetness in the back of her throat.

A shrill ringing, faint but discernible in her darkened tomb, startled her, soaking her already chilled body in a sheen of perspiration. She listened intently. The sound was coming from above her and off to the left of where she lay. If she could trust her senses, despite her condition, she knew what she was hearing. It was the phone in her kitchen. Her newly installed phone. It rang two more times before the voicemail picked up and the only sound was her own heartbeat pounding in her ears.

She knew where she was now. She was lying on the floor of her own root cellar. Although her earlier foray into the root cellar had been brief, she now recognized the hard-packed earthen floor, the lingering smell of decay.

A few days ago, when Audley had pulled out the nails securing the trap door, she'd scrambled down just a few rungs of the rickety ladder. She had to use a flashlight to check out the space as there were no lights down there. She had been disappointed by what she saw. A few broken-down wooden crates were stacked haphazardly in one corner. Nothing else. She'd hoped to sense the earlier ripple of energy she'd felt when she first explored the house, but there was nothing, just an empty room.

Now that she was stuck down in the dark space, she was glad no other energy was down there with her. Especially one laced with such strong negative emotions.

What had caused her to abandon her need for a hot bath to run down into the cellar? Had she heard something, sensed something that was urgent enough to send her down into the dark? In her rush to get down here, did she stumble and bang her head? Or did the ancient ladder given way beneath her feet, causing her to tumble down into the darkness below?

Turning her head slightly, she scanned above her. Even the small movement sent spikes of fresh pain blossoming at the back of her head. She inhaled sharply, holding her breath until the sharpest edges of the pain subsided.

If she'd come down here of her own volition and somehow fallen off the ladder, the trapdoor to the cellar would still be open. She should be able to see the light from her kitchen filtering down the hall. But the darkness was profound.

She knew Audley would eventually come in the morning, but she had no idea what time it was. She could be waiting a few hours or a whole night before her handyman showed up for work. Would he hear her cries for help down in the cellar, or would he leave after finding she wasn't home?

Her throat clicked dryly.

She sought out the cross around her neck and felt the coldness of the stone the cross was carved from.

With slow deliberate movements, she reached around to the back of her head and gingerly felt around where it throbbed. She winced when her fingers made contact with a hard lump at the base of her skull. She pulled her hand away, her fingers wet and sticky.

Moving with infinite care, she inched herself into a sitting position. Her efforts were rewarded by a wave of nausea. Her head weighed a ton, and she held it in her hands until the throbbing eased enough for her to gather her thoughts.

The ladder. She needed to locate the ladder in the pressing

darkness and get herself out of the cellar. She hoped it was still in one piece and its untimely disintegration not the cause of her fall.

She had no idea what corner of the room she was in, but the room wasn't large. The trapdoor would be near one of the walls, and she reasoned that if she'd stumbled off the ladder it had to be somewhere within a four-foot radius of where she'd fallen.

She raised her arms and felt the air around her, hoping her fingers would brush against the splintery wood of the ladder. Instead, she grasped only empty air.

Moving on all fours she inched forward, patting the air in front of her, but she kept coming up empty-handed. Every few paces she would stop and lower her head when the waves of dizziness threatened to overcome her, then she would move forward again searching for the ladder. Just when she thought she was moving in circles, her right hand brushed up against something solid. She cried out with relief when both her hands made contact with a rung of the ladder. Her hands danced forward, reading the shape of the wooden rails. The ladder was lying on the floor, not upright. With shaking hands she continued to map out the shape of the ladder until her fingers found the top. The wooden structure was intact. She had the means to escape, she just had to figure out where the trapdoor was and get the ladder back in place.

With a frustrated sigh she carefully sat back on her haunches, brushing her dirty hands on her thighs. She needed light to see by if she had any hope of getting the ladder upright and hooked into the wooden ledge at the lip of the trap door.

She was alone, injured, and had no way to call for help. Waiting helplessly in hopes Audley would show up on time and hope that he would investigate why the house was locked up and no sign of Lizzie was a long shot. If she wanted out she would have to do it on her own.

She thought about her connection to Vivienne. If she reached out to her across the ether, Lizzie could send her mentor a distress call. She knew Vivienne wouldn't hesitate to send someone from the order to rescue her.

Rescue her from her own house. Admitting she had gotten herself into trouble when she hadn't even spent one night in her new home would be admitting she needed the protection of the order. Worse, it would mean her decision to move out to the middle of nowhere was a complete folly. No, the humiliation would be worse than being stuck in the dark or taking the small risk of using her own talents to get herself out of her current mess.

Raising her hands, she called out to the element of fire. She waited for the humming vibration of her magic to call forth the glowing light into her palms, but nothing happened. Panic flickered in her chest. She'd been able to call up each of the elements as easily as she could draw breath. She tried again, but she remained crouched in darkness.

Perhaps her fall had done more to her than giving her a knot on the back of her head.

Fumbling with the catch on the silver chain, she let her necklace fall into her palm. She cautiously reached her hand into the inky blackness and dropped the charmed necklace onto the floor a few inches away. Without the protection of her charm, her power was now unbound.

Gathering her energy, she sent her magick out again, calling to the fire element once more. And once more, nothing happened. Not even a glimmer.

She had feared her powers her whole life, had tried to deny their existence, tried in vain to deny that part of herself. Now they were gone.

She shook her head as if to deny what was happening, and was rewarded by a fresh bolt of pain. Raising her hands in supplication she tried to draw her powers out, and for the fourth time she failed to conjure even a flicker of light. She was deeply and truly panicked now. A familiar sensation fluttered in her chest and she gulped air. She hadn't suffered from a panic attack in months, but she hadn't forgotten what the early sensations felt like.

Scraping her fingers into the earth, she pulled her focus away from her body and out towards the ether. She searched for Vivienne's energetic signature, waiting for the click inside her brain that signaled she'd connected with her mentor's thoughts, but there was nothing but blackness and an echoing emptiness. Her ability to link with Vivienne was gone too.

Tears of frustration dampened her cheeks, and a dread more profound than she'd ever felt enveloped her, driving a coldness into her core. She was well and truly trapped in the basement of her own house.

CHAPTER FOURTEEN

Dropping her hands onto her thighs, Lizzie sobbed into the darkness, the thick earth walls muffling the sound of her despair. She didn't hear the front door open, but even through her hiccupping sobs she sensed the house change to welcome its visitors. It felt as if the house had sighed, even down in the bowels of its structure. She cocked her head, listening intently.

Then she heard them; the distinct shuffling footfalls of her handyman, Audley. She opened her mouth to call out when she heard a set of uneven footsteps following close behind his. She'd only met him once, but she recognized the sound Jon made with his cane, the sound of a lighter step on his injured leg followed by the step of his good leg, punctuated by the sharp rap of his cane tip on the wooden floor above.

She followed their progress into her kitchen and still she hadn't called out. Having Audley find her in such a ridiculous state was okay, but having Jon see her this way brought a rush of heat to her face. As embarrassing as it was going to be, she didn't really have a choice. She couldn't stay stuck down in her root cellar.

"Audley," she called out, her voice barely a whisper. She cleared her raw throat and tried again. "Help, I'm down here. In the root cellar."

She continued to yell to her would be rescuers, her voice becoming hoarser with the effort. The footsteps stopped somewhere near the kitchen and she called out again. Quickly now she heard them approach until they were right above her head. Silt drifted down on her from the joists, sprinkling her face and stinging her eyes. There was a creak of hinges as the cellar door was heaved open.

A pool of soft light flooded down around where Lizzie crouched. She'd been sitting directly below the trapdoor. Looking up into the opening, she blinked several times. The light momentarily disappeared as a welcomed figure leaned down into the open hatch. The light was behind him, throwing his face into shadows.

"Ms. Bennet, watcha doin' down in the cellar?" Audley asked as he hung his head down through the opening.

"I'm not really sure," she replied. "But I'd be grateful if you could get me out of here."

Another head appeared through the hatch. "Lizzie, are you hurt?"

She leaned back from the shaft of light and into the shadowy gloom of the cellar. Brushing at her face, she hoped she didn't look as bad as she felt.

"Nothing's broken, but I've managed to give myself a rather hard knock to the head. The ladder is down here with me, and in my present condition I don't think I can manage to get it back into place." Even the effort of speaking left her breathless.

"We'll have you out in no time," Jon said. "Audley, a rope."

"Sure thing, boss."

Audley disappeared from Lizzie's view. She could hear him shuffling around above her, and minutes later Jon fed a rope down to her. She grasped it, her stiff fingers struggling to close around the rough hemp.

"Can you manage to tie the rope to the top of the ladder? If you can't I can try and lower Audley down to help."

She almost said yes to bringing Audley down, but she knew Jon was still hurting from his injuries, and as small as Audley was, it would still take a great deal of strength to lower her handyman down to help her.

"No, that won't be necessary. But I wouldn't mind a flashlight if you have one handy. It's a bit dark down here."

More shuffling sounds, then Jon lobbed a flashlight down to her. It landed with a soft thump near Lizzie's knee.

Just having the light from the flashlight renewed her energy. Even the pain at the back of her skull had subsided. She quickly looped the rope on the top rung and crawled out of the way as Jon and Audley hauled the ladder upright and back into place.

Once the ladder was secured, Audley nimbly scrambled down. He grasped Lizzie by the arms and gently helped her stand. The movement caused an explosion of stars to zip crazily in front of her eyes. She held tightly to Audley's thin arms until her vision cleared.

Audley's familiar scent of stale marijuana was as reassuring as the sight of his plain features and his crumpled work clothes. Her gratitude was so overwhelming that if she'd had the strength she would have hugged him tightly.

"You head up the ladder first and I'll be right behind you makin' sure you don't fall back down. Okay?"

"Okay." She smiled at him. In the unsure half-light of the cellar, his eyes looked sad or worried, Lizzie couldn't decide which.

The two of them did an awkward waltz across the dirt floor with Audley holding her by the waist as he shuffled backwards into position at the foot of the ladder.

Lizzie felt Jon's eyes on her as he watched the procedure from his position up in the hall. Her hands shook as she placed them on the rung just above her head. With cautious slowness she made her ascent, conscious of Audley's chest pushing gently on her back, his arms on either side of her, his hands sliding up the rails near her shoulders. Even if she picked this moment to pass out, Audley's embrace would save her another tumble down the ladder. She had a new appreciation for her handyman.

As her head and torso emerged through the cellar door, Jon stood up with the help of his cane, holding his good arm out to her. Placing her feet on the solid floor of her hallway, it felt like the most natural thing to step into Jon's outstretched arm and allow him to cradle her against his chest. The curve of her body seemed to find its natural fit in the compliment of Jon's broad chest and the angle of his trim waist. He gave her a gentle squeeze and she settled in closer against the soft cashmere of his brown sweater. It smelled of laundry soap and aftershave.

She would have liked nothing more than to close her eyes and stay within Jon's encircling arm, but the thwack of the trapdoor as it dropped closed and the scuffling sound of Audley's work boots on the wood floor pulled her attention back to her handyman.

"Ms. Bennet, shouldn't we do something about that cut on your head? Seems to be bleeding," Audley said, shifting closer to her.

"Yes, let's get you where the light's a little better and get that looked after," Jon said.

Reluctantly she straightened her shoulders and stepped back, creating a few inches of space between her and Jon. The two men guided her down the hall.

"Mind your step," Jon warned as they skirted Audley's open toolbox and the coil of rope on the floor.

They made their way into her kitchen. The light of early morning draped the house in its lemony disposition, making her primitive kitchen and her make-do camping chairs seem like the most comforting space she could imagine. Although the house was cool, it was perceptibly warmer than the damp hole she'd woken up in.

"What time is it?" she asked no one in particular as the two men deposited her in one of the camping chairs at the table.

"A little after eight," Jon replied.

She'd spent the whole night down in the cellar.

"Let me take a look at your head. Audley, there's a first-aid kit in my truck."

Audley trotted out of the house, but not before patting her awkwardly on the shoulder. His concern brought a small smile to her lips.

"What brought you here so early? I don't usually expect Audley to show up until around ten."

"That would be my doing," Jon said as he moved behind her.

Her heart raced as she felt his fingertips brush her hair away from the contusion on her scalp, his touch so gentle she barely felt any discomfort. As he probed around the base of her skull, a delicious shiver tingled down her neck where his fingers brushed the skin.

"I wanted you to take a look at the kitchen plans I'd drawn up. I'm going to Nelson today to pick up supplies for another job, and if you signed off on the plans, I could pick up supplies for your job too. Save me another four-hour trip through the mountains. I figured you for an early riser, and that you wouldn't mind me dropping by if it meant we could get started on your kitchen."

"Mmm, that makes sense," she murmured. As she settled into the chair, her frayed nerves relaxed under Jon's touch. Her gaze lazily followed the grain of the wood on the table, admiring the dings and dents from years of use. Her eyes lit on her front door key lying in the middle of the table, and a large leather briefcase placed off to the side.

"How did you get in?" Her tongue seemed too big for her mouth and her words came out slurred.

"The door was unlocked." Jon stopped his examination of her head and rested his hands on her shoulders. A sinking warmth seeped down her shoulders. She stifled a small sigh of pleasure.

"You must have forgotten to lock it behind you, which was a good thing as it turned out. If it had been and you hadn't answered the door, I would have assumed you were sleeping and Audley and I would have left you in peace. He wouldn't have come back for a couple of hours."

Jon removed his hands and she straightened up. The cold returned to her body. She longed for him to touch her again.

"Well, I think you're going to survive," he announced. "You've got a nasty goose egg and the skin's split, but I don't think you're going to need stitches."

Audley returned with a clatter of his work boots on the hardwood. He handed Jon the first-aid kit, then took a seat next to Lizzie, his eyes large and curious. "So how'd ya get stuck down there with the trapdoor closed like that?"

"I haven't a clue. I'd just returned from town and was standing by the sink getting a drink of water, and the next thing I knew I was lying on the ground down in the cellar." Lizzie reached out to touch her key on the table and noticed how dirty her hand was. The fingertips on her right hand were sticky and crusted with dried blood and dirt. She pulled her hand off the table and gave her fingers a vigorous scrub against her thigh.

"You don't remember anything?" Jon asked as he rummaged around in the first-aid kit.

She slowly turned her head, as the bump on her skull was still wreaking havoc on her equilibrium, to look up at Jon.

"Nothing. Just an odd sweet smell."

"It was the witch," Audley said. "She lured you down there and closed you in."

She turned to look at Audley. The quick shift of her gaze sent bright sparks of light across her vision.

"Sure enough, it was the witch of Grey House. People that have had the misfortune of seein' her swear they smell a sweet aroma before she appears. They say it's the smell of the herbs and things she used to make her potions."

"Audley, that's enough."

"But how else would you explain how she got down there with the trap door closed? There's no way to prop the trapdoor open when you go down...you have to lay it flat on the floor. It can't accidently close when it's layin like that. And the smell, how do you explain that?"

"I said that's enough; can't you see you're scaring her?" To Lizzie he said, "Now let's see to that cut."

He stepped behind her, but instead of attending to her wound, he placed his hands on her shoulders again. Her limbs slackened as a delicious warmth spread through her body, leaving her pleasantly numb. She was drifting effortlessly on a warm current of air. Any discomfort in her body dissolved like gossamer webs in the breeze.

Leaning over so that his mouth was near her ear, he spoke in a soothing tone. "You're all right now. No harm has come to you."

"Yes," she replied her voice thick.

"And you trust me, I'm your friend."

"Yes."

"As your friend you can tell me anything. And what you tell me will remain our secret."

She was trying to get her mouth to form the word yes one more time, but the muscles in her jaw didn't want to cooperate. Not that it mattered...Lizzie was floating in such a pleasant dream.

"Now, where shall we begin?" he said, stroking the curve of her neck with his thumb. Lizzie slipped further down into the warm womb-like dream. "Perhaps let's start with what is missing. Lizzie, where is that pretty little necklace you had on the other day? You know the one I mean, the one shaped like a cross carved from a lovely blue stone." His voice slipped through her ear like warm honey.

She'd finally managed to open her mouth to tell him it was down in the cellar when someone called out from the porch.

"Hello in the house," called out Grandma Faye's melodic voice, followed by a sharp rap on the front door.

The knock on the door startled Lizzie and the room spun drunkenly. She grasped the edge of the table to keep herself upright.

For a moment neither Jon nor Audley moved. "Get the door," Jon ordered, and the handyman sprang to life.

He opened the door for Grandma Faye. She stepped over the threshold, the bells on her ankle dancing musically beneath the bright orange skirt she wore. A pink shawl was draped over her shoulders, and she carried a large wicker basket covered in a blue checked cloth, her arms looped through the handles.

She gave Audley a cheerful smile. "Good morning, Audley. I heard Lizzie had you working on the place. Are you keeping out of trouble?"

"Yes, Grandma Faye."

"And you aren't indulging too much in your pastime, I take it. Because it wouldn't do for you to show up to work muddle headed, now would it?"

"No ma'am," Audley mumbled, looking down at his feet.

He stepped back to allow her into the cottage, the smell of fresh bread following in her wake. Three steps in she stopped. Looking at Lizzie, her warm smile faltered.

Lizzie squinted at Grandma Faye. For such a small woman she seemed to take up too much space, and use too much air. Even the way she was dressed, with her orange skirt and pink shawl, was loud and garish, jangling Lizzie's nerves. She wanted to tell her to go away, but Lizzie's ability to speak seemed beyond her.

"Jon, it's been awhile."

"Grandma Faye," Jon replied with a nod of his head.

Grandma Faye turned her attention to Lizzie. "Well my dear, you look a little worse for wear. What happened to you?" She handed her basket over to Audley, and with a swish of her skirt, she came to stand between Jon and Lizzie, effactually pushing Jon out of the way so he had to take a step backwards. Lizzie tried to ask Grandma Faye what she was doing in her cottage, but all that came out was a mumble. She watched the old woman give a sharp glance to Jon and then Audley.

"Seems she took a fall down the cellar ladder. We found her this morning down there with the trapdoor closed. But other than a bump on the back of the head, she seems to be doing okay. She'll probably have a killer headache for a while," Jon said.

"Let me take a look."

Granma Faye crouched down in front of Lizzie. She placed her smooth hands on either side of Lizzie's head and looked her in the eye. "Do either of you have a small flashlight handy?" she asked the two men while she continued to stare at Lizzie. Lizzie heard Audley move down the hallway and returned moments later, handing the old woman a small penlight. "This will do nicely," she said, taking the flashlight from Audley and shining the small beam directly into Lizzie's eyes. Lizzie flinched.

"Are you experiencing any nausea or headache?"

Lizzie thought the questions were rather silly. Of course she had a headache, she'd taken a tumble down a ladder, whacking her head in the process.

"I'm a bit dizzy, and for obvious reasons my head hurts."

Nodding her head, Grandma Faye rose and stood behind Lizzie as Jon had done earlier, and with cool meticulous fingers, she examined Lizzie's head. Lizzie shivered. She sat quietly while Grandma Faye made her assessment.

"Jon's right, you don't need stitches, but we need to get the wound cleaned, and let's see what I can do about getting the swelling down. Your pupils are responsive, so that's a good sign."

Grandma Faye came around the table and took the basket from Audley's hands. He was still standing in the middle of the room, a look of confusion on his face. Jon, in the meantime, had stepped away from the kitchen table and was standing by the fireplace, his good arm leaning up against the rough-hewn mantle.

With quick efficient movements, Grandma Faye unpacked several fresh loaves of bread from the basket, placing them on the counter. "Audley, fill this with plantain. I saw a plentiful patch near the old shed." Audley took the proffered basket, his mouth hanging open. "And don't bring in clods of dirt when you pick them. Give them a good shake before putting them in the basket." The handyman stood where he was, giving a beseeching look to his boss. "Off you go then." The old woman gave him a gentle push as if dealing with a small child. Audley took a stumbling step backwards, then scrambled out the door.

Grandma Faye turned her attention to Jon. "I see there's wood laid in the grate." She pointed to the fireplace. "I think you can handle getting that lit. It's freezing in here, and Lizzie's in shock and needs to be kept warm." She flung her shawl off her shoulders and with one graceful movement settled it around Lizzie's shoulder. "And once you're done here, Jon, see to the fire in her bedroom."

With Jon thus engaged, Grandma Faye rummaged in the kitchen, pulling open cupboards and drawers.

Lizzie put her elbows on the table and rested her sore head in her hands. Her thinking seemed clearer, and with Grandma Faye's shawl around her she was warmer, but she still felt slightly odd. Not quite herself, which would be expected considering what she'd just been through. She watched Jon as he put a match to the kindling, the crackle of the wood igniting, briefly filling the silence, followed by the sound of running water from the kitchen sink.

Moments later, Grandma Faye returned to the table, placing an enamel bowl filled with warm water and a stack of folded dishrags near Lizzie's elbow. Lizzie recognized the waffle pattern as the new ones she'd purchased during her trip to Revelstoke. She hadn't even had a chance to use them yet.

Grandma Faye hummed a lilting tune under her breath as she set about soaking one of the clean dishrags in the bowl. After ringing it out, she carefully dabbed at the back of Lizzie's head.

Lizzie winced as the warm cloth made contact.

"So how did you manage to get yourself stuck down in the root cellar?" Grandma Faye asked.

She repeated her tale, including the strange smell that was present before she blacked out. She withheld the more important piece of information regarding her powers. She'd have to wait until she was alone with the old woman to give her the distressing news.

As Grandma Faye administered to Lizzie's head, Lizzie's faculties returned, her thoughts clear and precise. "If Audley and Jon hadn't shown up when they did, I still be stuck down there."

"How fortunate for you they did," Grandma Faye said, ringing out her cloth. Lizzie watched as the water in the enamel bowl turned pink.

Grandma Faye took the bowl from the table and returned to the sink for fresh water. Lizzie rubbed her temples. Something had happened down in the cellar, more than her powers evaporating, something else that was just as significant. She just couldn't recall what it was even with her thoughts returning to normal. She blamed it on the pounding headache.

Audley entered the cottage, huffing as he tried to catch his breath. He presented Grandma Faye with her basket full of the dark green leafy weeds she'd requested.

Jon silently moved off to kindle the fire in Lizzie's bedroom.

"You can give those a good rinse under cold water and then

place them in a large bowl. I spotted one in the cupboard to the left of the sink that will do nicely," said Grandma Faye. She joined Audley at the kitchen counter, opening cupboards and rattling the cutlery drawer. Lizzie listened to the movements behind her, but was content to watch the fire in the hearth. There must have been a few apple wood logs on the fire from the downed fruit tree Audley had cleared up earlier in the week, for the air in her cottage filled with the sweet smoke as the flames licked higher in the firebox.

She closed her eyes for a moment, imagining the movement in the kitchen was in preparation of a meal. She spun out her daydream, populating her cottage with friends gathered to share a meal. A meal whose ingredients she had harvested from her own gardens. A pie for dessert sat cooling on the counter, the apples that formed the filling plucked from her own fruit trees that grew alongside her veggie garden.

"Here we are." Grandma Faye's return to Lizzie's side interrupted her charming daydream. She opened her eyes and peered down at the Pyrex bowl filled with finely chopped greens. She wondered in dismay if Grandma Faye expected her to eat the strange green fibrous concoction. She tentatively poked the thick green mush. It was cold and wet.

"It's plantain. I'm using it as a poultice for your head."

"You're going to put a weed on my goose egg?" Lizzie vaguely recalled reading about plantain in the book on local plants she'd bought at the bookstore the day she found Rose Cottage.

"The 'First Nations' people prized it for its ability to bring down inflammation, and its antiseptic properties. More importantly, it quickly stops blood flow and promotes the repair of damaged tissue. Which in your case is just the ticket," said Grandma Faye.

"That's a relief; for a second I thought you were going to make me eat it."

"Oh, the young fresh leaves are delicious in a salad or lightly steamed as a side dish. I'll make some for you later."

Lizzie made a noncommittal sound.

Grandma Faye gathered a handful of the chopped herbs, and after giving them a squeeze to remove some of the moisture applied them to Lizzie's head, using another of Lizzie's brand new kitchen cloths to hold the poultice in place.

"Lower your head a bit, dear," Grandma Faye instructed as she applied the poultice. "That's better," she added as she held the macerated herbs to the wound.

The wet herbs were cool against Lizzie's head. While Grandma Faye held the poultice in place with one hand, she rested her other on Lizzie's shoulder. "Let's see if we can do something about the pain," she whispered into Lizzie's ear.

From the palm of her hand that cupped Lizzie's shoulder a steady warmth emanated, flowing up her neck to her head. Almost immediately her headache abated. She felt relief mingled with gratitude for Grandma Faye's unscheduled visit.

With her head still bowed, she spoke to Grandma Faye. "What brought you here this morning?"

"Providence, no doubt," Grandma Faye said, removing the poultice and refreshing it with more herbs from the bowl. "I was headed to town to deliver an order of bread when I spied the gate to your place standing open. I had made you a loaf and was going to drop it off on my way back from town, but I felt drawn to bring it to you now. I never question those kind of urges, and as you can see my presence was needed."

Grandma Faye removed the poultice, and with a clean kitchen towel gently dried the area around Lizzie's wound. "That should do the trick. Now a few steri-strips to close the wound and you're as good as new." The old woman riffled through the first-aid kit Audley had left on the table and procured the little bandages. She applied then with expert hands.

Lizzie raised her head as Grandma Faye busied herself at the kitchen sink, washing and putting away the bowls and rinsing out the dishrags. When Lizzie straightened up in her chair, she noticed Audley was still standing in the center of her living room staring at her. It wasn't until moments later, when Jon returned from lighting the fire in the bedroom, that Audley seemed to come to life, rushing to his boss's side.

"Well, I guess if there is nothing else you need done, we should leave you in the capable hands of Grandma Faye."

"Yes, you've both been most helpful, but what she needs right now is some rest."

Audley spoke. "Shouldn't she go to the hospital? What if something got knocked loose in her brain?"

"Lizzie's tougher than she looks. She may have a slight concussion, but I'll monitor her over the next twenty-four hours, and if anything changes I'll call Doc Connelly."

Lizzie cleared her throat. "But your bread delivery, aren't your customer's expecting their orders? Go, I'll be fine by myself. Like you said, I'm stronger than I look, and I'm already feeling tons better. You can stop by on your way home and check on me if that would make you feel better about leaving."

"No, Audley is right. Someone needs to make sure you haven't given yourself a concussion. From what I see you should be fine, but it's better to be on the safe side."

"If you're worried about Grandma Faye's customers, Audley will gladly deliver your orders," Jon said. "Seeing as he's not going to work here today, it's the least he can do to help out, right Audley?"

"Right boss. I'll just go get my tool box." He hurried down the hall and began gathering up his tools.

Grandma Faye loaded up the bread back into the now empty basket, covering the golden loaves with the blue and white cloth, and handed it over to Audley when he finished collecting his toolbox. She put one loaf aside for Lizzie.

Jon approached the table and reached for his briefcase.

"But the kitchen plans," Lizzie said, suddenly remembering what had brought Jon to her cottage in the first place. "Don't you want me to take a look at them?"

"We'll do it another time, when you're feeling better."

"But it'll mean an extra trip to Nelson. If the plans are in your briefcase let me take a look."

Jon hesitated. "If you insist." He snapped open the clasps of the briefcase and pulled out several sheaves of paper, laying them out on the table in front of her.

There was a schematic drawing detailing the electrical and plumbing, a floor plan showing the layout of the cabinets and appliances, and a colored elevation depicting a simple and elegant country kitchen. There was even a cost breakdown of the materials. Lizzie was in love. It was the kitchen of her dreams.

"Jon, the kitchen is beautiful." She looked up at his smiling face. "It's even better than I imagined it would be."

"I thought simple, white, shaker-style cabinets would be fitting with the style of the cottage, and we'll be able to keep the farm sink, but I'll replace the faucet with a goose-neck model. It's easier to fill pots and things than the old one. And as you can see from the drawing, I'll rewire and install another breaker so we can move the fridge into the kitchen proper and give you a stove. Seeing as you don't have natural gas lines out here it will have to an electric range, but I think it will more than do the job."

"And you've kept the woodstove." She touched the floorplan with her finger. During their initial conversation about the kitchen reno, she'd forgotten to mention to him that she wanted it to stay, and was pleased he'd incorporated it into his plans.

"I'm glad you approve," Jon said, gathering up his papers and slipping them back into his briefcase.

"Oh yes. It's the most exquisite kitchen I've ever seen. Now that I've seen the plans I can't wait."

"Well, you won't have to wait too long. If you sign off on the cost and the plans, I can pick up what I need today and order the cabinets. Audley and I can have the install done in a couple of weeks." He pulled out another paper and a pen from the bottom of the briefcase and presented them to Lizzie.

She scrawled her signature and handed them back to him.

"I guess we'll be off then," Jon said, picking up his briefcase and nodding to Audley.

Suddenly Lizzie was struck with the need to have both Audley and Jon stay. It was a ridiculous thought, but having them here with Grandma Faye despite the circumstances made Lizzie long for the odd mix of companions populating her kitchen to remain. It reminded her of her time at the hotel with Madison, Gideon, and Vivienne. With an overwhelming sense of regret, she realized how much she missed her surrogate family.

"Audley, Jon, thank you for coming to my rescue. I am in your debt," Lizzie said, a strange unnamed emotion clogging her throat.

Audley's only response was an odd bob of his head before he scurried out the door with his toolbox in one hand, Grandma Faye's basket in the other, and the coil of rope slung over his shoulder.

"You're welcome. But in the future you might want to avoid getting near any root cellars," Jon said with a smile, then followed his handyman out.

As Jon closed the door behind him, the house settled around the two women, the only sound the crackle and pop of the logs on the hearth.

"Grandma Faye," Lizzie said.

"Yes, child?"

"Do you think I could have a glass of water? I'm awfully thirsty."

* * * *

Lizzie had to be content with sucking on ice chips from the glass of crushed ice Grandma Faye handed her. The old woman had insisted that filling her stomach full of cold water when she was still nauseous was just asking for trouble.

After somewhat slaking her thirst, Lizzie took up Grandma Faye's suggestion to lie down. She was tired, but on the way to her bedroom, she stopped off at the bathroom to wash her face and arms. The thought of slipping between her new clean sheets when she was filthy wasn't appealing. She washed quickly, noting her reflection in the bathroom mirror.

Only a few months ago she'd stood in front of the mirror at the nearby resort cabin she'd been staying at and had looked at a decidedly less attractive reflection of herself. After destroying the demon sent by the still unknown warlock, she'd come back to the cabin bloodied and soaked to the skin.

Other than the dirt and the bump on her head, she looked pretty good. However, she was tired and the short walk from the kitchen to the bathroom drained what little energy she had left. Sleep called to her like a lover.

As she drained the dirty water from the sink, she realized she'd spent her first night in her cottage, just not in the way she'd intended. With a rueful smile she headed to her bedroom, anticipating the sweet relief of lying down for a while.

She stifled a yawn as she walked down the short hall, running her hand along the wall for balance. Grandma Faye was back in the kitchen, but Lizzie noted she'd been in her bedroom while Lizzie was washing up. Her nightgown was laid across the foot of the camping cot, the bed had been turned down, and Grandma Faye had found the extra sheets Lizzie had left folded on the top of her suitcase and had strung them up over the windows and the french door to darken the room.

The subdued lighting and a comforting fire blazing in the

hearth was all the enticement Lizzie needed to crawl into bed. She shed her clothes, leaving them in a pile on the floor, and carefully slipped her nightgown over her head and climbed into bed.

She slowly lowered herself onto her side. The inflatable mattress shifted to accommodate the weight of her body. Her heavy lids drooped and she closed her eyes with a sigh. Before sleep overcame her, she heard Grandma Faye's confident footsteps down the hall. Forcing herself to open her eyes, she saw Grandma Faye standing in the doorway.

She held a kitchen towel and a bag of frozen peas from Lizzie's freezer. She approached Lizzie, and leaning over her propped the frozen peas wrapped in the towel on the pillow next to her head, and with gentle motions let the weight of the bag rest against the back of Lizzie's head. Lizzie shivered and pulled the blankets under her chin.

"Thank you," she murmured, feeling the pull of sleep calling her down.

"You're welcome. Now rest for a bit. I'll be waking you in a couple of hours just to make sure you didn't give yourself a concussion."

"Grandma Faye, something happened down in the cellar," Lizzie whispered. She was so tired she needed to tell her what had happened to her magick.

"What, my child?" Grandma Faye asked, rearranging the blankets neatly around Lizzie's chin.

"My powers, they're gone," she managed to murmur. She felt Grandma Faye's cool hand on her forehead before she slipped into unconsciousness.

CHAPTER FIFTEEN

Lizzie opened her eyes and stretched. The air mattress squeak as she moved. Although the inflatable camping bed was temporary until her real bed was delivered, it was proving to be less comfortable than she'd anticipated judging by the stiffness in her lower back and the hip she was lying on.

She shifted onto her back, and as she did, something cold and lumpy pressed against her neck. Reaching behind her, she pulled out the bag of frozen peas wrapped in a towel. The bag was still cold but the peas had begun to thaw. She pushed herself up into a sitting position and dropped the make-shift cold pack on the floor.

"Good morning," Grandma Faye said. "Or should I say, good afternoon." She turned over the book she was reading and rested it in her lap.

She was sitting next to the fireplace in the rocking chair that normally sat next to the woodstove in the kitchen. Lizzie's new sheets were still in place over the window frames and the french door where Grandma Faye had hung them, and the filtered light of the late afternoon seeped around their edges. The fire was banked, and the orange glow of the dying embers cast a flickering light across the hardwood floor.

"Can you tell me your name?" Grandma Faye asked.

"Lizzie Bennet," she replied, and before Grandma Faye could ask the rest of the questions, Lizzie supplied the answers. "I'm thirty-five and I live at 3797 Quail Hollow Road, British Columbia.

You are my neighbor, Grandma Faye, and you keep waking me up and asking me these annoying questions because I was stupid enough to fall down into my own root cellar and whack myself on the head." She smiled at her friend. "Did I pass?"

"With flying colors. How does your head feel?"

Lizzie gingerly felt the back of her head. There was a slight tenderness, but the golf ball sized knot at the base of her skull had gone down to a barely noticeable lump.

She was hoping it was her own unique talent that was the cause of her clear-headedness and rapid healing, and not just Grandma Faye's poultice. If she still had the power to heal maybe her other powers would return too. Her chest tightened at the thought of not having her powers anymore.

She reached to her throat to touch the cross at her neck, but her fingers found only the bare skin of her throat.

"My necklace," she said, flinging back the bed covers and swinging her legs over the edge of the mattress. "Where's my necklace?" She searched the stacked boxes she'd placed next to the bed to use as a nightstand, but the only thing that was on it was a glass of water that once had been full of ice chips and the penlight Grandma Faye had used to check Lizzie's pupils every time she woke her to ask her questions.

She stood up and tossed back the bedcovers, searching the mattress for her necklace. Grabbing at the pillows, she pitched them off the bed. Her necklace wasn't there.

"You weren't wearing it this morning, but you did have it on yesterday when I met you on the road. I remember thinking what a beautiful stone it was." Grandma Faye stood up and put her book on the mantle.

Grandma Faye's words twigged her memory, and she sat back down on the edge of the bed. She'd left it down in the cellar when she'd tried to cast a spell and had failed. Climbing back down into the dank, little space was the last thing she wanted to do, but she needed to get her necklace back.

"It's down in the cellar where I left it," Lizzie said. She put her head in her hands. "I took it off when I discovered I couldn't cast an illumination spell."

Her powers. Could they really be gone for good?

She shivered despite the warmth in the room.

Grandma Faye joined her on the edge of the bed. The cot's metal frame groaned under the added weight of the old woman. Grandma Faye patted Lizzie's knee.

Lizzie looked down. She noticed Grandma Faye was barefoot. She had perfectly proportioned toes, graceful arches, and skin that unlike her hands were smooth and unblemished. The feet of a young woman. To her amusement each little half-moon shaped nail was painted a glossy red. They looked like rubies against the dark hardwood floor.

"Are you quite sure you've lost your powers? Because when I was attending to your wound this morning I could feel your magick and it felt quite strong."

Lizzie raised her head, searching the woman's wrinkled face.

"I don't know. I don't feel any different. But when I tried to summon the fire element there was nothing. Not even a flicker of magick."

"Well, there is one way of being sure. Try it again." Grandma Faye pointed to the water glass. "Levitate the glass. I've already showed you how to do that one, and it's a beginner's spell."

Lizzie hesitated. She really shouldn't be using her magick until the warlock was captured. But if she couldn't cast she'd know for sure that her powers had abandoned her. Could she live with being ordinary? Wasn't that what she'd wished for since she was old enough to realize she wasn't like everyone else?

"Yes. Okay. Just a simple spell and then I'll know for sure." Lizzie sat up straight and turned her focus to the glass next to the bed. She raised her hands to summon the air element. She stared at her shaking hands.

"Lizzie, what are you waiting for? There's no need to be afraid."

Lizzie drew in a breath and closed her eyes. She almost cried out in relief as she felt the ripple of power cascade down her body. Confident now, she called out and was rewarded as a pale yellow orb appeared floating inches above her open palm. Sending her focus to the water glass, she felt the air current shift and the glass trembled on the box. She narrowed her focus, blocking out the room and Grandma Faye as she willed the glass to rise.

The water in the glass rippled slightly as the glass floated up into the air.

"I did it," Lizzie exclaimed. "My powers are back." In her excitement, her concentration wavered and the glass tipped dangerously in the air.

Lizzie shot out her hand and caught the glass seconds before it crashed to the ground. Water splashed over the rim and onto her hand. "Okay, I need to work on my focus." She laughed. "So why couldn't I cast down in the cellar?"

Grandma Faye shrugged. "Maybe the shock of the fall had something to do with it."

Lizzie thought about the other times she'd had to use her magick when she'd been hurt or frightened, and she'd never lost her ability, not even when she'd thought she was going to die in her stand-off with the demon. What happened down in the cellar didn't make sense.

"Maybe," Lizzie said. She'd have to figure out the mystery later, for now she needed to go back into the cellar and retrieve her necklace. Everything else could wait until she had it securely around her neck again.

"You must be hungry," Grandma Faye said, pushing herself off the bed. "I hope you don't mind, but I took the liberty and went through your cooler and cupboards. I could whip you up an omelet, and there's fresh bread with your name on it."

"I would like nothing more than to have a hot shower and something to eat, but before I do anything I need to get my necklace."

"Surely that can wait until you've had some nourishment. It's not like it's going anywhere."

"I know it may seem silly, but I'm used to having it with me. It's a family heirloom and means a great deal to me." Her hand snuck up around her neck, touching the hollow of her throat where the cross usually rested.

"Yes, I can see that. Why don't I just pop down and get it for you while you jump in the shower?"

Grandma Faye made to leave the bedroom, but Lizzie leapt off the bed and grabbed the old woman's shoulder.

"No, that wouldn't be a good idea." The look on the old woman's face had her scrambling to smooth the furrows that appeared between Grandma Faye's eyebrows. "It's a kind offer because I don't relish going back down into that spider infested hole, but I don't think it would be safe for you to pick it up."

Grandma Faye tilted her head and rested her hand on the doorknob.

"Sorry, I'm not being very clear. My mother placed a ward on it. The only way it would be safe for you to hold it is if I willingly handed it over to you."

"Oh, I see. You're right, best for me not to touch it. Well, I'll leave you to get dressed. I'll be in the kitchen." The old woman left Lizzie to change.

Lizzie dug through her suitcase at the foot of her bed and pulled out what she needed. She dressed quickly and proceeded out into the hall.

Grandma Faye was standing at the kitchen counter grating cheese into a bowl. Putting down the metal grater, she joined Lizzie in the hallway.

"Let me do this," she said, leaning over to roll up the threadbare carpet runner. "You may be feeling better, but there's no need to push it."

Lizzie smiled at Grandma Faye's back. She wondered if she would become as bossy when she'd lived alone for a while. Without waiting for Lizzie's help, the old woman yanked open the trapdoor. She let it fall open, and it made a substantial thwack as it contacted the floor.

The slightly metallic smell of loamy earth filled the hallway. Lizzie reached over and flipped on the hall lights before peering down into the mouth of the opening. Even with the late afternoon sun spilling down the hall from the kitchen windows and the illumination of the sconces along the corridor wall, the light puddling at the base of the ladder only extended a few feet beyond the last rung.

Lizzie hugged herself and rubbed her upper arms, dispelling a faint chill she felt despite the sweater she'd put on. From where she stood she studied the ladder, making sure the hooks at the top were secured properly in the ledge designed to hold the ladder in place. It looked fine. Lizzie shifted positions and craned her neck to see farther into the root cellar. She caught a glimpse of the faint shine of silver just at the edge of the shaft of light pooled on the packed earth floor. It would be easy to go get her necklace. It was just sitting a couple of feet from the base of the ladder. She need only make the quick climb down, take two steps, grab her necklace, and then climb back up. Easy.

"Is there something wrong? Do you sense something down there?" Grandma Faye asked, peering around Lizzie's shoulder into the hole in the floor.

"No, no. I was just thinking maybe a bit more light would be wise. I'll be right back."

Lizzie walked towards the kitchen but detoured into the mudroom. From the shelf above the washing machine she took down two large, lantern-style flashlights. She turned them both on, satisfied when they both worked. She fiddled with the dial on one of them, playing with the intensity of the beam.

Fear kept bumping against her chest, unnerving her. If Madison was with her she'd give her a friendly punch on the arm and tell her it was time to put on her big girl panties, hustle her butt down into the cellar, and get her damned necklace.

She missed Madison everyday, but the longing intensified standing in her back porch fussing over flashlights. She was stalling and she knew it. She'd thought the recent challenges in her life had made her fearless. Apparently she was only brave when she was protecting others. When it came to herself and her own needs, she reverted to her old ways.

She ground her back teeth together.

Moving out to the middle of nowhere was a stupid idea, perhaps the dumbest she'd ever had, prophetic dream or not. She'd sunk most of her savings into buying and renovating Rose Cottage. She had no place else to go. She had no one she could turn to. She needed to make this work.

But she'd never make a go of it if she was going to be a shrinking violet at the first sign of a challenge. There had to be a simple, logical explanation as to how she ended up locked down in the root cellar, why her powers had disappeared, and why the thought of going down there again made her hands slippery with sweat. As soon as she'd retrieved her necklace, had a shower and something to eat, she'd figure it out. And everything would be fine. Just fine.

She fumbled one of the flashlights and it crashed to the floor. "Shit."

"Is everything all right in there?" Grandma Faye's voice floated down from the hallway.

"Yes, I just dropped the flashlight." Lizzie swiped at the flashlight on the floor. *Okay Madison,* she thought. *I've got my big girl panties on. Let's do this.*

Armed with the two flashlights, she crouched down near the trap door. Handing one to Grandma Faye, she sat down and swung her legs over the opening.

"Could you hold yours down into the opening as I climb down?" she said. She placed the second flashlight on the floor near the opening.

"I could come down with you if you like."

"No, that won't be necessary. I'll be down and back up in a matter of seconds. I can see my necklace from here, it's just at the bottom of the ladder."

As much as she wanted Grandma Faye to accompany her down into the dark, she also wanted her to stand guard over the trapdoor just in case.

In case what? Lizzie thought. She didn't really believe Audley's conviction that the Witch of Grey House had pushed her down into the cellar and closed the trap door. She didn't feel any presence or malevolent energy rising up through the cellar door. Still, she had shivers down her spine. If anything should happen while she was in the root cellar, she'd rather have her capable neighbor standing at the ready instead of having both of them stuck underground.

The longer she waited, the stronger the urge to pull her feet back out of the trapdoor became. She had battled a demon by herself in the middle of a forest…she couldn't possibly be scared of an empty room beneath her house.

"It's now or never, Lizzie," she whispered to herself. She exhaled loudly, and before she could think any more about her growing fear, she placed her right foot on a rung of the ladder and with one swift movement, she grasped the top rung and swung herself over the opening.

Threading her arm through the handle of the lantern, she climbed down into the darkness. The lantern swayed on her forearm, making the strong beam of light dance in drunken circles. She counted the rungs as she went to block out her thoughts.

When her feet touched the dirt floor, she had to stop herself from scrambling back up the ladder. The root cellar brightened considerably as the beam of Grandma Faye's lantern shone down through the opening above Lizzie's head.

Tilting her head back, she looked up at the old woman. Grandma Faye was lying flat on the floor with her torso hanging over the opening, holding her lantern down into the space to give Lizzie as much light as possible.

Grandma Faye gave her a little wave with her free hand. Her reassuring grin and the child-like wave was so comical Lizzie smiled in spite of herself. She waved back then turned to where her necklace lay.

Stooping over to pick up her cross, she glanced into the corner of the root cellar. The light from the two battery powered lanterns was strong enough to illuminate the far corner of the space. It was directly opposite to where Lizzie had lain in the darkness. A white mold bloomed in the corner where the two walls met, its feathery tracery growing halfway up the wall like a lattice carved from snow

Lizzie gasped, her fingers suspended just inches above her necklace. She hadn't been trapped down in the cellar alone. There had been a woman. A woman with blank staring eyes.

There was movement on the ladder behind her and the discordant jangling of tiny silver bells. The light from Grandma Faye's lantern danced wildly, then grew brighter.

Lizzie remained bent down, her hand still outstretched to pick up her necklace as Grandma Faye rushed in front of her, her lantern held out at arm's length.

"What is it? Did you see something?"

"There was a woman, crouched in the corner over there." She gestured with a nod of her head towards the empty corner of the cellar. Lizzie scooped up her cross and stood up, keeping her gaze on the corner of the root cellar.

Grandma Faye swung her lantern in the direction Lizzie had indicated. "I can feel something, but it doesn't feel like a spirit. Is she there now? Do you still see her?"

"No, no she's not here." She clutched her necklace to her chest. "I saw her when I was trapped down here. Or I dreamed her. I'm not sure." Taking a step towards where she'd seen the woman, she held up her own lantern, making the white mold glow against the dirt walls.

"Could Audley be right? Was I trapped down here with the Witch of Grey House?"

"I don't know." Grandma Faye walked into the corner and placed her free hand on the wall. "I don't feel anything." Holding her light aloft, she walked the perimeter of the root cellar. Her bare feet made a soft patter on the hard packed earth, accompanied by the ever present sound of bells from her anklets.

Lizzie stared into the corner, trying to remember the details of the apparition. She could only recall the woman's eyes. Empty eyes.

The sound of Grandma Faye's silvery bells stopped abruptly. Lizzie turned to look at her neighbor. She was standing by the ladder, her lantern raised above her head. The color had drained from her face and her gaze fixed at the floor joists above.

"Grandma Faye?"

The old woman remained motionless, her eyes wide. The lantern cast deep shadows across the old woman's face, turning her pleasant features into a ghoulish mask.

Lizzie's scalp prickled with fear. She didn't want to look. With dream-like slowness, she swiveled her head up to the ceiling.

CHAPTER SIXTEEN

Lizzie wasn't sure what she was looking at, but there was something sinister in the crude shapes and slashing lines above her. Painted on the ceiling of the rough-hewn joists and floorboards of the rooms above, in what looked to be ordinary white house paint, was a collection of geometric shapes and swirls held within a pentacle. The wide brush strokes were executed with an uneven hand, adding to the coarseness of the design.

"What is it?" Lizzie whispered.

"Black magick." Grandma Faye held her lantern higher as she examined the shapes above her. "I don't recognize these symbols, and I didn't make the connection earlier because it's been ages since I've come across anything remotely like this. But I know black magick when I feel it."

"I don't feel anything."

"We need to get out of here now," Grandma Faye said.

"No wait. Cast a spell."

"What?"

"Just try something simple. This thing on the ceiling may be the reason I can't use my magic down here."

Grandma Faye looked at the ladder and back at Lizzie. "Okay, quickly then."

Lizzie nodded and placed her lantern on the floor. Both women held out their hands. Just as before, nothing happened with Lizzie, but in Grandma Faye's palm a golden ball of light shimmered. She closed her hand and the light winked out.

"Now, let's go."

Lizzie didn't argue. Pocketing her necklace, she then slung her lantern on her forearm and scrambled up the ladder with Grandma Faye close behind.

As soon as they were both clear of the opening, Lizzie dropped the trapdoor closed. Standing over the secured hatch, her feet planted like a fighter, she held out her hand once more. The blue orb in her palm danced and shimmered with the power of her magick before she closed her hand into a fist.

"Now we know what caused your magick to disappear." Grandma Faye gathered the two lanterns and returned them to the mudroom.

Lizzie waited until Grandma Faye was out of sight before stamping her foot in triumph over the trapdoor. Then she laid the carpet runner back in place, hiding the cellar from view.

Lizzie was chilled and still hadn't had a shower since yesterday morning, but she skirted the bathroom and headed into the kitchen to find Grandma Faye.

The two women moved wordlessly around the kitchen, each bound in the silence of their musings. Grandma Faye stoked the woodstove, meticulously feeding the thinly split logs into the firebox. An oily chemical smell rose from the pristine blackness of the newly polished stovetop.

After washing her hands at the kitchen sink, Lizzie filled the cast iron kettle that had been part of what she had inherited in the sale of the house. She stood watching the kettle boil, the heat from the stove warming her arms and the front of her legs, but it couldn't penetrate her core where a shard of ice had settled just below her breast bone.

While she waited for the water to boil, Lizzie dug out her necklace from her pants pocket and secured it around her neck. She rubbed the cool stone with her fingers.

Without needing to ask, Grandma Faye located two cups

and saucers and the small jar of honey. When she could hear the dance of water inside the kettle, Lizzie rinsed out the Brown Betty teapot. She sank into the ritual of making tea, the cool of the fat bellied teapot resting in the curve of her hands, the heat of the steam on her face as she filled it with just enough hot water to warm the inside. She absorbed herself in the calming rhythm of swirling the water around to heat the earthenware pot, dumping the water in the sink, measuring out the tea leaves, and filling the pot from the boiling kettle. The steam now carried the aromatic smell of bergamot.

When the tea had steeped, Lizzie poured out two cups, adding a generous tablespoon of velvety honey to both cups. Sister Collette, the nun who had raised her, said in a crisis the two best things were strong sweet tea and time.

The two women sat across from each other, regarding the contents of their teacups. Lizzie placed her lips tentatively on the edge of her cup before returning it to the table to cool. She held on to the handle, rubbing the curve of it with her thumb.

"They really did kill her, the Witch of Grey House. They trapped her down there with that spell and left her to starve to death." Lizzie felt sick.

The wood stove had warmed the kitchen, adding to the domestic peace of the cottage. It was hard to believe her charming little stone house kept such a sinister secret down below.

"Yes, it appears the legend is true." Grandma Faye took a delicate sip from her cup.

"So you believe I saw her down there and that she wasn't just a hallucination triggered by hitting my head?"

"I believe you saw something down there. Why would anybody go through all the trouble to cast such dark magick and to make it so permanent as to paint it on if not to trap someone or something? That spell was meant to stay in place as long as the house is standing."

142

"If her spirit is trapped down there, we have to release her."

"I agree, if that is what you saw. She may not be a ghost at all but an event echo."

Lizzie gave her a questioning look as she drank her tea.

"When she appeared to you did you feel a cold spot? Did you hear anything? Did she try to reach out to you or communicate in any way?"

"No," she answered to Grandma Faye's barrage of questions. "I don't think she even saw me. She just stared out into the darkness with such blankness in her eyes, like she'd given up and was just waiting for death."

"Sounds like what you experienced was an echo, not an apparition."

"The difference being?"

"An apparition is a spirit who hasn't crossed over, either by choice or because they've become trapped. An echo is just that, a replaying of past events. Have you ever walked into a place and felt an instant like or dislike for no apparent reason?" Grandma Faye sipped her tea.

"Yes." Lizzie thought of the first few moments she'd stepped over the threshold of her home. With Rose Cottage, she fell in love with it without questioning the rightness. Even after finding the strange sensation coming from the cellar, she still loved her cottage and, as strange as it seemed, she felt that it loved her back.

"Buildings and even outdoor locations store events in their bricks and mortar, or even the earth itself. If you are sensitive enough you can feel, hear, or even see the past events, like listening to a recording or watching a movie. When the energy of a building is disturbed—for example, when someone starts a renovation—it can be like hitting the play button on a recording device. The spell on the ceiling is probably holding the energy there too."

"So when I started fixing up the place I triggered the release of the event echo." Lizzie took a long swallow of her now cool tea.

"That would be my guess."

"Is it possible to erase or cleanse the house of the memories? To stop them from replaying?"

"If I knew what those symbols on the spell were it wouldn't be a problem. I'd cast a counter spell to break it, and then we'd perform a cleansing ritual. Although its existence doesn't seem to pose an active threat to you as long as you stay out of the cellar, the fact that it renders your magick useless when you're down there is enough reason to do whatever we can to get rid of it."

"It is odd that it affects me but not you."

"Yes, you must have something in common with the Wise Woman of Grey House for it to shut down your powers."

"I couldn't guess what that would be. I mean, I'm a witch like her and like you. But if the black magick doesn't affect you then it must be something more than just using the craft that links us."

"Maybe there's a hereditary link?"

"As in I'm related to her? That's highly unlikely." But was it really? Lizzie pondered. She was an orphan; she didn't even know her mother's name or where she came from.

Lizzie reached across the table, picked up the teapot, and refilled their cups. "The odds that I'd move into a cottage in a place I'd never heard of and have it turn out it was once owned by my ancestor is a bit too farfetched, even for me."

"Maybe, but I can't think of any other thing you may have in common if not heritage. Until we have a little more information it's all just speculation. Our priority should be to break that spell. As soon as I get home I'll check my Book of Shadow to see if I can find anything that resembles those symbols."

Lizzie spluttered the mouthful of tea she'd just taken. "Sorry," she said, wiping her chin. "You actually have a Book of Shadows?"

"Yes, of course I do…all wise women worth their salt have one." Grandma Faye sat up straighter, tilting her head slightly so she looked down her nose. "Mine has been in my family for five generations. How can you be a wise woman and not have a book of shadows?"

"Well, I just recently came to understand exactly what I am, and I have no family as far as I know to teach me or pass anything down. I had a few months of training, but other than that I'm still rather new at this whole thing."

"Well, for a complete novice you have a natural aptitude for the craft."

Lizzie shrugged. She'd been told that very thing by her mentor, Vivienne. The fact she alone had managed to track down the demon and kill it proved her talent, a talent that seemed more apt to hurt and kill rather than heal. She was building up quite a list of casualties in her wake, her own husband being the first on the list.

Lizzie stomach growled noisily. Grandma Faye put aside her cup. "It's time for supper. We aren't going to solve anything on an empty stomach. Eggs fine with you?"

Lizzie smiled as her stomach rumbled again as if in answer to Grandma Faye's question. "I would love some. What can I do to help?"

"Nothing, I think I can handle it. Why don't you get yourself into the shower? You'll feel better."

After a quick shower and a change of clothes, Lizzie came back into the kitchen drawn by the smell of frying butter and aromatic herbs.

It was just a little after six in the evening, but the lingering light coming through the kitchen window had faded, the proximity of the mountains cutting the sunset short. Grandma Faye had turned on the overhead lights, pushing the coming darkness back behind the windowpanes.

The table had been set with Lizzie's mismatched plates and the box set of stainless steel cutlery she'd picked up at the hardware store. Grandma Faye had found the iced tea in the cooler and had poured them into heavy restaurant-style tumblers.

Lizzie sat down to her first real meal in her new home. Her vision blurred as Grandma Faye placed the plate of food in front of her. She couldn't believe her neighbor had managed to create such a beautiful feast with the meager offering in her pantry. She wondered if magick was involved in conjuring up such a delightful dinner from the supplies she'd picked up at the grocery store.

Lizzie groaned as the first mouthful of the light, buttery omelet melted on her tongue. "This is amazing," she said between mouthfuls.

"I'm glad you like it. Although, it would be a great deal better with fresh eggs. I'll bring you a dozen eggs from my coop next time I pop by."

"I'd appreciate that," Lizzie said, scraping the last morsel off her plate.

"Or I can give you a few of my hens. You have a lovely shed standing empty. I'm sure with just a few improvements, Audley could have it ready for chickens in no time."

"Chickens? You want to give me chickens." Lizzie hadn't thought about populating her little acreage with livestock, but suddenly the idea appealed to her immensely. As a child, growing up in the isolation of the convent, one of her duties was to collect the eggs from the henhouse. The thought of recreating a piece of that idyllic existence delighted her.

"You'd love them. They are dear little creatures and don't take a lot of work. Imagine going out to get fresh eggs every morning. And they are great little earth movers, perfect for turning your garden over every spring."

"It's a very generous offer and I'm tempted, but do you mind if I think about it for a little while?" Lizzie stood up and began removing their empty plates.

"Not at all." Grandma Faye joined Lizzie at the sink. She grabbed a fresh tea towel while Lizzie filled the sink with hot soapy water.

As they washed and dried the dishes, the two women's conversation circled around from chickens to the Witch of Grey House, and the problem of undoing the black magic. They rehashed the events, going over every detail, but as Grandma Faye stacked the last dish in the cupboard and Lizzie swept the kitchen floor, it became all too obvious that for tonight at least, nothing was going to be resolved.

Seated back at the table, feeling slightly drowsy from her full stomach, Lizzie accepted a fresh cup of tea from Grandma Faye. She had just raised the cup to her lips when the memory of standing at the sink filling a glass at the tap flashed in her mind's eye. She fumbled the teacup in her hand as the memory flooded back, then placed it down, rattling it against the saucer.

"What is it?" Grandma Faye said, half rising from her chair.

"I just remembered something. Right before I woke up in the cellar, I was getting a glass of water at the sink and I smelled something, almost like perfume but more cloying, a sickly sweet smell. Can a spirit conjure up a smell instead of a cold spot like you mentioned?"

"Yes, people have reported noticing the smell of perfume or tobacco smoke right before the appearance of an apparition. Is that what you think you smelled?"

"I think so. Maybe the containment spell is limiting her ability to interact with the living other than for brief moments. My gut is telling me what I saw down in the cellar wasn't an event echo, but her spirit." Lizzie felt the familiar sting of tears. She gulped her tea and swallowed hard around the lump in her throat. "She seemed so forlorn, so very sad."

147

"Do you think it was her ghost who lured you down in the cellar and trapped you?"

"No, I didn't feel anything like anger or vengeance, just hopelessness. I think it was my own stupidity that trapped me down there." Despite consuming several cups of tea, Lizzie stifled a yawn. "I have no recollection of what happened between smelling the perfume and waking up in the cellar, but I could have gone to investigate the source of the smell and accidently fell down the ladder, dislodging it as I fell. I was so tired when I got home. Knowing how I just wanted a hot bath and bed, instead of pulling the hatch fully open, I probably just held it open and climbed down a few rungs of the ladder to take a peek. So conjecturing I'd slipped and actually closed the hatch on myself isn't that farfetched." Lizzie hesitated. "I don't think a ghost had anything to do with my own klutziness."

A wave of guilt hit her in the solar plexus. The reason she'd been so focused on a hot bath was because she'd spent the afternoon rescuing a dog. She'd completely forgotten about Bear. The poor dog had undergone a complicated surgery and she hadn't given him a passing thought. With a sinking feeling, she also realized that he was now *her* dog. She'd never had a pet before, and it didn't bode well if she couldn't even remember that she now had one.

Grandma Faye reached across the table and put her hand on Lizzie's. "What is it? Do you sense the witch?"

Lizzie's shook her head. "No, nothing. Sorry, I just realized I now have a dog. I can't believe I forgot about Bear. Did the vet call?"

"Oh yes, she called this afternoon while you were sleeping. The surgeries went well and Dr. Laurie said he was recovering nicely. You can call her tomorrow morning for an update on how he's doing. Sorry I didn't mention it earlier, but it slipped my mind."

"Mine too, apparently." She used the back of her hand to hide a jaw-cracking yawn. "Excuse me."

"I should be going," Grandma Faye said, getting up from the table. "It's been a long day for both of us, and I need to get home and lock up my chicken for the night and give the goats their evening rations. Goats like routine, and they can get a bit feisty if I'm late."

"Goats? You have chickens and goats?"

"Yes. Although the goats are pets more than anything. The three of them are dry does, but they needed a home. So now I have three goats."

"Dry does?"

"Haven't been bred, so no milk. I have an idea…why don't you come with me and you can meet my barnyard menagerie yourself, and you could spend the night."

Lizzie smiled. "I appreciate giving me an out if I was too scared to be alone." She crossed over to the kitchen counter and handed Grandma Faye her basket. "And I'd be lying if a part of me doesn't want to take you up on the offer, but…."

"But, this is your home." Grandma Faye took her basket from her, returning her smile.

"Yes, and I refuse to let what the villagers did to that poor woman chase me out. I won't abandon her."

"I understand." Grandma Faye patted her arm.

"I'll walk you out," Lizzie said, softening her tone.

Arm-in-arm they headed over to Grandma Faye's truck. The sun had disappeared behind the mountains and the sky glowed violet, inviting the stars to come out and play. Grandma Faye gave her a hug. When they stepped apart, Grandma Faye held her by the shoulders. "If you change your mind about spending the night, call me. I left my number by the phone. I'll come and get you no matter what the hour. It can be a bit tricky finding my place in the dark."

Lizzie nodded.

Grandma Faye climbed into the truck and rolled the window down. "I'll shut the gate behind me," she called out before gunning her truck to life. She raised her voice over the rattle of the engine. "Think about the chickens, Lizzie. Imagine fresh eggs for breakfast every morning," she called out as she disappeared down the driveway.

Lizzie watched the taillights from Grandma Faye's truck until the trees lining the driveway obscured them from view.

A light breeze moved her hair, bringing a chill to her neck as she listened to the rattle of the gate being closed. As the sound of the truck faded into the night, Lizzie realized two things; one, it was easier to be brave when she had someone with her, and two, how profoundly dark the night could be without the comfort of street lights.

She was only a dozen feet from her front porch, but she could barely see the outline of the steps leading to her front door. She wished she'd brought one of the lanterns with her. She'd turned to head back inside when an owl called out from the deepening twilight. She yelped, scrambled up the stairs, and slammed the door behind her.

She leaned against the door to catch her breath. She was grateful Grandma Faye wasn't around to witness her cowardice. This was the first night she was going to spend truly alone. Even during the months she'd spent at the resort cabin she hadn't felt a sense of isolation, because she knew the hotel and its staff were a quick ten-minute walk away, or she could just pick up the phone for the front desk.

She'd been so consumed with the details of restoring her new home she hadn't put much thought into what it would be like at night, by herself, with just the forest and the night creatures as her neighbors. And a ghost in her root cellar trapped by black magick, she reminded herself. Was she completely nuts to think living in such an isolated place would be best for her, despite being guided to find the cottage?

"I'm courageous and powerful," Lizzie chanted as she secured the front door. "I slayed a demon on my own. I'm a force to be reckoned with," she continued to chant as she checked every window and door to make sure they were locked.

Walking down the hall she skirted the cellar door, keeping close to the wall. In her bedroom, she checked the french doors and windows, then threw several logs on the fire.

"I am not afraid, I am not afraid," she whispered as she changed into her nightgown and straightened up the bedcovers from her early search for her necklace.

"I am not afraid," she said, pulling the covers over her head to block out the glare of the light she'd left on.

CHAPTER SEVENTEEN

Despite her fear of being alone the night before with what she now knew was in her cellar, upon waking she'd felt a bit foolish. The black magic painted on the aged timbers wasn't aimed at her, and the Witch of Grey House never harmed her. If anything, she'd just tried to let Lizzie know she was there, so really Lizzie had nothing to fear. She had only her clumsiness to blame for her ordeal in her cellar. She flicked off the light she'd left burning by her bedside before shuffling into the kitchen to make coffee.

Even with the cool reasoning of her logic, she couldn't stop herself from quickening her pace as she walked over the cellar door.

In the kitchen, the bare windows allowed the sunshine to flood the main living space. Dust motes danced in the open space of her unfurnished home, and the air smelled smell of last night's fire. She plugged the electric kettle in to make her French press coffee, and threw a few slices of Grandma Faye's bread into the toaster. She was craving eggs with her toast, but she didn't have the patience to fuss with the woodstove.

When she'd found out there wasn't a proper stove in the cottage, she thought it would be quaint and charming to fix meals on the woodstove, but after only a day she realized the folly of her original plan. Now she could hardly wait for her new kitchen; more importantly, her electric range. She loved the charm of the woodstove, but not the inconvenience of trying to cook something when she wanted it quickly.

She ate slowly, waiting for the time to pass so she could call Grandma Faye at a reasonable hour. Even though her friend said the symbols didn't look familiar, Lizzie held out hope she'd found something in her Book of Shadows that could break the spell.

Sitting at her kitchen table, drinking a strong coffee liberally doused with sugar, she realized she desperately needed to furnish her bare cottage. She couldn't wait to find an overstuffed sofa for the living room, a large rag rug for in front of the fireplace, and several bookcases she planned to fill with books. The kitchen table needed proper chairs, and she couldn't sleep forever on an inflatable bed. The basics she could buy from the big box stores in Revelstoke, and her bed was due to be delivered any day now, but the pieces she hoped would infuse her home with a sense of place were things that had a history and the comforting patina of time. When she called Grandma Faye she'd also ask her if she knew the best places to look for antiques, even though Birdie would have been the most logical one to ask.

She was a bit puzzled with Birdie. She'd been so helpful and efficient during the sale, even sending her a list of trades people to start the renos, and promising to give her the name of her aunt's antique shop. She had sounded excited about taking Lizzie there.

Lizzie had called the realty office several times to set up their shopping trip, but no matter what time of day she called she only ever got the answering machine. She'd left several messages for Birdie but she'd never returned any of them.

Her eyes roamed over the empty space, alighting on the cooler and a few small boxes shoved against the far wall. Her bare house echoed her own emptiness.

Blinking back tears, she got up from the table and poured herself another cup of coffee. She missed her childhood home, even with the unconventional arrangement of living in a cloistered nunnery.

When she'd first set eyes on Rose Cottage, a part of her thought she could recapture the sense of security and love she'd felt with Sister Collette, the nun who'd cared for her. She still loved her cottage and felt within the marrow of her bones it was her place, but without family what did she really have?

Had the Witch of Grey House ever felt lonely? Had she ever despaired of her decision to move out to the middle of nowhere by herself?

To stave off her growing sense of despair, Lizzie turned her focus to cleaning up her meager dishes and making another pot of coffee. She knew from the past how quickly feelings of loneliness and despair could turn into a darkness that held only one kind of relief. She'd been down that road before and ended up in the hospital. She wouldn't do that to herself again.

She had a mystery to solve and a soul who needed her help. And soon a dog to care for. She shook her head. Why did she keep forgetting she now owned a dog?

Sipping her fresh coffee, she glanced at her watch. With relief she realized it was late enough to call Grandma Faye. She'd meant what she'd said to her friend the night before…this was her house and she was prepared to fight to claim it back from the past horrors it had witnessed.

Grandma Faye answered on the first ring. The old woman's warm honeyed voice dispelled some of Lizzie's sense of loneliness. She may be living by herself in the forest, but she'd already found a kindred spirit, and all she needed to do was pick up the phone to feel the connection.

"Good morning. I take it you had an uneventful night?"

"Slept like a log." Lizzie couldn't bring herself to admit she'd slept with the light on. "Any luck with your Book of Shadows?"

"Sorry to disappoint you, but it was a long shot. There isn't anything that even remotely resembles that spell. I didn't think there would be, but I went through every page just in case."

Lizzie let out a frustrated sigh. "Then it's hopeless."

"Why are you giving up before we've even started? I don't belong to a coven, but I'll reach out to a couple of other hedge witches I know to see if they recognize the symbols."

Lizzie shook her head, "Hedge witches?"

"You are a babe in the woods, aren't you?" Grandma Faye chuckled. "A hedge witch is one who practices her craft alone. She doesn't belong to a coven. We hedge witches tend to be a private lot and can be a bit standoffish, but in a pinch we do stick together. It would be best if we had a picture of that thing in the cellar. Do you have a camera?"

"No, but my cell has one. I can use that."

"Good, just shoot me a text with an attachment and I'll get right on it. I'll post it on the hedge witch forum and see if we get any bites."

Lizzie pressed her lips together to stop from laughing at the image of solitary witches huddled in front of their computers, sharing spells and incantations. "How do you have an Internet connection at your place and I can't even get a cell signal here?" she asked, struggling to suppress her laughter.

"It's a satellite connection. It's a bit dodgy at times, especially when we're socked in with fog or heavy rains, but it works more often than not. Anyway, I'll also check the forum archives to see if there is anything helpful."

"The archives...why didn't I think of that sooner?" Lizzie said.

The order had an extensive archive filled with arcane texts, all dealing with magick. If there was anyone who could dig up the information it would be Gideon. But her excitement soon fizzled as she realized she couldn't reach out to him, not now anyway. Call it hurt pride or just hurt, he hadn't tried to contact her since the day they had kissed. The day he'd turned his back on her. She couldn't bring herself to be the one to make the first contact.

She knew she could call Vivienne with the request, but she felt her resistance to even do that. When she'd left Toronto to deal with the demon on her own, she'd made it clear she didn't want the order meddling in her life anymore. She had to prove to Vivienne and herself she was capable of solving this on her own. If Grandma Faye and her cyber community of witches didn't turn up anything, then she'd reach out to Vivienne, but only as a last resort.

"Hello? Lizzie, are you still there?" Grandma Faye's voice pushed into Lizzie thoughts.

"Yes, sorry."

"What did you say about archives?"

"I was just thinking aloud." The two pieces of toast she'd eaten for breakfast sat like heavy lumps in her belly. She couldn't share with her friend what she'd been thinking, but another idea occurred to her that could be just as helpful.

"While you are researching the symbols, I could see if I could dig up anything on the witch. Surely the village office has census records and property titles. I think it's just as important to find out who the witch really was. We need to know her name."

"Those kind of things would be located in the basement of the library, not the village offices, but good luck with that."

"Why? Aren't those documents public record?"

"Yes, but you already know how much the people of this fair village like outsiders, and they like them even less if they go snooping around in their not so perfect past. The only reason they don't bother me is because I keep to myself and I sell them something they want. So don't be surprised if they don't throw open the doors to the archives for you, especially if you tell them what you are looking for. The villagers like to maintain a squeaky clean image of the past, more palatable for the tourists who come to spend their money in town."

"I promise to be discreet." Lizzie felt herself rising to Grandma

Faye's challenge. Now more than anything she was determined to find out who the witch really was. "I should get going. Seeing as I'm heading into town anyway I'll send you the pictures from my cell as soon as I get there."

"Did you want me to come over to help with the pictures?"

"No, I better do it now before Audley shows up. He's already ten minutes late, so that means he should be here in the next fifteen. The last thing we need is having him find out what we are doing and blabbing it to the whole village."

"You've got a point there. Your handyman gossips worse than the old women at the quilting club."

After assuring her friend she would be careful not to trap herself down in the cellar again, she hung up the phone and scurried to gather up what she needed.

Armed with her cell phone and the two battery-operated lanterns, she headed back down to the cellar. The need to hurry before Audley appeared steeled her nerves as she voluntarily climbed down into the darkness one more time.

In the glow of the lanterns she snapped a few pictures on her phone, and when she was satisfied she'd taken a clear enough image she climbed back out without incident.

She put away the lanterns, and was just replacing the carpet over the cellar door when she heard the familiar rumble of Audley's van pulling up. She slipped her phone into her purse and quickly poured herself another coffee just as Audley knocked on the door.

"Good morning," she said with what she hoped was a casual breeziness, even though her heart was knocking against her ribs. "Did you want a coffee? I just made a fresh pot."

"No thanks, Ms. Benett. Jon's asked me to double-check some measurements for the kitchen, and he wants it done ASAP." He kept his eyes glued to the floor as he walked past her into the cottage. Putting down his toolbox next to the kitchen table, he then pulled out a tape measure and a scrap of paper from the back pocket of his baggy jeans. Instead of heading straight to measuring, he stood staring at his feet.

She sipped her coffee and waited for him to say something, but he just rocked slightly on the balls of his feet.

"Is there something else? If you changed your mind I could get you that coffee." She gestured with her own cup, but he still wouldn't look up.

"What? No, no coffee, thanks." He finally turned to face the kitchen cabinets, but stopped short of actually measuring anything. "How's your head, Ms. Bennet?"

"It's fine. Just a little tender this morning, but nothing a couple of aspirin won't fix."

"Good, good. You took quite a tumble down that ladder, and I was worried about you." He said this with his back towards her. The metal of the tape measure rattled as he started measuring the space the current cupboards occupied.

"I really do owe you for coming to my rescue," she said, walking over to him and placing a hand on his shoulder.

He shuffled sideways, causing her hand to slide off his shoulder.

"You don't owe me nothing. I'm just glad you're okay." He set about taking his measurements in earnest. She backed away to let him work.

"After you've finished in here, I was wondering if you had time to look at the shed near the house and give me your opinion on what it would take to get it ready as a chicken coop."

"You planning on getting chickens?" For the first time since he arrived, Audley turned to look Lizzie in the eyes.

"Yes, I think they would be a lovely addition to the acreage. Grandma Faye offered to give me a few of her hens, and the more I think about it the more I want to have them. So if you could take a look at the shed I'd appreciate it."

"So you really are going to stick it out here, by yourself?"

"This is my home. Why wouldn't I stick it out?"

"I thought maybe after what the witch did to you, you wouldn't want to stay out here all by yourself."

"If that what's bothering you, you don't have to worry about me. There is no such person as the Witch of Grey House. She's just a made up story."

"But how do you explain how you ended up down in the cellar?"

"It was nothing more sinister than my own curiosity and clumsiness. My memory is a bit foggy due to the bump on my head, but I'd guess I heard something when it was probably just the house settling. I wasn't paying attention when I climbed down, and I more than likely pulled the ladder down when I fell." She thought she'd lied convincingly, but there was still worry in Audley's eyes.

"I don't mean to upset you, but I think you're wrong. That witch is still in this house, and I don't think she wants you here. It's not safe for you being out here on your lonesome. And now you be wanting chickens, and you don't even have a guard dog or nothing to protect you and your property." A strange look passed over Audley's face, and he pressed his lips into a tight line.

This was the most words she'd ever heard coming from her handy man, and the only time she'd seen him infused with any kind of emotion it had been with devotion for his boss. She wasn't sure how to take his obvious distress over her safety.

"That's where you're wrong. I've adopted a dog. And that reminds me, I need to call the vet." She didn't add that up until that moment she'd forgotten all about Bear, again.

She left Audley to finish up his measuring and placed the call to the vet in the relative privacy of her bedroom. As she dialed Dr. Laurie's number, she pondered Audley's earnest concern for her wellbeing. She was surprised by the warm glow of affection she felt for the strange little man in her kitchen.

* * * *

Lizzie pulled into the vet clinic's parking lot with mixed emotions. She was relieved to hear Bear was doing so well, considering what he'd gone through, but she couldn't deny the acidic burn in her stomach telling her she may have taken on more than she could handle.

Bear still had a few weeks at the clinic until he'd be released into her care, and then she'd be the one responsible for looking after him until he completely mended. She'd never even owned a gold fish, and now she was responsible for a hundred and twelve pound, convalescing dog. He was hers and she his for the rest of his life.

Lizzie hated the smell of hospitals, and the clinic's recovery area with its bank of metal cages carried with it the stomach churning odors of antiseptic and sickly sweet anesthetic. She breathed through her mouth to lessen the effect of the smells.

Bear was housed in one of the lower cages because of his size. Except for a brown tabby curled up in one of the upper cages, her dog was the only patient.

Lizzie hunkered down and waited for Dr. Laurie to open the door. Bear was wearing the requisite plastic cone around his neck to prevent him from licking his wounds. The collar pushed his thick ruff of fur up around his face, making him look a little like a dandelion seed head. The illusion was accentuated by the fact his lower body had been shaved. She made soothing sounds as she hazarded a closer look at his lower half.

His right leg was in a cast, and the inside of his other leg still had a gaping wound where he'd been dragged across the gravel road. Dr. Laurie had explained there wasn't enough skin left to close it. It had been cleaned and debrided, but needed to be watched for any signs of infection.

Lizzie could handle both the sight of the cumbersome cast and even the raw pinkness of the deep abrasions. But it was the metal appliance attached to his left leg that made the backs of Lizzie's knees weak and tingly, and made her grateful she was already kneeling on the floor. The appliance looked like a crude metal handle attached directly to the outside of his leg. Where the screws entered the skin the flesh oozed a yellow substance that had crusted along the metal in some places.

Dr. Laurie joined Lizzie on the floor and ran her hand affectionately down the dogs back as she explained how the surgeries had gone. She was able to place internal pins and screws on Bear's right leg, but because of the location of the break in his left, the external fixation was her only option. She reiterated that with time and care Bear would make a full recovery. Because his right hipbone had been sheared off he'd walk with a slight limp, but the vet assured Lizzie the dog would adapt to it, and overall it would barely affect his mobility.

Lizzie rubbed Bear's ear between her thumb and forefinger while the vet went on to explain how to clean his leg wound and around the pins where they entered his flesh. Her words rolled off Lizzie in a garbled tumble. The only things she'd ever cared for were plants and cut flowers. It all seemed too much.

Dr. Laurie touched Lizzie's forearm. "Lizzie, have you ever had a pet before?"

"Is it that obvious?" she said.

"Well, you do have a rather terrified look on your face. There's nothing to worry about. The most important things this dog is going to need are love and gentle exercise when he's able to walk. The wound care and all the rest is just a matter of following instructions. We have handouts detailing what you need to do, so take a deep breath...it's all going to be okay."

Lizzie gave her a weak smile and turned her attention to Bear, who had raised himself up so he was lying on his belly instead of his side. He had to twist his large body awkwardly so his back legs remained stationary. He leaned the considerable weight of his head into her probing fingers, encouraging her to give him more scratches, his large tongue lolling to the side of his black rubbery lips. Something shifted in her chest, and she laughed at his big goofy face.

When the hour was up, she told Bear she would be back in a couple of days. She gave him one more scratch behind the ear, promising him a treat at her next visit. He replied by licking her hand with his warm pink tongue. Whatever her misgivings about taking him home, they melted away with each slobbery dog kiss.

CHAPTER EIGHTEEN

Lizzie managed to park her truck directly in front of the library, as there was only one other vehicle on the street. But before she went inside the classic white structure with its stately black trim, she pulled out her cell and sent the email with the photos off to Grandma Faye. She'd given her friend what she needed to do her part in releasing the witch; now it was Lizzie's turn.

Making her way up the wooden steps of the library, she reminded herself to watch what she said. As she swung open the heavy wooden door with its leaded glass panes, she discovered it was the first building she'd come across in the village whose interior had been recently renovated. The walls were a soft moss green, while the thick window casings and moldings over the door were painted a creamy white. The light oak bookcases still smelled faintly of varnish, but underneath that was the comforting smell of books.

She strolled across the original hardwood floors, which had been refinished to a glossy shine, and towards the circulation desk. The young woman behind the desk had her back to Lizzie, unpacking boxes of books and loading them onto a trolley situated behind the counter. Lizzie had become accustomed to the fashion sense of the village, which tended to run to flannel shirts, khakis or jeans, and functional footwear even for the women. She wasn't prepared for the visual assault when the woman, upon hearing Lizzie's footsteps approach, turned to face her.

The young woman's chestnut hair was twisted into two small buns, one on either side of her head. Colorful ribbons were threaded through each one, the ends hanging down in streamers that fluttered when she moved. Her cheeks and the bridge of her nose were liberally sprinkled with freckles. They were too dark and obvious in their placement to be anything other than drawn on with an eyebrow pencil. She wore an acid green top with tiers of ruffles down the front.

"Good morning," she said, placing an armload of books on the trolley. "What can I help you with today?" When she smiled she revealed that her two front teeth had been blacked out.

Lizzie struggled to keep her face neutral. "Yes, hello. I recently moved here, and I was interested in reading up on the local history."

"Oh, of course." The librarian left the stack of books on the counter and came around to the other side. "You're the woman who bought Grey House. Bet you want to find out about the witch. I'm Amanda." She grabbed Lizzie's hand and gave it two vigorous pumps before releasing it.

"Lizzie Bennet," she replied. So much for keeping her purpose a secret.

"No way, seriously?" Amanda put her hands on her hips and laughed. "We have the complete collection of Jane Austens if you're interested," she said, her wide grin showing off her two blackened teeth. Lizzie tried not to stare. "I don't think anybody's checked them out in ages. Well, at least since I've been here, and that's coming on three years. But, I suppose with a name like yours you're already acquainted with Miss Austen's work."

"Yes, indeed I am." Lizzie's gaze wandered down to Amanda's legs and feet. This time she couldn't help but stare. The librarian was wearing a pink tutu, black tights, green, orange, and black striped knee socks, and on her feet were thick-soled Doc Martin's with pink laces. She looked like a cross between Heidi and Pippi

Longstockings.

Following Lizzie's gaze, Amanda looked down at herself and fluffed out her tutu with her hands. "It's for this afternoon's storybook hour. Preschoolers. It helps to keep the kid's interested if I dress up in costumes."

"Oh, of course."

"Follow me, I'll show you where the local histories are kept." Amanda led Lizzie to the farthest corner of the library, where the periodicals were organized. "We only have three books on the village. Here we go," she said, leaning down to pull out the books from a lower shelf and handing them to Lizzie one at a time. "This one's a bit dry but well researched, this one has some great early photos of the village, but it was self-published so the editing is appalling. This one goes into more detail about the great fire and some of the prominent characters of the time. I suppose I should push this one, seeing as it is published by our head archivist, but in my opinion the writing's a bit overblown, more like reading a trashy romance than a history." Amanda lowered her voice as she spoke, glancing over her shoulder down the stacks.

Lizzie peered down through the bookshelves following the librarian's gaze, but there was no one there.

"Don't tell Maryanne I said that. She very proud of her book, and I'd never hear the end of it if she heard what I said."

"Not to worry, your secret's safe with me." Lizzie cradled the three thin volumes in her arm. "I know its Saturday, but are the archives open today?"

"Sort of. Maryanne left me in charge. She took today off because her Melvin passed away yesterday, and she wasn't up to coming in."

"I'm sorry for her loss. Were they married for long?"

Amanda shot her a quizzical look, then let out a laugh. "No, no, Melvin was her cat. Maryanne's husband is doing just fine. Or as fine as one could be married to the Queen of the

Archives." Amanda motioned for Lizzie to follow her down the stacks. "Melvin was a lovely grey tabby, but he must have been a hundred years old if he was a day. He hung out down in the archives and occasionally came up here to sleep in the sunshine. He had a good life as far as cats go, but I'm going to miss him all the same. Anyway, why don't I sign out your books before we head down to the archives? I don't know if I have a volunteer coming this morning, and it'll save you waiting for me to finish up with my preschoolers."

Amanda took her back to the circulation desk, where she issued her a library card and checked out her books, then she led her to the archives.

Lizzie tucked her books under her arm and followed Amanda to a large metal door at the back of the building. A hand written sign on the door declared Village of Barton Historical Society and Archives. Resting her hand on the latch, Amanda turned to Lizzie. "Don't tell Maryanne what I said about Melvin. About missing him."

"Okay," Lizzie said.

"If she thinks I've gone soft she'll run roughshod over me." Mindful of her beribboned hair, she removed the key hanging around her neck from a lanyard and unlocked the door. "I don't mind giving her the space in the basement, but now she wants even more for a museum. If she manages to secure the funding, which is iffy, she'd going to completely take over this building, not to mention building an ugly addition onto the back." Returning the key around her neck, she opened the door.

A stairway led down into the darkened basement. As Lizzie followed Amanda over the threshold, she let go of the door. It swung closed, plunging them into darkness. For a split second a rush of fear shot along her nerve endings before Amanda located the light switch, illuminating the stairwell and the landing below.

"Sorry, forgot to warn you about the door. Shuts

automatically." Amanda headed down the stairs, her thick-soled boots clunking loudly on the treads as she went. Lizzie followed obediently behind, keeping a firm hold on the banister.

Once in the basement, the librarian hit a few more switches and a small bank of florescent lights flickered to life. The clear unforgiving light spilled in tight pools, but left large areas in darkness. In the quiet of the basement, the hum of the lights sounded like the chirring of cicadas.

The archives took up the same footprint as the library above, but from Lizzie's vantage point, the high metal shelves running the perimeter of the cinder block walls and populating the remaining floor space seemed more like a maze than an organized layout. None of the shelves had any labels indicating what was held in the numerous file boxes and plain brown manuscript boxes. The catacomb of recorded memories infused the still air with the dusty threads of peoples' lives long forgotten.

Lizzie hugged herself and followed Amanda over to a small wooden desk and chair. The desk faced the stairs, so whoever sat there could see anyone coming down into the archives. A ledger bound in faded brown leather was centered on a felt blotter, along with a gold pen and a desk lamp with a green glass shade that sat on the top edge of the blotter. The only personal object was an ornate gold framed picture of a large grey cat. It must have been taken to commemorate Melvin's birthday, as the cat was wearing a small cone-shaped birthday hat, and placed in front of his paws was a cupcake with a candle in it. The cat peered at the camera with withering indignation.

Tucked between the wall and the desk was a wicker pet bed. Folded neatly at the bottom of the basket was a blue flannel blanket littered with an array of cat toys.

"You need to sign in or Maryanne will have my head," Amanda said, flipping open the ledger.

Lizzie did as she was told, noticing the last visitor to the archives had been four years earlier.

Amanda leaned on the desk and surveyed the shelves. "I'll give you the lay of the land and then I should head back upstairs. I'm not supposed to leave anyone down here by themselves, but you look responsible enough. Promise you won't steal anything."

"Promise," Lizzie said, giving her a smile she hoped said honesty and integrity, not that she planned on stealing anything.

Amanda remained leaning on the desk. "Okay, here's the five cent tour. These shelves here," she said, pointing to the closest ones, "hold the photographic collections. The most recent near the front. I think they go back to the late 1800s. The middle shelves are where you'll find all the back issues of the newspapers. They start in 1910. We lost the earlier editions when the newspaper office flooded back in sixty-two." Amanda rested her hip on the corner of the desk, the crinoline of her tutu rustling like bird wings as she moved. "Next we have the school records." She indicated the next set of shelves with a flutter of her fingers. "These won't be of much use to you if you want to find out about Grey House. It's these last two shelves you should focus your efforts on. The municipal records are all stacked down there. Everything from the voters' lists, Land Registry Office title transfer books, assessment and collectors' rolls, and maps and plans. The title transfer books will have what you're looking for." Amanda pushed herself off the desk and fluffed up her tutu. "I'm assuming you're trying to find out if the witch was the original owner of your house."

"Yes, I'd like to know if she really existed."

"Or if she's just a story made up to scare kids at Halloween?"

"Yes."

"Well, good luck. I've never heard of anyone refer to her as anything other than the Witch of Grey House, but then again I've only been here a few years. If a record exists pertaining to our witch, then this would be the place to find it."

"Thank you. I'll start there then."

"Normally Maryanne pulls the boxes and watches over the documents being viewed, but seeing as you promised not to steal anything, I'll let you handle it on your own. Besides, if you do, I know where to find you." She smiled, her blacked out front teeth making it look more like a ghoulish grin than a friendly acknowledgement. "You can use her desk, just make sure you put everything back where you found it."

Amanda headed for the stairs, then stopped. Pirouetting around to face Lizzie, she said, "You might want to steer clear of the back shelves. That's where the museum artifacts are kept." She turned back to the stairs and sprinted up them, her Doc Martens thudding on the stairs. "Wouldn't want you to freak out down here by yourself," she called out, her voice echoing down the stairwell.

"Pardon?" Lizzie peered up the stairwell, catching a glimpse of Amanda's pink tutu disappearing as the door clunked closed. Shaking her head, she placed her purse and library books on the corner of the desk before wandering over to the farthest metal shelves where Amanda had indicated would be her best bet of finding something.

She ran her finger along the boxes at eye level, noting the dates written in magic marker. They were organized by decade and cryptic abbreviations. Scanning the wall of boxes, Lizzie figured out she needed to look at the boxes marked TT for title transfer. These boxes were on the lowest shelf, and Lizzie bent down and scanned each one. Birdie had said the house had to be at least a hundred and fifty years old, so she pulled out the appropriate box, dislodging years of dust into the air.

Back at the archivist's desk, she placed the box on the floor and pulled off the lid. Inside was a small stack of bound ledgers. Lizzie gently lifted out the first one and placed it in the middle of the desk. She switched on the lamp and the shade glowed a soft green. Melvin watched from his vantage point, the look of boredom unchanging.

The ledger's cheap leather showed cracks along its grainy surface, and even with Lizzie's careful manipulation the binding crackled as she opened it. The thick yellowed pages were filled with columns of hand written entries, the once black ink faded to a reddish-brown but still legible, although it took Lizzie a few pages of scanning to be able to decipher the intricate flowing script that was typical of the era.

Using her finger as a pointer, she ran down the first column looking for the lot description that matched her property. She had no luck with the first book or any of the following in the box. Carefully replacing the ledgers in order, she closed up the box and returned it to its place on the shelf.

She repeated the procedure five more times, and each time she came up empty. She'd gone all the way back to the 1880s and forward until the 1920s, but found no description that even remotely matched her property on Quail Hollow road.

Half-heartedly she pulled out the next box, covering the 1870s, and diligently took it back to the desk. As she flipped through each book, the feeling of futility blossomed into full-blown disappointment when she finally dug out the last plain black ledger in the box.

She'd noticed that as she moved back through time the ledgers had gotten bigger, the quality of the leather bindings finer, the feel of the pages smoother and thicker under her fingers. It was hard for her to imagine that the sleepy little village she now called home had once been a thriving town by the look of all the property that was purchased and developed.

Each entry listed the property's legal description, the name of the person purchasing, and their occupation. There were merchants and business men, farmers, occupations linked to the railway and lumber, and to her surprise even ranchers. She couldn't imagine ranching in such difficult mountainous terrain. The fire that ripped through the town two decades later must have been massive, the destruction so complete that the village never fully recovered.

Squinting at the page before her, she tilted the desk lamp, shining a bright spot directly on the entries, hoping to make them more legible. Although the quality of the books had gotten better with age, the handwritten entries had become harder to read as the ink had faded and in places was completely illegible. There was no entry for her property.

Her eyes burned and she had a crick in her neck from hunching over the desk for so long. Frustrated, she leaned back in the chair, shoving the ledger across the blotter. She pushed the book harder than she intended and it skated across the blotter and over the polished wood of the desk. It hit Melvin's picture, sending it flying over the edge.

Lizzie scrambled to grab the frame before it hit the floor, but she wasn't fast enough. She cringed, waiting for the brittle sound of breaking glass, but it never came. She scurried around the side of the desk and peered down. The picture had fallen in the soft flannel blanket inside the wicker cat bed. Breathing a sigh of relief, she picked up the frame. As she lifted it up, the backing, which must have come loose in the fall, fell back into the wicker basket, along with several sheets of folded paper.

Placing the picture frame carefully on the desk, she crouched down to retrieve the backing and the papers. As her fingers brushed the thick paper, she recognized the feel and weight of them. She scooped them up and sat back down at the desk. Cradling them in her lap, she glanced at the empty stairwell. She was still alone in the archives, but the hammering in her chest told her she'd found something important, important enough that Maryanne had wanted it hidden from prying eyes.

She carefully unfolded the first piece of paper, and the sight

171

of the now familiar columns and handwritten entries made her heart beat even faster. Her eyes flitted down the page—she couldn't make herself slow down, so strong was the feeling of discovery—and there it was, halfway down the middle of the page, the legal description of her land purchased from the Crown. And next to it a name; Emma Hawksworth. Under occupation was listed widow. Through all the ledgers she'd plowed through, Emma's was the first woman's name she'd come across. This was her Emma. The woman who had lived at Rose Cottage. She'd purchased the land in the spring of 1882.

Her hands were damp with perspiration, so she wiped them on her thighs before unfolding the second sheaf of paper. It took a few seconds for her brain to digest what she was reading, and she finally made sense of the columns, names, and numbers. It was a census dated the same year as when Emma purchased the land. There on the page, in faded ink the color of a sepia photo, was Emma Hawksworth, residing at 3797 Quail Hollow Road. She was listed as the only occupant.

With furtive glances at the stairwell, she unfolded the remaining documents. They were all census records dating from 1883 to 1893. They weren't the complete records for those years, just the pages containing Emma's name.

Lizzie sat back in the chair, the last piece of paper cradled in her lap. She'd found what she'd been looking for, and in turn it had raised more questions than answers. By all accounts Maryanne took such obvious pride in maintaining her little archival domain that for her to hide a part of her village's past only strengthened Lizzie's conviction that the legend was true. The villagers had murdered Emma.

She took up the paper in her lap and reexamined it. Running her finger along the left-hand side of the document, she felt only the straight, smooth edge of the paper. It hadn't been carelessly torn, but meticulously cut out. She examined each of the sheets of paper in turn and found the same smooth edge where it had been removed from the bound ledgers. That's why she hadn't noticed the pages missing from her earlier search. Maryanne had excised the pages so cleanly, no one would have spotted it if they weren't looking.

Was the archivist alone in her subterfuge to hide the dark past of the village, to obliterate the sins of their forefathers? Or was she part of a village-wide cover-up, to keep their quaint little village palatable for the tourists?

She refolded each piece of paper and placed them back in their hiding place. With infinite care she secured the backing on the frame. She had no idea if she'd put them back in the order in which they'd been placed, but she hoped that Maryanne would never have cause to check them in the future.

She straightened the photograph near the corner of the desk. Melvin stared back at her, unperturbed by her discovery. The florescent lights flickered, the hum of the ballasts startlingly loud in the silence of the basement. Lizzie looked up and then back at the stairwell. There was no one there.

In the past her uncontrolled power had been known to affect lights and electronics, but the power surge wasn't coming from her. She sat huddled in the office chair, not sure what to do, when the lights resumed their normal intensity and the hum toned down to what it had been before. She'd had enough of basements.

Returning the ledger she'd been looking through back into its box, she scurried down the aisle and slid the box back into the empty hole on the shelf. She had every intention of retrieving her library books from the desk and leaving, but as soon as she slid the box home she was seized by the urge to look at the rest of the census records. Specifically, the census for 1894. She just had to be sure.

Remembering what Amanda had told her, she knew what she needed was shelved on the next aisle over. Instead of heading back the way she'd come, she walked to the end of the aisle. The light was poor at the back of the archives, and as she glanced to her left she let out a startled gasp.

She'd forgotten Amanda's earlier warning, and now found herself nose to nose, or more accurately nose to snouts, with a two-headed pig. She was grateful for the thick glass walls of the jar it was floating in, separating its rubbery snouts from hers. She stepped back from the gruesome sight floating in its murky formaldehyde bath. From a safe distance, she surveyed the other items littering the shelves that ran along the back wall.

These must be the artifacts the archivist intended on displaying in the museum, but to Lizzie's eyes the strange collection resting on the shelves looked like they would be more at home in a curiosity shop. A moth-eaten stuffed porcupine listed dangerously on its wooden plinth; a collection of dusty blue bottles sat next to what looked like a bear skull that had only one tooth. There was a stack of postcards from the turn of the century, and a few calligraphed handbills advertising a sale at a mercantile store long closed for business.

She took a few more steps away from the aisle she needed to go down as she perused a fan carved from what looked like ivory, by far the most intriguing item in the museum's collection. She spied several model trains and an apothecary jar filled with small rounded teeth. Lizzie leaned over to get a closer look. They looked like children's teeth.

She shuddered, backing away from the collection, and turned the corner. She shrieked and stumbled back into the shelves, smacking the back of her already tender head on the hard edge of the shelving. A bright explosion of stars danced before her eyes. The blue glass bottles rattled as they knocked together. She raised her hand and was seconds away from calling down her power when she realized what she was looking at.

"Shit." Her voice sounded harsh in the quiet of the archives.

She rubbed the back of her head where it throbbed.

A mannequin was propped up against the wall, her hand outstretched in supplication asking for someone to put some clothes on her naked form or to put her out of her misery, Lizzie wasn't sure which. Judging by the stylized arms and legs and the thick painted eyeliner on her crumbling face, she looked like she'd come from a department store in the sixties. Her head was angled away from Lizzie looking down the aisle of boxes, a matted wig sitting askew on her head. A large crack ran down the side of her face facing Lizzie, adding to her morbid countenance.

Lizzie skirted around the mannequin, shaking her arms out to relieve the tension. Quickly scanning the shelves, she spotted the box she wanted and yanked it off the shelf. She could feel the mannequin's eyes staring at her, and before she gave in to the urge to look behind her, she scuttled back to the safety of the desk and the warm green glow of the desk lamp.

She found the ledger she needed and flipped it open to the surnames starting with H. This time she also focused on the inside edge of the pages as she scanned down the names. There was no Hawksworth listed, and no missing pages. She had been counted in the census the year before. Emma had moved into Rose Cottage in 1882, and the last time she'd been counted in the census was 1892. Then she just disappeared from history. The archives didn't have birth and death certificates, but she doubted Emma's death would have been recorded.

She replaced the box, avoiding the back shelf entirely. Scooping up her library books and purse from the desk, she pushed in the chair and gave Melvin one last look. To her eyes, the desk looked just as it had before her discovery. She turned, switched off the desk lamp, then scrambled up the stairs.

She struggled with the door for a moment before realizing she'd pushed down on the grab bar on the wrong side. Banging through the door, she stumbled into the welcoming brightness of the light-flooded library. The sound of children's laughter and Amanda's singsong voice as she read aloud was a stark contrast to the quiet of the catacombs she'd emerged from.

She stood for a moment in the periodicals, hidden from view from the preschoolers and Amanda on the other side of the library. She had found what she'd come for; the witch of Grey House had existed, and she had a name. She wasn't a made-up story to scare kids at Halloween, she wasn't a myth weaved into the folklore of the village. She had lived, and she had been murdered for no other reason than she was different, an outsider. Not just killed, but starved to death in the darkness, alone.

Lizzie leaned her head against the end of the stack closest to her. Closing her eyes, she took a deep breath, breathing in the aroma of fresh varnish from the shelves. The smell of newness filled her with thoughts of her own renovations in her cottage. She promised Emma, as she stood alone amongst the books, that she would do everything within her power to release her spirit, to let her rest and to banish the pain that remained locked into the dirt walls of her cellar.

"Emma," she whispered. She heard a soft whisper of sound as if in reply.

Opening her eyes, she noticed a book sticking out ever so slightly from the others on the shelf. Impulsively she plucked the tattered looking volume up and slipped it into her purse.

She had every intention of returning the book she'd just secreted away. When she was done with it, she'd just slip it in the after-hours book return when the library was closed. She'd promised Amanda she wouldn't take anything from the archives and she hadn't. Besides, she was just avoiding any more unwanted speculation the book would cause if she'd checked it out.

As Lizzie casually made her way to the exit, she noticed that other than the preschoolers and the head librarian, she was the only other patron in the library. She'd almost slipped out the door unnoticed when Amanda suddenly turned from the crowd of children seated at her feet and winked at Lizzie, not skipping a beat in the flow of her story.

Lizzie gave her a flustered wave as she sailed out into the fresh air, cutting off the sound of Amanda's voice as the leaded-glass door swung shut.

CHAPTER NINETEEN

"Lizzie, she's over to your left," Grandma Faye said. "Go get her."

"Where?" Lizzie raised the fishing net over her head and scanned the waist-high ferns she was standing in. "I can hear her, but I can't see her."

This was her third attempt at capturing the chicken. Each time she was sure she had lowered the net down on the feathered creature, only to be rewarded by a frantic shriek from the chicken and a flurry of wings as the indignant hen flew deeper into the forest.

Audley had done a fine job of rehabbing the old shed into a chicken coop, complete with a fenced-in run. He'd even fastened chicken wire to the top of the run as per Grandma Faye's instructions, to protect the small hens from becoming lunch for the eagles and osprey that flew overhead. But Lizzie hadn't realized all the safeguards in the world wouldn't keep a strong willed chicken from escaping.

The chickens she was used to as a child were large docile Orpingtons, not the petite and spectacularly colorful Banties Grandma Faye showed up with. When she'd left the enclosed chicken yard with her new charges duly installed, she hadn't thought she needed to be on her guard when she walked through the chicken wire and wood gate. She hadn't noticed the gold Seabright hen shadowing her until it was too late and the bird had literally flown the coop.

Lizzie had stared in amazement as the russet and black bird took flight. Without missing a beat, Grandma Faye had jogged to her truck and produced a fishing net on a long aluminum pole. She handed it to Lizzie and instructed her to go after the wayward chicken.

"Just there," the old woman said, pointing. "About two feet from where you're standing."

Lizzie focused on the area Grandma Faye pointed at. She could hear the hen's soft clucking. It was a melodic sound, as if the hen was humming to herself as she strolled in the summer sunshine without a care in the world.

Readjusting her grip on the net's handle, Lizzie crept over to the sound. The thick carpet of ferns swayed slightly two feet in front of her. Sweat stung her eyes and made her T-shirt cling uncomfortably to her back as she struggled through the ferns.

She felt ridiculous brandishing a net intended for scooping up fish while stalking a chicken through the bracken and ferns behind the coop. She swiped her forearm at the beads of perspiration dotting her forehead, and in the process her weapon got stuck in a pine branch above her head.

As she wrestled with the entangled net, she let out a frustrated sigh. This was not how she'd planned on spending her day, not by a long shot. Nor her week, for that matter. She had wanted to find out what the symbols in her cellar meant so she could rid her house of the black magic and release Emma's spirit. But the day after her visit to the archives a gaggle of workmen descended on her with orders from Jon to start ripping out what little she had of a kitchen. It turned out Jon had been more successful at getting a rush order through than he'd anticipated, and the kitchen cupboards were scheduled to be delivered later today.

On top of her kitchen being in shambles, the fridge and bed she'd ordered both arrived mid-week. She'd spent most her time dealing with deliveries and stepping around piles of lumber and spools of electrical wires littering the cottage, while trying to avoid the burly men filling her cottage with sweat and the lingering odor of pot while their work spread plaster and saw dust everywhere.

And then there was Audley. Ever since her tumble into the cellar, Audley had been following her around like a puppy, asking her how she was feeling and if she'd had any more run-ins with the Witch of Grey House. She had no desire to share with him what she'd found out about Emma Hawksworth. And no matter how many times she reassured him she was fine, it didn't stop him from following her and asking if she was okay.

To get away from the chaos and her moon-eyed handyman, she drove into town every day to visit Bear. He was doing remarkably well. Dr. Laurie suggested that if he kept showing such splendid improvement he would be able to go home with Lizzie in a few weeks.

When not crouched on the floor of the vet clinic hanging out with her dog, she worked in her garden planting spring crops of lettuce, peas, and spinach.

The only thing she'd manage to accomplish in regards to her ghost was reading the slim volume she'd liberated from the library. It was an odd little book containing a few chapters on the practice of Wicca and a detailed section on conducting séances to communicate with the dead. She wasn't sure if a séance would work, but she thought it couldn't hurt.

Lizzie gave the net a sudden hard jerk. There was a loud crack as the branch it was ensnared on broke in two, one end of it remaining trapped in the net. The sound frightened the hen that had been standing right at Lizzie's feet. In her attempt to get the net free of the tree, she hadn't noticed the chicken had wandered so close. It flew up into Lizzie face in a flurry of wings and bright orange beak.

Dropping the fishnet, she backpedaled through the ferns,

holding her hands up, struggling to keep her balance as the thick stems of the ferns caught at her jeans and snagged her ankles. She felt the sharp edges of the hen's feathers scrape against her cheek before she watched in amazement as the chicken flew up into the tree.

"Really," she said in exasperation. Hands on her hips, she peered up into the tree. The chicken settled on a branch fifteen feet above Lizzie's head and began preening itself. It stopped for a moment and peered down at her, a challenge in its tiny black eyes. "Fine," she shouted up at the bird. "If you are so keen on becoming someone's dinner, stay there."

Snatching up the net, she stomped out of the forest dragging the net with the tree branch still in it, picking up a few fern fronds along the way. Dropping the net at Grandma Faye's feet, she glared at her friend. Not that the old woman noticed Lizzie's exasperation, as she was doubled over, her shoulders shaking with laughter.

"It's not funny," Lizzie said, then clenched her teeth to stop from smiling.

"Oh, yes it is." Grandma Faye straightened up and swiped at the tears streaming down her wrinkled cheeks. "You should have seen the look on your face when Ginger Chicken flew into the tree."

"Ginger the chicken?"

"No, Ginger Chicken, like the Chinese food dish," Grandma Faye said, gathering up the fishnet. With one swift twist of her wrist she pulled the twig free of the net, and then began picking out the fern leaves.

"You named her after food? Isn't that a bit ghoulish?"

"Not at all. The color combination of her feathers reminded me of the dish, which happens to be my favorite. But it also describes her personality to a T. Like ginger, she's a bit sweet with a dash of spicy zing, and as you've just experienced firsthand, she can be very saucy."

"I see your point." Lizzie looked back towards the forest, trying to catch a glimpse of the roosting bird in the trees, but the thick pine and cedar bows camouflaged her location. "So how do you propose we get *Ginger* Chicken out of the tree and back into the coop where she belongs? And don't you dare suggest I climb up there after it, because that's not going to happen."

"But it might be good for a few more laughs. And they do say laughter is good for the soul."

"Well after this morning, I think your soul has got its fill. But seriously, how am I going to get her down from there?"

"Go talk to her. Lay down the law. And after that I think we should take a break."

"You want me to reason with a chicken? Wouldn't it be simpler and far more effective if you just cast some sort of spell and levitated her down?"

"I could, but it wouldn't be right. We never use magic to force someone to do our bidding. That's when you start heading into black magick territory."

"But it's just a chicken, for heaven's sake. And besides, we are doing it for her own good."

"She might disagree with that last statement. And it doesn't matter if she were a child or a chicken. Every living thing has free will, and it does the world more good than harm when you give them the freedom to choose their destiny."

"So how was scrambling after her with a net giving her a choice?"

"She didn't let you catch her, did she?"

"Oh, I give up. I'm thirsty and you're giving me a headache," Lizzie said, and turned on her heels. She trudged back into the forest with Grandma Faye's childlike giggle ringing in her ears.

CHAPTER TWENTY

Lizzie squinted up at the tree. Ginger Chicken was just where she'd left her. She had her feet tucked up under her and her feathers fluffed out, making her look larger than she really was.

"This is ridiculous," she murmured. Clearing her throat, she spoke. "Ginger Chicken, I can imagine that it's quite lovely up there in the tree, but it's not safe. There's eagles and osprey that would love to have you for their dinner, not to mention coyotes and weasels. If you come down, I promise to take good care of you. The chicken coop is large and airy, with pretty nesting boxes full of fresh bedding. Please come down."

The chicken stood up from the branch and stretched its amber and black wings. Lizzie couldn't believe Grandma Faye's ludicrous suggestion had worked. She took a step closer to the tree to make sure she would see where the chicken would land.

Instead of taking flight, Ginger Chicken turned around, her scaly little feet moving with ease on the rough bark of the tree limb until she was facing away from Lizzie. Then, fanning out her tail feathers, she pooped, her missile landing with a liquid splat on Lizzie's shoulder.

Lizzie looked in disgust at the bird poop oozing down her shoulder towards her bare arm. Her nose wrinkled at the acrid smell. "Fine, I'm done being nice." She shook her finger up at the hen. "Get eaten by a coyote for all I care. I'm not wasting another minute on you."

Lizzie fled the forest, swiping furiously at the fern fronds in her way. She heard Ginger Chicken cackling from her roost as she tramped her way back to Grandma Faye.

"Reason with a chicken, you tell me. Fat lot of good that did. I'm going to go change."

"That seems wise."

Lizzie narrowed her eyes at her friend, daring her to even think about cracking a joke or bursting into laughter. Grandma Faye's face remained stoic, but Lizzie noticed the twinkle of amusement in the old lady's eyes.

She left her friend by the coop and stormed towards the house. As she came up to the cottage, what had once been her kitchen cupboards lay in a heap of splintered wood littering her driveway She let out a huff as she stepped onto her porch.

She could hear the steady kachunk-kachunk of a nail gun and the muffled beat of music. When she flung open the front door a cacophony of men's voices, blaring music, hammering, and the metal zing of a table saw surrounded her. She glanced around at the chaos. Two men were busily nailing strips of wood along the walls, to which her new cupboards would eventually be secured. Another stood at her kitchen table measuring lengths of wood, then cutting them down to size on a compound miter saw.

In the corner of the kitchen, she stared in amazement at a large hole in her floor. The floorboards were stacked neatly to one side, and a man's torso disappeared down the gaping hole between the floor joists.

If it weren't for the strong desire to rid herself of the chicken poop she now wore, and the need for a chilled bottle of water, she would have left her cottage and slammed the door on the whole mess.

"Audley," she called out for her handyman who was nowhere to be seen. None of the workmen looked up from what they were doing or moved to turn down the blaring music coming from a portable boom box on the floor. "Audley." She raised her voice over the noise as she stepped further into her cottage.

Lizzie's head throbbed. She just wanted to change her T-shirt and grab a bottle of water, not maneuver through a construction minefield.

The familiar face wearing its customary look of bewilderment appeared from the doorway of the three-season porch, his hair sticking up in odd little tufts. He wandered into the kitchen carrying two lengths of black PVC pipe under his arms. When he caught a glimpse of her, he dropped the pipes on the floor and scurried over. The pipes clattered hollowly against the hardwood, and rolled to a stop when they hit the kitchen table's leg.

As he approached, the musky smell of pot almost overpowered the stinging ammonia emanating from her shoulder. Breathing through her mouth to avoid taking in the combined miasma of stink, she wondered with irritation if he even owned a comb or had been introduced to a bar of soap recently.

"Why is there a hole in my kitchen floor?"

"Oh," Audley said, looking behind him at the man currently wriggling out of the hole. "That's so the plumber can run new pipes for your water and waste lines. We had to install new water lines for the dishwasher, and Jon said it made sense seeing as we were going to be under the house to run a new waste pipe too."

"But why did you have to rip up my floor to do it?"

"There's no other way, Ms. Bennet. Your house don't have a basement that extends under the whole length of the house, and there's no outside access to the crawl space unless you wanted us to hack through the stone foundation. But not to worry, I took the boards out careful, and I'll put them back so's you'll never know they was ever torn up. You'll see."

"Fine." She crossed her arms over her chest.

Audley sniffed the air, wrinkled his nose, then took a shuffling step away from her. "You might want to take care of that," he said, pointing to the drying spot on her shoulder. "You smell like you've rolled around in the chicken coop."

"Thanks, I hadn't noticed," she said through clenched teeth. Now she was getting hygiene advice from her handyman.

Stepping around Audley, she maneuvered over the plastic pipes and went straight to her bedroom. She dug out a clean tee from her suitcase and locked herself in the bathroom. She stripped out of her soiled shirt and turned the tap to fill the sink. Instead of warm water filling the basin, all she got was the hiss of air through the pipes.

She groaned. The plumber was working on the pipes. The water had been shut off. Pulling the clean shirt over her head, she left the bathroom and ducked into the three-season porch. Her sparkling new fridge was temporarily housed in the porch until the new wiring was in place, and then she could move it into the kitchen proper. Snagging two bottles of water, she snuck out the back door and made her way around the house to the coop.

Grandma Faye was sitting under a large pine not far from the coop, a red flannel blanket spread beneath her in the benevolent shade. A wicker hamper nestled near her feet, its contents neatly arranged on the blanket. She smiled and waved at Lizzie as she approached. Her heart lurched in her chest and her purposeful stride faltered.

Another image superimposed itself on the scene in front of her. Instead of Grandma Faye sitting on the picnic blanket, it was Sister Collette, the nun who had raised her, who she saw waiting under the tree. The two of them would spend lazy summer afternoons reading in the shade of the ancient oak at the corner of their walled garden. After one or two stories, Lizzie would curl up on the blanket, the scent of honeysuckle and verbena following her into her dreams as she had her afternoon nap.

Lizzie shrugged off the memory before the sadness could overtake her, and flopped down on the blanket next to Grandma Faye. Handing Grandma Faye one of the water bottles, she then took a deep pull on her own water and surveyed the contents of the hamper laid out between them. There was a large silver thermos, two delicate white china cups, a plate of sliced lemon loaf, and a pint of small glossy red strawberries.

"Here, you might want to use this," Grandma Faye said, handing her a pink paper napkin.

Raising her eyebrows, Lizzie took the proffered napkin.

"You missed a spot," Grandma Faye answered Lizzie's silent question, pointing to the dried chicken poop still stuck to her arm.

"Stupid chicken. Stupid plumbers shutting off my water," she muttered under her breath as she dampened the napkin with water from her bottle. She scrubbed furiously at her arm, shredding the damp napkin and leaving a red mark on her upper arm. She wadded up the napkin and tossed over her shoulder.

Grandma Faye removed the top off the thermos and poured the steaming contents into each of the teacups. She handed one of the white china cups to Lizzie. She took the teacup, holding it carefully by the foot of the bowl before grasping the delicate handle. The steam carried the scent of lavender, and she glanced curiously inside her cup. Against the bone white bowl of the cup, the tea was a pale purple.

"Lavender tea?"

"A hot drink on a hot day will cool you down faster than cold one, and the calming nature of lavender would be beneficial right now."

She ignored her friend's comment and sipped her tea instead, surprised by the intense flavor.

As they drank their tea, the women watched the chickens scratch around in the dirt of their yard, each one occasionally pecking at the handfuls of grain Lizzie had scattered earlier. A handsome cooper and green rooster with an extravagant glossy black tail kept watch over his harem from a stump placed in the center of the yard.

"The white and black hen, just there," Lizzie said between sips of tea. "She has the same markings as Ginger Chicken the way each feather is outlined in black. Except, of course, she's white while that rude chicken up in the tree is russet. You called her a Gold Seabright, so what is that one?"

"She's a Silver Seabright."

"She's beautiful. Her feathers look like an inlayed mother-of-pearl. What's her name?"

"She doesn't have one, nor do the rest with the exception of Ginger Chicken. A few of these are her babies. All of them were born in very early spring, so I haven't named them yet. They're yours now, so that job falls to you."

"Mmm," Lizzie murmured through a mouthful of lemon loaf. "If that's the case, I think I shall call the silver one Miss Pearl."

For the next hour, the two women drank tea and nibbled on strawberries in the shade as they debated and decided on names for Lizzie's new flock. Grandma Faye held out the last piece of lemon loaf for Lizzie.

"No thank you, I'm stuffed." She lay down on the blanket with a contented sigh, looking up through the pine boughs at the intensely blue sky.

Grandma Faye rearranged her flowing skirt before reclining on the blanket to join Lizzie in looking up through the trees. "So did you want to talk about what's really bothering you?"

Lizzie put her hands behind her head. "Let's see…my chicken ran away ten minutes after I got her, I've been pooped on by said chicken, my kitchen looks like a bomb went off, and I'm sick of eating cold sandwiches from the Done-Rite Deli for the last week. Oh, and did I mention they've ripped up my kitchen floor? I think those things would put most people in a foul mood."

She looked over at Grandma Faye and noticed her smiling at Lizzie's pun. The old woman turned her head back to look up at the sky. "I wasn't referring just to this morning. This whole week you've become increasingly on edge. But if you don't want to talk about it, it's okay."

Lizzie's irritation crept back. "What do you want me say?" She sat up. Was she really out of sorts over a chicken and a bunch of workmen who were doing their best to put in her new kitchen?

"Nothing. But if your heart's heavy because of Emma, I'm confident we'll figure something out. There's been some lively debate on the hedge witch forum, and if there is anyone who knows anything about this spell it's only a matter of time."

Not for the first time Lizzie thought about reaching out to Vivienne and the order for help. She knew she was being stubborn, and that her pride was probably the source. No, she'd give Grandma Faye and her cyber witches a few more weeks.

The rooster, now dubbed Henry, let out an ear-piercing alarm call. Immediately several of the hens flattened themselves on the ground while a few fast-thinking ones ducked into the safety of the coop. A winged shadow floated across the chicken yard.

Lizzie looked up in time to see a large raven sail by. She pushed herself on all fours and squinted against the sunshine. Could that be Quinn? Her Quinn?

The raven flapped its wings and sailed up into the sky until it was a tiny dot of black against the blue. Lizzie sat back down, the heaviness in her heart returning.

"Who's Quinn?" Grandma Faye asked, sitting up.

Lizzie hadn't realized she'd said his name out loud. During her stay at the Halcyon Resort the raven had been her constant companion, showing up at her window twice a day. On the last night, before she was to move to the cottage, she'd bought him a special meal of bagels and cream cheese. She'd even cut up her offering into small bite-sized pieces to make it easier for the raven to eat. She'd talked to the bird, telling him she was moving and would love to have him continue his visits. She'd even pulled out a map and pointed to where her cottage was.

189

For the first few days after she'd moved she'd kept an ear cocked, listening for the familiar sound of his beak tapping on the window announcing his arrival. But he never came.

"Who's Quinn?" Grandma Faye asked again.

Lizzie dabbed at the moisture at the corners of her eyes. Horrified, she looked at the tears on her fingertips. What was happening to her? Was she becoming the avian version of a crazy cat lady? Was she really that upset about a bird? But he wasn't just any bird. Twice during her ordeal, when the demon had hunted her relentlessly, his kind had come to her aid. Quinn himself had been present when she'd faced the demon and destroyed it. She had thought she'd shared a special bond with his kind and a unique relationship with him.

Lizzie shook her head. She'd made fun of Grandma Faye's suggestion to talk to a chicken, and here she was feeling upset that her bird friend hadn't found the time to fly down and visit her in her new cottage after she'd asked him to.

"He's a raven," she said sheepishly. "He used to visit me when I was staying at the resort. I was hoping he'd show up here. I even told him where I was moving to." She was too embarrassed to tell her friend about showing him the map. "So you see, I suck at talking to birds. They don't listen."

Grandma Faye opened her mouth to reply, but the sound of a large truck struggling up the drive diverted both women's attention. Lizzie looked over her shoulder as the flatbed parked near the rubbish pile on her driveway. Several tie-downs secured an array of large boxes with the name of the kitchen cupboard manufacturer printed in big blue letters.

"Looks like my kitchen cupboards have arrived. The gods be praised, I might actually have a working kitchen by this evening."

From the tranquility of the shade, the women watched a young man climb out of the cab of the truck. With a clatter of boots on the front porch, Audley greeted the delivery truck and the two men had a brief conversation before Audley disappeared back inside the cottage. Minutes later he came out again, followed by the rest of the work crew. Two dollies were rounded up from the back of Audley's cube van, and a makeshift ramp made of plywood was laid across the front porch steps. With surprising speed and efficiency, the men unloaded the truck and maneuvered the large boxes into the cottage.

"Did you want to go and take a look?"

"No, I don't think I could take going back into that chaos. I'd rather wait until it's all done and I can admire the finished results."

"Well then, we have a whole glorious day full of possibilities. What shall we do?"

Lizzie shrugged. She thought about all the things she should be doing; weeding the garden, finding a bolt cutter to remove the padlock on the barn door so she could finally take a look inside, ridding the attic of the cobwebs and dust she hadn't gotten to. All things she had absolutely no desire to tackle.

"Let's go on a road trip. Two daring young women, racing down the mountain roads, the wind in our hair." Grandma Faye flipped her grey braid coquettishly over her shoulder.

Lizzie laughed. "Sounds like fun. I haven't had fun in a long time. Where should we go?"

Grandma Faye collected the teacups and placed them inside the wicker hamper. "By the end of the day you'll have a brand new kitchen, but all you have for furniture in your cottage is a kitchen table and a bed. You'd mentioned the other day that you wanted to check out the antique stores in the area. Why not today? I know several great stores between here and Nelson, and the drive is beautiful."

"Birdie had promised to take me, but she's not returning my calls, and every time I stop by the realty office it seems to be closed." Lizzie handed Grandma Faye the cake plate and gathered up the napkins that had been scattered across the blanket by the breeze. The chickens began to sing softly as they scratched at the soft ground. Henry arched his neck and let out a full-throated ka hee haw.

"That settles it then. Antiquing we shall go," Grandma Faye said, putting the thermos inside the hamper and closing the lid.

"Wait, we can't go. What about Ginger Chicken? We can't just leave her running around the forest. And seeing as I've no talent talking to birds, maybe I should climb the tree to get her down."

The chickens singing turned into excited calls, punctuated by Henry's crowing.

"Oh, I don't think that's going to be a problem," Grandma Faye said, looking past Lizzie's shoulder. Lizzie turned to see what she was looking at.

Out of the forest stepped Ginger Chicken, calling out to her flock mates. She tottered straight over to the chicken coop and stood expectantly at the door to the run, waiting to be reunited with her family.

"I think you possess the gift after all," Grandma Faye called out to Lizzie as she strode over to the chicken coop to let the wayward chicken back home.

CHAPTER TWENTY-ONE

Lizzie drifted past the empty chicken yard. The flock had been shut up safe within the coop hours before. The wind tugged at her short nightgown and blew her hair into her eyes. All was silent but for the wind frolicking through the trees, enticing the forest surrounding the cottage to dance and sway to its mischievous tune.

She stepped in the direction of the barn, following the pulse rising up through the dew-dampened earth, the heartbeat cadence of the Great Mother urging her into the forest.

A velvet fog collected in the small dells scattered around the open field between her house and the barn. Slipping through the fog, she felt its cool caress against her bare legs. Coming to the edge of where the forest began, she didn't hesitate to slip between the dark outline of the tree trunks into the deeper bruised darkness within.

Here her feet touched the springy softness of the moss carpeting the forest floor, her footsteps leaving faint impressions as she went. Her right hand reached out to caress the trees as she passed, the rough bark kissing the palm of her hand. She could feel the pulse through the trees as her fingertips alighted on the next curving trunk. Each swaying-branched sentinel sent out the throbbing call of the earth through the interconnected web of their roots sunk deep into the loamy soil like a relay.

Deeper she plunged into the forest, the darkness neither impeding her progress nor sending her off course. Sure footedly she followed the siren call until the trees began to thin out, the spaces between their trunks widening to allow the moonlight to emboss the arching curves of rock and outstretched tree limbs with silver filigree.

He was there waiting for her in the small glen, as she knew he would be, ready to begin their ancient dance one more time in an endless spiral of the times before and the ones yet to be. At the opposite edge of a circle of white stone he stood bare-chested, his arms at his side. The stones glowed beneath the moonlight as if emitting their own internal white-hot fire.

She entered the circle at the same time he did, each of them avoiding the line of stones dividing the circle into four. They came together in the center, their breathing synchronized.

He reached out and caressed her cheek, sending a shiver of anticipation down her body and centering between her legs.

"Beloved," he whispered. They held each other's gaze. The black of his pupils contrasted with his irises that burned bright with the color of sea and sky.

Oh, how she'd missed her lover's gaze.

They stepped in closer, his broad muscled chest crushing her breasts, his arousal firm against the gentle swell of her belly. The heat of him radiated through the slim cotton of her nightdress.

She answered with a kiss, the searing heat of it driving her into a frenzy of desire. In the silvery moonlight, his skin shone like burnished bronze in contrast to the glowing whiteness of her own. Her hands wandered down the curve and dip of his biceps, down his forearms until she held his hands.

Stepping back, she lowered herself to the ground, pulling him down on top of her. His skin smelled of wood smoke and earth. What little clothes covering their hungry bodies were scattered around them in a frantic push to feel skin on skin.

They embraced in a tangle of limbs, exploring hands, and hungry searching mouths. She opened her body and soul to him, her cry of pleasure breaking the stillness of the night.

The earth welcomed the lovers, surrounding them with her song. Her children of two worlds united once again. The Great Mother was pleased.

CHAPTER TWENTY-TWO

She was hung over. The morning light shining through her eyelids made her head ache. She threw the quilt over her head and buried herself deeper into the cocoon of blankets. She groaned as the slight movement of the mattress made her stomach flip. She didn't think she'd drunk too much last night, but by the way her body hurt and her mouth felt stuffed with cotton she'd obviously over indulged. She'd never been hungover in her life and she vowed not to do it again. It was worse than the concussion. She could only hope her ability to heal quickly also applied to self-induced pain.

Last night she and Grandma Faye had celebrated the completion of Lizzie's new kitchen renovation and May Day with a home-cooked meal provided by Lizzie, and a couple of bottles of red wine compliments of Grandma Faye. One too many bottles, if the thwacking in her skull was any indication.

She thought about spending the day in bed, not moving until her body felt at least half-human, but she'd overslept and her chickens needed to be let out for the day and fed their daily rations.

The tapping in her head got louder. Her cloudy brain registered the sound, but it took a few seconds before her synaptic process shifted into gear. The sound wasn't the result of a hangover...there was someone in her bedroom.

The tapping started again. It sounded like the clip of high heels against stone. Then she heard the rustle of fabric, like crisp taffeta, as if her dainty-heeled intruder where wearing a long skirt.

Was it Emma? Grandma Faye and Lizzie had spent the better part of the night discussing Emma Hawksworth over the now regretted bottles of wine. Had invoking her name and stirring up the energy of the house with the last of the renovations caused her to materialize in her bedroom?

Lizzie strained her ears beneath the quilt, trying to pinpoint where the footsteps were originating from.

Tap-tap-tap.

The sound came from over by the fireplace, and she was positive it wasn't a ghost but a flesh and blood human that was making the noise.

The remnants of last night's bacchanal evaporated in a wash of adrenaline as all of her senses went of high-alert. In one swift movement, she flung back the quilt and sat up, her hands thrown forward as she called forth her powers. Her palms tingled with the buildup of energy and the air crackled with electricity.

"Eep," she squeaked, and flung her hands out to the side, drawing down her power before she blasted Quinn. The raven was perched on the mantle, one glittering black eye staring at her calmly. Unconcerned by Lizzie's movements, he aimed his sharp beak at a stone on the chimney breast and pecked at it. Tap, tap, tap.

"Quinn, how did you get in here?" As she asked the question, she suddenly became aware of the chill air caressing her breasts and arms. She looked down at herself and emitted another squeak of alarm. She was completely naked under the blankets. Wrapping the quilt around her shoulders, she slipped off the bed.

Her joy at seeing her friend was tempered with the mystery of how he'd gained entry into her cottage. At the resort, he'd always tapped on the window and waited patiently for Lizzie to open it for him. She glanced around her bedroom. All the window sashes were securely latched, and the french door's bolt was in the locked position.

She may have been a bit tipsy when she said goodnight to Grandma Faye, but she distinctly remembered checking all the doors and windows before retiring for the evening. She'd locked up her cottage tight as a drum.

She padded over to the fireplace, but not before bending over to take a cursory look under her bed for her missing nightgown. It wasn't there or anywhere in her sparsely decorated bedroom. The cold floorboards made her bare feet ache, and they hurt as if she'd run a marathon in her sleep.

Quinn shuffled across the mantelpiece towards her, his tiny black nails scraping against the wood. Clutching the quilt around her with one hand, she snuck her other one out from under the blanket and gently stroked Quinn's back with her finger. His feathers were silky, his body solid under her touch. He fanned out his tail feathers, exposing a gap where one was missing. It was a feather he'd left for her on their first meeting that now sat by her bedside table.

"So big boy, how did you get in?"

With a ruffle of feathers she now recognized as what she thought was the rustle of fabric, Quinn launched himself off the mantle and onto the floor.

He walked through her open bedroom door and down the hall. Gathering the quilt tightly around her, she followed him out, careful not to step on the length of quilt that puddled around her feet.

Despite not feeling her best, she couldn't help but smile as she watched the raven's tottering steps, his head jutting forward with each step. Which reminded her, her hens were probably eager to get out of the coop and have their breakfast, but not before she started a pot of coffee. She needed coffee.

As she passed the bathroom, she paused to see if she'd left

her nightgown on the floor, but it was nowhere to be seen. The raven kept up his pace towards the kitchen, and Lizzie shuffle-hopped around the quilt tangled at her feet to catch up.

As she neared the kitchen, she caught a whiff of something sweet, a sugary smell laced with peanut butter, as if someone had recently baked a batch of cookies. Her step faltered. Gooseflesh rippled across her skin and fear tingled at the base of her skull. All thoughts of coffee and chickens evaporated as she stood at the end of her hallway looking into the kitchen.

CHAPTER TWENTY-THREE

She watched in disbelief as Quinn stepped around shattered dishes and tangled piles of silverware scattered over the wide-plank floor. Broken glass was everywhere. Quinn pecked at a cellophane package of raisins before abandoning it in favor of a large jar of peanut butter, the cracked plastic jar oozing oily brown goo.

Her brand new kitchen.

When she'd gone to bed, she'd left her beautiful kitchen spotless. The dirty dishes loaded in the dishwasher, the wineglasses left in the dish rack to dry, and the leftovers stacked neatly in the fridge.

She stared at the mayhem. The dishwasher and fridge doors were ajar, their contents mingled with the broken crockery on the floor. Gone were the wineglasses and the dish rack from the counter. Every single cupboard door was flung open and all the drawers pulled out.

A large bag of flour had been upended on the kitchen table in a great powdery heap. The mismatched kitchen chairs she'd picked up antiquing with Grandma Faye were tossed around the living room. The front door stood open, and the windows in the living room were thrown open too.

Stepping further into the kitchen, she grasped the quilt tightly in front of her. Taking a deep breath, she sent out her energy in cascading waves. Locking her eyes on the broken jar of peanut butter, she turned her other senses not on her physical surroundings, but to the energetic world around her.

She searched for any unwelcome energy signatures in her house, or even the faintest ripple of magick. There was nothing to detect. She sent her energy further out across her property. The only sentient beings other than the inhabitants of the forest hitting her psychic radar were her and Quinn.

Puzzled, she pulled back her energy to within its normal range. Could this level of destruction be caused by a spirit? Did Emma see her as a threat instead of someone who wanted to help her?

Quinn continued foraging for his breakfast as Lizzie's eyes roamed over her vandalized kitchen. She needed to call Grandma Faye. She started over to the phone when the wind rocketed through the open windows and door, slamming into the pile of flour. The flour lifted off the table in great white flurries, the air quickly filled with a fine gritty fog.

She made a frantic move to close the windows when she saw him standing in the doorway, his silhouette filling the doorframe blocking out the light. With the light behind him and a haze of flour obscuring his features, she only had a brief impression of her intruder.

She had no time to think. Throwing both hands in front of her, the quilt falling to the floor at her feet, she sent a flash of energy furling out from her fingertips strong enough to knock the man off the porch or worse. Too late she noticed the man standing in the doorway was leaning on a cane.

"Jon," she called out. Running towards him, she skidded to a halt when instead of being lifted off his feet by her magick, Jon swayed slightly but remained upright in the doorway.

She would have sworn her aim had been true, but somehow Jon remained unaffected. She didn't have time to puzzle what had gone wrong with her magick as the ball of energy she'd thrown ricocheted back towards her. When the wave of her magick hit her, she was so surprised she didn't make a move to deflect it. Behind her, she heard Quinn let out several angry caws, followed by the flurry of wings as he flew out of the path of the bolt of energy.

If she hadn't been wearing her necklace, the powerful magick she'd released would have done her a serious injury. Instead, the charm held and protected her from the destructive powers she'd unleashed, and the cottage took the brunt. The stone walls absorbed most of the blast, and the foundation shuddered as the magick passed through it. The floor boards rippled beneath her feet, causing the broken plates and cups to chime discordantly before the energy dissipated.

"Lizzie, are you hurt? We must've had a rockslide on one of the nearby mountains."

Jon's voice snapped her into action.

"I'm fine," she said, turning from him as he stepped over the threshold. She grabbed at the quilt, throwing it over her, praying the flour filled air had hidden her nakedness from him. "Close the door," she called out, pulling the quilt tight. "I'll get the windows. Watch where you step, there's broken glass and plates all over the floor." She coughed in the flour-clogged air. Her hip knocked against a small end table and it clattered to the floor.

Jon followed her lead, joining Lizzie in a frantic dash to close and latch all the windows as the dervish-like wind continued to swirl around the cottage. With the last window securely shut, a loud silence filled the cottage. Even Quinn had stopped his angry caws from the top of the fridge where he'd sought refuge.

Flour still floated in the air, but without the wind as its dance partner, it had slowly begun to settle back down onto every surface. Now everything, including her and Jon, was coated in a fine powder.

Jon held her by her shoulders. She could feel the heat of him even through the thick quilt. His calm grey eyes searched her face.

"Are you sure you're okay?" he asked, rubbing her upper arms through the fabric of the quilt. Lizzie felt a reassuring warmth spread through her.

"What the hell happened?"

The shock of seeing her destroyed kitchen and the apparent misfire of her magick seemed of little importance. She leaned into him and looked up. His hair had turned white with flour, and with his cane, he looked like an old man with a young man's face.

"I'm fine. As for what happened to my kitchen, I don't know. When I went to bed last night, everything was perfectly normal. I woke up and found Quinn in my bedroom, and it wasn't until we headed into to the kitchen to put the coffee on that I knew anything was amiss."

Jon's hands stiffened and he gripped her arms a little too tightly. "Who's Quinn?"

She realized that trying to explain she was going to put the coffee on for herself and feed the raven breakfast sounded ludicrous, so she settled for the simplest answer. "He's behind you on the fridge." She looked over to her winged friend. He was leaning over the edge of the fridge, his head lowered, his feather puffed out around his neck and chest.

"Quinn's a crow?"

Before Lizzie could correct him, Quinn launched himself off his perch and straight at Jon. Quinn screamed in what Lizzie could only describe as the bird version of rage. He flew at Jon with his claws and beak, aiming for his face.

Despite his injuries, Jon managed to wield his cane in the air with a surprising swiftness and swung at the raven. He missed the bird by inches, but it didn't stop Quinn's attack.

She yelled at both of them to stop, but neither man nor bird listened. The air filled with the flap and flurry of wings, flashes of beak and claw, and the swoosh of Jon's cane as it slashed through the air.

Struggling to keep the quilt wrapped around her, she tried to insinuate herself between Quinn and Jon before either one injured the other. But she couldn't get her hands around the cane Jon wielded high above his head, and Quinn kept circling and flapping just out of her reach.

Quinn had looped over their heads and was about to take another dive at Jon when the front door opened. There was no furious wind this time, just the short round silhouette of her friend in the doorway.

"What in heaven's name is going on?" she said, then ducked as the raven flew over her head and out the door. She straightened up and strode into the cottage. "I take it that was Quinn," she said matter-of-factly as she shut the door with a firm hand.

Lizzie nodded and pulled at the quilt that had slipped down during her attempt to break up the fight. Wrapping it tightly around her chest, she tucked in the loose end.

"Did the two of them do all this damage?" She threw her head in Jon's direction as she made her way over to Lizzie's side.

"No I didn't," Jon said, brushing at the flour in his hair, trying to regain some of his composure. "It was like this when I showed up. I was helping Lizzie when then that idiot bird started attacking me. Wouldn't be surprised if it has rabies."

Lizzie crossed her arms over her chest and stuck out her chin. "He does not have rabies. He was just trying to protect me."

"Protect you from me? I was helping you, remember?" He stepped back from the two women, brushing flour off his shoulder. "If that dumb crow was so intent on protecting you, why didn't he go after whoever did this to your kitchen?"

"I don't know. Maybe he didn't come through the window until after the intruder left. And he's not a dumb crow, he's a raven," she shot back.

It was Grandma Faye's turn to step into the fray. Holding

her hands up like a referee, she looked sternly at both of them. "Enough, you two."

Lizzie held back the urge to stick her tongue out at her friend.

Grandma Faye looked at Lizzie. "Now tell me everything."

Lizzie recounted everything that had happened since she woke up: from finding Quinn in her bedroom, to discovering the mess in her kitchen, and the arrival of Jon. She left out that she originally thought Quinn was the ghost of Emma prowling around her bedroom, and that she'd used her magick on Jon and the subsequent misfire. As soon as Jon left, she'd fill in her friend on all that had really happened.

Grandma Faye listened without interruption until Lizzie was finished. "So, can you tell if anything's missing? This could have started out as a robbery, and when the thieves couldn't find anything of value, like a TV or a computer, they resorted to vandalism."

Lizzie took a moment to survey the damage more closely. She scanned the kitchen, then turned to face the living room. None of the living room furniture had been touched except for a small end table Lizzie had knocked over in her rush to close the windows.

"No, nothing's missing, just dumped in the middle of the floor. Wait a minute," she said walking over to the cabinet to the right of the sink.

The tail of her quilt left a clean path through the flour-coated floor. The right side door was only partially opened, and Lizzie caught a glimpse of something scrawled on the face of it. She closed the door and let out a sound of dismay. Whoever had vandalized her place had gouged something in the smoothly painted finish of the wood door. They'd used something sharp and wide to carve two words, leaving splintered jagged edges along each letter.

"House? Out?" She read the words on the cabinet door.

"What does that mean?"

"Close the other door, Lizzie." Grandma Faye's voice sounded flat. Lizzie did as she was told. The three of them looked in silence at the complete message scored into the wood with a crazed manic hand.

My House, Get Out.

CHAPTER TWENTY-FOUR

She gave the bathroom door a hard kick, satisfied by the way it shuddered in its frame. As she tramped across the floor she kicked the tail of the quilt she still wore out of her way.

"Asshole," she huffed as she put the fresh change of clothes she was holding in her arms on the little wooden stool positioned next to the claw foot bathtub.

After finding the angry warning gouged into the kitchen cabinets, Jon had insisted they call the police. Lizzie had told him no and another argument ensued. If it wasn't for Grandma Faye ordering Jon to start cleaning up the mess and suggesting Lizzie freshen up while the old woman tended to the chickens, Lizzie had no doubt she and Jon would still be standing in the kitchen nose-to-nose, bickering like children.

Just the thought of the police descending on her cottage and poking around in her life made her tremble with rage. The last time she'd been interviewed by the police had been around the circumstances of her husband Ian's death. The policeman had all but accused Lizzie of killing Ian, even though he'd stepped out into traffic in a drunken stupor and had been hit by a bus.

No police, she'd insisted. She wouldn't subject herself again to that kind of scrutiny. Having the police crawling through her things and no doubt spreading gossip around the village made her blood pressure rise just thinking about it.

The whole reason she'd moved out to Rose Cottage was to be alone, to be anonymous and finally at peace, not having to be anything to anyone. And now someone had violated her sanctuary. The worst part was they had invaded her home while she slept down the hall.

Why hadn't she heard anything? Yes, she'd had a bit too much wine with dinner, but she wasn't falling down drunk, nor did she pass out when she went to bed. But how then could she have slept through the sounds of silverware crashing to the floor and china being smashed?

She refused to believe the spirit of Emma would have done something so malevolent. No it was probably someone or several someones from the village who thought it would be fun to terrorize the newcomer. But that still didn't explain how they had gotten in. None of the windows and doors showed any signs of a forced entry.

She flung the shower curtain around the tub, turned the water on, and waited for the spray of water to heat up. She listened to the water pinging off the bottom of the cast-iron tub.

When steam began to fill the bathroom she shrugged off the quilt and kicked it aside. She made to step into the tub when she glanced down at her foot. She froze with her left leg suspended over the rim of the tub. She cocked her head and stared harder at her naked limb. Finally she lowered her leg back down on the floor. Both her legs were covered in a crosshatch of thin scratches and smudges of earth, as if she'd walked through a bramble patch. Dried flakes of dirt clung to her feet, and something was stuck between her toes. She bent down and plucked at the fuzzy green material and held it up to her face. It was moss.

She spun around to the mirror, gripping the cool surface of the porcelain basin to steady herself as she examined her reflection. The mirror had already begun to fog over, but even before her face was obscured by the warm mist she took in her disheveled hair dusted with flour and the smudges of dirt that caked one shoulder.

Then the dream with all its explicit details flooded her senses. The man in the forest, her standing in the circle of stones. The intense longing for him that went beyond the thrumming sexual need that invaded every cell of her being. Her very existence seemed to hinge on her reuniting with him. She was at once intrigued and appalled at her own imagination.

Had she really slept-walked into the forest in the dead of night, all the while having an extremely erotic dream? For even now, recalling the details, she felt her knees grow weak with desire and the slickness of her arousal between her legs.

Her nightgown. Had she stripped it off in the forest as she walked unconscious into the night? She'd experienced the unnerving effects of her reoccurring dream of Rose Cottage and the resulting sleep deprivation, but she'd never had a history of somnambulism. This new form of mental imbalance had her gripping the sink until her knuckles turned white.

Then she felt the gentle familiar push deep in the recesses of her mind.

Vivienne.

Vivienne was trying to link with her.

She took a deep steadying breath.

Pushing herself away from the sink she stood up straight, banishing all thoughts of the dream and focused on her mentor's psychic call. She felt the opening of the link as a mental click, as if two parts had joined together, and in her head she heard the reassuring voice of her friend.

Lizzie are you all right? Do you need help?

Sorry, Vivienne, I'm fine. Some vandals broke into the cottage. I was upset at finding the mess and I must have let my guard down, sorry.

Vandals? Were you alone when it happened?

No, I wasn't even home. And it was probably just a few bored teenagers causing mischief. Nothing was stolen, they just made a mess of my kitchen. Turns out the house has a bit of a reputation. I've got my neighbor and the local contractor here to help clean up the destruction.

Are you sure it was just bored teenagers? I can send someone up your way to check it out. They could be there in under an hour.

No, really Vivienne. I've have everything under control and it was really nothing. I hope I didn't pull you away from something important.

Nothing too serious, but I do need to get back to it. I think I may be able to swing a little visit soon.

I'd love that. I can't wait to show you the cottage and to spend time with you. I've missed you.

I've missed your company too, but if things stay the way they are I should be seeing you before too long. Take care, Lizzie.

You too.

Lizzie withdrew her energy and felt the link break like a small tug. Before she could step into the shower, a sickening thought occurred to her. If she had left the cottage in the middle of the night, had she left the front door wide open? Had she unwittingly provided the opportunity for whoever had been watching her house to waltz in and destroy her kitchen? And they must have been watching her house for the first opportunity to gain access. She shivered uncontrollably. With measured slowness she stepped over the rim of the tub and into the spray of the showerhead, gripping the edge like an old woman as the bathroom continued to fill with steam.

CHAPTER TWENTY-FIVE

Lizzie drove back up the winding road from the landfill after leaving behind several garbage bags containing the contents of her kitchen. She was finally alone and alone with her thoughts, not a comfortable place to be considering recent events.

The whole time she, Grandma Faye, and a much subdued Jon had filled bag after bag with the ruined foodstuffs and broken dishware, the daunting and somewhat heartbreaking task of cleaning up what had been her beautiful kitchen had distracted Lizzie from sorting out why she was now sleepwalking, and what this new behavior could mean. And she needed to tell Grandma Faye about her suspicions that someone had been watching her cottage, about her magick going haywire again, and her midnight stroll through the woods.

Although Grandma Faye met her at the landfill in her own battered truck filled with several more bags of Lizzie's broken crockery, they didn't have time to talk privately. The dump was bustling with villagers dropping off their weekly garbage. It was the most activity Lizzie had seen in the village since she'd arrived. Everyone was exchanging good afternoons and catching up on the latest goings on with their neighbors. There was a festive atmosphere among the stinking heaps of garbage and the growl of the heavy machinery as they pushed and flattened the growing piles of trash.

Even the landfill attendant hovered around needlessly when he realized Lizzie was the new occupant of Rose Cottage. She kept sidestepping his prodding questions about why she moved to the cottage, and she downplayed his mention of the Witch of Grey House. She was relieved when he finally toddled off to deal with the ever growing lineup of vehicles waiting to pay their fees before heading to the drop off area.

She had only managed to tell Grandma Faye there was more to what had happened that morning. Grandma Faye gave her a knowing nod before tossing the last of the black plastic garbage bags over her shoulder.

"I've the bread orders to deliver and then there are several errands I must run. I'll meet you at the cottage for an early dinner. Say about five?" Before Lizzie could even think about what she would need to pick up at the grocer's, Grandma Faye added, "Not to worry, I'll be bringing dinner with me. You need to only supply the details of this morning."

Lizzie followed Grandma Faye's truck as they left the dump, but they drove off in different directions once they reached the village. Lizzie glanced at the truck's dashboard clock. She had the whole afternoon to kill before Grandma Faye was due at the cottage. She would definitely have to stop at the grocery store and buy paper plates and plastic cups until she felt like spending the day in Revelstoke to replenish the china and plates she'd lost.

Still making a mental list of the supplies she needed, she drove past the grocery store and headed up the hill towards the vet clinic. Restocking her kitchen could wait. She suddenly needed to spend time with her dog.

Once at the clinic, she took the now familiar route past a series of glass-fronted metal cabinets filled with vet supplies, and rounded the corner to the bank of cages in the recovery and observation area. She glanced down at the bottom row to the cage that was Bear's. Her heart skipped a beat when she saw it was empty, then she heard a rhythmic thump coming from behind her. She turned around, a smile stretching across her face.

Bear was lying on a large green plaid dog bed sandwiched between a metal office desk and a tall cabinet used to store rolls of bandages. Gone was the awkward plastic cone around his neck, and the lower half of his body already sported a fuzzy growth of new hair. The open wound on the leg not encased in a cast had almost completely healed, leaving behind a pink raised scar where no hair grew. He was definitely on the mend, but the biggest change in Bear was the sparkle in his dark eyes.

"Look at you," Lizzie said, crouching on the floor next to him. "I see you've been sprung from jail. And who found you such a comfy bed?" Before she could reach over and give him a scratch on the head, Bear surprised her by heaving his body forward and standing up. He swayed momentarily, taking the weight of his body on his front legs, then proceeded to hop forward in an ungainly stride until he had covered the small distance between the dog bed and Lizzie.

"Hey there, big fella," Lizzie said, clutching handfuls of his ruff and leaning into his chest to support him. He towered over her. This was the first time she'd ever seen him standing, and the sheer size of the dog was astonishing. From her kneeling position he could have rested his chin on her head if he had been so inclined. Bear was most decidedly an appropriate name for him.

When he lowered his head, she didn't move out of the way as he gave her a slurpy lick. Lizzie chuckled and wiped the wet kiss off her face with the sleeve of her sweater. "It's good to see you up and about, but I'm not sure you should be walking just yet." She attempted to guide him back down to a lying position, but it was like trying to move a mountain.

"Hi there, Lizzie," Dr. Laurie said as she pushed through the far door leading from the surgery. She was wearing green scrubs, and a mask dangled from around her neck. A patient chart was tucked under her arm. "How do you like the surprise? He's been trying to get up and walk out of his cage over the last few days, so I took another set of x-rays and he is healing faster than I thought possible. It's astounding. It's only been a week and a half since the accident. I wouldn't have believed it, but I was the one that took the x-rays and gave him a thorough exam. His bones can definitely handle weight bearing, and it'll actually help him heal even faster. I was going to call you about his progress, but I knew you'd be coming soon so I thought a surprise would be more fun."

Dr. Laurie patted Bear's head before taking a seat at the desk. She jotted something down in the chart, then swiveled her chair to face Lizzie and the dog.

"Come on, Bear, there's a good boy. Can you show Lizzie what you can do?" she said, leaning forward and patting her thighs in encouragement.

To Lizzie's astonishment, he hobbled over to the vet and rested his head in her lap. Dr. Laurie gave his head a good scratch.

"Good dog. Now go lay down."

Instead of returning to his bed, Bear pushed his big black nose in the vet's palm, then turned his head so that he was looking at the bottom drawer of the desk. Swinging his head back towards Dr. Laurie, he stared intently into her eyes. Dr. Laurie leaned back in her chair and laughed.

Encouraged, Bear repeated the same gestures, nudging her hand, staring at the desk drawer and then back at her.

"Okay, okay," she said, then leaned down and opened the drawer. "I'm afraid I've been spoiling your dog." She smiled sheepishly as she pulled out a bag of dog treats. She held one out to Bear, who gobbled it down in two bites. "That's all you're getting, so don't even think about asking for another. Go lie down."

Bear obeyed this time, and with a loud sigh flung himself down on his bed. Lizzie scratched his chest and he rolled over, exposing his belly, his plaster encased leg sticking up at an absurd angle.

"After what he's been through he deserves to be spoiled," Lizzie said, rubbing the dog's tummy.

Dr. Laurie stood up and pushed the chair under the desk. "If this big fella keeps improving as quickly as he has been, you should be able to take him home as early as next week."

Unlike her previous talk with the vet, the idea of bringing her dog home to the cottage didn't fill her with worry anymore. Looking down at him, she realized she was excited about him sharing her life. She couldn't wait until next week.

After the vet left to deal with her other patients, Lizzie stayed by Bear's side until he'd nodded off to sleep and began to snore, a deep resonating rumble that made Lizzie smile. She tiptoed out of the back room leaving her dog to slumber, dreaming of dog treats no doubt.

Back in the village she again detoured from the grocers to wander down the pet aisle of the hardware store. She filled two carts full of essentials her dog would need for his homecoming; a blue dog collar and leash, metal food and water bowls, dog toys, treats, grooming brushes, dog shampoo, and two large dog beds. She'd cleaned out the shelves in the pet section by the time she was done.

It was the first time all day she felt a lightening in her heart. She knew the healing she'd given Bear when she'd found him on the road was responsible for his rapid recovery, but she had no idea how much her magick had helped. It pleased her that finally her magick had done some good instead of the destruction she was used to.

She could already imagine his big furry presence in her cottage, and she couldn't wait to take him on daily walks through the woods. The whole incident of her kitchen faded in importance next to imagining Bear leaving the clinic and coming home.

215

Buoyed by these thoughts, she quickly shopped the grocery aisles for the staples to replenish her cupboards.

She swung her truck back onto the main road to go home, the cab filled with shopping bags. As she drove through town she rolled down her window, allowing the warm breeze of a perfect spring day to play across her face. The air was laced with the smell of lake water and the greenness of sap rising in the trees. Her stomach growled loudly when she picked up the scent of french fries and grilling hamburgers as she approached the local takeout joint. The Burger Hut had been closed over the winter season when Lizzie had first arrived, but today it was open and doing a bustling trade.

The building was a small white A-frame with red trim, set well back from the roadway to allow for a large gravel filled area dotted with picnic tables, as there was no seating in the building itself.

Lizzie hadn't eaten anything all day, and although she had bags filled with everything she needed to fix a meal when she got home, she was too hungry to wait, the smell of fried food too enticing to pass up.

What little parking was available at the hut was already taken, so she pulled into one of the side streets and trotted across the road. As she approached the building, several teenage boys who had been draped across a nearby picnic table rose as one group. They followed her closely enough to make her uncomfortable.

She took her place in line and aimed her attention to the menu posted on the outside wall, scanning down all the selections. Out of the corner of her eye she watched the group take up a position against the wall nearest her, sucking loudly on their sodas, the sound sending gooseflesh down her back. Their movements reminded her of a wolf pack on the hunt.

She forced herself not to react to their proximity, and instead refocused on the menu in front of her. Deciding on a cheeseburger and vanilla milkshake, she stepped up to the order window and waited for the waitress, who was serving a customer at the opposite order window.

One of the boys kicked at the gravel, sending a stone skittering towards Lizzie and bouncing off her leg. She turned with deliberate slowness and stared at the offender. He gave her a smirk and then slowly licked his lips.

"Can I take your order?"

Lizzie turned away from the young men and heard them sniggering before she focused on the young woman in front of her.

"Can I take your order?" The young waitress repeated the impatience clear in her voice.

"Birdie?" The last person she'd expected to be serving burgers was the highly efficient young realtor. Birdie had even mentioned that the sale of Rose Cottage would go a long way in impressing her boss and securing her position at the realty office. Lizzie blinked hard, trying to take in the image of Birdie now standing before her in her red polyester uniform, her raven hair hidden under a hair net, her face scrubbed clean of her dark eye makeup. She looked even younger than Lizzie remembered, but there was a new weariness around her eyes.

"Oh, Miss Benett." Birdie lowered her head and fiddled with her order pad and pen before meeting Lizzie's gaze.

"What are you doing here?"

"Working."

"But what about the realty office?"

"It just didn't pan out. Sales were slow and my boss decided to close the office over the summer, so here I am."

"But surely you'll go back in the fall. When things pick up."

"We'll see," she shrugged.

"Order up," a gruff male voice boomed from the fry kitchen at the back.

217

Birdie looked over her shoulder, then back at Lizzie. "Look, I'm kinda busy right now, so if you wanted to order I have to get back to work."

"Just a vanilla milkshake, thanks." Lizzie had lost her appetite.

Birdie quickly made Lizzie's milkshake and slid it across the counter without meeting her eyes. "That'll be $3.50," she said. Lizzie handed over her money.

Taking the milkshake she no longer wanted, she strode across the picnic area and toward her truck. She veered slightly to avoid the pack of boys that had resumed their position at their picnic table, but she was close enough to hear a hiss as she passed.

"Witch."

The word floated across the few feet between her and the teenagers. It was just one word, but the menace behind it was clear.

Her heels dug into the gravel as she marched towards her truck. The back of her neck burned but she kept her head high. She'd almost gotten her temper under control when she spied three words keyed into the blue paint of the driver's door. The words *Go Home Witch*, scratched in a childish hand, had an uncanny resemblance to the warning on her kitchen cupboard.

Her hand trembled as she flung open the driver's door, and she was about to climb in when the smell of root beer flooded her nose. Ice cubes lay scattered across the seat; an empty drink cup lay on its side in the foot well. After putting her own drink on the roof of the truck, she scooped up the melting ice and threw it onto the ground along with the empty cup. She didn't once look over her shoulder, but she knew she was being watched.

Upending a grocery bag full of paper plates on the passenger's seat, she spread the bag over the sodden fabric of the driver's side, and plucking her milkshake from the roof of the truck she climbed in. Slamming the door, she then gunned the engine and tore off out of the parking lot.

As she barreled down the highway her anger rose, but she kept a tight check on her powers. She wasn't going to accidently endanger herself because of her emotional state. But she wasn't going to sit back and allow the backwater hillbillies to frighten her out of her land and her home. If it was a fight they wanted it was a fight they were going to get. And they had no idea what they were up against.

Approaching her property, she could see the gates at her driveway standing open. She knew she'd closed them behind her when she'd left for the dump. It was too early for Grandma Faye's arrival, and if Jon had come by again to tell her what she should do she was going to be ready to give him an earful. She'd spent fifteen years married to a man who thought it was his birthright to tell her what to do and how to be. She'd fought hard and battled through her fears to finally win the right to govern her own life, and by the Goddess she wasn't going to let Jon and his arrogant attitude push her around.

Stamping down on the accelerator, she tore up her driveway, already formulating her argument with Jon. As she cleared the trees lining the drive, she slammed on her brakes, narrowly missing the grill of the police cruiser parked at her door.

CHAPTER TWENTY-SIX

After gathering a handful of shopping bags Lizzie jumped out of the truck, slamming the door with her hip. She marched up to the police officer who was leaning against the side of his cruiser lazily smoking a cigarette. He took a drag before addressing her.

"You Lizzie Benett, owner of Grey House?" he asked, smoke billowing out of his mouth as he spoke.

"Yes, and you are?" she said, making her way around his vehicle and towards the porch.

He followed behind her, his police-issue boots thundering on the wooden steps. He leaned against the door jam, eyeing her as she struggled to get the key in the lock.

"You know you should really get those locks changed," he said, ignoring her question. "Easy as pie to pick these old ones. You just need a simple set of tools, even a screwdriver would work."

Lizzie finally got the door open and whipped around to face him, the handles of the heavy shopping bags digging into her fingers. "So I've been told." He wasn't much taller than Lizzie, and she barely had to raise her head to look him in the eye. "So did Jon call you?"

"He may have done. Said you'd been burgled and asked if I could take a look around. I've already checked the doors and windows and they don't appear to be jimmied. Like I said, those locks are pretty easy to pick."

"Well, as you can see I'm fine, the cottage is fine. Nothing was stolen. You've wasted a trip out here, so if you don't mind, I have a lot of shopping that needs to be unpacked and I have a guest coming for dinner." Lizzie stepped over the threshold, but stopped just inside when she realized the officer had followed her in.

"Please don't smoke in here," she said, straining to keep her tone polite.

He took another drag on his cigarette before flicking it on the porch, crushing it under the heel of his boot before stepping back inside.

Lizzie frowned at the dark smear of ash and shredded tobacco littering her newly painted porch, then turned her back on the police officer. She could feel the crimson tide of her anger rising up her neck and inflaming her cheeks. Striding over to the kitchen, she heaved the heavy grocery bags onto the counter. She still had several more bags to bring in, but she wasn't about to leave the officer alone in her home. Instead, she began unpacking her groceries, studiously ignoring his presence.

The constable, who still hadn't told her his name, strolled in a lazy circle around the perimeter of the living room, checking the window latches as he went.

"You should think about getting new locks on the windows too," he said. He brushed past her and walked down the hall. Inching open the bathroom door with the toe of his boot, he leaned forward and looked in.

Lizzie turned from unpacking her groceries, a can of tomatoes clutched tightly in her hand. She watched him close her bathroom door, and when he started for her bedroom, she took a step towards the hallway.

"There is no need for you to go down there," she said. "The only room vandalized was the kitchen." He ignored her again and stood in the doorway of her bedroom, taking his time as he surveyed the small room.

She was about to head after him and insist he leave when he turned slowly and sauntered back down the hallway, his thick-soled boots making a hollow sound as he walked over the trapdoor to the root cellar.

"This cottage has way too many old windows, and that french door would be easy to break down. You've set yourself up to be in a very vulnerable position. Especially since it would take a while for me to respond to an emergency call with you living so far out of town."

"I can take care of myself." She placed the tin of tomatoes in the cupboard and continued unpacking her groceries.

"I wouldn't be so sure of that. If you had an accident you'd be all alone; there would be no one to hear your calls for help. It's an easy thing to slip getting out of the bath and hit your head. Even knock yourself unconscious. Happens more often than you'd think."

"Or take a tumble down the root cellar," she said.

"My point exactly. You obviously heard what happened to the last woman who lived out here by herself." He crossed over to Lizzie and leaned against the kitchen counter. He stood close enough for her to smell the stale cigarette smoke and cheap aftershave rolling off him in waves. "It would be a shame if the same thing happened to such a sweet thing like yourself."

He reached out his hand as if to touch her face. She recoiled out of his reach. His last words hung in the air, and her earlier annoyance with him was replaced with the tingling of fear.

She swiped at the two bottles of wine she'd just unpacked and held them by their necks. She wasn't sure if she could actually use them as weapons against a man with a gun, but their weight was reassuring. She backed up towards the fridge, giving herself a few feet between herself and the constable. "Was that a threat?" she asked, keeping her voice steady even though she could feel her racing pulse throbbing in each fingertip gripping the bottles.

She didn't want to use her magick but she sensed her options were running out. Grandma Faye wasn't due to arrive for at least another hour, and he was right when he'd said that no one would hear her cries for help. But he was wrong when he assumed she was helpless.

A slow smile spread across his face and he pushed himself away from the counter. Adjusting his belt, he sauntered over to her. "Now why would you say such a thing? I'm merely doing my duty to make sure you're safe." He was still smiling as he closed the distance between them.

As she inched backwards, preparing to draw her powers up, the temperature in the room dropped suddenly. A rash of gooseflesh broke out on her bare arms. The constable felt it too and stopped in his tracks. The color drained out of his face, his ruddy complexion turning alarmingly pale. He stared at Lizzie for a moment as if she was the source of the cold, the cocky expression he'd worn moments ago changing into one of confusion, then fear. His eyes widened and he whirled around to face the hallway, his hand fumbling to his belt, his fingers struggling to release the leather strap holding his revolver. Before he could draw his weapon his arms went limp at his sides.

Whatever was causing his terror, Lizzie couldn't sense it or see it. Other than the dramatic drop in temperature, she felt nothing.

She took a half step towards the man, the wine bottles still firmly clutched in her hands. "Constable," she called out, her breath forming a white vapor in front of her as the temperature continued to plunge. He stood staring off down the empty hallway. She tried to get his attention again, but he was unresponsive. Cautiously she maneuvered around the kitchen table until she stood at his shoulder.

She followed his gaze down the hall but there was nothing there. Slowly placing one of the wine bottles on the table so as not

223

to startle him, she reached out with her hand and gently touched his shoulder.

"Constable, are you okay?" she asked in a low even tone. He didn't acknowledge her, just continued to stare down the hall. She could see trails of perspiration on his face, and where Lizzie had touched him his shirt was damp. She tried gently shaking him, but that too had no effect.

Lizzie struggled with what to do next. Moments before she had felt threatened by the constable, and was seconds away from using her magick to stop what she was sure was going to be some kind of physical attack. Now she found herself trying to help him.

She was about to give him another shake when he broke out of his trance. His movements were so sudden Lizzie let out a yelp and stepped out of his way. Raising her hand, she began to draw her powers, unsure of what his next move would be.

But he simply looked at her, a bewildered expression playing across his face. Brushing past her, he walked with deliberate slowness to the front door, and without a backward glance headed off down the front porch. Lizzie followed at a distance and watched from her open doorway as he climbed into his police cruiser, started up the engine, and drove away.

She stood in the doorway until the sound of his car faded in the distance. Stepping back inside, she shut the door, dug out the skeleton key from her purse, and secured the door. She realized she was still holding one of the wine bottles, and crossed over to the fridge to put it away.

The air in the cottage had started to return to normal. She could no longer see her breath forming a white vapor, but it was still cool within the stone walls. Lizzie shivered.

She knelt down in front of the fireplace hearth and stacked a handful of kindling in the firebox, as she'd seen Jon do, and lit a match. Her hand shook and the flame at the end of the match chattered until it caught the wood.

She watched the flames slowly spread while she replayed what just happened. She thought by now she would take any strange occurrence in stride, especially after what she'd been through, but that wasn't the case. Adding a few small sticks of wood to the growing flames, she held her hands towards the warmth of the fire. Once the fire was established, she stood up on slightly shaky legs and went to the bedroom to get a sweater.

Heading back into the kitchen, she stopped in the hallway and sent out her energy. She narrowed her focus to pick up on anything, even the slightest difference in the energy of the house, but there was nothing there.

Pulling back her energy, she rested her hand on the wall.

"Emma, if that was you earlier, thank you," she whispered. She stood a moment waiting for a reply, but none came.

Instead, there was a knock on the door. The sound broke the silence of the cottage and her heart knocked against her chest. Had the constable come back?

She stood in the hall, unsure of what to do, when another knock sounded. She thought about waiting out whoever was there, but she gave her head a shake. She could take care of herself, she'd proven that time and time again. When was she going to stop having her first reaction to a threat or the unknown be fear? Some habits seemed hard to break. Besides, she reasoned, the constable would hardly give a polite knock and wait patiently for her to answer the door. More than likely he'd have broken it down or ordered her to open it.

Leaving the safety of the hallway, she was going to open the door when she glanced at the clock in the kitchen. It was well past the time she was expecting Grandma Faye. Relief rushed through her. She needed Grandma Faye's comforting presence.

She flung open the door, a smile of welcome already spreading across her face. Instead of Grandma Faye, she found herself staring into a pair of green eyes. Ones she'd gazed into in

225

her dream.

CHAPTER TWENTY-SEVEN

Lizzie inhaled sharply. The man from her dream, the one she'd met in the forest, was standing on her front porch. She hadn't made him up. The floor tilted dangerously beneath her feet, and she clutched at the doorframe to steady herself.

As she wavered between inviting him in and slamming the door in his face, he spoke. He was definitely real.

"Hello again." His voice was deep and melodic. Lizzie felt the two words resonating in her breastbone like the low notes on a cello. The sound ignited an intense longing, making her heart ache.

She felt his heartbeat even though they stood several feet apart. The pulse and beat of blood rushing through flesh and sinew became one. One breath, one beat, one thought. She wondered if she wore the same look of awe and confusion as he did. He stepped forward tentatively, a question in his almond-shaped eyes.

Lizzie answered his unspoken question with a nod, opening the door wider and stepping back to let him in. He moved forward, stopping a few feet from her. He smelled like the forest: a combination of cedar and pine and the darker scent of moss and water.

His clothes were freshly laundered by the look of the knife-sharp pleat running down his khaki's and the smooth starched-like appearance of his button down shirt. His pants fit him snuggly and were a bit too short in the legs, barely brushing the tops of his hiking boots.

"I believe this is yours," he said, holding out a small bundle. His voice made her think of the silvery rush of water over dark stones, and sent a shiver up the back of her neck.

She slowly pulled her gaze down to his outstretched hand. He had the hands of an artist, his fingers long and elegant but strong. She knew the feel of them on her skin, their urgency as he explored her body, the skill they possessed in arousing every cell of her body. Her cheeks burned from the memory even as her body yearned to feel his touch again. The cottage was suddenly too warm.

She plucked her nightgown from his hands, making sure she didn't touch him. Clearing her throat, she looked down at the neatly folded cotton shift. "How did you know where to find me?" She was also about to ask how he knew the nightgown was hers, but if memory served her, it was pretty obvious.

"It was surprisingly simple," he said. "I made my way back to the stone circle and found your nightdress, so I knew I hadn't dreamed you. Then I set out in the direction you first appeared from in the clearing. This cottage was the first house I came across, so I figured the odds of this being your place were pretty good. There aren't many people living out here."

"About last night. I'm not sure what happened, but…." She rubbed the thin fabric of her nightdress between her thumb and forefinger. "What I mean is, I know *what* happened, but how did we both end up at that circle?"

"I don't know. I'd woken up suddenly feeling an odd sensation, like a pulling. There was this urgency that I needed to be somewhere, and I couldn't resist it. I just had to go."

"Me too. It was like the forest was calling out to me, like it was—"

"Singing," they said in unison.

"What exactly was that?" Lizzie asked.

228

"I don't know. But they say that these old forests hold the ancient magick in them still. Perhaps because of Beltane we got caught up in it."

"Beltane?" Feeling the need to put some space between her and the beautiful stranger, she stepped over to the kitchen table, placing her nightgown on its scrubbed surface.

"Yes, last night was Beltane. The celebration of fertility."

"About that. What we did, I just…."

"Yes?" he said, his face open, his eyes questioning. He didn't try to move towards her.

"You need to know that I don't usually wander around at midnight in the forest, and, you know…." She felt foolish trying to explain this to a man who last night she had rolled around with in the pine needles in wild sexual abandon.

"Make love to a stranger by the light of the moon."

"Yes," she giggled nervously. "And I don't even know your name."

He glanced over her shoulder, his eyes roaming over the kitchen counter where she'd started unpacking her groceries. "I'm called Wren," he said, looking at her again. "Wren Maxwell." He stuck his hand out.

"Lizzie Benett," she replied, suddenly feeling giddy. She shook his hand. When he let go she had the sudden desire to grab his hand again, to pull him near her. She didn't think it possible, but her cheeks burned even hotter. She regretted lighting the fire.

"I seem to have caught you in the middle of unpacking," he said, gesturing to the bags littering the countertop. "I should probably go, I just wanted to return your nightgown."

"Yes, thank you for that." She didn't want him to go yet. She searched for something to say, to keep him in her cottage just a few more minutes. "So do you live nearby, are you one of my neighbors?" She wandered over to the kitchen counter and started pulling out cans and jars, lining them up in a row.

229

"No, I'm not from around here. In fact, I just arrived yesterday." He joined her at the counter, watching her as she continued to pull out cans. "My camp is stationed a couple of miles up into the mountain behind your place. I'm doing a study on the saw-whet owl."

He reached over and picked up a super-sized jar of peanut butter she'd just pulled out of a bag. He inspected the label, then held up the jar to her. "That's an awful lot of peanut butter for one person. Is it really that good?"

"It's not just for me." She took the jar from his hand and put it away in a cupboard. "There's a raven that hangs around here, and he's partial to peanut butter on toast." She knew that sounded absurd, even a little crazy, but she didn't want to go into a drawn out explanation as to why she had befriended a raven, or more accurately why Quinn had befriended her. His response wasn't what she anticipated.

"Of course," he said without a hint of sarcasm, and handed her another can to put away.

"So how long have you been with the Department of Fish and Wildlife?" He gave her a startled look and she laughed. "You're wearing your uniform. I noticed the insignia on the breast pocket of your shirt. And you did just say you were studying the owls here."

"For a second there I thought you were fae and I had inadvertently stumbled across an enchanted cottage."

"No such luck. Would you cast me in the role of good witch or bad?" she asked, putting the last of the groceries away.

"Definitely good." The smile he gave her made her tingle right down to her toes.

She glanced at the clock on the stove. Grandma Faye would be there any minute, and she still had more groceries in the truck to bring in.

Wren followed her gaze. "Wow, is that the time? I should be

off."

"No, you don't have to go. Why don't you stay for dinner? A friend is coming over, and I know she wouldn't mind if you joined us."

"As enticing as the invitation is, I've overstayed my time here. There's a few nesting sites I need to check before the owls wake for the evening. Perhaps another time."

She was disappointed by his refusal, but at the same time relieved she wouldn't have to introduce him to Grandma Faye. She wanted to keep him all to herself for just a little while longer.

The sun was already tipping behind the mountains and the shadows had begun to lengthen as they walked out onto the porch. Lizzie wondered if she'd ever get used to how fast the sun set. There were no lingering sunsets with the mountains crowded around her.

As they said their goodbyes she half expected him to kiss her, seeing as just last night they had been so intimate with each other. What she didn't expect was for him to take her hand gently in his, and with a courtly bow brush his lips across her knuckles. He looked up into her eyes as he stood up.

"Until next time," he said.

She watched him amble across the driveway in the direction of the barn as she rubbed her knuckles against her mouth where his lips had touched. She wanted to call out to him but had no idea what she would say. The familiar rattle of Grandma Faye's truck chugging up her driveway pulled her attention from Wren. She saw him turn and look down the drive before she too turned to look. She sighed. So they were going to meet after all.

She stepped off the porch just as Grandma Faye pulled in behind Lizzie's truck. Lizzie waved at her friend and opened the passenger-side door. The enticing aroma of roasted chicken and freshly baked bread escaped from the interior.

"Sorry I'm late," Grandma Faye said. "Could you take the

salad, and I'll grab the hamper?" she said, pointing to a large yellow Tupperware bowl sitting on top of a wicker basket on the passenger's seat.

"Sure, but first I'd like to…." Lizzie had turned to introduce Wren, but no one was there. There was no way that he could have disappeared so quickly. Just moments before he'd been standing in the open watching as Grandma Faye's truck pulled into view. Lizzie scanned the area but she saw no movement.

"What?" Grandma Faye had jumped down from the truck and had walked around to Lizzie. "You'd like to what?"

"Nothing," she said. "Except thank you for making what smells like the best dinner I'll ever have."

She let Grandma Faye lead the way back inside the cottage, and before she closed the door, Lizzie looked one last time in the direction where Wren had been standing.

A part of her was relieved that he would remain her secret a little longer, but another part of her wondered if she'd just imagined the whole encounter.

CHAPTER TWENTY-EIGHT

Lizzie shifted her foot on the stone hearth and leaned farther back in the rocking chair, resting her arms on the curved wooden armrests. The enormous amount of food she'd eaten and several glasses of wine she'd consumed had left her contentedly drowsy, despite the disturbing start to her day and the still unanswered questions the events had brought up.

Over roast chicken and delicately grilled vegetables, she told Grandma Faye about sending out her magick at Jon when she thought he was an intruder and her apparent misfire. She shared her theory of the break-in, but she couldn't bring herself to tell Grandma Faye about Wren.

They both agreed the vandalism to her kitchen and truck was most likely the work of the bored and high-spirited teenaged boys she'd encountered at the Burger Hut. As far as Lizzie's second occurrence of her magick going haywire, the two women had exhausted every angle and hypothesis, from the black magick slowly draining Lizzie of her power the longer she stayed in the cottage, to her simply miscalculating her aim.

After dinner, Grandma Faye settled before the fireplace in the scarred leather chair the two women had purchased on their day of antiquing. Lizzie elected to bring over the rocking chair from the kitchen to sit in, as her new couch was still sending out puffs of flour every time she sat on it. She'd have to take the cushions outside and beat them to get them clean again. For now, the hard-backed rocking chair would do.

The night pressed against the windowpanes and the warm glow of the fireplace made Lizzie reluctant to turn on the electric lights and break the spell. Instead, she lit several beeswax candles and placed them on the kitchen table and the fireplace mantle. The air was soon infused with the fragrance of beeswax mingled with wood smoke.

For the moment, each woman sat staring into the fire, watching the flames flicker and the wood shift as the coals glowed, creating fantastical shapes and images. Sometimes Lizzie would see the outline of an animal in the glowing embers, a horse or a dog, and then a log shifted sending a shower of sparks up the flu. Lizzie followed the bright red and orange lights until they winked out, and when she looked back into the flames she saw a face: one with luminescent green eyes. She shook her head and the image dissolved, leaving mere wood and embers and dancing firelight.

"Here, let's finish this off. Hand over your glass," Grandma Faye said, picking up the almost empty wine bottle that sat on the floor between them.

Lizzie held out her glass as Grandma Faye divided the last of the wine between them. Lizzie took a sip of wine, rolling it around in her mouth before swallowing. "I had an uninvited guest when I got home this afternoon."

"Spirit form or human?" the old woman said over her wine glass.

"Oh, definitely human, all too human. It was the local RCMP officer. A rude, aggressive brute of a man."

"Mmm, that would be Constable Whitby by your description. He grew up here. Bit of a bully from what I've seen."

"That's putting it mildly."

"What was he doing here?"

"I can thank Jon for that. I specifically asked him not to involve the police, and he completely ignored my wishes."

"Jon seems like a man that is not easily dissuaded when he

234

sets his mind to something. Maybe he was just concerned about your safety."

"That may well be, but Whitby is the last person I'd call if I needed help. In fact, his visit was more threatening than the damage the teenagers did to either my kitchen or my truck."

"What happened?" Grandma Fay said, placing her wine glass on the stone hearth, the glass making a soft clink against the stone. Angling her body, she turned to face Lizzie.

"Nothing really, just some veiled threats that as a woman living out here alone I'm not safe. It felt like it could have come to something more, except…."

Lizzie looked into the fire, watching the flames dance as she recalled the specifics of Whitby's strange reaction. "He tried to touch me. His energy was giving me the creeps, and I was trying to get some distance between us just in case I needed to use my magick, when the temperature dropped dramatically. Then he saw or heard something down the hallway, and then just turned and left. He looked like he'd seen a ghost."

She looked over at Grandma Faye. Her blue eyes looked almost navy in the firelight, dark and intense.

"Maybe he did. You said the cottage felt cold before his abrupt departure?"

"Yes, and it wasn't like a draft. It was so cold in here I could see my breath. It didn't last long. In fact, as soon as he left the temperature began to return to normal."

"It's not uncommon for a distinct drop in temperature to precede a spectral appearance. Maybe it was Emma, coming to protect you."

"I thought about that, but if the black magick in the cellar was supposed to trap her down there, how did she manage, or her spirit manage, to come to my aid up in the main part of the house?"

Grandma Faye retrieved her wine glass and took a delicate

sip before returning the glass to the hearth. "I don't know. If only I knew more about what those symbols mean and what the intention of the spell was, I'd have a better grasp on what's going on. Although there has been some heated debate about the symbols on the hedge witch forum, nothing helpful has come of it."

"Between the villagers trying to scare me off and finding out I'm sharing my house with the trapped spirit of a murdered woman, I'm starting to think coming out here was a bad idea."

She picked up the poker and jabbed at the fire, sending fresh sparks up into the flu. She threw on a new log before settling back in her chair.

"You're not thinking about leaving, are you?"

"Not a chance. I was meant to find this cottage. It was waiting for me; it needs me as much as I need it, and I'm not going to be scared off by a bunch of dim-witted teenagers or a bully of a constable. Besides, if I don't help Emma, who will?" As she spoke she leaned forward in her chair, her hands fisted on her thighs. "I'm not the shrinking violet the people of Barton think I am, and it's about time I started pushing back."

"What do you plan on doing?"

Maybe it was time to put aside her stubbornness and reach out to Vivienne for help. "I'm not sure, but the first thing I need to do is protect myself from any more intruders."

"You mean changing the locks?"

"And give the villagers the satisfaction of showing I'm scared? Not a chance. I was thinking something more up my alley and yours."

"Magick then." Grandma Faye smiled and raised her glass.

"Magick," Lizzie replied, then picked up her wineglass and clinked her glass with her friend's. The crystal chimed and resonated in the air like a bell summoning the elements.

CHAPTER TWENTY-NINE

Lizzie faced the living room window, arms upraised, palms facing the glass. Planting her feet squarely on the floor, she drew her powers up into her hands until her fingertips vibrated with energy. Then using her left hand, she sent her magick out, filling the window with a web of energy the radial arms of which touched the window frame on all sides. With her senses open to the invisible energy surrounding her, the ward she was placing on the window glowed a deep luminescent violet.

Grandma Faye let out a low whistle from her position behind Lizzie. "You have got to teach me that one. I didn't know it was possible to place a ward without casting a circle first, or without using an athame. There's more to you than you let on, Lizzie my girl."

"If you feed me another meal like the one we just had, I'd happily tell you all my secrets," she said with a smile as she moved to the next window and began setting up the next ward.

Within fifteen minutes Lizzie had placed wards on all the windows, the back door leading off the mudroom, and the french doors in her bedroom. During the process Grandma Faye followed behind silently.

Now both women were back where they'd started, standing just inside the threshold of the front door. Lizzie put a finger to her lips as she pondered what to do.

Grandma Faye spoke for the first time since Lizzie had started the process. "Is there a problem?" she asked. Even though she spoke in a normal voice, the sound startled Lizzie. "Sorry, I didn't mean to break your concentration." Grandma Faye moved to stand next to her.

"It's okay, you didn't. I was going to put up a standard ward as I did with all the other doors and windows, but I realized I could be creating a problem." Grandma Faye raised her eyebrows questioningly, and Lizzie went on to explain. "At the last place I stayed there had been wards placed on the front door for my protection. But when I needed to gain entry to help a friend who was in serious trouble, the ward worked too well and stopped me from going in right away. I lost precious minutes removing the ward, and as a result my friend paid the price. I don't want that to happen again, or to inadvertently block myself from my own home."

Lizzie tried not to dwell on the panic she'd felt that night as she stood outside the condo, while inside Madison was being attacked by her abusive boyfriend. If it hadn't been for Miss Sweetie, a large gentle man who worked as a cook at the women's shelter Lizzie volunteered at, Madison's injuries would have been much worse. But Miss Sweetie had paid for his bravery by receiving severe injuries of his own.

Lizzie squeezed her eyes shut, trying to banish the memory and the feelings of remorse and sadness that always seemed to follow. Madison had not been grateful for what Lizzie had done, and hadn't spoken to her since that terrible night.

"What about using the simplest form of protection? Sometimes simple is best."

It was Lizzie's turn to throw her friend a questioning look.

"I have to give credit to whoever taught you all this fancy spell work," the old woman said, gesturing to the windows. "But they seem to have missed some of the basics of being a well-equipped witch." Lizzie looked at her blankly. "Lizzie dear, salt. Salt is all we need. A simple line across the threshold should do the trick. Mind you, it's not as convenient as a permanent ward, as you will always have to keep replenishing it, but if you need to get inside, as the one who placed the ward you simply have to brush it away with your foot to break the line of protection."

Lizzie smacked her forehead with the heel of her hand. "Of course, I can't believe I'd forgotten that." Lizzie hunted through her cupboards and produced a box of sea salt that had been part of her groceries she'd just picked up that day. Within minutes she'd laid a line of salt along the outside of the front door, all the while holding the intention that the salt should provide protection against anyone who wished her harm, barring them from entering. She felt her spell infuse the salt as she poured the remaining line of protection.

CHAPTER THIRTY

Lizzie picked her feet over the uneven ground, mindful not to dislodge her traveling companion's perch on her shoulder. She was surprised by the strength of his grip, but his claws never penetrated the knit of her sweater or caused her a moment's discomfort.

Quinn leaned his sleek feathered body against her cheek as she made her way past the barn. His feathers were like silk against her skin, and she was astonished by the heat radiating off his compact, muscled body.

For the first time since she'd moved in she felt energized and fully rested, having slept through the night. She would have slept even later if it had not been for Quinn tapping on her bedroom window.

No one had broken into her cottage in the middle of the night, her kitchen was just as she'd left it the night before, and she hadn't taken off to wander the forest without her clothes on. It was definitely a good day.

She moved through the forest with confidence, the way to the stone circle still clear in her mind. When the forest abruptly ended to give way to the small clearing, Lizzie hesitated before stepping out of the protection of the trees.

But Quinn didn't. She felt the raven gather himself up before launching into the air. She turned her head away from him as the sharp edges of his wing feathers brushed against her cheek.

He landed on one of the nearby stones of the circle. Cocking his head, he eyed the first rock then proceeded to hop to the next one, slowly making his way around the circle, all the while emitting a series of clocks and chortles as he went. To Lizzie it sounded as if he were talking to himself as he examined each stone he landed on before hopping to the next one. She wished she could speak raven.

Quinn had made his way halfway around the circle before Lizzie gathered herself and stepped over the moss covered stones and into the circle itself. It looked a little different in the daylight with the sunshine playing across the clearing, shifting the light and shadows. The last time she'd been here the full moon had washed the circle in its silvery light, and the patches of stone not covered by moss had glowed like bleached bones in the dark.

The spongy earth gave way slightly as she wandered towards the center, following a line of stones that made up one of the spokes dividing the circle into four sections. She felt the ancient power of the circle with each step she took. It carried the same sacred pulse she had sensed in the hallowed spaces of churches.

She stopped abruptly and looked down at her feet. There on the ground in the spot where she and Wren had made love was a definite depression in the soil; a slight hollow in the soft earth created by the weight of their bodies. If she had even the slightest doubt of Wren's existence she was now looking at proof that they really had met in the circle under the full moon.

She rubbed her knuckles over her lips. "Wren," she whispered into the morning air. She held her breath. The trees danced slowly in the breeze shifting the light across the circle. Quinn had completed his circuit and now stood on a stone facing Lizzie. He cocked his head and looked at her with one dark eye.

She let out her breath. She chided herself for her apparent disappointment that Wren hadn't magickally stepped out of the curtain of trees as he had done before. She turned and strode out of the circle, calling over her shoulder, "Let's go, Quinn."

In two powerful wing beats he landed back on her shoulder. She waited for him to find a comfortable position, and once he'd settled down, his black claws finding purchase in the fabric of her sweater, she set off towards the front of the property and her garden.

No sooner had she opened the rickety gate to her garden than she heard the unmistakable growl of Audley's van roaring up the gravel road beyond the stone wall of her property, followed by the sound of a finely tuned engine. She heard both vehicles stop just outside her property, and then the sound of Audley opening and closing his van door as he went to open the gate.

Perhaps she should have put a ward on the front gate too, one that would keep out a certain chauvinistic bullheaded contractor who disregarded her wishes.

She swore under her breath and swatted at the garden gate. It shuddered against the wooden gatepost and swung back open.

Her sudden movements dislodged Quinn from her shoulder, and his claw dug painfully into her shoulder before he took off. Cawing loudly at her, he settled in a high branch of a hemlock near the garden. She wasn't expecting Audley, and the last person she wanted to see right now was Jon. So much for spending a peaceful morning in her garden.

She marched over to the driveway, hoping to stop Audley before he drove up to the cottage. As she approached the hard-packed sand of the drive she waved frantically in an effort to stop him, but he misinterpreted the gesture and waved back at her as he continued to drive up to her house, with Jon's truck following close behind.

Muttering to herself, she strode up to the cottage just as Audley was opening the side door of the van.

"Good morning, Ms. Benett," he called out cheerfully. "We've brung you a surprise," he said before ducking inside the van. He scrambled out of the van backwards, holding her new cupboard door aloft as if it were some sacred offering.

Her irritation dissolved and she returned Audley's childlike glee with a beaming smile. "How wonderful. But Jon said it would probably take at least a week to get a replacement."

"Normally it would have," Jon's voice came from behind her. She turned to face him, but he was looking past her at the house. His eyes narrowed and his lips disappeared in a thin white line. When he pulled his gaze away from the cottage his face was rearranged into a pleasant smile. "You were in luck, as it turned out. When I called the factory in Vernon they had just gotten a cancellation on a kitchen reno with the same style cabinets, so they had what we needed in stock."

"But it's Sunday. How did you manage to get it here? Surely they didn't courier it out all this way on a Sunday."

"No ma'am, Jon went and got it himself. Drove out yesterday afternoon and back the same day. He said he wanted to make things right for you after what the witch did to ruin your kitchen."

"But that's over a six-hour drive."

"Seven and a bit when you include the ferry stops," Audley corrected her.

She didn't want to feel gratitude towards Jon, she wanted to be mad at him. "You didn't have to do that. It could have waited until the manufacturer could send it out."

"It could have, but I wanted to get your kitchen put to rights so you wouldn't have a visual reminder of what happened," Jon said, leaning on his cane as he took a step towards her.

"Thank you for that," she said, then looked past Jon's shoulder at Audley. "The door's open if you wanted to take that inside."

"Sure thing," Audley replied. He thumped up the porch steps, his tool belt jangling as he walked.

As soon as Audley was inside the cottage, Lizzie turned her attention back to Jon. "There's something I need to discuss with you."

"What's up? You seem upset."

"How very astute of you."

"I don't understand. I thought you'd be pleased to have your kitchen restored as soon as possible." As Jon spoke he closed the gap between them. Lizzie took a step backwards, but stopped when her back came in contact with Audley's van.

"I am pleased about the cupboard; this has nothing to do with that. I'm angry that you called the police about the vandalism, especially when I specifically asked you not to." She glared at him when instead of looking apologetic, a playful smile turned up the corners of his mouth.

"Let me get this straight; you're mad at me because I was worried about your safety and I asked the authorities to come check your cottage to make sure you weren't vulnerable to danger." The smile had vanished from his face and his grey eyes looked hurt.

A pang of remorse pierced her heart as she shifted her irritation to herself for not being able to stay level headed. Despite her efforts, it seemed every time he came too close to her, her equilibrium shifted. Even now she felt a strange helplessness rise, a desire to be protected like some frail Victorian lady overcome by strong emotions.

She took a deep breath and kept her gaze steady on Jon. "I don't need protecting. I can take care of myself." He closed the gap between them, resting his cane against the side of the van. Slowly, deliberately, he placed both hands on her shoulders.

Her heart fluttered and a dreamy warmth spread down her arms. In the distance she could hear Quinn cawing insistently. His rasping calls pulled her back from sinking deeper into a delicious drowsiness.

"More to the point…," she said, struggling to get her thoughts straight, "you had no right to go behind my back and disregard my wishes. I said I didn't want the police brought in, and you completely ignored what I said. I'm not a child, Jon, and I don't appreciate being treated like one." As if in agreement with her statement, Quinn's caws got louder.

"Can you blame me for worrying about you?" He lowered his head to hers and whispered in her ear. "I care about you, Lizzie. Surely you've noticed that by now. I just wanted to keep you safe."

His breath tickled her neck and her skin broke out in gooseflesh. Her head swam with confusion.

"Jon, if I've given you the impression—"

His lips pressed down on hers, cutting off her words. She tried to turn her head to the side, to break their kiss, but he'd placed both hands on either side of her head, making escape impossible. She couldn't breathe and his lips pressed aggressively against hers, and when she felt his tongue pressing into her mouth she gagged.

She tried to push him away but her strength seemed to have drained away. Her efforts to escape only seemed to inflame him more and he pressed himself against her, grinding her shoulder blades into the side panel of the van.

Quinn's cries became louder, then she felt the beating of his wings above her head. She squeezed her eyes shut as sharp wing feathers brushed against her cheek. Suddenly, Jon broke away. She pushed hard against Jon's chest and he stumbled backwards, nearly losing his footing just as Quinn swooped again, black claws extended. The raven left behind a deep line across Jon's high forehead. The line darkened as blood filled the deep furrow.

Now free, Lizzie sidestepped so she was clear of both Jon and the van. No longer trapped, she felt her anger rise in a clear bright wave.

Jon stared at the ground for a moment as a drop of his blood pattered onto the sand. He straightened up and swiped at his forehead, then stared at his fingertips, now stained red. For a moment his expression looked quizzical, as if he didn't understand what had happened to cause his injury. Then his eyes narrowed as he looked up at the raven. He curled both hands into fists, the knuckles turning white.

Quinn cawed, the anger in his voice unmistakable. He had landed on the top of the van and was hunched down, ready to strike at Jon again. Jon grabbed his cane but Lizzie snatched it first.

"Don't you dare," she growled, holding the cane against her breast. To Quinn she also issued a warning. "That's enough." But her voice didn't hold the anger that she'd aimed at Jon. "I'm okay," she whispered to the bird.

The raven let out one more angry caw, bobbed his head, then flew off into a nearby tree. She could feel Quinn watching her from his vantage point in the trees. She had no doubt that if Jon tried to even step towards her, Quinn would launch himself at him again.

"I think it would be best if you leave, now," she said, holding out Jon's cane. He pulled it roughly out of her hands. The cut on his forehead was still bleeding and he wiped it with the back of his hand, leaving a smear of blood across his brow.

Jon took his time positioning the cane and shifting his weight to his good leg before pulling back his shoulders and walking to his truck. As he passed by Lizzie he whispered something to her. She wasn't sure what he'd spat at her as he walked past, but it sounded like "you ungrateful bitch."

It was her turn to clench her fists, but instead of fighting the urge to pummel her contractor, she was forcing herself not to send a white hot ball of magick into Jon's back. She held back as she watched him climb into the cab of his truck. The hairs on her arms stood on end, and little balls of energy crackled off her fingertips.

She kept her arms rigid at her sides until he gunned the engine and roared down the driveway. Not until he was completely out of sight and the smell of exhaust had dissipated from the air around her did she trust herself to raise her hands.

Instead of hurling a ball of destructive energy she vigorously shook them, releasing sparks like tiny fireflies into the air. With concentrated effort she took a deep breath and pushed the rest of her unspent magick into the sand at her feet.

Without her anger or her magick to sustain her, Lizzie legs gave way and she leaned against the van for support. She kept her head down until she heard the clatter of Audley's feet descending the porch stairs. She looked up to see him busily fiddling with his tool belt, trying to get the screwdriver he held in his hand back into the leather loop of his belt. He didn't look up until he was almost on top of Lizzie.

"Sorry that took so long, I was having trouble getting the cupboard door level...." His voice faltered as he looked up at Lizzie, then over to where Jon's truck had been parked. "Where's Mr. Ryan?"

"He had to leave suddenly," Lizzie said. She pushed herself away from the van as Audley opened the sliding side door. Audley unhooked his tool belt, slung it onto the floor of the van, and slid the door closed.

"Did Mr. Ryan say where he was heading?"

"No, but maybe you should try back at his office," she said. Lizzie didn't know what else to say...the truth seemed too bizarre even to her.

As Audley headed towards the driver's side door, a terrible thought hit her. After rejecting Jon's advances she doubted he'd send Audley to do anymore work for her. She had not only come to rely on her quirky little handyman, his shuffling walk, the constant smell of pot smoke that followed him, but he'd become part of her new life, a constant. It wasn't just the exceptional work he'd done on her cottage bringing her dream to life, but he'd become a friend. Other than Grandma Faye he was the only one she could count on, and she looked forward to his arrival. The loss of his presence in her small circle of friends was a sad reminder that anyone who entered her life, it seemed, was destined to leave almost as soon as they appeared.

"Audley," she called out to stop him before he left.

"Yes, Ms. Benett? Was there anything else you needed done today?"

"No, no there's nothing more to do. I just wanted to let you know how much I've appreciated everything you've done for me. You are an amazing handyman, and without you my cottage would not be as beautiful as it is."

"It's nothing, just doing my job."

"It is something to me, and I wanted to make sure you knew how I felt." She wrapped her arms around him and gave him a hug. She felt him hesitate and then return her embrace. Before she broke away, she planted a kiss on his stubbly cheek.

When she drew back, he blushed fiercely and she had to resist the urge to pat his cheek. He cleared his throat and looked down at the ground. "Well, I'd best be off."

He climbed into his van and started the engine. Leaning out the open window, he smiled at Lizzie. "See ya later, Ms. Benett." He drove away before waiting for her reply. She watched the white van until it rounded the curve of the driveway.

"Goodbye, Audley," she whispered to the empty driveway.

CHAPTER THIRTY-ONE

Lizzie collapsed on the porch steps. Quinn followed her and took up position on the porch railing. She looked up at him through shimmering eyes.

"Thanks," she said, the word catching in her throat. He chortled his reply, dipping his head, then started preening himself.

Cradling her face in her hands she took loud hitching breaths, willing herself not to cry. She still wasn't sure what had happened. Jon was as stubborn as a mule, but during their short acquaintance he'd been thoughtful and even kind. But when she refused his advances his violent reaction had shocked her.

"What am I going to do?" she muttered into her hands.

"About what?"

Lizzie whipped her head up and around at the sound of Wren's voice. He strode across the driveway, coming from the direction of the barn. He looked like he'd dressed in a hurry, his shirt untucked and buttoned wrong so one shirttail hung lower than the other.

"Nothing," she said from her seat on the step, swiping at a tear that slipped down her cheek.

"It doesn't look like nothing," he said, stopping a few feet from her.

Quinn, who had been quietly grooming himself on the porch rail, lowered his head and gave a squawk. She'd seen how he'd reacted to Jon, and now it looked as if he was going to attack

Wren. Quinn hunkered down on the railings, puffing out his neck feathers in agitation.

She'd opened her mouth to warn Wren when he shifted his gaze over to the raven, and then he did an extraordinary thing. He bowed deeply, never taking his eyes off the bird.

Quinn took flight just as Wren straightened up from his bow. Instead of ducking out of the way, Wren held out his arm. To Lizzie's astonishment, Quinn alighted on his forearm with a gentle grace.

Man and bird eyed each other. Quinn chortled and made a series of little popping sounds deep in his throat. Wren nodded his head a few times, then smiled at the raven. It looked to Lizzie as if they were carrying on a conversation. When Quinn had finished his vocalizations, instead of flying off, he nimbly walked up the length of Wren's arm and perched on his shoulder.

"A friend of yours, I take it," Wren asked as the raven started to preen the hair on the back of Wren's neck.

"And yours too, by the looks of things. His name is Quinn."

"Oh, the one with the peanut butter habit?"

"Yes, one and the same," she laughed.

Wren let the bird groom him for a few more minutes, then turned his head to the side, trying to avoid the raven's nimble beak. "Hey there Quinn, that tickles," he chuckled. The raven stopped his ministrations and flew back to the railing. Wren took a seat next to her on the stoop.

"So why so glum?"

"It's just...." She was going to tell him exactly what had happened, but she couldn't get the words past her lips. She looked down at her hands. "I had a disagreement with someone I thought was a friend. It's left me a bit rattled, that's all."

"I can see that," Wren said, cupping her chin in his hand and gently lifting it so she had to look at him. His blue-green eyes burned like candle flames. Butterflies danced in her belly. She turned her head so his hand was no longer on her chin.

"Why are you here? I mean, what brought you to my doorstep this morning? Shouldn't you be out counting owls?" It came out sharper than she'd intended.

"The owls are sleeping at this time of day. I do most of my work at night when they are up and about. As to why I'm here, I thought it was obvious. I wanted to see you again."

He reached out to her again and this time she didn't pull away. Wren's fingers felt cool against the heat of her face. With the softest touch he traced a line down her jaw, trailing his fingers down her throat. She knew what question he was asking in the intensity of his gaze. She replied by leaning in and kissing him gently, tentatively. He responded in kind, both of them exploring, taking their time.

As their kiss became urgent, more insistent, she felt Wren's hand continue down her throat and sneak under the fabric of her sweater to dance over her collarbone. She leaned in further, encouraging him, suddenly desperate to feel his hand against her breast. When his hand found her stone cross, she felt a jolt of heat from the stone. Her eyes flew open.

Instead of releasing her necklace, Wren's hand clutched tighter, trapping a handful of her shirt under which her pendant lay. The silver chain bit into the back of her neck as Wren increased his grip. She'd forgotten about the protective charm around the stone…he'd touched it without her permission.

"Wren, take your hand off…," she started to say, but the look on his face made her stop.

His brows were furrowed and his eyes were blank and unseeing. Wren's skin was pale to begin with, but now it had gone a ghastly grey, making his aquamarine eyes glow brighter.

She grasped his wrist, intending to pull his hand away, but the second she made contact a flash of light obliterated everything around her.

Images bombarded her vision; a woman sitting at a table with Wren. They were surrounded by high wooden bookshelves. Light streamed down from windows high above. The woman was laughing. She looked familiar, but as Lizzie strained to put a name to the face, the image dissolved and was replaced by another and then another. Each image moving faster until they became a blur of color and movement. Vertigo overwhelmed her, and along with the spinning colors came a waterfall of feelings; joy, happiness, confusion, fear, searing pain, deep heart pounding panic, and then darkness.

* * * *

In the cottage the phone was ringing. Lizzie remained on the porch steps, leaning her shoulder against the railing. It was raining. The porch roof shielded her upper body from the raindrops, but there were wet patches darkening the legs of her jeans and her feet were already soaked inside her sneakers. On the fourth ring the phone went silent as the call was shuttled to her voicemail. The phone message could wait.

Swiping at the tears streaming down her cheeks, she looked at her damp fingers, trying to remember why she was crying. She blinked, then looked around. She was alone on the porch. She was positive Quinn had been with her just moments ago. Heaving herself up, she shuffled to the front door, her feet making wet squelching noises with every step.

It wasn't until she stepped inside the cottage that she found the anchor to attach her sorrow to. Seeing the brand new cupboard Audley had just installed brought everything back.

She remembered her hot indignation at Jon for calling the police, his confusion at her anger, the kiss, and everything that came after. Her cheeks burned with a mixture of shame and anger.

No, she wasn't sad about Jon…this emotion she reserved for Audley. Like the past repeating itself, she'd destroyed yet another fragile thread of connection with someone she'd begun to regard as a friend.

Moving like an old woman, she picked up the receiver and dialed in to check her messages.

CHAPTER THIRTY-TWO

"Come on, Bear, there's a good boy. Hurry up before I get washed away." Lizzie gently tugged on the leash, but the dog refused to move from his refuge on the porch.

He looked dismally at her then out at the pelting rain. Lizzie was standing at the bottom of the stairs, leash in one hand, umbrella in the other, the rain beating a hard tattoo on the fabric of the umbrella. Twilight was fast approaching, and Lizzie just wanted her dog to do his business so they could both get back inside where it was warm and dry.

Quinn was peering out through the open living room window. Even the raven didn't want to go out in the wet dreariness. Instead he cawed his support from the comfort of the cottage.

She would have stayed inside too and just let Bear go out by himself, except every time she'd let him out he refused to budge off the front porch. Even with the ramp Dr. Laurie had installed over one half of the porch stairs to make it easier for the dog to leave the house, he wouldn't go out in the rain unless Lizzie used encouragement…gentle tugs on his leash and bribery with a cookie.

It had been raining for three days and showed no signs of letting up, so Lizzie had become an expert on how to get her 112-pound dog outside to go pee. Although it was almost June, the rain was cold and relentless, turning the sky a deep and ominous grey. The cloud cover was so low Lizzie felt if she reached up on tiptoes she would be able to brush the clouds with her fingertips.

The warm days of May that had tantalized Lizzie when she'd first moved out to the Kootenay's and led her to believe she had moved to paradise had left when the rains started. Grandma Faye had assured her this was typical late spring weather, the rains arriving at the end of May and into the first part of June. She warned Lizzie that by the end of August she'd be wishing for the cool rain. Lizzie hoped what her friend said was true, because at the moment she was weary of the grey and dampness.

Lizzie was thankful Bear's cast had come off before he'd come home, because she couldn't imagine having to deal with a cast in this much wet. Dr. Laurie was still unable to explain his miraculous and speedy recovery, but his last x-rays had confirmed that his bones were sound. And Lizzie had no compunction about keeping the real reason a mystery.

Even without the cast Bear walked with a pronounced limp, but she had a suspicion her dog was delaying his calls of nature not just because of his hitching gait, but because he hated the rain. She couldn't blame him. His long fluffy fur was more like wool, and as soon as it got wet, instead of repelling water like a Labrador retriever's coat, his immediately soaked up the water like a sponge, plastering his coat against his body in long wavy strands. It probably added twenty pounds to his frame, and it took hours to dry even when Lizzie went after him with a towel.

Thunder rumbled in the distance although she couldn't see any flashes of lightning. Looping the handle of the leash around her wrist, she dug out a cookie from the pocket of her yellow slicker. Lizzie held it out in front of her.

"Come on big guy, come down and go pee pees for Mommy," she said, and then laughed. Three days in and she was already using that high-pitched singsong voice people reserved for animals and babies.

Either the fact that he couldn't hold it any longer or the promise of the cookie was enough to make him endure getting wet. Bear hobbled over to the ramp, gave a loud chuff, puffing out his ample jowls, and slowly negotiated the ramp. He kept close to Lizzie so he had some protection from her umbrella, and nudged her leg with his nose.

"No, no cookie until you've gone to the bathroom, you know the drill." Lizzie smiled down at the dog, holding the cookie out of his reach. "Away you go." Bear lowered his head and shuffle hopped over to the grass at the edge of the driveway, with Lizzie following at the end of the lead.

While Bear sniffed the wet grass, Lizzie turned to look back at the cottage. She'd found out quickly that her dog was shy when it came to matters of his bowels, and wouldn't do the deed until she looked away.

In three days she'd also learned that he preferred to sleep with his dog bed near the head of her bed and not at the foot, where she'd originally placed it, he liked to have a cookie before retiring for the evening, and although he liked his ears scratched, he much preferred a thorough belly rub.

The leash slackened in her hand as Bear made his way back to her. She turned and held out the cookie, which he gobbled down in one bite. Lizzie slowed her pace as they approached the ramp and Bear moved his massive body up the wet boards.

Once inside, Lizzie unclipped the leash and hung it on the hook beside the door. Bear didn't bother to shake out the rain from his fur, and instead plopped himself down on the second dog bed she'd purchased, which was positioned in front of the living room fireplace. He let out a satisfied groan, rather like an old man, as he found a comfortable position on his bed.

The heat from the fire crackling in the hearth would help to dry his fur, but Lizzie still needed to towel off as much of the moisture as she could. The cottage smelled of wet dog and the lingering aroma of the stew Lizzie had made for dinner.

Lizzie peeled off her wet slicker and gave it a quick shake out on the porch before hanging it on the hook next to the leash. She shut and bolted the door, then closed the window sash now that Quinn had moved to be near the dog. Her two animal companions had hit it off instantly, and except for Quinn's reluctance to follow Bear out in the rain they had been inseparable.

As she rubbed the towel over Bear's broad back she felt the twinges of boredom creeping in. She hadn't seen a soul for three days, and coupled with the rain she was beginning to feel the beginnings of cabin fever. The chickens required very little from her, and it was too soggy to even think of planting anything.

Grandma Faye had spent the last few days with an elderly shut-in in the village, but she'd given Lizzie the number where she could be reached if she needed her. Except for the first visit from Wren at her cottage she hadn't seen him either. And as she expected, she hadn't heard from Jon or Audley. Not that she ever wanted to cross Jon's path again, but she missed her handyman. Everywhere she looked, in every room, she saw Audley's work and skill. Not having Audley around also made her realize a rather huge oversight on her part. And when Dr. Laurie delivered Bear her insight was confirmed.

When the vet suggested a ramp would make Bear's coming and goings from the cottage easier, Lizzie had to admit she didn't own a power drill, or a hammer for that matter. It was the vet who had managed to build a ramp, using leftover wood from a cottage reno and Dr. Laurie's own well-stocked tool kit that she kept in the back of her SUV. Lizzie's only contribution to the construction project was handing the vet a screwdriver.

To her dismay, she knew she was ill prepared for the life she had so desperately wanted. A life away from prying eyes and the pressure she felt when she was under the order's protection to be something she wasn't. Yes, it was safer for her to live in the woods, but she'd been relying on Audley to do all the work requiring tools and saws, and she'd came to expect Grandma

Faye's deliveries of bread, meals, and wisdom. If Lizzie was really serious about living out her days in her woodland cottage she needed to learn some basic skills of self-sufficiency.

So over dinner she made a list of tools and a separate list of the things she needed to learn. The list was extensive, and so were the questions she needed to ask Grandma Faye, but that had only eaten up an hour of her time. She'd already put the chickens to bed, and with Bear's bathroom needs taken care of the evening stretched out interminably before her.

Leaving Bear to dry out by the fire, she threw the now sopping towel in the laundry hamper and then plucked a dog biscuit from the glass jar on the counter. She also poured a handful of dried cranberries into a bowl for Quinn, these being his second favorite food next to peanut butter.

After she handed out the snacks to her companions, she sat down in the leather chair before the fire and picked up the cheap paperback copy of *Pride and Prejudice* she'd left open on the armrest. She couldn't focus on the story, and after flipping through three chapters without retaining a word she discarded it on the side table, her fingers brushing over the hard cover of the book she'd stolen from the library.

She picked up the slim volume and reread the section on making contact with the spirit world.

Why not? she thought. It seemed simple enough, and she had everything she needed to perform the ritual. Although she hadn't discussed the idea with Grandma Faye, what harm could it do? And if it could help Emma then it was worth trying. Besides, she didn't have anything better to do with her time.

Perhaps she'd known the secret to releasing Emma the moment she slipped the book into her purse before leaving the library. If Emma's spirit held any memory of her death, perhaps she herself knew the meaning of the symbols. She may be wrong in her assumption, but at least she had to try.

She knew there was a slight risk in using her magick, but if the warlock was still searching for her the order would have let her know by now. And the order believed the blast of magick Lizzie had sent to him through the ether had damaged his ability to not only sense her presence, but to perform any magick of his own. It was a small risk, especially as she was going to keep her powers confined to her cottage, and one she felt comfortable taking if it meant Emma would cease to relive those dark and painful days before her death.

Although it would have been nice to have Grandma Faye present, for company more than anything else, now that Lizzie had made up her mind to contact Emma she didn't want to wait. She quickly gathered everything she needed and placed them on the kitchen table; a bowl of sea salt, a wineglass full of water, a fat beeswax candle, a box of wooden matches, and the book opened to the incantation.

Raising her arms in supplication, she called down the elementals. As the first luminescent vapor appeared it suffused her with pure joy. Oh, how she missed their presence; it felt like coming home. The whitewashed walls of her cottage were colored over with the palest shades of yellow, red, blue, and green as she called each of the directions.

Bear raised his head from his dog bed but seemed content to stay where he was. Quinn flapped his wings and flew the few feet to land on the back of one of the kitchen chairs. He'd been with her during her encounter with the demon, he'd seen her call the circle into being before, and had stood guardian as she did battle.

She smiled over at him. "Not to worry. This time we aren't hunting demons, just helping someone from the spirit world. But I thank you all the same." Thunder cracked close enough to rattle the windows in their frames. Quinn stayed where he was.

Lizzie lowered her head and focused her attention and her

magick on bridging the worlds of the living and dead. Raising her head, she spoke in a clear determined voice. "To the spirit of Emma Hawksworth, I reach out to you now and invite you to join me in this sacred circle. I mean you no harm, I only want to release you from your torment."

The temperature in the room dropped dramatically, and even with the fire roaring goosebumps broke out on her arms.

"If you are here with me now let me know. Tap on the table or move an object. Please do something to show your presence."

In the middle distance between the kitchen table and the leather armchair a mist appeared. Lizzie watched transfixed as the white vapor solidified into the shape of a woman. Her outline was hazy at first, as if she were drawn by an inexpert hand, and then Emma stood before Lizzie in great detail, as if she were alive. Well, not quite stood, as the hem of her skirt floated a good three feet off the floor.

Lizzie recognized the woman as the one she'd first seen down in the cellar, but gone was the dead expression and the ragged and dirty clothes. She wore a similar style of dress as before, but instead of green it was a deep crimson color, and over her shoulders she wore a russet colored shawl embroidered with gold leaves. Her manifestation was so complete Lizzie could pick out the individual stitches of golden embroidery thread that made up the pattern of foliage.

"Emma," Lizzie said.

The apparition nodded then smiled. Her expression held such warmth and affection that Lizzie felt a pang of regret that they would never meet in this world.

Lizzie cleared her throat. "I've summoned you because I want to help. The binding spell trapping your spirit here. If you know what the symbols mean tell me please." She spoke rapidly, not knowing how long Emma's spirit could maintain her appearance.

Lightning flashed outside, illuminating the trees along the

driveway. Seconds later a clap of thunder followed close in its wake.

Emma clasped her hands in front of her, floated a few feet up in the air, then settled back down so that she was eye level with Lizzie.

"If you can tell me, please, I want to help." Emma shook her head as another flash of lightning lit up the cottage. "No you don't know what they mean, or no you can't?" The ghost shook her head again, this time pointing to Lizzie. "Me? I can release you?"

The ghost shook her head again, her smile never wavering. She had begun to fade. Lizzie gripped the edge of the table, trying to will the ghost to stay visible. "Don't go. If there is something I can do to help tell me."

The apparition became solid again, her calm face suddenly looking startled. The ghost turned abruptly, facing the living room windows. Looking over her shoulder at Lizzie, she spoke. "The Dark One knows."

Lizzie's mouth fell open. She hadn't expected the spirit to speak, and in such a clear tone as if she were flesh and blood. But she didn't have time to ponder this as the ghost turned back to the window and raised her hands. In that instant all the outside shutters slammed closed, even though there were eye hooks securing them open.

"Reveal your history, heal his sorrow," Emma spoke, then disappeared as a flash of lightning and a clap of thunder occurred simultaneously.

Lizzie screamed as the cottage plunged into darkness.

Chapter Thirty-Three

A cold nose nudged Lizzie's hand. She reached out and scratched Bear's head and opened one eye. She heard water running somewhere in the house. A wet tongue slurped across her face.

"Ugh," she spluttered and sat up, scrubbing her face with the sleeve of her nightgown. She swung her legs off the couch. "While I appreciate the affection, your breath leaves a lot to be desired. Especially first thing in the morning." Bear cocked his head, his quizzical expression making her laugh. "I suppose you want breakfast?" He backed up slowly, giving her room to get up. "Well, you have to wait five minutes...I need coffee and you need to go out first." She patted the dog's head then wandered over to the kitchen.

She hadn't slept well, as the storm had raged all night and the power had remained off. After the initial lightning strike had hit during the séance, it had taken several minutes for her heart to stop hammering in her chest and the bright spots that danced in front of her eyes to disappear. As soon as she was able she'd armed herself with a flashlight, and against her better judgement she and Bear had crept out to the front porch. When she had reassured herself that the lightning hadn't caused a fire and the chicken coop was still standing, she decided to spend the night on the couch. She knew it was silly but she felt safer in the main part of the house, as far away from the cellar as possible.

Still half asleep, she grabbed the coffee carafe and headed

over to the sink to fill it. The faucet was already running, the cold tap opened up all the way. She spun around, looking for signs of a break in, the carafe still in her hands. All the windows were latched, the shutters remained closed over the windows, the door was shut, the deadbolt engaged, and the magickal wards still in place.

She shut off the water and put the carafe on the counter. Heart pounding, she inched towards the mudroom. Bear clumped across the floor to her side, tongue lolling. Her senses were on high alert, but she resisted the need to send her energy out to search for any hint of lingering magick. Emma's warning rang through her mind. *The Dark One knows.*

Knows what? About who she really was? About the black magick in her cellar? Could the Dark One be the warlock that had tried to kill her? Lizzie feared she may have gotten in over her head. Perhaps it was time to call Vivienne after all.

She peeked her head into the mudroom but nothing was amiss. As she tiptoed down the hall she could hear water running in the bathroom. She inched the door open and stuck her head in. The bathroom was empty but the tub and sink faucets were running. While she turned off the sink tap, Bear leaned into the bathtub and slurped water from the gushing faucet. She let him take a few more slurps before turning it off.

Bewildered, she stepped into her bedroom and looked around. Everything was where it should be, the french doors closed tightly. The window facing the front of the house had its shutters closed like the rest of the house. She retraced her steps to the kitchen with Bear following at her heels.

"Emma, did you turn the taps on? If you did, why?" There came no reply. She couldn't detect any ghostly presence, no cold spots, and no strange vapors.

She grabbed the phone and started dialing the number Grandma Faye had left for her. It wasn't until she put the phone to her ear that she realized the phone was dead. Putting the receiver back in the cradle, she flicked on the kitchen light. Nothing happened. The power was still out.

She didn't know who the shut-in was that Grandma Faye was looking after, so going to see her wasn't an option. She supposed she could drive into town to use her cell to call her.

She couldn't help but see the humor that such a powerful organization like the order, which went through the trouble of installing a phone that couldn't be bugged or traced, hadn't thought about the fact that a cordless phone would be rendered useless during a power outage.

She took in a deep breath, making sure the barrier between her and Vivienne was still strongly in place. She was shaken by Emma's warning, but now that she'd calmed down she didn't want to bring in the order. Logically it made sense; they had untold resources, talented powerful witches in their service and people who would protect her, but her instincts were telling her not to send out a distress signal. Not yet.

Her instincts. She needed to honor what she was feeling. Wasn't that the reason she'd moved out here, hadn't her instincts brought her here? She had wanted to live out in the wilderness, to be alone, to have time to discover who she was in relation to herself, to stop listening to everyone else and follow her own powerful magick.

Yes, she would figure this out on her own, but she would have appreciated Grandma Faye's knowledge and her presence if only to reassure herself.

She needed a clear head to figure this one out, and that meant coffee. But without power she'd have to do it the old fashioned way, with boiling water and her French press. After starting a fire in the woodstove and placing the cast iron kettle in place, she threw her slicker over her nightgown and donned her rubber boots. When she opened the door she was pleasantly surprised to see a clear blue sky and sunshine. She didn't grab Bear's leash, just held the door as he followed her outside.

As she stepped off the porch she surveyed the damage from last night's storm. Bear wandered past her to sniff at the fallen branches littering the driveway and grassy area surrounding the cottage. From what she could see the branches had been the only casualty from the storm winds. She walked around the house and noticed one tree at the back of the cottage had fallen, snapped halfway up its trunk.

Although the rain had stopped the ground was saturated, and even though the sun didn't pack a lot of heat the comparative warmth of its rays caused the dampness to rise up from her feet, and with it the smell of cedar and wet earth. Water drops clung to the tree limbs, sparkling in the sunshine.

Lizzie breathed deeply, stretching her arms in the air. It felt good to be alive.

She let out the chickens before looking over the rest of the property near the house. All the girls looked none the worse for wear after having to endure the storm in their coop. They came as one clucking fluttering flock into the chicken yard, scrambling after the feed Lizzie scattered on the ground.

She left Bear snuffling around the driveway as she headed down to assess her garden. The rickety garden gate was lying flat on the wet grass, and other than a few rain bedraggled lettuce leaves everything else looked fine. Again she was reminded not only did she not know how to do the simplest of repairs, she didn't even own a hammer or nails to fix her gate.

She leaned the broken gate against the garden fence and wandered down the driveway. By the time she made it to the front gate she heard the wind, as if it were a powerful locomotive heading straight for her, before it began to toss the tops of the trees.

She turned to the sound and marveled as she watched the

wind as a living breathing thing make its way through the trees and towards her. She squinted up at the sky, her brows furrowed as she spotted the dark clouds moving back over the property. More rain was on its way. She sighed and checked the gate. It was locked and holding firm in its stone posts.

She rejoined Bear, who was still on the driveway. He'd nudged a large tree limb out of the way and was pawing at the sandy ground.

"What did you find?" She peered over him at the place where he'd been scratching.

A blackened line squiggled across the driveway like a garter snake. She traced her finger along its path to where it ended, her hand touching something solid just underneath the sand. Brushing the top layer of blackened sand away, she plucked up a tube-shaped piece of glass. Melted grains of sand fused into an uneven texture across the surface of the tube.

The lightning strike had turned the sand into glass. Remembering what it felt like to be that close when the lightning hit made her shiver in the mild sunshine.

She glanced down at where the piece of glass had been. Just a few feet separated where the lightning had hit and the house. The wards she'd placed on the cottage wouldn't have protected her or her animal companions from such a powerful force of nature.

She curled her fingers over the tube of glass. Would a warlock be able to conjure up weather and direct it at someone? Maybe she wasn't as safe in the middle of nowhere as she'd thought.

When the first fat drops began to plop onto her head, she hustled Bear back into the house. He didn't need much encouragement.

CHAPTER THIRTY-FOUR

By four o'clock, Lizzie couldn't stand being inside a minute longer. The power was still out and she'd kept the woodstove going all day to keep the house warm and to make her meals. The rain hadn't let up and she'd exhausted every conceivable chore to occupy her time inside. She'd even written copious notes about what had happened the night before. But even rereading them hadn't given her any ideas on how to help Emma or what her cryptic message meant. Instead it only made her irritation grow.

She'd briefly entertained the idea of jumping in the truck and heading for town to use her cellphone to call Grandma Faye. She even had the truck keys in her hands before she stopped herself. Her friend was busy taking care of someone who was ill. Lizzie wasn't in any immediate danger, and if she'd accidently given Emma more power the worst the ghost had done was turn on the cold water taps.

Grabbing her slicker and sou'wester from the pegs at the front door she stepped out into the rain. She figured a walk was just the thing to burn off her excess energy. Bear gave a slight whine when he realized he wasn't coming with her.

"I'm just going for a walk to get the mail," she said to her dog. "You can't walk that far just yet, and it's too wet anyway. Besides, you've got Quinn to keep you company, and I won't be more than twenty minutes." She patted him on the head and tried to ignore the pathetic look he gave her as she shut the door.

She left one of the front windows open, to allow fresh air in in case Bear got too warm with the cook stove burning, and to allow Quinn access to the outside if he needed it, but not wide enough for her dog to squeeze his head through.

When she reached the mailbox she was surprised at how full the little cubby was. She only gave the envelopes a cursory glance before stuffing them in the inside pocket of her slicker to keep them dry. Other than junk mail it looked like the majority of the correspondences was bills. She still had a substantial amount of savings in the bank that would last her a while if she was careful with her spending, but eventually she'd have to figure out a way to bring in an income. But that was a worry for another day.

With her mail secure and dry inside her slicker she turned for home. The sound of her footfalls on gravel and the patter of the rain on her hat created an almost meditative state as Lizzie's mind finally stopped its constant loop of thoughts. Instead of trying to worry out the solution to her current problems, she just let them slide by her consciousness and put her attention to the sound of the rain, the sway of the trees, the smell of wet sand and earth, and the tug of the wind on the brim of her hat.

As she opened the gate on her property, her vision wavered. At first she thought it was just the rain making the trees and the driveway shimmer, but then she saw a gossamer net overlaid over everything, its thin filaments glowing in a golden sheen. She inhaled sharply and the vision was gone.

Lizzie stood with her hands at her sides, the rain forgotten. For in that brief moment when the vision revealed itself to her she understood what she'd just seen. Everything—from the trees, to the blades of grass, each individual particle of sand, the birds roosting in the trees—was all connected to the golden net.

More astonishing was everything wasn't just interconnected, but communicating with each other through their energy and the luminescent energetic web. Every living thing and things she'd never considered living, like the rocks and the dirt, had an intelligence no different than hers.

Tears sprung into her eyes, to be washed away with the rain pelting her face as she turned her face skyward. Although she no longer could see the web of life, she felt just the faintest thrum of the energy as it pulsed through the air and ground.

Humbled, she strode to her cottage, feeling the earth through her rain boots. Before she stepped inside the cottage she sent out a silent prayer of gratitude.

"Hey guys, I'm back. I told you I wouldn't be gone long," she said, throwing the stack of mail on the narrow hall table. She shook out her hat and coat on the porch before hanging them up on the pegs next to the hall table. When there was no sound of feet shuffling over to greet her, she turned to look at the room.

The fire in the cook stove was still burning, as evidenced by the warmth of the room and the smell of hot cast-iron. There was a breeze coming in through the window she'd left open, keeping the room comfortable instead of overly warm. Everything was just as she'd left it, except there was no dog or raven.

"Bear," she called out. She surmised Quinn may have flown out the window, perhaps needing, like she had, a spurt of exercise to fend off cabin fever. Bear must have gone into her bedroom. When she didn't hear the dog coming down the hall, she was just about to go find him when she heard something clatter on the floor above her, followed by footsteps.

She stopped next to the kitchen table and looked up. There it was again. Someone was up in the attic. No, it sounded like more than one set of feet. Fear and anger sluiced through her in equal measures. If they had done anything to harm Bear she would strangle them with her own hands.

Moving slowly and as quietly as she could, she grabbed the ash shovel that stood next to the stove. Gripping the handle tightly, the sweat on her palms already making her hold on it slippery, she edged towards the hallway. She kept to the wall beside the stove so that if there was someone in the hallway they couldn't spot her until she was ready.

She heard more footsteps from above, the sound of something being dropped on the floor, and then the distinctive squawk of a raven. Before she lunged around the corner, she cocked her head and listened to the commotion upstairs. She heard Quinn chortle, then more footsteps. No, not footsteps, nails on hardwood.

Somehow, Bear was upstairs. There was no way he could have gotten up there on his own. Even if the stairs had been pulled down the incline was way too steep for him to negotiate. And she hadn't lowered the stairs to the attic in a week.

How had someone managed to get her dog stuck in the attic? And more importantly, how did they get past the wards on the windows and doors? And were they still in the house? She took a deep breath to steady her nerves, then jumped into the hallway brandishing the coal shovel.

There was no one in the hallway, but the stairs had been pulled down. As she snuck towards the stairs, Bear peered down through the opening and let out a friendly woof. Lizzie put her finger to her lips, trying to get him to be quiet, but instead he pranced on his front legs and let out another playful bark. Waving her hand up at him to shush him only made him let out another friendly hello.

If there was someone still in her house, someone clever enough to get past her magickal security system, she'd just lost the element of surprise. She didn't have any choice but to use her magick now.

Using her powers, she quickly scanned the cottage. The only two creatures who were in her house were the two she'd left before going to get the mail. From her position in the hallway, she also used her magick to check that the wards were intact. As far as she could tell, they hadn't been broken or tampered with.

Just to be doubly sure she checked the bathroom and her

bedroom. Everything was just as she'd left it. Even though she'd left the living room window open for Quinn to slip out, the ward on the window was intact. She quickly powered down her energy and lowered the shovel. There was no one in the house. So how had her 112-pound dog with a broken leg ended up in the attic?

She retraced her steps back to the attic stairs. Bear was still looking down at her with what appeared to be a goofy grin on his face. Climbing up the steps, she was rewarded by a sloppy dog kiss as soon as her face was level with his.

"I'm glad to see you too," she said, climbing the rest of the way up. "But how the hell did you get up here?" She ran her hands over his body, examining his legs in particular to see if he'd been injured. He seemed fine, nothing re-broken or pulled.

Bear wasn't about to tell her how he had managed his feat, and as she puzzled the more important question of how she was going to get him down, Quinn, who had been up in the rafters, sailed down and tottered over to where a twig lay on the floor. She watched as Quinn waddled over to the stick, picked it up in his beak, and then flew to the ceiling, this time perching on a rafter just above her head. She craned her neck to see what he was going to do next. Bear woofed at the bird and pranced on his front legs. Then Quinn tossed his head and released the twig.

It clattered to the floor several feet from where Lizzie stood. Bear's front paws scrabbled to find purchase on the hardwood, then he trotted after the stick at a speed Lizzie worried wasn't good for his still mending bones. But her dog didn't seem bothered in the least by his injuries as he grabbed the stick in his mouth and trotted back to sit just underneath where Quinn was perched. He dropped the stick and looked up at the raven, letting out a hearty bark.

Quinn chortled in response and flew down to retrieve the stick. He then repeated the process of flying up to the rafters and launching the twig in the air for Bear to retrieve.

Lizzie laughed and backed out of their way as they continued to play fetch. She needed Grandma Faye's help to get Bear down, there was no question about it. Lizzie could levitate a glass of water by herself, but she'd need her friend to help manage the dog. She wasn't sure she could hold the spell if he started to struggle against it, and she didn't know enough about magick to know if there was something that could be cast to immobilize him until he was safely on the ground. She didn't want to think of what would happen if she dropped him from a ten-foot height.

She hadn't been under the protection of the order and Vivienne's tutelage long enough to learn anything useful about wielding her power. All she really knew how to do was place wards, call the elementals, and throw destructive balls of energy, none of which would help her now. It looked like she was going to have to drive to town and call her friend for help after all.

She'd be gone for at least an hour, so before she left she'd have to bring him up his water dish. And it was quite warm up in the rafters. She had knelt down at one of the low windows to open it for fresh air when she spied Grandma Faye's truck pulling up in the drive. She was so relieved she jumped up, skirted the dog as he went scrambling for the twig Quinn had just thrown, and clattered down the stairs.

She flung open the door just as Grandma Fay came around the side of her truck. The old woman wore a man's oilskin coat a size too big and the color of sand, and on her head she wore a clear plastic rain bonnet tied neatly under her chin.

"I'm so glad to see you," Lizzie said, rushing down the porch steps, not bothering with her raincoat.

The old woman smiled at Lizzie. "I figured you might need a little help coping with the power outage."

"No, no that's not what I mean. I've done an incredibly stupid thing and now I need your help. I know I shouldn't have gone ahead without you, and now I've somehow given Emma the power to move things. And I don't know how to help Bear without hurting him. I'm so stupid."

"Slow down, Lizzie, and catch your breath. What stupid thing have you done? You've given Emma the power to do what? And what's wrong with Bear? He looks well enough to me." She looked past Lizzie's shoulder. "Don't ya, big boy? Grandma Faye's brought you a nice big soup bone."

Lizzie followed her friend's gaze and watched in astonishment as Bear stood on the porch wagging his tail.

CHAPTER THIRTY-FIVE

Lizzie sat at the kitchen table trembling uncontrollably while Grandma Faye bustled around preparing dinner. Bear was lying on his dog bed in the living room, contentedly gnawing on the promised soup bone.

When Lizzie had first spotted Bear standing on the porch as if nothing was amiss, she felt the world slide sideways. She grabbed Grandma Faye's amble upper arm to keep herself from pooling onto the wet driveway, her words coming out in a chaotic tumble.

Immediately Grandma Faye took control of the situation, hustling Lizzie and Bear back into the cottage and out of the rain. After both women made sure Quinn was down from the attic they closed up the stairs. Then Grandma Faye plunked Lizzie down at the kitchen table and told her to sit quietly until she'd drunk a whole cup of strong sweet tea.

As Lizzie did as she was told, Grandma Faye filled a cooler with bags of ice she'd picked up in town and put anything from the fridge that would spoil quickly in it. Then she pulled out the leftover stew from the night before and set it on the stove to warm, and started to mix up a batch of biscuits. While she stirred the stew and rolled out the biscuit dough she kept up a running monologue about the man she'd been caring for, who'd been recovering from a recent hip replacement surgery, and the source of the power outage, which was a lightning strike that hit a transformer up in New Denver.

"Knocked the whole area out from New Denver to Edgewood," Grandma Faye said, popping the biscuits into the oven.

Lizzie lifted her teacup with both hands and smiled at the back of her friend as she stood at the stove. It was apparent to Lizzie that Grandma Faye's first reaction to any crisis was tea and whipping up a meal.

Grandma Faye tapped the wooden spoon on the edge of the stew pot, then placed it on the spoon rest. Wiping her hands on the apron she'd liberated from Lizzie's cupboard, she sat down at the table. "So start from the beginning. You did a séance to call forth Emma to see if she could help us find out about the binding spell. Is that right?"

"Yes. At the time I thought it was a good idea, but now it seems I've made her more powerful, and now she's turning on my cold water taps and levitating my dog into the attic."

"But what possessed you to hold a séance in the middle of a lightning storm?"

Lizzie shrugged, not understanding the sudden firmness in Grandma Faye's voice. "Seemed as good a time as any, and I was tired of not making any headway on the problem."

Grandma Faye shook her head. "Don't you know that the electrical charges of a storm not only heighten a witch's power, but it thins the veil between this world and the afterlife, giving more power to the spirits?" She narrowed her eyes, and Lizzie tried not to squirm under the old woman's disapproving stare. "You didn't know, did you?" Her voice softened.

"No," she replied.

Grandma Faye slammed her hand on the table, making Bear lift his head, his bone momentarily forgotten. "Those nuns who raised you didn't do you any favors. You can't be practicing the craft without the basics, or you're going to get yourself into a heap of trouble."

275

"I think I already have." She took a mouthful of tea to fortify herself. Lizzie had to come clean about her past, about all of it, including the most recent dealing with the order and the reason she'd come all the way across the country to the middle of nowhere. She needed an ally; someone to guide her who didn't belong to the order, someone she trusted.

"Before I tell you about last night I think I need to start at the very beginning. About my birth, about everything that's come before."

* * * *

Telling her story was easier than she'd imagined. And once she began she found the words poured out of her like quicksilver. There was so much to tell, not just the facts of her life but her fears, her capacity for revenge, the rage she'd felt always simmering under the surface. And Grandma Faye listened.

She explained about her mother arriving at the cloistered nunnery in the last stages of labor, and her death while giving birth to Lizzie. She told of her unorthodox upbringing by Sister Collette at the priory, of being sent away at eighteen, banished from the only life she'd known. And how she'd found out just the past winter how some of the rubies from her mother's necklace had been used to pay off the nuns for agreeing to raise Lizzie.

Lizzie talked through dinner and while doing dishes. Grandma Faye only interrupted the flow of Lizzie's words when she needed clarification. Lizzie continued to talk as both women put the chickens to bed for the night and hauled in another load of wood.

Around the lump in her throat she spoke of her intense loneliness, her sense of not belonging, and her attempted suicide that ended her up in the hospital. She spoke of her marriage to Ian, of his drinking and violence, of her own isolation, and fear of her growing powers. That because of her uncontrolled magick she in a sense drove her husband to his death, out onto the icy streets to be hit by a bus as he stumbled in a drunken rage.

She recounted the night her flower shop burned to the ground and how if Gideon, a member of the Order of the Triple Goddess, hadn't intervened she would have unleashed a power so destructive she'd would have killed everyone near her.

She explained how in her fear she'd inadvertently left her body, her soul ending up trapped in a limbo-like plane of existence called the *In Between*. Her physical body would have died if not for Gideon's mother Vivienne using her skill to go and retrieve her.

She poured out her story of her reoccurring dreams of Rose Cottage, a result of her soul's journey to the *In Between*. The cottage, a place she didn't know existed until she found it. She told her about the warlock that had sent a demon to hunt her down, and her rescue by the Order of the Triple Goddess.

The only break in Lizzie's narrative occurred when both women changed into their pajamas once Grandma Faye announced she was spending the night. She had her overnight case with her from her stint with her shut-in.

Both women reconvened in the living room, and Lizzie picked up her tale where she'd left off. Grandma Faye sat in the leather chair by the fire, resplendent in a pair of men's silk pajamas printed in a swirl of blue, orange, and green paisley. Lizzie had opted for a pair of grey sweatpants and an oversized T-shirt. She curled up on the couch, hugging a pillow to her chest with Bear nestled at her feet, Quinn perched on the back of the sofa as she began the second part of her story.

She wasn't sure which aspect of her past was harder to tell. The part where she'd put a man in a coma while rescuing her young friend from being beaten to death, only to have her friend want nothing to do with her? Or the part of the story where she'd given into her passion for her young guardian, and just as they had crossed the line from guardian and charge to lovers he'd rejected her.

But as Grandma Faye lit the candles and put another log on the fire, Lizzie pushed ahead with her story.

When she finished her tale of coming out to the Kootenay's by herself, battling the demon, and doing serious harm to the still unknown warlock, and finding and buying Rose Cottage, she was exhausted. But as she stretched her arms above her head and repositioned herself on the couch, she also felt a deep pool of calmness she'd never felt before. She knew it wasn't as simple as confessing her sins and having her slate wiped clean—there were some things she'd never forgive herself for—but there was a restorative power in laying bare her soul to someone she trusted.

Lizzie blew out a long breath. "So now you know exactly who and what I am. And what I'm capable of," she added. She hesitated before looking in her friend's eyes, afraid of what she might find reflected there: shock, disgust, pity.

"You've been through more than most but less than some, I'll grant you that. But you must guard against judging yourself so harshly. It can quickly become a crutch and an excuse for not living up to your potential."

Lizzie smiled at both the acceptance and admonitions of Grandma Faye's words. "Vivienne used to say the same thing."

"Well, Vivienne is a wise woman then, isn't she? We all have a dark side, Lizzie, whether we have a talent with the craft or not. It's part of the human condition. It's acknowledging this part and choosing the light that makes us rise above it, to transcend. But pretending it doesn't exist is like trying to walk on your hands when you have two perfectly good feet."

"I understand what you're saying, but I put a man in a coma, and if Gideon hadn't stopped me I would have killed him."

"Because you were trying to save your friend and your anger got the better of you. You can't live your life afraid of who you are. I know you don't want to be a part of the order, but at the very least you need more than the rudimentary training you received from Vivienne. You need to test the limits of your capabilities and learn the laws of magick, the consequences of say, holding a séance during a thunderstorm."

Lizzie looked into the fire, letting Grandma Faye's words sink in. She'd turned her back on the order because she'd wanted to be normal, to live an uncomplicated life like the rest of humanity. But then she'd chosen to go after the demon herself. And lately she'd been using her magick more and more. But she wasn't like other people, she never had been. Although living at Rose Cottage was proving more challenging than she'd thought, it was also showing her just who she was, flaws and all. And wasn't that what one of her goals was; to find out who she really was in relation to just herself and no one else? Now she had a choice to make. She could keep denying what she was or embrace her magickal side.

She didn't know who her mother was but she did know her legacy; her history was one of witches and wise women. If she turned her back on that, wasn't she just as bad as the villagers who had condemned Emma to death because of her witchcraft? She needed to honor the women that had come before her, the women whose history ran through her veins, and she had women here with her now that could teach all she needed to know.

The only way she was going to truly live was to embrace who she really was: the witch of Rose Cottage.

"Will you teach me?"

"Of course I will. I will share with you all I know of the craft, but there may come a time when you will need Vivienne's skill too." She held up her hand to stop Lizzie's protest. "Not now, but perhaps in the future. Just keep the possibility open, that's all I ask."

Lizzie nodded.

"Now tell me exactly what happened during the séance."

Lizzie stifled a yawn. "I wrote everything down. My head's a bit fuzzy and I'll probably forget something in the retelling. Best if you read it first and then we can discuss it." Lizzie unfurled herself from the couch and slowly straightened her legs, being careful not to step on the sleeping dog stretched out below her. Reaching out to the side table at Grandma Faye's elbow she picked up her journal, thumbed through to the entry she wanted, and handed it to her. Grabbing one of the heavy silver candlesticks, she placed the burning candle on the side table next to Grandma Faye to give her more light to read by.

"While you go over my notes I'm going to make some coffee. We have so much more to talk about, and if I don't get some caffeine in me I may drift off to sleep."

Leaving Grandma Faye to go over her journal, Lizzie pulled out her French press and tin of coffee. After checking the firebox, she threw in a few more sticks of wood to get the stove hot enough to boil water. She closed the heavy cast iron door with a clank and went to the sink to fill the kettle. She glanced at the clock on the wall.

"Oh my god, your chickens and goats. They're still outside and it's after midnight."

"Not to worry," Grandma Faye said, looking up from the journal. "They're all tucked in for the night. When I knew I'd be spending time in town I asked Audley to stay over at the cabin and take care of the livestock. He does this for me from time to time."

Lizzie made a face at the sound of Audley's name. It made her sad to know she'd never be able to call on him in such a way. Not with the way things ended with Jon.

"He's not a bad sort. He may indulge on a little too much weed on occasion, but he's trustworthy. And I'm not about to judge how a man deals with his pain."

Lizzie had no idea what pain her friend was referring to, but she wasn't judging her former handyman. "I like Audley too, it's his boss I have a problem with. He and Jon stopped by a few days ago to install the new cabinet door. And let's just say things got a little strange." Lizzie poured the hot water into the French press and watched as the grounds mixed with the hot water, creating a brown slurry. The aroma helped to calm her nerves.

"Oh, Jon; well, that's another story. There is something about him that reminds me of a used car salesman. Now that your kitchen is done it might be best to steer clear of him."

Lizzie slowly pressed the plunger down on the press. "That's not going to be a problem. He showed me his true colors, and it wasn't pretty."

Grandma Faye raised her eyebrows.

Lizzie felt the heat of embarrassment on her cheeks as she poured out two cups of coffee. She gave one to Grandma Faye before returning to her perch on the sofa. Lizzie looked into her cup then up at the old woman. "He made a pass at me, and when I shut him down he didn't take it well. If it wasn't for Quinn I'm not sure how it would have ended." She stroked Quinn's back and he squeezed his eyes closed in pleasure. "As it was, he stormed off after calling me an ungrateful bitch."

"Are you worried he may come back and try again?" For the moment Lizzie's journal lay forgotten on Grandma Faye's lap.

"No, I don't think he would harm me. I think his pride was wounded. He seems like the type of man who is used to getting his way and having women fall at his feet."

"Well, I'd rather you be safe than sorry. If he so much as drives by your place you are to call me immediately. Is that clear?"

"Yes, Mother," Lizzie said with a smile. She thought her friend was overreacting, but it felt good all the same to have someone worry about her. "So getting back to Emma, what do you think?" Lizzie drank her coffee.

"It sounds like she's a benevolent spirit. Haven't heard of

many ghosts who could draw that much power that they appear in solid form and communicate. Or maybe it was the storm boosting her power. And if your account is accurate, she not only gave you a warning, but I think she may have saved you from the lightning strike."

"I think you are right. At least that was my take on it. She slammed the shutters on the windows to shield me from the flash of light, but my gut is telling me she also did something that made the lighting strike the driveway and not the house."

"Where exactly did it hit?"

"Your truck is parked right over the spot."

"My, that was close."

"Look what it did to the sand. Bear found it this morning." Lizzie extricated herself from the couch, stepping over the dog, and plucked the strange glass tube from the mantel piece where she'd placed it. She handed it over to Grandma Faye, who turned it over in the firelight.

"I think this is called a fulgurite. Imagine the power and heat required to turn sand into glass." She handed back the artefact and Lizzie returned it to its place on the mantle.

"I don't need to. The blast was bone rattling." Lizzie sat back down. "Whatever she did I'm grateful to her, but why must ghosts be so vague? If she was trying to warn me, why not give me a name instead of telling me the Dark One knows? I don't have a clue who the Dark One is or what it is he knows. Is she referring to the person who trapped her in the cellar? He'd have to be a warlock if he knew how to cast a binding spell like that. And so what if he knows? He's been dead for over a hundred years…how is that supposed to help us?"

"Maybe she wasn't referring to her own plight, but yours. What about the warlock that hunted you recently? Perhaps she's warning you that he knows where you are."

"If that's the case then what about the second part? What am

I supposed to remember, and why the hell would I want to heal the warlock's sorrow? It makes no sense."

"No it doesn't. But if my hunch is right and Emma was referring to your warlock, then maybe it's time to admit we are a bit out of our depth. Maybe it's time—"

"Don't say it."

"But I must. If there is a possibility Emma is referring to the warlock that went after you and not the one that trapped her in the cellar, then it's time to call in the order." The candlelight flickering threw deep shadows across the contours of the old woman's face, making her features appear as if they were shifting and changing appearance. "I know you want to prove to Vivienne and yourself that you can manage your own life, but I think we need the order's help."

"I don't think the warning was for me," Lizzie insisted. "If the warlock was actively seeking me I would have been told by now, even with the power out. The order would have dispatched someone here if I was in any danger. They still have seers working around the clock to find the warlock, and they are still protecting me from him. But I will concede, the order does have resources that we don't in helping Emma. I'll go into town first thing tomorrow and call Vivienne on my cell."

Butterflies frantically beat their wings in her stomach, but not because she was going to talk to Vivienne. She knew exactly who in the order would be helping her with Emma's problem. She took another sip of coffee and stared at the fire, trying not to see Gideon's face in the flames.

Chapter Thirty-Six

The power had come back on in the early hours of the morning, and Lizzie could have called from home, but she needed to send Vivienne the photo of the spell that was on her cell anyway so she headed for town as promised. She chose to park in the empty lot fronting the public beach. The long stretch of sand was deserted, the rain keeping everyone away.

Lizzie sat in her truck staring at the phone clutched in her hand as the rain pattered on the roof of the truck and corrugated the surface of the lake. Before she placed the call she centered herself and made sure that the energetic walls around her thoughts and emotions were solid.

She needed to be careful Vivienne didn't sense her feelings about living here; about the townspeople's not so subtle message that she wasn't welcome. The last thing she needed was to admit to her mentor that living at Rose Cottage and turning her back on the order had been a mistake. Although it was true she was beginning to doubt the rightness of her decision, she wasn't about to abandon her little cottage, the life she was trying to forge for herself, and her friendship with Grandma Faye.

And then there was Wren. She still wasn't sure what to make of him, and she wasn't about to let Vivienne take a peek at the emotions swirling around a mental picture of the two of them making love in the stone circle.

When she felt centered and calm she turned on her phone and pulled up her directory. Tapping Vivienne's name, she connected the call. As was her habit, Vivienne picked up on the third ring.

"Lizzie, how are you?"

"I've been better," Lizzie replied. Those were not the words she'd planned to say, but hearing Vivienne's voice conjured up the powerful woman behind it, and the soul connection they shared. Keeping truths from Vivienne wasn't easy. "I'm not in danger or anything," she said, backtracking. "There's just been a few challenges and adjustments I've had to deal with. You know the kind of thing, city girl moving out to the country. Nothing a little time and experience won't fix." Lizzie looked down at her free hand and saw she was crossing her fingers.

"Mmm," was all Vivienne replied. "And there is nothing else going on, nothing that needs my attention?"

Lizzie thought she heard a smile in Vivienne's words but she couldn't be sure. She uncrossed her fingers. "Yes, there is, but it's not a huge deal and I didn't want you to think I'd gotten in over my head." So much for keeping her thoughts private. Lizzie bit her lip.

"Lizzie, you've proven you are very brave and capable of many things, but it's okay to admit when you need a little help. Now tell me what I can do."

Lizzie gave Vivienne a brief account of her first contact with Emma's spirit, the discovery of the binding spell in the cellar, the help she'd received from Grandma Faye, and what had happened during the séance. She held back on her hunch that Emma had protected her cottage from being struck by lightning. If Vivienne even suspected that the lightning was anything but an act of nature she'd have the whole order swarming around the cottage.

"And you've never felt any dark energies around Emma's presence?"

"No, if anything I think she's protective of me." She told Vivienne how Emma had scared off the local police when he'd tried to threaten her. "And there is something else. For some reason the binding spell affects my powers. If I'm down in the cellar they don't work at all. And I've noticed recently even when I'm in the main part of the house my magick is unpredictable."

"Does it affect Grandma Faye's magick in any way?" Lizzie was relieved Vivienne hadn't asked why she was using magick in her house to begin with.

"No, just me. Grandma Faye looked through her Book of Shadows to see if there was any mention of the spell, but there was nothing. After the séance she suggested we talk to you."

"And I'm glad you trusted her judgement."

"There is one more thing I should probably mention. Emma said something to me just before she disappeared, something that makes no sense. She said 'The Dark One knows, reveal your past and heal his sorrow.'"

There was an ominous silence on the line before Vivienne replied, and when she spoke her voice was firm. "During any of this did you sense anything familiar, anything that reminded you of the warlock who hunted you?"

"No, nothing. If I had I wouldn't have wasted time calling you, I'd have linked with you right away. And I would have welcomed every member of the order if it meant finally capturing that man. I wouldn't put Grandma Faye in danger. I may not want to be part of the order, but I'm not stupid."

"No, you are many things; strong willed and impulsive to name a few, but not stupid."

Lizzie opened her mouth to shoot back a retort, but snapped her jaw shut, clenching her teeth. At least Vivienne hadn't told her to calm down. And wasn't her mentor right? She was impulsive and strong willed. And if she was being honest with herself, she would add easily frustrated and overly sensitive.

She rubbed her eyes. "Sorry, I didn't mean to snap at you. I'm just feeling a little overwhelmed."

"It's okay, no need to apologize. So who do you think Emma

was referring to?"

"I've been thinking about it all morning. What if the person who placed her in the cellar and bound her spirit to the cottage is the dark one she is talking about? Maybe his spirit is trapped just as she is, but not from a spell but from remorse at what he did. Maybe in releasing her we can help heal his sorrow so he too can move on."

"It's plausible. But what about her reference about you revealing your history?"

"I know it doesn't make sense, unless...." Lizzie paused, trying to collect her thoughts. "I know this is going to sound far-fetched, but what if Emma and I are related? That her history is mine, and that is why my magick is affected by a spell designed to trap her."

"That could be the answer. Fate can be a rather tangled web. Maybe it was Emma's spirit that gave you the vision of Rose Cottage in the first place. Or your shared DNA means you already held the memories of Rose Cottage within you."

If Vivienne's conjectures were right, it meant Lizzie had a link to the past to a blood relative. She'd lived her whole life not knowing who her mother was, having no one to call family. Could Emma have given birth to at least one child? But how had the child escaped when Emma had not? And how would Lizzie track down this child when no record of her existed?

"We may be on to something. But the first thing to do is figure out the binding spell. You said you took a picture of it."

Vivienne's voice cut through the storm of questions swirling in Lizzie's mind. "Yes, hold on a sec." Lizzie put Vivienne on speaker while she called up the image and sent it off. Switching off the speaker, she put the phone back to her ear.

"Let's see what we have then." Vivienne's voice sounded farther away as she checked the screen on her phone. There were a few moments of silence as Lizzie imagined Vivienne examining the photo. Lizzie watched the lake as a blue heron swooped down and settled on a diving platform anchored out in the middle of the iron grey lake. The bird reminded her of an ancient Buddhist monk with his robes wrapped around him against the rain, his head tucked down in deep meditation.

"This is odd." Vivienne's voice snapped her out of her reverie. "I've never seen anything quite like it. What makes you think it's dark magick?"

"Grandma Faye said it was the way it felt. That it had the unmistakable energy of darkness."

"With her experience she would know. I'll send this off to Gideon. If there is anything in the libraries, he'll find it."

Lizzie could have kept her mouth shut, never said what was on her mind. But she couldn't let it go. Maybe Vivienne should add stubborn to her list of Lizzie's qualities.

"So Gideon's not back as a guardian?" Such a simple question...so why was her heart hammering in her chest?

"No, he is still at the archives. He had his hearing before the elders and they brought down their ruling. He's banned from guardianship for at least two years, and if he wishes to rejoin he must begin as an apprentice."

"Oh," was all Lizzie said. She couldn't think of what she could say to make any of it better for Vivienne, especially since she was the cause of Gideon's problems.

"But I don't think he will. He is where he has always wanted to be, and he seems happy."

Happy? The word filled her with anger. He had used Lizzie, whether he was aware of his motives or not, to get out of his responsibilities as a guardian and pursue his own path. Being used hurt more than the rejection. Had he even seen her as a person, or just a means to getting what he wanted?

"Well, I'm glad everything turned out well for him." She stared hard out at the rain, willing the walls around her emotions to stay strong.

"I'm sorry for the way he treated you."

Vivienne's words came as a surprise to her. When Gideon had crossed the line with Lizzie and broken his vow to the order, Vivienne hadn't blamed Lizzie but she'd been protective of her son. Her apology helped to soften the humiliation burning her cheeks.

"I know my apology can't undo the way he treated you. I am disappointed he hasn't shown you more compassion or respect. I raised him to be better than that. At least I thought I had."

It was strange for Lizzie to hear the sadness and confusion in her mentor's voice. It was her turn to extend the balm of healing to her friend.

"It's not your fault. In wanting to please you he'd placed himself in an untenable situation of following what he thought you wanted for him, instead of what his heart wanted to do. I really don't think he intended to be so callous with me. I know first-hand how our motives can get muddled when we are afraid of disappointing the ones we love."

"Perhaps it is as you say. And I do understand the need to follow one's destiny, but I wish he'd done it with a bit more courage and integrity."

"Don't condemn him too harshly. It's not like he broke my heart…he just bruised my ego." The truth of what she'd just admitted washed over her. Holding on to her hurt about Gideon was more about embarrassment and pride than any true feelings of betrayal. "But I do miss his friendship and his company."

"I think he misses that too, but he doesn't know how to mend what he's done. And I think his guilt is stopping him from doing something about it. It's times like this that I want to shake him by the shoulders and tell him to stop being such a big baby. But what do I know, I'm just his mother."

Lizzie laughed and Vivienne joined in with her deep-throated chuckle. "It is absurd, isn't it? I'm and elder of the order, powerful magick at my disposal, and I am helpless to understand my own child. Or to make him see what a nitwit he's being." Both women laughed harder.

"When you give him the information about the spell, tell him that I trust he will crack the mystery and that I look forward to hearing it from him." She closed her eyes and let out a breath, a feeling of lightness infusing her body. "And tell him I consider him a friend and always will." With those simple words Lizzie felt the last binding strings of emotional pain dissolve.

CHAPTER THIRTY-SEVEN

The rhythmic slap of the windshield wipers lulled Lizzie as she drove home. Her mind wandered gently over the terrain of her conversation with Vivienne, and the truths about herself she'd revealed. Asking Vivienne for help wasn't as bad as she'd anticipated. In fact, it had given her a measure of comfort to know Emma's release was imminent given the resources of the order. And as far as Gideon was concerned, her anger about the way he'd treated her was gone. It was more than time to let go of that festering thorn, and when she'd plucked it out she realized the letting go had been easier than the holding on. And now she had so much to look forward too; new skills to learn, new challenges to embrace.

So wrapped up in her thoughts, Lizzie was startled into wakefulness when she pulled up to the wrought iron gate of her property. She had no memory of the drive home. She left the truck running, scooted out to open the gate, drove through, and then securely latched it before driving up to the cottage. The air smelled of wet sand and a slight fishy odor from the lake.

Turning off the engine, she peered across the seat through the rain splattered passenger window. The front door of the cottage was standing wide open, even though she distinctly remembered shutting the door and turning the key in the lock.

Instead of fear, she felt outrage and a fierce protectiveness. If someone had hurt Bear…. She couldn't finish the thought. In one swift movement she flung open her door and leapt out of the truck. Rushing up the steps, she pulled up the magick coiled within, preparing to defend her dog and her home.

She had left a light burning in the kitchen when she'd left that morning, and the pale light gave her the advantage as she was standing in the relative darkness of the porch. As she pushed the door open wider, she stepped over the threshold, adrenaline and magick pumping through her veins.

She almost kicked the wicker basket that lay on its side just inside the door. Bits of cellophane littered the floor, a big green bow that looked like it had been chewed and spit out lay near the stove, a glass bottle filled with a deep red liquid rested on its side against the leg of the kitchen table, and a handful of apples and oranges were scattered over the floor. She powered down her magick, shaking her head at her feathered and four legged friends.

"What have you two done?" she said, scooping up the basket. Bear and Quinn both glanced up at her, their expressions indifferent to her annoyance, turning their attention back to the pie plate that had all but been licked clean.

She rescued the pie plate from her dog and the bird. "I can't believe you ate the whole thing." From the lingering scent of cinnamon and apples she assumed the plate had once contained an apple pie. "You know you're both going to pay for this. When you have tummy aches and the squitteers, don't expect any sympathy from me." Instead of looking contrite, Bear looked longingly as she placed the pie plate in the sink. Quinn studiously ignored her and started pecking at stray pastry crumbs littering the floor.

She gathered up the fruit, placing it in a bowl on the kitchen table, then retrieved the bottle from the floor. The handmade label said the deep ruby liquid was a strawberry wine. She placed it on the counter and scooped up the cellophane and bow. She found a hand-written tag peeking out from under the leather chair by the fireplace.

Welcome to Barton, compliments of the Ladies Auxiliary, the tag read.

Lizzie pondered the irony of the house warming gift. Since moving to the Kootenay's her house and truck had been vandalized, she been threatened by the local cop, called a bitch by her former contractor, and now she was getting a warm welcome and a gift basket, or what was left of it, from the women of the village. Shaking her head, she threw the packaging in the garbage.

"So how did the basket get in here?" She turned to the only other inhabitants of the cottage, but they didn't offer up an answer. Bear was slurping from his water bowl and Quinn had retreated to the arm of the couch and was preening his tail feathers.

"I know I locked the door behind me," Lizzie said to herself, and retraced her steps to the front door. She opened it and examined the salt line. It had definitely been disturbed, the line of protection broken. She had laid a fresh line before she and Grandma Faye had left that morning.

The thick line of the salt would have stopped anyone who wished her or any inhabitant of the cottage harm, so the broken line of salt could only have occurred if whoever had dropped off the basket was friend, not foe. But again, she knew she had locked the door when she left. The person who had dropped off the basket, upon finding no one home, more than likely would have left it by the door where it would stay dry under the porch.

That left only one other person, or should she say spirit, who could have unlatched the door so that Bear could have dragged the basket inside.

After restoring the salt line, she grabbed a broom and swept up the remaining crumbs from the floor. "Emma, I appreciate the thoughtfulness of not wanting the basket outside," she spoke to the air around her. "But next time could you just leave the door locked and let me deal with it?" Nothing stirred in the air around her and the temperature in the cottage remained steady.

"As for you, you little piggy," she said to her dog, who was now curled up on his bed by the hearth. "Time for you to go outside. Raining or not, you need a potty break, and seeing as you are in my bad books right now, I'm not going to wait around for you to do your business." She scratched the top of his head affectionately and clipped on his leash. "Let's go," she said, tugging on the leash. Slowly Bear got off the pillow, letting out a low groan that sounded almost human.

"Maybe next time you'll think twice about eating a whole pie." Bear hung his head in what Lizzie thought looked like shame, and ambled outside with Lizzie leading the way.

CHAPTER THIRTY-EIGHT

Lizzie sat up abruptly, knocking her book from her lap. She blinked and looked around the cottage, her eyes heavy with sleep, her thoughts sluggish and confused.

Bear hadn't stirred from his bed in front of the fireplace and was snoring loudly. She heard a softer snore, more like a wheeze, coming from the couch. Turning sideways, she spied Quinn asleep on the back of the sofa, his head hidden under his wing.

The only other sound was the persistent ticking of the mantle clock. She glanced at it, noting the time.

It couldn't be that late.

Lizzie scrubbed her face with both hands, trying to banish the groggy feeling and the sense of disorientation. She squinted at the clock again. It was after midnight.

Her mouth felt full of cotton and her throat clicked when she swallowed. She reached over and picked up the mostly untouched strawberry wine she'd poured herself earlier when she'd sat down to read her book before dinner, but the sickly sweet smell caught in her nose, making her gag. She put the glass back down on the side table.

She would have sworn that only a few minutes had passed since she'd poured herself her drink and settled on the couch to read. She couldn't recall feeling tired when she'd opened her book.

Slowly getting off the couch so as not to dislodge her sleeping crow, she put another log on the fire. Neither crow nor dog stirred as she moved about the cottage.

She padded in her socks over to the kitchen light, her feet barely making a sound. Her fingers found the switch already in the on position. She toggled the switch up and down but nothing happened.

"Not again," she sighed. She picked up the phone and hit the talk button. Nothing but silence greeted her on the line. If power outages were going to be par for the course living in her cottage, she'd have to get herself a generator. Or forgo the modern amenities like her fridge and opt for an icebox and her root cellar for keeping things cold. At least she could be thankful she was on a gravity fed water system. Even with the power out she had running water.

She poured herself a glass from the kitchen sink and downed the ice cold water in several greedy gulps, giving herself a chest freeze in the process. She left the tap running and splashed several handfuls of water on her face. Scrubbing her face dry on a tea towel, she couldn't banish a strange feeling that something wasn't right.

"Shit," she said aloud. "The chickens. I forgot to lock them in for the night." She knew from experience when dusk arrived, her chickens would take themselves into the coop without her help, but the door from the coop to the chicken yard would still be open, letting in the drafty night air. Grandma Faye had also warned her about the mink, raccoons, and skunks that liked to slink around at night and wiggle through the smallest of spaces. A single mink could devastate an entire flock in a matter of minutes.

Before donning her slicker and gum boots she scooped up the large flashlight from the laundry room and turned it on. She didn't really want to go there alone, especially with the power out. She wouldn't even have the porch light to illuminate the darkness, just the small beam of her flashlight.

She walked over to her sleeping dog and called out his name. He didn't move. Kneeling down she gently shook his shoulder. "Bear, time to get up."

He finally stirred and opened one heavy lidded eye, only to close it again.

"Bear, come on. I need you to come with me."

Her dog had started snoring again.

"You know, you're not turning out to be such a good guard dog. All you seem good at doing is eating your weight in dog biscuits, not to mention pies that aren't yours." Bear snored through her tirade. "Fine, stay where it's nice and dry, but don't expect any cookies any time soon."

She turned her back on her sleeping companions and stepped out into the night, closing the door behind her. She hesitated a moment and swung her flashlight in the direction of the chicken coop from the protection of the porch. The beam of light illuminated the raindrops in its path, turning them into silvery beads. The light didn't quite make it to the chicken yard, but from the quiet of the night Lizzie knew all the chickens had gone to bed.

It was less than a hundred feet to the coop, but once she stepped off the safety of the porch the hair on Lizzie's neck stood on end. She shivered. Panning the beam of light in a circle she squinted through the raindrops. There was nothing out there, or if there was the nocturnal hunters were adept at hunting on silent feet.

Lizzie scurried across the slippery grass, and after fumbling with the latch, stepped into the chicken yard, swinging the gate closed. The dirt in the yard had turned to a soupy mess from all the rain, and her foot skidded in the slippery muck. She pin wheeled her arms in an effort to stay upright, her free hand reaching out to the solid wall of the coop, stopping her fall. The chickens let out an angry squawk at Lizzie's clumsy thumping about.

"Sorry girls, it's just me," she said before unhooking the hatch-like door and sliding it closed. She heard them giving her an angry admonishment for disturbing their sleep as the door slid all the way down. Before leaving the yard she let the flashlight beam run the perimeter of the enclosure just to make sure there wasn't a stray chicken left outside. Ginger Chicken not only had a penchant for escaping, she liked to hang out by herself after her companions had gone to bed. But a quick survey revealed an empty mucky yard.

Just to be on the safe side she closed the gate to the yard and entered the coop from the human sized door at the front of the henhouse. She cupped the end of the flashlight to dim the beam before stepping inside. Her presence still garnered her some angry clucks as she panned the light across the roost. She did a quick head count. All her chickens were inside and safe. Spreading her fingers a little wider, she let more light spill out as she ran the beam across the floor. There were no dark shapes huddled in the corner, no one but chickens resided in the coop.

"Goodnight ladies. Sleep tight."

She was reaching out to open the door when she heard the snarling growl of an engine break the silence of the night. She froze, her head cocked as she listened to the sound grow louder as it moved up the driveway and past the coop. She knew the sound the vehicle made wasn't a car or a truck. It sounded to her like a motorcycle. Her heart knocked against her ribs, but it wasn't fear making her grip the flashlight tighter. It was anger.

There was only one reason why someone would be sneaking onto her property in the dead of night, and that reason couldn't be good. It had to be the teenager who had harassed her at the Burger Chalet. Him and his buddies. The fading sound of the engine told her they were heading towards her barn. She had visions of them spray painting the side of the building with crude epitaphs, or worse, setting fire to the structure.

Well, she wouldn't let that happen. If they had come like thieves in the night to scare her off, they were in for a surprise. If they wanted to dare each other to sneak onto the property of the witch of Rose Cottage, then it was their lucky day. Because she was going to give them a chance to experience magick up close and personal.

Locking the coop behind her, she skirted the wire fence of the coop and followed in the direction of the barn, keeping the flashlight pointed to the ground. She saw the distinct tire tracks in the wet sand and the trail in the wet grass where they had driven towards the barn. It wasn't a motorcycle. There were two tire tracks evenly spaced that dug thick grooves in the wet sand. Too small to be a car. *Some kind of ATV*, she thought as she detoured into the woods.

She wanted the element of surprise, so she veered towards the stone circle with the intent of coming around the barn from the other side. Keeping her hand cupped over the flashlight beam, she stood for a moment to draw up her magick and connect with the earth. There was no moon to light her way, as the low rain clouds had obliterated even the stars in the night sky. She would need all of her talents to negotiate through the woods and circle around to the barn without getting lost or tripping over a fallen branch.

When her powers unfurled and she felt the pulse of the earth rise up through her feet, everything around her changed. Instead of dark shapes of trees looming a few feet in front of her, she saw every tree and plant outlined in varying colors of energy. Everything was illuminated, even the rocks and small forest creatures lurking in the undergrowth. She snapped off the flashlight and picked her way through the forest in an arc that would bring her around to the side of the barn.

Her anger and her powers propelled her forward. She didn't feel the cold kiss of rain on her cheeks as she sidled around the side of the barn…there was only a building outrage at whoever had dared to come onto her property uninvited.

She was halfway down the side of the barn, hugging the wall, when she heard the sound of the large sliding door being pushed open. She stopped moving, her hands gripping the rough boards of the barn.

They had gotten inside. How did they know to bring a bolt cutter to cut off the locks she herself kept forgetting to do? And what were they intending to do once they got inside?

Her blood boiled. Pushing herself off the wall she marched around the corner, her hands held high, each one holding a glowing ball of blue light.

A large bright swath of light spilled out from the open doorway and across the wet grass. She narrowed her eyes, looking for her targets. Instead she found her handyman.

CHAPTER THIRTY-NINE

Large industrial lights illuminated every square inch of the barn. Just inside the doorway, an ATV was parked on the spotless concrete floor. A trailer hitched to the back of it was piled high with what looked like hay bales encased in black plastic. She could hear the tick of the engine as the metal started to cool. Two Gerry cans stood off to the side.

Audley was in the process of throwing one of the bales onto the trailer when she stepped out of the darkness.

"Audley, what are you doing here?"

At the sound of her voice he dropped the bale mid-swing and it thumped to the ground. He peered at the doorway and into the night, a look of bewilderment on his face.

Lizzie lowered her hands to her waist and stepped through the barn.

"Don't, Ms. Bennet. Stay where yous are," Audley shouted, but his warning came too late.

Lizzie walked straight into a ward placed around the door, and the power of it threw her backwards through the air.

She slammed into the wet ground, knocking the wind out of her. Raindrops splashed in her face and into her open mouth as she tried to catch her breath.

"Are yous all right?" The musk of pot overwhelmed her as Audley's rough hands gently grasped her shoulders.

Lizzie blinked raindrops out of her eyes as she finally caught her breath.

There was a ward on her barn, powerful magick, one that wasn't hers.

Audley helped her to sit up and she almost gagged at the strength of the pot smell surrounding him. She scrambled awkwardly to her feet, stepping back from Audley as she did. The smell wasn't just coming from her handyman, it was wafting from the barn as well.

"You're running a grow-op in my barn," she said with equal parts anger and indignation. "How dare you."

"You can't be here." Audley wrung his hands, ignoring her accusation. "You're supposed to be in the cottage." He seemed to be speaking more to himself than to Lizzie. "If you'd just stayed where you were supposed to be you'd have been safe."

Fear prickled down the back of her neck and she raised her hands again, drawing up her powers.

"Audley, I don't want to hurt you. Take your drugs and leave. I promise not to tell the police if you just go now." She prepared to throw her magick at the man that she'd come to regard as a friend.

He dropped his hands to his sides and looked at her as if he were pondering her proposal.

"You know you can trust me, Audley. I won't say a word to anyone. Just get on the ATV and go."

"He's not going anywhere." A voice spoke behind her. "And neither are you."

Audley looked past her, his eyes now holding a look of resignation. The cold bite of metal pushed against her temple as she struggled to turn and release her magick towards the man behind her.

"I wouldn't do that if I were you."

The stranger jammed the muzzle of the gun hard against the tender flesh of her temple. Lizzie stood still. She didn't have to turn around to know who the man with the gun was. She recognized his voice and the stench of cigarette smoke on his breath.

"I can put a bullet in your head faster than you can throw your spell, so I suggest you power those down. Your death is supposed to be an accident…a candle left carelessly burning, the whole cottage in flames, no survivors. But I will shoot you if I have to," Constable Whitley said, gripping her neck with his free hand, his fingers digging painfully into her skin. "Lower your hands, bitch."

Pushing her magick down into the earth, she took a ragged breath, trying to order her thoughts.

"Do you have to be so rough with her?"

"I'll do what I want to her," Whitley replied, shaking Lizzie by the neck to make his point. "Instead of worrying about her you should worried about what he is going to do to you when he finds out you screwed up. Get me a zip tie from the barn." Audley didn't move. "Now!" he roared, digging his fingers deeper into Lizzie's neck.

She flinched when her skin tore under the pressure of his sharp fingernails, but she didn't cry out. She watched Audley scramble back into the barn and over to the workbench that stood against one wall. Grabbing a thin plastic tie from a pile stacked in an old coffee can, he held it out to Whitley.

"But Miss Bennett never caused no harm. Why don't we do like she said and just get outta here? We can make the delivery and the boss will get his money." The zip tie quivered in his hand. "She won't tell no one, will you, Miss Benett?" He chanced a look at Lizzie. "And you'll leave and never come back, right?"

"Sounds like a great plan, Audley. Why don't we go back to the cottage and help her pack? Make sure she gets off safe and sound. Fuck, you're as dumb as a post. Of course she'll rat us out, if not to the police then to her little witchy friends. I'm not about to allow a bitch like her to ruin my career. And what do you think the boss would do to you if you let her go? What would he do to your precious Cathy?"

Audley blanched at the constable's threat. Panic rose in Lizzie's throat as she realized her slim chance of survival had vanished.

"Finish what you started and the boss will never have to know about your screw up."

"I can't. The wards she's placed on the cottage won't let me get in now. Not after what I've just done. And we're going to be late meeting the boats. They won't wait. If we let her go she won't tell. Right, Miss Bennet?"

"Yes," she whispered, her voice cracking.

"Jesus." Whitley jammed the gun muzzle harder into her temple. "That's not going to happen. Hands behind her back, and make sure you zip that nice and tight."

She fought against Audley as he guided her arms behind her back, but with his strength, Whitley's hold on her neck, and a gun digging into her temple, without her magick she was no match for the two men.

"Tighter," Whitley ordered. "You don't want her getting loose."

Audley hesitated a second before she heard the zing of the plastic teeth and the hot fire of pain on her wrists as the plastic cut into her skin.

When Audley spoke it was barely above a whisper. "What are you going to do with her?"

"The boss said he wanted her gone, and as far as I'm concerned it doesn't much matter how we do it. The fire will destroy any evidence anyway."

Something warm trickled down her wrists, trailing a thin line across her palms before the rain washed it away. Her fear tasted like metal at the back of her throat, but the biting pain at her wrists helped to cut through her panic. She closed her eyes and inhaled, slow and even.

Reaching out with her thoughts, she searched for her mentor.

"I'm sick of standing out here in the fucking rain. And we're running out of time. Put her in one of the stalls and we'll deal with her later."

Audley grabbed her by her bound wrists, but didn't push her immediately towards the barn. She felt a tug at her wrists, then a frantic sawing motion on the plastic. When Audley gently nudged her forward the pressure on her wrists had slackened.

Lizzie just needed a few more seconds. She dug in her heels and struggled against Whitley's hold on her neck as both men pushed her towards the barn. She felt the familiar tug and the flow of energy as the link was established.

"I've have had just about enough from you," Whitley growled in her ear as he moved the gun away from her temple.

Vivienne, help me..., she called out with her thoughts as Whitby slammed the butt of the gun down on her skull.

CHAPTER FORTY

Something warm and wet dragged across her cheek. She heard a low whimper before another pass of a wet tongue brought her around. Opening her eyes, she looked up at a big black nose. She was lying on her side, her hands still bound behind her, the smell of dust and old hay filling her nostrils. She was in one of the empty horse stalls.

Bear lowered himself until he was eye level with her. She tried to speak his name but her mouth had been taped shut.

Bear nudged her with his nose and scuttled back, issuing another urgent whine. She tried to oblige him, but lying on her side with her hands tied behind her back she couldn't find enough leverage to get in a sitting position.

She shook her head, a move she instantly regretted as her world tilted and spun. She squeezed her eyes shut until the spinning stopped.

When she opened her eyes Bear had moved in closer, and using his nose he pushed his head under her shoulder. Wedging his upper body underneath her shoulder, he leaned his weight into her and slowly stood up, pushing her into an upright position.

Once she was sitting up she scooted across the floor, grateful Audley hadn't thought to bind her feet. When her back made contact with the rough boards of the stall she pushed and wiggled herself into a standing position, her shoulders in agony at the movement.

She strained against the binding at her wrists but they

wouldn't give, and only caused more pain for her efforts. She tried to wiggle her fingers but they had gone numb. Whatever Audley had done to the zip tie before Whitley had knocked her out had loosened it, but not enough for her to break or stretch the plastic and free her hands.

Planting her feet, she straightened up the best she could and started to draw up her powers, but instead of feeling a surge of energy she felt the air constricting around her. She stopped and the weight around her lessened. The ward on the door wasn't the only magick at work in the barn.

She wasn't sure how to convey to her dog what she wanted him to do with her mouth still gagged, but it turned out she didn't have to. Bear moved around her and put his mouth on the plastic at her wrists. She felt the scrape of his teeth as he clenched the tie in his jaw. In unison, they both pulled in opposite directions. Lizzie screamed as the plastic dug deeper into her wrist, the duct tape muffling her outcry.

Finally she felt the tie snap and she tumbled headlong across the stall, falling in a heap into the dusty straw. Bear stood over her, his doggy breath warm on her face.

Peeling on a corner of the duct tape at her mouth, she then braced herself and ripped it off in one pull. Her lips burned and her face stung like she'd been bitten by a thousand fire ants. She tasted blood.

With one hand on Bear's broad back and the other pressed against the worn boards of the wall, she eased herself upright, trying to make as little noise as possible. She listened intently as she crept along the side wall towards the stall door, but all she heard was the rain clattering on the roof and the wind whistling through the siding of the barn.

Peering over the stall door, she looked down the barn aisle in both directions. The barn housed six stalls, identical in size to the one she'd been thrown into. At the end of the short aisle there

307

was another barn door facing the back of the property and the forest beyond. That would have been her safest route, but she could see a shiny padlock securing the door from the inside.

Bear had to have gotten in somehow. In their rush to meet the boats, Audley and Whitley must have left a door ajar. But how Bear managed to walk through the wards was something else she didn't understand. She prayed to the Goddess that she could get out the way her dog had gotten in.

Reaching over the stall door, her fingers found the sliding bolt. Nothing happened when she touched the cold metal. She was grateful for small mercies; her captors hadn't thought to secure it with a ward. They knew she was a witch, but they obviously didn't know about her ability to recover quickly from injuries.

Easing the bolt back, she then swung the door inward, cringing when the rusty hinges shrieked. She held the door open, but waited before stepping through. There were no footfalls to indicate someone was coming to investigate the sound. It looked as if she was alone.

She slipped through the door with Bear following at her heels. His nails clicked loudly on the concrete floor. When she came to the end of the aisle she entered the small open space where the ATV had been parked. Both doors were closed.

She looked down at her dog. "How did you get in?" she whispered. He looked up at her and gave her a big doggy grin, his tongue lolling out to the side.

Approaching the man door first, she took a cautious step towards it. Maybe they had left this door open and ward free. Bear could have snuck in and the wind could have shut it behind him. It was as good a theory as any.

She tried one more time to call up her powers, but as soon as she did the air around her thickened, pressing against her skin. Her magick fizzled like a short circuit. She dropped her hands and gulped a lungful of air as the atmosphere lightened.

She held out her hands and slowly approached the door. What she felt made her heart sink. Even without her extraordinary talents she knew there was a ward in place by the way the fine hairs on her arms stood up the closer she got to the door.

She walked over to the larger door that had been open when she'd discovered Audley, but it too made her hair stand on end the closer she got to it. She had managed to get out of her bindings, but she was still well and truly trapped.

But how did her dog get in?

She knelt down in front of Bear, digging her fingers into the thick fur around his neck. "Let's go home, Bear," she said in a sing-song voice. "Let's go get a cookie. Do you want a cookie?"

The dog's tail wagged enthusiastically and he took a few steps away from her, his front legs held out stiffly as he jumped a few inches off the ground. "Yes, let's get you a cookie." He replied by giving her a woof, and headed for the man door she'd already assessed as being charmed. Maybe she'd been wrong about the ward. She started to follow him when she heard the rattle of a door handle. She'd run out of time.

Scanning the nearly empty barn for something to use as a weapon, she spied a few farm tools propped up on the opposite wall. She raced over to them and grabbed a pitchfork, but as she lifted it up the tines fell off the rotted handle and clanked to the floor.

As she looked for something else to use, the whole door shuddered in its frame. Lizzie threw a panicked look over her shoulder at the door when she noticed Bear was gone.

She dropped the useless pitchfork handle to the floor and clutched at a shovel. Whipping around, the shovel held aloft, she snuck behind the door. She was just about to lower the shovel with all the force she could muster when Bear trotted in, his fur lightly sprinkled with rain.

309

She was so shocked at the reappearance of her dog she failed to use the few seconds she had to lower her weapon down on Audley as he followed close behind her dog.

"Don't, Miss Bennet, please don't," Audley said, holding his hands above his head. "I'm here to rescue you, and we don't have much time before Whitley realizes I've sneaked off." He spoke in ragged gasps, his face a deep crimson as if he'd run the whole way from the beach. His hair was plastered to his skull, water running down his face in rivulets.

"Rescue me. Are you kidding me? So far, by my count, you've drugged me, tied me up, gagged me, and did nothing to stop Whitley from cold cocking me," Lizzie panted, still holding the shovel aloft. "Bear, shouldn't you do something? This man tried to kill me."

Bear cocked his head, and instead of lunging at Audley or even growling, he licked Audley's hand.

"Really, Bear? He's the enemy."

"No I'm not." He held his hand out to her. "If we don't go now it will be too late, and then you *will* be dead. Please."

She heard the fear in his voice. But it was the sound of an approaching ATV that convinced her to trust her handyman. Audley heard it too and his eyes widened. Lizzie stepped towards him. "How do I get through the ward?"

"Take my hand, and don't let go until we've walked over the sill." He held his hand out to her. She dropped the shovel, knowing it would be useless against Whitley's gun, and grabbed Audley's outstretched hand. She felt the rough scrape of his callouses as he closed his fingers around hers in a bone crushing grip.

"Come on," he urged, and led her out into the night.

CHAPTER FORTY-ONE

As she stepped across the threshold, all the hairs on her body stood on end as an electrical buzz danced over her skin, making her nose itch. As soon as they were clear of the door, she pulled her hand out of Audley's grip.

The growl of the all-terrain vehicle's engine filled the air, muting the steady drumming of the rain. They both turned to look towards the cottage and driveway. The rain was coming down in torrents, and the darkness obscured the path to the chicken coop and beyond. The light from the ATV's headlights bit into the night, two bright eye's searching for its prey. It was headed directly towards them.

"Run," Audley said, pushing Lizzie towards the forest. This time she didn't argue. She tore off into the darkness with Bear at her side.

She'd only run a few yards before her feet slipped on the wet grass. She stopped and looked back. Audley was still standing by the barn, his body outlined by the light spilling out of the door. The ATV was gaining ground, its headlights fast approaching Audley.

"Audley, hurry up," she shouted over the noise of the approaching vehicle. The sound of her voice seemed to snap him out of his trance. He ran towards her, his arms waving frantically.

"Go, Miss Bennet, I'm right behind you."

She dashed into the forest, but didn't get very far before tripping over an exposed tree root. Grabbing frantically at a nearby tree she broke her fall, her hands gripping the wet crumbly bark. If she were to have any hope of navigating through the dark woods she needed her magick at full power, unhindered by the ward on her necklace.

Tearing at the silver chain around her neck, she yanked as hard as she could. The chain slipped through her fingers and onto the mossy ground.

Through ragged breaths she called up the energy from the ground, opening herself up to its power, at the same time letting loose her own magick. She'd lost precious seconds, but now she could see everything illuminated by their own energy fields. It was like looking at an old photographic negative. Unhindered by the darkness she plunged deeper into the forest, Bear, a shimmering shape of undulating gold and silver, running a few feet ahead of her.

She knew even in her heightened state she wouldn't be able to outrun Whitley…they hadn't got enough of a head start. She just needed to gain a bit of distance so she could draw up her powers to their full strength and take careful aim. She'd only have one chance at stopping Whitley.

Suddenly the roar of the ATV's engine died, and all she could hear was the drumming of the rain and her crashing footfalls. Then she heard it; the crack of gunfire. She stopped running and looked behind her. She couldn't see Audley, not even with her magick.

Someone crashed through the forest close behind her. A shout, a growl of frustration. It wasn't Audley's voice she heard. She felt the intense fear of prey being pursued by a predator. Bear was a few yards ahead of her and she launched herself in his direction, flying past the trees.

Whitley was almost upon her, his thundering footsteps just off to her right. How could he negotiate the dark reaches of the forest so quickly? She could only manage it because of her magick.

It hadn't occurred to her that maybe she wasn't the only one who possessed the abilities. She'd assumed the boss they had referred to was the one who knew how to weave wards, but perhaps all the men working for him practiced the dark arts.

She could see the outline of the stone circle glowing and throbbing like a heartbeat, guiding her. A few more feet and she'd have reached the edge of the stones. Another crack sliced through the night, echoing through the woods. Her right shoulder erupted in a burning sensation of ice and fire, and she bit down to keep the scream from escaping her lips.

She sprawled to the ground just inside the stone circle, slamming her injured shoulder into the wet ground. This time she screamed.

In one fluid move, Bear leapt over the stones and turned to face the direction where Whitley was crashing through the trees, closing the distance. Lowering his head, the great ruff of fur around his neck standing out like a huge mane, he growled menacingly, his teeth bared. His incisors gleamed in the moonlight as he stepped towards the edge of the circle just as Whitley broke through the clearing.

Rolling onto her knees, Lizzie then pushed herself up into a crouch. Whitley stood a few paces away, turning his head slowly, scanning the small clearing. She blinked through the rain, raising her head to look at him. She understood now how he'd managed to track her so effortlessly through the darkness. On his head was a pair of goggles with huge protruding lenses. He looked like a hybrid of man and machine. He was wearing night vision goggles.

"There you are, bitch," he said, his head swinging in her direction, pinning her with the bulging unblinking lenses of the goggles. As he raised his gun, Bear launched himself at Whitley.

"Bear!" Lizzie screamed as Whitley pulled the trigger. One moment Lizzie was watching her dog sail through the air on a collision course with Whitley, the next her dog disappeared. Lizzie ducked involuntarily as the bullet whizzed past her head. She heard the thwock as it imbedded itself in a tree behind her.

Whitley let out a guttural sound, swinging his gun wildly in front of him, searching for her dog. He was nowhere to be seen.

Anger replaced fear as Lizzie pulled herself into a standing position, swaying slightly, the edges of her vision graying. She ignored everything—the pain in her body, the relentless rain, the fear that rolled over her in waves—and focused on pulling her magick into her left hand.

It came when she called it forth but it felt different, weaker than it should be, the bullet wound in her shoulder hampering her abilities. She knew she would have just one chance of hitting Whitley before he let off another shot, and she prayed her magick was strong enough.

Raising her left hand that now held a flickering blue light, she let out a laugh. Even to her own ears it sounded hysterical. Whitley raised his gun again, the muzzle pointed directly at Lizzie's chest. If this was to be her last moment, she wasn't going out alone.

Before either of them could do anything, all the hairs on her body stood at attention, a feeling akin to what it had felt like to walk through the ward on the barn, but a thousand times more intense. There was a pressure, as if a shock wave passed around her. She swayed, trying to keep her feet underneath her, and seconds later she watched Whitley do the same.

Instead of pulling the trigger, Whitley looked past her and over her shoulder. She was just about to turn around when Wren spoke. "Don't turn around, Elizabeth. Close your eyes."

His voice held such power and authority that she did as she was told. Even with her eyes closed the burst of light was so intense she raised her good hand to cover her eyes.

She heard Whitley yowl. Not a cry of triumph, but one of

pain. A pulse of energy enveloped her as the bright light winked out. She didn't jump or pull away when Wren took her hand, his strong fingers gently curving around her palm. She tried to make her fingers grasp his hand but they wouldn't respond.

"Elizabeth, you can open your eyes now," Wren said, his voice urgent put not panicked. "I cannot be the one to end this. You must do this; use my energy, let it flow through you."

Lizzie looked around for Whitley. He was stumbling around like a drunk, frantically clawing at the straps that held his night vision goggles securely to his head, his gun nowhere in sight.

She did as Wren asked, not once taking her eyes off Whitley, who was still screaming in pain but had managed to throw off his night goggles. He pressed the heels of his hands to his eyes.

As the warmth of Wren's energy flowed up her arm and into her body, she was suffused with such power that the pain of her injuries dissolved in the glowing perfection of his energy. The blue light she'd summoned earlier grew bigger, the color more intense, golden threads sparking in its center.

She'd never felt power like this before. Raising her hand, she drew back her arm. She knew with complete and cold certainty if she let fly the energy undulating in her palm, Whitley would not be as lucky as the last man she'd used her powers on. No, if she threw this energy at him he would be nothing but dead.

Deliberately turning from the anger roiling in her chest, she powered down the energy in her hand until the deep color lightened to the pale blue of a morning sky. She breathed in, and on the exhale she lobbed the light at Whitley. He gasped when it hit him square in the chest, but instead of flying off his feet as he would have done if Lizzie had hit him with the full force of her power and anger, he merely crumpled to the ground and remained there.

With the last of the fight gone out of her, her legs gave way, and she would have collapsed on the mossy ground if Wren hadn't been there, holding her now by the waist.

A wet nose nudged her good hand and she looked down. Bear was standing at her side. With Wren's help she slowly lowered herself to her knees and dug her fingers into Bear's thick fur, now hanging in wet ringlets around his shoulders. She picked out a stick and a few leaf bits stuck to his back, the whole time checking his body for injury. He was unscathed. She kissed his wet nose and was rewarded with a slurpy dog kiss.

After Wren helped her stand up again, he left the circle and headed towards Whitley's prone body. Without Wren's energy supplementing her own, all of her injuries came alive, from the lacerations on her wrists to the gunshot wound in her shoulder. But she was alive.

She held onto Bear's broad back when the grayness threatened to swamp her vision, before joining Wren next to the man who had tried to kill her. Bear followed silently.

"Is he dead?"

"No, just unconscious," Wren said.

She didn't ask how he knew without kneeling down to check for a pulse. "We should probably tie him up in case he comes around. There are zip ties in the barn."

Wren looked at her quizzically.

"To bind his wrists," she said.

"There's no need," he said, lifting up his shirt to reveal an intricately tooled leather belt around his waist. He wasn't wearing his fish and wildlife uniform. Instead he had on a light colored loose-fitting tunic and dark trousers. The rain had plastered his shirt to his skin, and she could see the outline of his broad chest and powerful arms. She noticed with some curiosity that he was barefoot.

He quickly undid his belt, and after rolling Whitley onto his side, bound his wrists behind his back. Once that was done, Wren propped the unconscious cop under the boughs of a huge cedar tree to give him some protection from the rain.

Wren stood up and addressed her. "Elizabeth, we've got to get you back to the cottage and attend to your injuries. You're bleeding." He took her gently by her left hand. "Let's go. This man poses no danger to you now."

While she'd been watching Wren secure Whitley she'd become very tired, the drag of sleep making her limbs heavy. But when he mentioned her injuries she felt a jolt of panic instantly pulling her back from her magickal sleep that would bring about her remarkable healing.

"Oh my God, Audley. He shot Audley." She stumbled towards the direction of the barn before Wren caught her. "We need to get to the barn."

"Who's Audley?"

"He's my handyman. He was a part of all this, but he tried to rescue me. He faced Whitley alone to give me more time to escape, even though he knew Whitley had a gun and he was unarmed. We have to go."

Lizzie tried to pull away from Wren but his grip was too firm.

"We are going but you are too weak to walk," Wren said matter-of-factly, and proceeded to scoop her up in his arms.

He traced his way through the trees as if he'd traveled the route a thousand times, his feet never stumbling even though the cloudy night sky still hid the moon. He moved with grace and speed, as if he wasn't carrying her at all.

Leaning her head against his shoulder she could hear his heartbeat, strong and slow. He smelled of cedar and moss and rain. Before she knew it he was placing her gently on her feet.

Audley's body was only a few feet from the barn. Light spilled out from the door they had fled through, splashing a band of light across his legs, the rest of him remaining in the shadows. He had landed face down with his arms splayed out at his side.

"Audley," she whispered as she let go of Wren's arm and

knelt before her handyman. Despite what she now knew he'd done to her, tears clogged her throat. He'd come back to save her and sacrificed himself on her behalf. "Help me roll him over."

With Wren's help she gently positioned Audley on his back. Brushing mud and leaf matter from his face, her fingers caressed it. His skin was cold to the touch.

"Please, please, please, don't be dead." She searched for a pulse at his neck, but all she could feel was the throbbing of her own heartbeat in her fingertips. "Wren, help him. Give him your energy like you gave me," she pleaded.

"I can't, Elizabeth. And even if I could it's too late. His spirit has flown and there is no calling it back."

"No," she screamed. "It's not too late." Drawing in a breath, she pulled up the earth's energy and expanded her perception. She struggled to keep the connection as the energy flowing up into her hands.

She could see Wren was right...there were no sparks of life emanating from Audley's body, just a dark void in the outline of his form. Still she persisted, placing her hand on his chest, willing Audley's heart to beat. Wren gently tugged on her good shoulder, pulling her away from Audley.

"Leave me alone," she screamed, trying to shake Wren off, but all it did was cause a shooting pain down her arm. "He can't be dead, he just can't," she said through clenched teeth.

"You heard what she said, get your hands off her."

Lizzie's powers faltered. Twisting her torso around, causing new ripples of pain in her injured shoulder, she shouted, "No Grandma Faye, it's okay, he's a friend." The grayness around her vision returned. She blinked around the dark threatening to swallow her and focused on her neighbor.

The old woman stood with her feet planted, a rifle aimed at Wren's chest. The oversized green plastic rain parka she wore billowed out around her, making her look like a giant green mushroom wielding a rifle.

"You can put the gun down, he saved me." As Lizzie spoke Wren stood up and turned to Grandma Faye.

If Wren was afraid Grandma Faye was going to shoot him he didn't show it. Instead he bowed deeply and spoke, "Esteemed Grandmother. It is an honor to make your acquaintance."

The effect of his words on her friend left Lizzie blinking, not from the relentless rain but from sheer puzzlement. As soon as he'd spoken Grandma Faye threw down her weapon as if she'd accidentally pointed a gun at the queen. She curtseyed, her voluminous skirt pooling around her. "Honored Light-Bringer, I am humbled in your presence," she said, rising from her curtsey.

In unison they spoke, "May the Goddess guide you, may Gaia protect and provide. May balance be your watchword and compassion rule your heart. So mote it be."

"Forgive me, Light-Bringer. Your kind hasn't honored us with your presence in several life times. I meant no harm, I was only protecting Lizzie. I received a call from the order saying they received a distress call from my friend." She stepped forward, her arms out at her sides, her palms facing down and away from Wren.

"The order is still in existence. That's good to know," Wren said, nodding. "And there is no need to apologize for caring about your friend. The one who wished her harm has been dealt with. But our Elizabeth has been injured and needs our assistance."

On hearing those words Grandma Faye scrambled to Lizzie's side, kneeling in the wet grass. "You've been shot," Grandma Faye said, surprise in her voice. She gently laid her hand just below the spot on her shoulder blade where the bullet had entered. "Did Audley do this to you?" She glanced over to Audley's body as she asked the question.

"No, he saved me. It was Whitley, he killed Audley too." Lizzie couldn't bear to look at Audley's body. She stared down

319

at her hands.

"And where is Whitley?"

"Tied up under a tree just outside the stone circle."

"Stone circle?" Grandma Faye asked.

"About two hundred yards from here." The darkness around her vision pushed in. "He and Audley are running a grow op in my barn. They were supposed to meet some drug runners up on the beach somewhere to make the delivery. They were going to kill me. I tried to reach out to Vivienne." Lizzie began to shake.

"You did, she heard your call. A team from the order should be here any moment. Come now child, we need to get you out of the rain and your injuries looked after." Grandma Faye gathered Lizzie in her arms.

Her body's need to heal itself won the struggle with Lizzie's attempt to stay conscious.

"I'm sorry, but I think you're going to need to carry me," she mumbled. She didn't hear her friend's reply as the darkness pulled her down.

CHAPTER FORTY-TWO

The warmth of the sun felt good on her bare shoulders. Sighing, she stretched her arms in the air, then sat on the top step of the porch and waited expectantly, her gaze focused on the driveway. The sun stood at high noon in a sky of saturated blue. It was always noon when she found herself in this particular dream plane.

She smiled as a figure approached her from the sandy drive, looking completely polished as always and out of place in such rustic surroundings.

"Vivienne," she called out, leaving the porch to greet her mentor.

They embraced before they both took a seat back on the porch steps.

"So what day am I on?" Lizzie asked.

"Day two."

"One more to go before I return. Are you there with me at the cottage?"

"Yes, as is Grandma Faye and your dog Bear. He hasn't left your side since you entered your healing time."

As if Vivienne's words had summoned him, the dog appeared on the porch, his big furry bulk insinuating himself between the two women.

"Bear," Lizzie exclaimed. "What are you doing here?" He slurped her cheek, making her laugh, then turned his massive head towards Vivienne.

"Hello handsome," Vivienne said, scratching him behind the ear. He settled between the two of them, letting out a deep sigh before placing his head in Lizzie's lap.

Lizzie ran her hand absently over his neck. She regarded her dog then looked at her mentor quizzically. "Have you ever heard of animals entering the dream plane of another?"

"Usually only if the animal is the familiar of a wise woman. Perhaps he's yours."

"No, I don't think so. Quinn is more likely my familiar according to Grandma Faye. Oh my God, is Quinn all right? When I left the cottage that night both he and Bear were asleep in the cottage, drugged as it turned out."

"Quinn's the raven?"

"Yes." Lizzie's heart quickened with anxiety.

"He's fine. It took him longer than your dog to come around, but according to Grandma Faye he's eating you out of your supply of peanut butter."

Lizzie laughed. Yes, if Quinn was back to eating his body weight in peanut butter, he was definitely feeling okay. She looked down at Bear, who was still resting his head in her lap. "So if he is not my familiar, why does he...," she indicated to Bear, "have the ability to visit me here?"

Vivienne gave her an amused smile. "I'll leave the explaining to Grandma Faye. After all, she was the one who figured it out. But I will tell you what you've missed while you've been here. My team and I arrived shortly after Grandma Faye found you and brought you back to the cottage. The team did a thorough sweep of the barn and found a very sophisticated and well run marijuana grow op beneath the structure. The business was probably raking in a least a few million a year."

"There is another whole level under the barn?"

"It was cleverly concealed in one of the horse stalls. There is a trap door that fits so cleanly that if you didn't know what you were looking for, you wouldn't have seen it."

Lizzie's eyebrows furrowed. Her recollection of that night was hazy at best, as if she'd been given only a few random photographs of the events, just quick images of Audley and Whitley subduing her, escaping the barn, running through the forest, and then seeing Grandma Faye wielding a shotgun. She knew there was more that happened that night, but she couldn't pull the sequences of events from her memory. She rubbed her temples in annoyance.

"Lizzie, is there something wrong?"

"I don't know. I can't remember everything that happened. Like pieces are missing."

"That not surprising, seeing how you were knocked on the head and shot. And Grandma Faye's told me this wasn't the first time you've received a blow to the head in recent weeks. Even with your quick ability to heal, that kind of head trauma can affect the memory. Give yourself time to heal. The memories are there, you just need to give yourself time to get stronger."

Lizzie steered her thoughts away from Audley's body lying cold and lifeless in the rain. That was one memory she wished she didn't possess.

"What is the order going to do with Whitley, now that he's in your custody?" It was a guess on Lizzie's part, but based on Vivienne's reply she knew she'd been right.

"He's been held for questioning. We are just waiting for him to recover from the magick you threw at him...he should make a full recovery in a day or two. When we are done we'll hand him over to the RCMP. We have a few members of the order within the police force. He'll pay for his wrongdoing and for the death of your friend, but your involvement will be kept out of it."

Lizzie shoulders relaxed. At least she hadn't put him in an irreversible coma like she'd done to Madison's boyfriend.

"From the type of ward we found on the barn it's clear a

warlock had his hand in all this, and Whitley doesn't possess even an ounce of magick nor the intelligence to set up such a well-run scheme," Vivienne continued. "Whoever he is he's very clever. He's managed to slip through our surveillance and is on the run."

"Both men had mentioned a boss, but never by name. So he's a warlock. Makes sense," Lizzie said.

"There's something else you need to know." Vivienne reached out and grasped Lizzie's hand. "When a spell or ward is cast, the caster leaves behind their unique signature, rather like a set of fingerprints. The person who placed the ward on the barn tried to disguise their mark. It was clever, but not clever enough, as my team had the layers unraveled in a matter of minutes. The magickal signature on the barn, we've encountered it before. The seer's working your case are certain."

Even on the dream plane Lizzie felt a coldness wash over her. She stared into Vivienne's dark eyes.

"Whoever put that ward on the barn is the warlock we've been trying to capture, the one who's been after you. So can you think of anyone you've been in contact with out there that felt familiar, or even made you feel uncomfortable for no reason? And had visible injuries?"

There could be only one man who fit the description, and Lizzie shuddered at the thought that she had willingly invited him into her home, her sanctuary.

"His name is Jon Ryan. He was the contractor I hired to work on the cottage." Lizzie pulled her hand away from Vivienne's. "I don't know why I didn't put it together earlier, or at least suspect something wasn't right with him. He has injuries, but he'd said they were from a car accident. And every time I was around him I didn't feel like myself, like I was dreaming or drugged. I can see it now, but at the time it was as if I couldn't think straight around him."

"He was probably using some kind of thrall. It clouds the mind and makes you susceptible to suggestions from the caster. Your necklace may have protected you from the full power of his magick. Otherwise this whole situation could have ended up much worse."

"But you and everyone in the order said the warlock couldn't cast because of how badly I hurt him, so how could he cast a thrall on me?"

"I don't know, I really don't. And I'm sorry we underestimated his abilities."

"And how did he find me out here? Why didn't he kill me the moment he realized who I was, what I was?"

"I think he didn't try to kill you because he didn't know who you were. He obviously figured out you were a witch, but not that you are the one he's been hunting. Your energetic signature has changed somewhat since we ventured into the *In Between* together. So he may have thought you were a witch he could exploit once he figured out what magick you possessed. And as far as how he could affect you, even with you wearing the necklace and him being injured, something just occurred to me. I know this is a strange thing to ask, but is it possible he managed to get some of your hair, or fingernails, or even blood?"

Jagged electric sparks crawl across Lizzie's scalp as she thought about Vivienne's question.

"Blood. He has my blood. The first time I met him I accidently dropped a glass bottle and somehow managed to cut myself. He cleaned the wound with a handkerchief. I remember thinking it was charming that someone would still carry a handkerchief these days. But it wasn't that bad a cut...there wasn't much blood."

"It only takes one drop, or one hair from your head, or a fingernail clipping. He didn't need to be in complete possession of his power to use this type of dark spell. Not once he had your blood. The blood would strengthen his connection to you and

325

increase the power of the spell, but it's still a thrall. It has its limitations, as the castor needs to be physically near the subject, but he still managed to use it to his advantage."

"Audley, the man Whitley shot, do you think he was under this thrall so that he would do the warlock's bidding?"

"I doubt it. It takes too much energy and concentration to keep the spell in place, even with someone's blood, and as I said, it only works when the castor is in close proximity to his victim."

Lizzie thought about what Vivienne had said, and then a new realization dawned on her as she remembered something Whitley had said that night at the barn. "Audley seemed to be incredibly loyal to Jon, but what I assumed was loyalty may have been fear. Whitley said something to Audley about the boss not taking kindly to Audley's screw up, and that he'd take his anger out on someone named Cathy. I think Jon was using this person as leverage to get Audley to do his dirty work. Vivienne, you must find out who this person is…they could be in grave danger now that Audley's dead."

"Could this Cathy be his girlfriend or wife? Some relation to him?"

"I honestly don't know. I never asked about Audley's personal life. Oh Vivienne, you must do something, and quickly. Find out who this Cathy is and get her out of harm's way before it's too late."

"I'll head the search for this Cathy person, and promise you I'll do everything I can to keep her safe." Vivienne stood up, preparing to leave.

"God, I wish I wasn't stuck here for another day. I want to help. It's the least I can do for Audley. He saved my life." Rising off the step, she followed Vivienne part way down the drive.

"Even if you could end the healing and join us, you wouldn't be in any condition to help. The best thing you can do for all involved is to stay here and come back to us when the time is right. But as you said, time is urgent and I must get back. I can't let this Jon Ryan slip through our fingers again."

Lizzie watched Vivienne walk down the drive and then suddenly blink out of existence. Turning back to where Bear was waiting for her on the porch, she felt more helpless than she ever had in her life.

CHAPTER FORTY-THREE

"Drink the whole thing and stop making that face," Grandma Faye said.

After handing Lizzie a cup, she started breaking eggs into a large bowl at the kitchen counter. Lizzie peered into the sludgy brown liquid and tried not to wrinkle her nose at the smell rising from the steam.

"It smells like old socks and has green bits floating in it... and you want me to drink this?" Quinn, who was perched on Lizzie's good shoulder, leaned forward and eyed the tea. When the steam reached his beak, he shook his head and jumped from her shoulder to the back of a chair farthest away from where Lizzie sat. "See, Quinn thinks it smells horrible too."

"Quinn doesn't have to drink it because he wasn't the one who was shot. Even with the work of the healers and your own healing abilities, your shoulder still needs more time before it's a hundred percent. The tea will help with that."

Grandma Faye's words stopped her from saying anything more. Yes, she'd been shot, but she'd survived. She drank the tea without further comment, trying not to grimace as she swallowed. It tasted as vile as it smelled. Her eyes burned with the hot sting of tears. She looked away from Grandma Faye.

"What did the order do with Audley? With his body," she whispered.

Grandma Faye stopped whisking the eggs and joined Lizzie at the kitchen table. "They took his remains with them."

"Why?" Lizzie felt a tear slip down her cheek. Bear, who had been sitting by her feet, put his head in her lap. She scratched him behind his ears. "What possible use would he be to them now?"

"We have to protect you, erase any evidence of what happened. And as far as I know Audley had no family, at least none that he spoke of."

"He mentioned someone called Cathy. Did Vivienne tell you? Maybe they are related."

"Yes, she told me what you said to her while you were in the *In Between*. And before you ask, Vivienne has a team already looking for her. If Jon has her or she's in danger, they will find her. And if she is related to Audley, they will return him to her."

Lizzie clutched her tea cup. She wanted to hurl it against the wall, but instead she took another gulp of the bitter liquid. "Audley is dead because of me."

"No he's not. Audley was mixed up with Jon way before you entered the picture. He chose to work for Jon, and maybe it was to protect this Cathy person, maybe it was to make some easy money, we don't know. But we do know that he could have chosen to let you die but he didn't. He defied Whitley and Jon and came back to rescue you. If you want to blame someone, blame Jon."

"Why didn't I recognize that Jon was a warlock? He was in my house, he worked on my kitchen, and I never once picked up on who he was."

"I've known Jon longer than you, and I didn't suspect or pick up on it either. He's very good at using his dark talents to mask his magick even with the damage that you did to him earlier. Vivienne mentioned he'd gotten some of your blood, so add to what he still could do, he had quite the arsenal to use against you."

She thought about what Grandma Faye said, swirling the remaining tea around in the cup. "Yeah, that's why every time he was near me my thoughts would get all foggy, like I'd been drugged."

"And it explains why your magick missed its mark when you sent it at him the day your house was vandalized. He was protected. He was also responsible for you ending up in the cellar...it wasn't Emma who lured you down there. He sent Audley in to chloroform you and put you down there, but you recovered from the drug before he managed to get you down the ladder. That's why you ended up with the injuries to your head. You didn't accidently fall down the ladder, Audley dropped you when you started to struggle."

"How do you know this?"

"Whitley. As soon as he regained consciousness he started singing like a bird. He ratted on all the major players in the drug operation, and it turns out a few were prominent members of the village."

Lizzie downed the rest of her tea and pushed the cup away. Despite the feelings of sadness and anger tumbling and knocking around in her chest, Lizzie's stomach growled loudly.

"You need to eat. Three days without food, you must be starving. And although it's after midnight, you're getting breakfast. The members of the order have eaten you out of house and home, and I haven't had time to replenish your larder." Grandma Faye patted her hand and resumed whisking eggs at the counter.

"Eggs are fine." Lizzie swiveled in her chair to watch her, being careful not to bang her injured shoulder. The lacerations on her wrists were healed, with just faint ghostly outlines encircling them. Grandma Faye had told her that the healers had removed the bullet in her shoulder, and although the wound had closed over it still required time to heal completely. When Lizzie had tested her shoulder the pain warned her not to push it.

"So everyone's gone?" she asked as she watched Grandma

Faye slide a generous pad of butter off a knife and into the hot skillet. The butter sizzled, filling the cottage with the comforting smell. Bear lifted his head from Lizzie's lap, his nose twitching.

"Yes, it's just us. But Vivienne did place a crystal grid around the whole property, and the seers are watching for any kind of intrusion. Plus a team is on alert and nearby if they need to be called in."

"Crystal grid?"

"It's similar to the protection ward you placed on the cottage, except it is reinforced by several large quartz crystals buried just below the surface. Very powerful magick." Grandma Faye placed several strips of bacon in a smaller pan, and as soon as they a started to sizzle Bear left Lizzie's side to sit near the stove, looking up adoringly at Grandma Faye.

"And what do you want, mister?" Grandma Faye said, waggling a wood spoon at Bear. He woofed in reply. "I suppose you're hungry too, from spending all that time with Lizzie. I guess I could find a few slices of bacon with your name on them."

Lizzie watched Bear dance in circles and then sit by the stove again. She couldn't help but smile.

"Vivienne said you figured out how Bear managed to join me during my healing time."

"Yes. Turns out Bear possesses magick."

"Magick? How? He's just a dog."

"Well, that's your fault."

"My fault?"

"Do you remember when we first met? When I came upon you treating Bear by the side of the road? I said I'd felt your power from my place.

"Yes."

"When you were healing him, do you remember blending your energy with him, maybe feeling his pain?"

"Yes."

"Because you acted intuitively and without proper training, you went too deep, connected too strongly, and left a bit of your own magick behind."

"How did you figure that out?"

"When I was bringing you back to the cottage after you fainted, he was following ahead of me, and then he just disappeared. At first I thought he'd just gone ahead, I wasn't really paying attention to him. But when I came to the cottage the door was shut and he was already inside." Grandma Fay plated the eggs and bacon and put it in front of Lizzie. Pouring a fresh cup of coffee, she placed it next to Lizzie's elbow.

"I didn't think too much of it at the time; I thought maybe the door blew closed with the wind. I figured it out before Bear decided to join you in your healing time. I'd come out to the living room to check on Quinn, and all the taps were turned on, even in the bathroom. I thought maybe Emma's spirit was acting up because you were hurt. I finally put it all together when the house was fairly quiet. Everyone had left except Vivienne, and she was with you in the bedroom. It was just me and the dog in the kitchen when I saw him levitate the cookie jar off the counter."

Grandma Faye pulled a plate out of the warming oven and dished it out to Bear in his bowl, adding a few strips of warm bacon.

"There you go, sweetie. Some sweet potato, rice, and bacon." She placed the bowl in front of Bear and he dug in with gusto. She placed a small plate of crackers and peanut butter on the table for Quinn.

"I've been watching him closely since you both woke up. He likes his water cold. So he turns the tap on to let me know he wants his bowl filled. The cookie jar I've hidden in the fridge; he hasn't figured out how to open it, yet."

"So you're telling me I accidently turned my dog into a spell wielding canine?"

"Apparently," Grandma Faye chuckled. Bear had finished his meal and walked over to the kitchen sink, looking at it expectantly. "Watch," Grandma Faye said.

Bear looked at Grandma Faye and then back at the sink. When Lizzie's friend remained standing by the stove, Bear sat down and eyed the taps. Lizzie watched in astonishment as the handle moved slowly until it was in the on position and water gushed from the faucet.

"See," Grandma Faye said, picking up Bear's water dish and filling it at the sink. She placed it at Bear's feet and he began to slurp noisily. "The only problem is he doesn't shut it off. Looks like you're going to have to teach him that one."

Lizzie eyed her dog while she sipped her coffee. "The day I discovered him up in the attic with Quinn, that was his doing, not Emma's. He and Quinn were playing a game with a stick when I found them. Somehow he'd used his abilities to get up there." Lizzie took another mouthful of coffee, hoping the caffeine would clear her thoughts. "And that's how he managed to come to me in the barn when I was tied up. I hadn't locked the cottage door when I went to put the chickens to bed, but I'd definitely latched it. Not to mention he just disappeared when I was looking for a way out."

"I think the word you are looking for is dematerialize," Grandma Faye said, pouring herself a cup of coffee and joining Lizzie at the table.

Lizzie rubbed her temples. "There's something else that happened. He did something when I was running into the woods, but I can't remember. Everything's a bit hazy still."

"What do you remember?"

"It's all disjointed. I definitely remember getting shot. It happened in the woods. And Bear attacking Whitley. But the next thing I remember is standing over Audley's body and you were there. I think I fainted shortly after that."

"It's not so unusual. You'd been hit on the head and shot. Plus, finding Audley dead. That's a lot for a person to process, even if you are a witch. Give yourself some time, I'm sure the memories will resurface." She patted Lizzie's arm and got up from the table. "Did you want any more food before I wash up?"

"No thank you, I'm stuffed. That was delicious." Lizzie pushed her chair away from the table.

"And where do you think you're going?" Grandma Faye said as she filled the sink with soapy water.

"I thought I'd help with the dishes. It seems the least I can do, seeing as you rescued me and took care of Quinn and Bear. And I have no doubt you've been looking after my chickens too."

"I don't need your help to clean a few dishes, so sit your butt back down, missy." Grandma Faye wagged a soapy finger at Lizzie. "And putting your girls to bed at night and feeding them is hardly a chore."

"Speaking of animals, who's looking after your place...?" Lizzie couldn't bring herself to say now that Audley was gone. The eggs and bacon she'd just eaten felt heavy in her stomach. She tried to steady her hand as she took another gulp of coffee, but the dark liquid trembled in the cup before she could bring it to her lips.

"I called a young girl from town, her name is Birdie Hapscomb. Nice young thing...don't know if you've had a chance to meet her. She was happy to oblige, as she seems to be between jobs."

"I do know her. She sold the cottage to me. I thought the sale of this house was her ticket to a full time job, but just after I moved in I saw her working at the Burger Shack. I'm not sure what happened, and she didn't seem like she wanted to talk to me at the time."

The two women remained silent, Lizzie finishing off her coffee while Grandma Faye stacked clean dishes on the dish rack to dry.

"She lost her job because of me."

"She wasn't supposed to sell the cottage to you."

Both women spoke at the same time.

Grandma Faye leaned against the counter, drying her hands on a dishtowel.

"Whitley told Vivienne that Eric Stubbs, the man who owns the realty office, was part of the drug ring, along with the bank manager. He pulled the file off the books, but obviously forgot about the one in the basement. The one Birdie found."

"But why not just buy the house? Or put the property in one of his lackey's names? If he'd done that I never would have come into the picture and spoiled all their plans."

"No, this way was perfect. There are no legal documents tying the property to Jon or anyone associated with his drug operation. No paper trail, no evidence. As far as the bank is concerned the property is a loss, since there is no development potential. No one wants to buy a run-down cottage in the middle of nowhere with a reputation of being haunted. When they realized Birdie's mistake and that you'd bought the property, they did their best to scare you off. You just proved too stubborn. Also, did you notice how you never once tried to get inside the barn even though you've been living here for over a month?"

"Yes, it was like I'd forget it was even there, except when I found myself walking in that part of the property. And then I would think that I needed to get the locks cut off, but as soon as I walked away it was like it didn't exist."

"It was because of the spell Jon placed on it."

Lizzie rubbed her eyes with the heels of her hands. So much had happened, things she couldn't remember. A part of her wanted to go back to the *In Between* and just forget all that had happened. Especially Audley. She looked up to see Grandma Faye staring at her.

"Go sit by the fire. I'll be right back...I just need to get more fire wood."

"I'll do it."

"No you won't. You need to take it easy, and it's still raining like cats and dogs out there, has been since that night." Grandma Faye threw on her rain poncho and headed towards the back door, but stopped and looked at Bear. "Come on, big boy, you need to go outside and do your business." Bear looked at Grandma Faye and back at Lizzie, but didn't move to follow the old woman. Grandma Faye put her hands on her hips, the plastic poncho crackling when she moved. "I know you don't like the rain, but you need to go outside. You can have a cookie when we get back."

Bear tilted his head at the word cookie and stood up. Lizzie expected her dog to follow Grandma Faye to the door, but instead he gave himself a shake and then disappeared. Even though Grandma Faye had told her what her dog could do, seeing it herself gave her a jolt.

"Did I mention your dog is a bit of a show off? We'll be right back," she chuckled as she stepped into the back room and out into the night.

CHAPTER FORTY-FOUR

Minutes later, Bear materialized back inside the cottage. Even his brief sojourn into the night had his thick fur already forming wet ringlets. He stood a few feet from Lizzie and gave himself a hearty shake, spraying water everywhere. Satisfied he was dry enough, he trotted over to his dog bed by the fire and lay down with a groan.

Lizzie shot her dog an annoyed look, but he was already sound asleep in front of the fire. Shaking her head, she followed Grandma Faye's earlier path out the back door, but before she stepped off the back steps the push of rain and wind made her grip the wood railing. Squinting through the curtain of water, she could see Grandma Faye's silhouette bending and straightening as she piled firewood into a wooden crate at her feet. The pool of yellow cast from the porch light highlighted only the lower half of the old woman's body and her rubber boots. The wind caught the edge of her rain poncho and it fanned out behind her like batwings.

Lizzie made to join Grandma Faye at the woodpile, but as she took a step anticipating one more wooden riser, her foot made contact with nothing but air. A brief shock registered in her limbs as her foot twisted beneath her on the ground. Lizzie felt herself falling and grabbed at the railing, wrenching her bad shoulder before ending up kneeling in the mud. She let out a cry of shock and pain.

She heard the clatter of logs and the crinkle of plastic as

Grandma Faye ran towards her, her rubber boots making a sucking sound with each muddy step.

"Lizzie, are you all right? Did you hurt your shoulder?"

She raised her head, and in the split second before her lungs expanded to answer Grandma Faye, Wren's face was before her eyes. He had taken her hand, said something to her. Then the vision was gone, leaving just rain and mud in her field of vision. She sat back on her haunches and looked up at her friend, shielding her eyes with her hand.

"I'm fine, just a bit clumsy. I miscalculated the number of steps." She allowed Grandma Faye to pull her into a standing position, careful not to jar her now throbbing shoulder.

"What are you doing out here?"

"I thought you could use some help bringing in the wood." Her thoughts still felt fractured…there was something about Wren. That night…had he been there?

"You came out in this without a raincoat and barefoot?"

Lizzie shrugged, looking down at her muddy feet. Why did she come out without at least putting on shoes?

"I appreciate the thought, but you can help by getting yourself inside. And stop pushing yourself. Do I need to bring up the point that you've been shot and not completely healed?"

"No," Lizzie replied, feeling like she was five years old.

"Go change into something dry and I'll be right in."

She obeyed, feeling fully chastised. Instead of helping, she'd delayed Grandma Faye in the downpour.

Lizzie waited in the mudroom for Grandma Faye, and held the door open for her as she struggled with the load of firewood. Lizzie bit her lip when the offer to help carry the box into the house almost slipped out.

Grandma Faye left the firewood just inside the door while she slipped off her poncho and left it to dry on a peg near the back door. As Grandma Faye toed off her gum boots, Lizzie began stripping out of her wet muddy clothes and threw them straight into the washing machine. A year ago she would have been too shy about her nakedness to strip down, even in front of a female friend, but so much had changed since then and her naked form was no longer an embarrassment to her. And besides, someone had attended to her for three days and changed her out of her clothes from that night and into a clean flannel nightgown. It was either Grandma Faye or Vivienne or both women who had taken such tender care of her while she lay locked in the dream plane of her healing time.

Shivering, she padded down the hall to the bathroom, leaving muddy prints on the hardwood as she went. She filled the basin and grabbed a clean washcloth to wipe her muddy feet, not wanting to risk balancing on the rolled edge of the claw foot tub to wash. She was still shaky from her fall in the mud, and more than that the gaps in her memory made her feel as if she wasn't fully herself, as if she'd left something vital back in the woods that night.

As she wrung out the warm washcloth her gaze flitted across the mirror, resting on her right shoulder. She played her wet fingers over the smooth skin. The bullet hadn't passed through her. She angled her body so her back was to the mirror and craned her neck. Even at her awkward angle she could see puckered red skin in the shape of a ragged circle the bullet had made.

While she tried to get a better look at her still healing wound, on their own accord her fingers danced across her collar bone, searching for the weight and comfort of her cross. Just a few inches, she thought, and the bullet would have hit her lung. Her fingers continued to search, as her mind was half a beat behind what they were telling her. When the truth finally registered she spun around to face the mirror. She moved too fast and had to grip the edge of the sink with both hands. When the dizziness subsided she raised her head and looked at her bare chest. She wasn't wearing her cross. Her eyes darted around the small room, but her necklace wasn't there.

Taking a seat on the closed toilet seat, she hurriedly washed and dried her feet. Her heart hammered in her throat as she entered her bedroom and began searching for her cross. A careful examination of the nightstand revealed nothing but a glass of water, a few brown vials of herbal tinctures, and a box of tissues.

Her necklace wasn't on the bedroom mantle either. Lizzie flung the comforter off the bed and tore at the bed sheets. She was tugging off a pillowcase, her shoulder sending her white hot lances of pain, when Grandma Faye spoke from the doorway.

"Lizzie, what are you doing?"

It wasn't the words that stopped her from tearing apart the whole room, but the slight fear she heard in Grandma Faye's voice. She turned around, hugging the pillow to her nakedness. She blinked as her vision wavered.

"My necklace, I'm not wearing it. Did you take it off me?"

Grandma Faye slowly walked into the room, her hands held up. "No child, you know as well as I do that with the ward on it no one but you can remove it. You weren't wearing it when I brought you in that night. Perhaps you took it off when you were trying to escape the barn." Grandma Faye took a few more steps, closing the gap between her and Lizzie.

"I don't remember. It would make sense though, if I was trapped and wanted to make sure I could access all of my power. Did the sweepers find it when they went through the barn?"

"I don't know. There was a lot of commotion while you were in your healing time; members of the order were all over the property and in the cottage. Someone probably picked it up and just forgot when they all raced out of here to find Jon." Grandma Faye now stood next to Lizzie and placed her warm hand on her shoulder. "Why don't you get dressed while I place a call and find out?"

Lizzie nodded, her throat too tight to answer. As quickly as she could, she threw on a worn pair of khakis and an oversized T-shirt. Grandma Faye was just hanging up the phone when Lizzie joined her in the living room. Even fully clothed, without her necklace she still felt naked. She had never been without her link to her mother...she'd only taken it off twice, and only for a little while.

She plunked herself down on the sofa, her hands wedged between her knees. "Well, do they have it?"

"They're not sure. I spoke to the head of the sweepers, and she's going to go over the inventory to double check, but as far as she knows none of her team found any necklace."

Lizzie stood and strode to the front door. She scanned the pegs for her raincoat but it wasn't there.

"Where's my slicker?"

"The sweepers took it, along with everything else connected to that night. Besides, it was ruined, had a big hole torn in it from a bullet."

She grabbed at a cotton jacket and flung it over her shoulders, thrusting her arms through the sleeves. She immediately regretted the aggressive move as a bolt of fresh pain from her shoulder made her wince.

"Where do you think you're going?"

"To find my necklace. I must have taken it off when Audley and I left the barn."

"You are doing no such thing. If you haven't already noticed from your most recent trip outside, it's pouring down and it's black as pitch out there. Even with a flashlight you are going on a fool's errand. You won't find your necklace, and you'll just come back wet and cold."

"You don't understand," Lizzie said, looking for her gum boots. She supposed the sweepers had taken those too. She bunched her hands into fists.

"I do understand. I understand the importance that necklace has to you because of your mother. I understand you've had many losses in your life and Audley's death has been a deep blow to you. But going out there now, even if you do find your necklace, won't bring Audley back."

Lizzie squeezed her eyes shut. She didn't open them until she felt her friend's gentle touch on her arms, stroking them lightly. "It's not your fault he's dead."

Lizzie nodded, and when Grandma Faye stepped in and gently embraced her she couldn't hold back the flood of grief. Lizzie's sobs shuddered through her body, and Grandma Faye slowly rocked Lizzie back and forth.

When her grief had played itself out and her tears had stopped flowing, Lizzie stepped back from her friend's embrace. "I'm sorry, I don't know why I'm behaving like an idiot." Lizzie scrubbed her face with the tail of her shirt. "I know my necklace won't bring any of them back. I don't know what's wrong with me. I've gone through a healing time before and I didn't feel so muddled like I do now."

"Go sit by the fire, and I'll go get us a piece of cake. I managed to keep two slices back from the members."

Lizzie shuffled over to the couch. "What kind of cake?"

"Chocolate, of course. Is there any other kind?"

Lizzie curled up on the couch, tucking her feet underneath her as Grandma Fay brought in a tray with fresh cups of coffee and two thick pieces of cake.

"Thanks," Lizzie said, taking her coffee and dessert and placing them on the side table. She wasn't intending on eating the cake, but the rich smell of chocolate and the sight of the thick creamy icing made her stomach growl. Taking a small bite, she followed it with a sip of coffee. "This is very good," she said, using her fork to take a larger chunk.

"I'm glad you like it; it's my grandmother's recipe."

Lizzie suddenly couldn't swallow the cake she'd just put in her mouth. She herself would never have the opportunity to bake a cake from her grandmother's recipe, or learn from the wisdom of her mother. She gave her head a slight shake, trying to dislodge the errant sorrow the thought had produced.

Taking a sip of coffee, she focused on Bear asleep in front of the hearth. She observed the stones that made up the fireplace, wondering if Emma was the one who'd labored to place them or if she'd hired someone like Audley to do the work. She gazed up at the rough-hewn mantle where her lightning glass lay. There was something propped up next to it, a roll of paper that hadn't been there before.

Lizzie got off the couch, careful not to step on her dog, then she plucked the scroll from its place. What she thought was paper felt soft and smooth under her hand. She held it out to Grandma Faye. "What is this?"

"I don't know," Grandma Faye said from her place in the leather armchair.

The fragile scroll was secured with a red silk cord that ended in ornate tassels. She brought it over to the kitchen table, and with infinite care she slowly released the cord and unrolled it with nimble fingers. Grandma Faye had come to stand next to her and leaned over the table.

Written on the vellum were words and symbols in an ink that had faded to a faint reddish-brown. Lizzie couldn't read the words, but she recognized the symbols.

"Is this what I think it is?" Lizzie asked, her voice rising in excitement.

"I think so. Wait a minute." Grandma Faye hustled over to the hall table and scrounged through her purse. Retrieving a pair of reading glasses she returned to the table. Perching the glasses on the tip of her nose, she peered down at the scroll.

"Yes, these are definitely the symbols painted on the cellar ceiling," she said, pointing to a series of shapes near the top half of the scroll.

"This must have come from Vivienne," Lizzie said. "With everything that was going on she must have placed it on the mantle and then forgotten to tell you."

"You're probably right. The cottage was swarming with people from the order, and when I wasn't with you I was busy preparing food for everyone. But I know for certain it wasn't here when we first brought you home. I lit the fire out here when the healers first began working on you, and I think I would have noticed."

Lizzie squinted at the unintelligible words. Her excitement dimmed. "So we have the spell to release Emma, but it is as good as useless if we can't read it. Why didn't Vivienne leave us a translation?" Lizzie gently fingered the soft edges of the scroll.

"Those nuns you lived with didn't teach you to read Latin?"

"No," Lizzie replied. "Can you?"

Grandma Faye snorted. "Of course I can." She nudged Lizzie out of the way and ran her finger across the first line. "Charm for unbinding. The procedure is quite simple, as I suspected. It's these symbols down here that are the key to removing the spell," she said, pointing to six shapes midway down the scroll.

Lizzie followed Grandma Faye's finger. The symbols were different than the ones in the cellar. As she stared at them they seem to rise from the scroll and float a few centimeters in the air. Lizzie squeezed her eyes shut and shook her head. When she opened her eyes again the symbols were back on the page where they belonged. Grandma Faye was intent on examining the scroll and didn't appear to notice Lizzie's discomfort.

"Do we need anything else for the ritual?" she asked.

"Mmm, let's see." Grandma Faye read through the charm, her eyes narrowed in concentration, the tip of her tongue poking out between her lips. "We just need the basic equipment for drawing the corners; candles, salt, water, and an athame."

"We have everything we need right here, except the athame. And I can draw the corners without one." Lizzie felt a surge of excitement, but it was instantly quelled when she remembered what had happened to her last time she was down in the cellar. "Except my magick doesn't work when I'm down there." She sat down hard on a kitchen chair, her frustration building. "I have everything else, but you will need your athame, as you have to be the one to do the ritual. I don't want to wait until the morning. Do you suppose we could go to your house and get the knife?"

"We don't have to. Really, Lizzie, we need to start on your education as soon as possible. If you'd been properly schooled you'd know a witch never leaves her house without her athame, a pouch of salt, her charms, and at least a few tea lights." Grandma Faye marched back over to her voluminous purse and pulled out a black velvet pouch. "But are you sure you want to do this now? We can wait until you've rested a bit more."

"Absolutely," she said, rising from her chair. "I've been resting for seventy-two hours. And if I can release Emma I won't wait another minute. I need to do this for her."

"I know," Grandma Faye said, rolling up the scroll. "Okay then, go get the candles, salt, and water, and I'll meet you down in the cellar."

CHAPTER FORTY-FIVE

Candlelight flickered across the dirt walls, the fragrant smell of beeswax filling the small space but not quite masking the odor of mildew and damp. The two women stood in the center of a salt circle, the four directions delineated by the placement of four pillar candles of beeswax. The piecrust table from the living room served as their alter, on which Lizzie had placed bowls of water and salt, another pillar candle, Grandma Faye's athame, and a box of wooden matches. Lizzie held up the scroll to the candlelight as Grandma Faye adjusted her reading glasses.

Whether because of the lack of illumination or the dampening of her powers due to the black magick above her, Lizzie couldn't see the elementals forming a protective barrier around the circle, but she knew they were there from the slight change in air pressure and the way the hairs on her arms and the back of her neck rose slightly each time Grandma Faye had called out to the guardians of the four directions.

With the circle complete, Grandma Faye spoke the incantation, her arms raised in supplication, her voice low and powerful. Lizzie held the scroll up as Grandma Faye read from it, but her focus was drawn to the air above Grandma Faye.

For a moment, nothing in the cellar seemed to change. Then the old woman picked up her athame and began carving out symbols in the air above her. Lizzie inhaled sharply, but her friend was so intent on what she was doing she didn't react to Lizzie's sound.

As the knife sliced through the air, the candle light winking off the polished blade, a faint green glow appeared in the air hovering just above Grandma Faye's head. As the words flowed from Grandma Faye's lips, the ball of green light rose to the ceiling, became more vibrant, and then attached itself to one of the white shapes painted on the ceiling. With each word spoken from the hedge-witch's lips more glowing orbs appeared, and as the black magick weakened, Lizzie watched as the glowing orbs took on the shape of the symbols she'd seen written on the scroll.

The ground below Lizzie's feet started to vibrate, the air sparked with magick. The energy rising from the dirt floor began to leech into the soles of her feet and swirl up her legs.

When Grandma Faye drew the last symbol in the air, Lizzie watched as it, like the previous ones, drifted to the ceiling and attached itself to its dark counterpart. And then the real magick began.

Both women stared at the ceiling, enraptured by the light display dancing over their heads. Electric colored shapes raced backwards over the painted symbols, sparking and flaring occasionally. The smell of singed wood mingled with the beeswax and damp. When the white magick had retraced over every symbol, all the energy coalesced in the center, creating a ball of intense white light.

Lizzie reached out her hand and Grandma Faye clasped it. Keeping their eyes locked on the ceiling, both women took several steps back so they were out from under the ball of light, but still within the protection of the circle.

The white orb began to spin, creating a dizzying display of light shards on the walls and floor. Energy crackled in the air, and Lizzie's own power surged within her. A high pitched whine pierced her eardrums but she held tight to her friend's hand. Both women ducked as the ball of light exploded, raining down pinpricks of light. But the sparks held no heat and fell onto their heads like the flutter of butterfly wings.

Straightening up, both women looked at each other, and with a quick nod from Grandma Faye they both faced the altar. They spoke in unison the words Grandma Faye had told Lizzie to say before they headed down to the cellar.

"Darkness has been banished and the light of the Goddess has prevailed. By the powers of three times three, the maiden the mother and the crone, we seal this spell with love and light, so mote it be. Now, we call upon the spirit known to us as Emma Hawksworth. Come before us and we shall guide you home."

No sooner were the words spoken than a spiral of grey mist emerged from the floor directly across from Lizzie and Grandma Faye.

"Emma," Lizzie whispered. "You are free to move on."

The grey spiral expanded, taking on an approximate form of a human, with a torso and legs and arms. Lizzie blinked and the outline of Emma became more distinct. Then the apparition became so solid she looked like she was casting a shadow.

"Is she here, Lizzie?"

"Yes, just to the left of the table. You can't see her?"

"No, but I feel her presence. We need to call the light now."

Lizzie nodded. She imagined a column of white light slicing down into the reaches of the dark cellar, just as Grandma Faye had instructed her before they had set about doing the ritual.

"Can you see the light?"

"Yes," Lizzie replied, her eyes glued to the ghost of Emma, who with each moment was becoming more corporeal. She wore the deep red dress she had been wearing the time she'd appeared to Lizzie during the thunderstorm.

"Emma, it is time for you to leave this earthly plane. It is time for you to return to your true home."

Emma smiled and nodded. Placing her hands on her heart, she looked at Lizzie and then at Grandma Faye. "Thank you."

Her mouth moved, silently forming the words.

"You're most welcome." Before guiding Emma into the light, Lizzie needed one last thing from the witch of Rose Cottage. "Emma, did the villagers bury your body down here?"

Emma frowned, then nodded.

"Could you show me where exactly? I would like to give you a proper burial."

Emma's gaze slowly shifted, looking past the two women. She raised her hand and pointed into the corner of the cellar where Lizzie had first seen her appear, where the odd white mildew grew against the walls.

"I promise you that your life will be remembered. Grandma Faye and I will honor you." Straightening her shoulders, Lizzie looked at the column of white light that danced behind Emma. "It's time now, turn around and enter the light. Peace and freedom awaits you there."

Emma glanced over her shoulder but made no move to go into the light. Instead she cocked her head to one side. "There is someone here for you," she said. This time Lizzie heard her voice clearly.

The spirit floated a few feet to the left, revealing another grey mist. What Lizzie had thought was some sort of ghostly shadow was another spirit.

Lizzie frowned.

"What is it?" Grandma Faye asked. "Has she gone into the light?"

Lizzie turned her head slightly towards her friend, never taking her eyes off the new spirit as it began to fill out into the distinct outline of woman. "There's another spirit here. Another woman, I think."

The woman was slightly taller than Emma, her hair worn long and cascading down her back. Her face was heart-shaped, but it was the eyes that made Lizzie's heart slam against her ribcage. She knew the shape of them, the way they turned up slightly at the corners, and the particular shade of grey that held a hint of purple like a sky threatening thunder.

And if she hadn't recognized the family resemblance, the necklace the spirit wore left no doubt who she was. It was Lizzie's cross that rested in the hollow of the woman's neck, but unlike the necklace's current condition, this one was complete with several crimson stones cut in the shape of teardrops. Dragon's tears.

Lizzie let go of Grandma Faye's hand and stumbled forward, knocking her hip against the altar. The pillar candle rocked then settled back down into place.

For the first time in her life, Lizzie gazed at the woman she'd never thought she'd meet.

"Mom." Lizzie choked out the word as tears pricked her eyes.

The spirit nodded and moved in closer, the candlelight revealing the transparency of her form. When she cupped her hand against Lizzie's cheek, Lizzie closed her eyes.

The flesh on her cheek tingled from the contact, and then for the briefest of moments Lizzie felt the solid warmth of flesh against her skin, and with it a sensation of overwhelming love. Lizzie would have given anything for that moment to last, but no sooner had she felt her mother's touch than it disappeared. Lizzie eyes flew open.

Lizzie watched Emma approach her mother, and the two spectral women clasped hands. Lizzie knew what they were going to do a half-second before they started moving.

"No," she called out. "No, please don't go." The words caught in her throat as her mother and Emma stepped towards the light.

Lizzie's mother looked over her shoulder and spoke. "Tell Wren it wasn't his fault." She turned away before Lizzie could respond. Still holding hands, the spirits merged with the light, and then the light too drew into itself and winked out.

CHAPTER FORTY-SIX

Lizzie stared at the spot where her mother had stood moments before. There was nothing but the dirt walls of the cellar. She hadn't realized Grandma Faye had approached her until she felt her hand on her arm.

"Lizzie, are you all right?"

She turned and patted the old woman's hand. "I think so," she said.

"Your mother was here with Emma?"

"Yes she was, but I don't understand why." With the back of her hand she touched her cheek where her mother's hand had rested. It was damp with tears.

She was about to tell her friend what else her mother had said, but she stopped short. Why would she ask Lizzie to tell Wren it wasn't his fault? What wasn't his fault? And how could her mother possibly know Wren? He had to be about Lizzie's age, which would mean he would have been an infant when her mother was alive. She needed time to process what that meant and whether or not she wanted to share it with Grandma Faye, which would also mean explaining who Wren was.

"It's not unusual for a spirit to attach itself to a loved one. Perhaps she's been with you all along, watching over you."

Lizzie felt comforted by the thought. "Perhaps you are right. But why would she choose now to show herself to me, and why did she choose to leave just when she let me know she was here?"

Grandma Faye shrugged. "Unfortunately, those are questions

351

we may never know the answers to until it is our time to cross over." Grandma Faye walked over to the table and picked up her athame. "We need to release the guardians and open the circle."

"Then we need to find Emma's body. She showed me where it is. I know it's been a long day for you, but I can't leave her remains down here a moment longer than they have to be."

"Many hands make light work," Grandma Faye smiled. "Besides, we owe her that much, don't we?"

Lizzie nodded, feeling her love for her friend growing.

"Can you work your magick down here now?"

"Yes, I felt it return even before the ritual was complete." To prove her point, Lizzie called up her powers and began releasing the elementals with the use of only her hands.

CHAPTER FORTY-SEVEN

Laying down the shovel, Lizzie knelt and used her hands to compress the earth around the area she'd just backfilled. The rains had stopped the morning Grandma Faye and Lizzie brought the remains of Emma out of the cellar, her yellowed bones wrapped in a new bed sheet with tiny blue flowers on the white background.

Satisfied she'd removed any air pocket from around the roots, she grabbed the galvanized watering can by her feet and soaked the dirt around the tree. Then she held each hand in turn under the spray of water, washing away most of the dirt caked to her fingers. Placing the empty can near the tree, she knelt down and dried her hands on the tops of her jeans. She glanced around, surveying her handiwork. The young sapling stood straight and true. With some careful nurturing it should take root in its new home, and once its branches had grown and its leaves filled out, it would provide lovely dappled shade, protecting Emma's resting place from the sun.

Lizzie had sprinkled some wildflower seeds over the raw scrape in the earth where they had laid Emma to rest. Over time the earth would heal its scar, and only the tree and a carpet of wild flowers would mark Emma's grave.

From this vantage point Lizzie had a view of her overgrown garden to her left and the cottage to her right. From her living room window Lizzie would be able to see the tree and be reminded of the woman who had come before her. A woman just like her, who had suffered at the hands of a village that wouldn't accept her.

But now she was in Lizzie's keeping, and she would not be forgotten. Lizzie had begun to write down Emma's story from the information she'd discovered at the village archives and her own experience, with the intent to send it to the order's archives so her place in history as a wise woman would be forever documented.

Except for Bear and Quinn, who were playing their version of fetch down by the garden, Lizzie was alone on her property. Grandma Faye had stayed with Lizzie until they'd gotten word from Vivienne just one day after laying Emma to rest that Jon Ryan was dead. She let those words tumble around in her mind. Jon was dead. The man who had hunted her for months was no longer a threat. It didn't seem real to her, not as real as Audley's death or seeing her mother's ghost in her cottage cellar.

For five days he'd managed to slip through the teams of men and women sent by the order to capture him. For a while it looked like luck was in his favor and he was going to evade them yet again. But Vivienne had been relentless, sending out teams from every chapter across the globe. It was near Hope, some six hundred kilometers from Barton, that Jon was finally cornered. According to Vivienne's account, rather than be taken in by the order, Jon had driven his truck over a cliff. The truck had exploded in a ball of fire upon impact, either by Jon's own magick or by the force of the impact. The order had recovered the burned out hull and the incinerated body of Jon. A team was running tests to confirm the charred remains were really that of the warlock.

Lizzie wouldn't deny she'd been relieved when she'd heard the news. She could live her life now without the fear of being hunted. More importantly, she could begin to use her magick freely; she could step into who she was and begin to live her life as a wise woman without the threat looming over her.

And her education was to begin later that afternoon. Grandma Faye had promised to start with the very basics of what it meant to be a witch, not just spells and incantations, but the more important connection with mother earth, her power, and her healing abilities.

Lizzie shifted her weight, resting her hip on the ground, and straightened out her legs. She watched Quinn fly off with a stick clutched in his claws. When he was several feet away from Bear he dropped the stick and returned to his roost on the garden fence, where Bear sat waiting. As soon as Quinn landed Bear tore off across the field, grabbing the stick in his jaw and running back to drop the stick below where Quinn sat. There was much cawing and barking as Quinn flew down to grab the stick and begin the game again.

Lizzie smiled. Her animal companions were a handful, especially Bear, but she loved them with all her heart and with a fierceness that surprised her. She hadn't figured out a way of training him not to turn on the taps when he wanted fresh water, so she was stuck with constantly filling his bowl and putting his cookie jar in the fridge. He hadn't used his ability to disappear lately, but that was by his choice and not by anything Lizzie had managed to do.

So much of her life felt expansive, there was so much that she looked forward to, but there were still clouds of doubt and unanswered questions floating around, threatening her positive outlook. As far as why Jon had hunted her or found her in the first place would always remain a mystery. Putting Emma's remains to rest and seeing her off into the light was something positive to hold onto, but it didn't take away the fact that Audley was dead, and that her mother's spirit was no longer with Lizzie.

And Wren. Why had her mother said those words? Lizzie had convinced herself that in her excitement at seeing her mother she had misheard her. It had to be some other name that sounded like Wren, Ben perhaps. Was it her father's guilt that her mother wished to relieve? Was her father's name Ben?

Her hand crept up to her neck, seeking comfort from her cross, but it wasn't there. Lizzie rubbed at the hollow of her throat. It still felt strange to not have the comforting weight of the stone resting there, and all the more reason she needed to start her lessons with Grandma Faye. She and Grandma Faye had scoured the forest and the barn looking for her necklace. Lizzie would keep looking, but for now it was lost to her.

A shadow fell across Emma's grave. Startled, Lizzie twisted her torso and half crouched into a sitting position.

"Sorry, I didn't mean to scare you," Wren said, moving off to the side so the sun was no longer behind him. He shrugged off his knapsack and placed it by his feet.

Lizzie looked up into his face. She felt a familiar pull in her belly, and she rubbed her already clean hands on the thighs of her jeans. "It's okay, I was just lost in my thoughts and didn't hear you come up."

"I didn't mean to intrude on a private moment," he said, indicating Emma's fresh grave. "I can come back later."

"No, I really could use some company right now." Lizzie patted the ground, indicating for Wren to take a seat. He was about to lower himself down next to her when Bear came bounding up, with Quinn flapping overhead.

Lizzie scrambled to stand up before Bear reached them, unsure how he would react to a stranger. Wren lowered himself down into a kneeling position, so as Bear approached they were nose to nose. She opened her mouth to call off her dog, but to her relief it wasn't necessary.

Wren smiled and scratched Bear behind his floppy ears, and was rewarded with a slobbery kiss. Wren laughed and swiped his face with his sleeve. "I'm going to assume you are a dog, but by the looks of you could also be a bear," Wren said, standing up.

He kept his hand on Bear's head, the dog leaning into Wren's leg as he continued to rub the dog's ear.

"Well, you are right on both counts. He's definitely a dog, but his name is Bear."

"And you must be Quinn?" Wren said, indicating the raven who stood on the grass. At the sound of his name Quinn launched himself in the air at Wren. Without hesitation Wren held out his arm and Quinn alighted on it as if the two of them had practiced the move before.

"How did you know his name?" Lizzie said slowly, rising to stand next to Wren.

"You'd mentioned him when we were in the kitchen unpacking groceries. He's the one with the peanut butter addiction, right?"

Lizzie rubbed her temples. The sensation of déjà vu was so strong.

"Hey, are you okay?" Wren said, rubbing her arm with his free hand, all the while being careful not to dislodge Quinn from his forearm.

"Mmm, I'm fine. Just a little light headed, I guess."

"You'd better sit down."

Lizzie nodded and plopped herself back down on the grass, her legs turning liquid beneath her.

"Off you go, Quinn," Wren said as he gently lifted his arm. The raven spread his wings and took flight, circled in the air, and landed near the grave. Bear trotted over to Quinn and laid next to his feathered friend.

Wren settled down next to Lizzie on the grass, and to her surprise took her hand in his. With his other hand he covered hers. She looked down at his hands, so strong yet graceful in the way his fingers tapered. Artist's hands. She could smell the forest on him, cedar and loamy earth.

"Grief is a slippery thing. One moment it has you in its grip, the next it flits away and for a brief moment we forget, only to have it come back with a fury when our defenses are down."

She snapped her head up so she was looking into Wren's eyes. They were the most unsettling color; in the bright sunshine they seemed to glow. Only someone who'd had a personal experience with loss would say such a thing. She could see that reflected in the strange firelight of his irises.

She nodded and looked over at the grave, slipping her hand out of Wren's clasp. She was about to say she wasn't close to the woman whose remains lay buried beneath the soil when she realized that wasn't true. She cleared her throat. "Her name was Emma Hawksworth, and she was the original owner of the cottage."

She went on to recount Emma's story, her life and her tragic end, but she carefully omitted how magick had played a part in the discovery of her remains, simply saying that Emma's remains were discovered when the renovations to her cottage unearthed her resting place.

"She must have been a courageous woman to choose a solitary life, especially out here and especially back then. I would have loved to have met her."

"Yes, me too," she replied, hoping her tone didn't reveal the lie. She had met Emma and she was an extraordinary woman. She only wished she had known her when she was living.

For a long time neither of them spoke, but the silence between them felt companionable. When Bear grew restless and stood up to wander down to the garden looking for his stick, Lizzie finally spoke.

"So how are your owls?"

"Oh, you know, doing owly things. Sleeping right now, hence the free time on my hands."

"Did you want to come inside? I could make us some iced tea."

"It's such a beautiful day after so much rain. It seems a shame to waste it inside. What would you like to do on this beautiful summer morning?"

Lizzie leaned back on her hands as she contemplated Wren's question. She was too unsettled to focus on gardening, but there was a restlessness in her bones that made her want to move instead of sitting around. She closed her eyes and let the warmth of the sun kiss her cheeks.

She opened her eyes to find Wren smiling at her, his blue-green eyes crinkled at the corners, a hint of mischief sparkling in the depths of his irises. His smile was contagious and she found herself grinning back at him.

"I'd like to go for a walk," she said. "I've over twenty acres to call my own, and so far I've kept close to the cottage. I've never even stepped foot on the west side of the property."

"Then a walk it shall be," Wren said. He stood up then held out his hand to her. He pulled her up and into him so that she had to place her hands on his chest to stop her forward motion. Beneath her fingertips she felt the quickening of his heart through the thick fabric of his shirt. When she felt her own pulse respond she stepped back, breaking the contact.

She turned to look at the cottage while he retrieved his knapsack. "I should go get a sweater," she said, starting towards the cottage, her legs feeling disjointed, her footsteps unsure.

"If we are going to be bushwhacking through your back forty, you might want to change into hiking boots."

Lizzie turned back to look at Wren.

"You do own a pair of hiking boots?" He gave her a crooked smile.

"Of course I do," she said with mock indignation. "I'll just be a minute. You can wait inside if you want." Lizzie scrambled up the porch steps, thanking her lucky stars she'd bought a pair of sturdy boots during her last trip into town.

She hadn't even taken them out of the box yet, but Wren didn't need to know that.

CHAPTER FORTY-EIGHT

Hiking through her property was the best antidote to her restlessness. There were four in the party; her, Wren, Quinn, and Bear. Quinn had chosen to ride on Wren's shoulder, and Bear kept pace with Lizzie as she followed behind. Once they had traipsed deep into the forest and started bushwhacking, as Wren called it, she felt her steps lighten despite the burning pain of new blisters forming on the back of her heels from her new hiking boots.

Turned out she didn't need her sweater, so she wore it tied around her waist. The effort of pushing through the thick bush had her perspiring after only a few minutes, despite the coolness beneath the canopy of trees.

But she was content. She hadn't felt such a deep sense of peace and oneness with her surroundings since the last time she'd been working with her flowers in her shop.

She had also made a few discoveries about the land that she now called home. After covering only about five acres they came across a rail fence, the wood silvery with age. So the carefully crafted stone fence only extended across the front of the property, and if Lizzie had to guess it ended where the rail fence met it at the corners. Just a small portion of her property was fenced, the rest was left wild and untouched. The trees growing within the fence line had the underbrush removed, and a heavy carpet of moss had taken over. Where Wren and she now traversed was thick with underbrush, fallen logs, and small saplings struggling to reach the light blocked by their bigger and older brothers and sisters.

Quinn had taken off when she and Wren clambered over the fence, flying back in the direction of the cottage. Bear found a portion of the fence where a rail was missing and shimmied his body through the opening, much to Lizzie's relief.

She wasn't sure how she'd explain to Wren if Bear had used his magick to dematerialize and then appear on the other side of the fence. He was definitely going to get an extra cookie when he got home.

They hiked walking side-by-side. Other times when the brush was too thick, Wren would take the lead, holding back low growing branches to allow her to pass. Bear trailed behind, stopping occasionally to sniff something that drew his attention.

When Wren noticed something he thought she'd find interesting he would point it out to her, whispering in her ear about what he spotted. He showed her where a family of skunks had made their home in a fallen log, deep gouges in a hemlock where a black bear had marked his territory, and the strange and otherworldly looking moss and lichen that populated the forest floor and grew on the trunks of trees.

They had just veered around a thick patch of ferns, where they had spotted a fawn tucked away safely until its mother returned, when Lizzie's foot caught on an exposed tree root and she stumbled, wincing slightly at the rawness of her blisters.

"Why don't we head back?" Wren said. "Before those blisters get too bad. If I'd known you hadn't actually worn those yet, I wouldn't have taken us so far," he said, nodding towards her feet.

"No, we haven't even come to the road yet. I'm fine. I just didn't see the root and tripped over it."

"Mmm. Okay, if you say so."

"I do say so." Lizzie stepped around him and headed off through the forest. She could hear him chuckling behind her.

"And I don't have blisters," she shouted back at him. She stepped down harder than she intended and grimaced as she felt the large blister on her heel pop, oozing a sticky patch of wetness onto her sock.

When she came across a cottonwood sapling blocking her path she held it out of the way, and just as Wren moved forward she let go. She heard Wren's surprised woof of air as the sapling thwacked him in the stomach. Letting out a peal of laughter, she took off through the trees, ignoring the burning at the back of her heels. Wren was close behind her, but she knew not to look back.

Her heart raced as she quickened her pace, and then she heard the equally strong rhythm of the land rising up through the earth, as if to join her on the merry chase.

When she was outside around the cottage, she could always feel the earth as a slight vibration, like a fluttering pulse that made the skin on the inner wrist tremble. But as she plunged through the wilder parts of the land, this sound, this drumbeat of life, became stronger, more vibrant. Without thinking she unfurled her energy and expanded her perceptions, her third eye opening up without effort. As she ran she could see the movement of small creatures, their energy signatures giving their locations away although they hadn't moved. She no longer watched where her feet landed. She didn't need to see where she was going, to find her footing or to avoid a fallen log or springy sapling. She and the forest were one.

Wren was just a few feet behind her, his movements quieter than she'd expected, but in her heightened state of perception she was able to track his movements with ease even though she hadn't glanced behind once since she'd taken off at a run.

As Wren closed the distance between them, Bear, who had joined the chase, overtook Lizzie, swerving around the tree with measured grace even with his bad hip.

But then what had started as a playful game turned dark.

Suddenly it was too close of a replay of the night she and Bear had dashed through the forest in fear of their lives. Gone was the dappled sunshine of a perfect summer day; she was running in the dark and the rain, Whitley in hot pursuit behind her.

She stumbled and fell to her knees, gasping for air as her long forgotten nemesis, a panic attack, enveloped her. She felt the pure terror of hearing a gunshot, knowing now it was Audley's death she was hearing, seeing Whitley with his alien-like night vision googles, Bear leaping to defend her.

Bear rushed to her side. He nudged her shoulder with his nose, emitting a soft whine when she didn't respond.

Her chest tightened and she couldn't catch her breath. Without the charm on her necklace to contain her energy, she felt her control slip. Her magick crackled, surging erratically in response to her fear. Bear whined again, taking a step back from her.

"Elizabeth." She felt the weight of Wren's hand on her back. "Are you hurt?" She shook her head in reply, but she couldn't suck enough air into her lungs to talk. "Take a deep breath, you need to slow down your breathing." She tried to do as he asked, but she couldn't. "Elizabeth, look at me." She raised her head and looked into his eyes; the effort felt like pushing through heavy currents of water. His eyes were more green than blue in the fractured light of the forest. The panic receded, the constriction around her ribs relaxed.

"That's it. Nice, slow breaths."

Lizzie kept her gaze locked on his, matching her breath with his, slow and steady. Her magick ebbed then stopped completely. When he gathered her into his arms she allowed it, needing to feel something real and solid to keep her anchored in the present, and not relieving the memory of that night.

She clung to him, the steady beat of his heart reassuring. He kissed the top of her head. "You are safe now, there is no danger here," he whispered into her hair.

He'd spoken words similar to her not long ago, in the dark and rain. A flash of memory. She and Wren were standing side-by-side, his aura blinding white in her peripheral vision.

She pushed away from his embrace. "That night. You were there. I remember now. It was you that saved me from Whitley, carried me through the forest when I couldn't make it on my own."

Wren regarded her with a mixture of confusion and surprise. They were kneeling on the spongy forest floor facing each other. "I'm sorry, Elizabeth, I don't know what you are talking about. What night? The night you found Emma's remains?"

"No, no," she said, shaking her head. "Before that, the grow op, the cop that was pointing a gun at me by the stone circle. You were there. Wren, tell me you were there."

"I'm not sure what you are talking about. What grow-op? And I've only been to your place once before when I helped you unpack groceries, remember?"

Lizzie rubbed her forehead. "But I remember you there." The more she thought about it the less certain she was. Grandma Faye had never once mentioned Wren being there that night. Was it possible that she'd imagined the whole thing, made up a story while she'd been in her healing time on the dream plane?

"I don't like seeing you so distressed, but I really don't have a clue as to what you are talking about. Perhaps it would be best if we headed back to the cottage." Wren didn't give Lizzie a chance to agree. Instead he stood up and offered her his hand.

"Yes," she replied, allowing him to pull her into a standing position. "I'm sorry if I frightened you, I've been under a bit of a strain of late, and I'm not quite myself."

"Does it have to do with the grow op you'd mentioned?"

"Yes," she replied, brushing pine needles off her pants before turning for home.

The trip back to the cottage took longer than the hike out. She walked slowly — Bear on one side of her, Wren on the other — trying hard not to limp from the broken blisters that made her socks stick to her heels.

She recounted the story of finding the marijuana operation, downplaying it as much as possible. The order had gone to great pains to cover up the whole thing, and in her confusion she'd let it slip. So she lied to Wren, omitting Audley's death, her being held at gunpoint, and the pursuit of Jon by the order.

She'd glanced at Wren a few times as she told her tale, and he seemed to believe her. He never asked any questions or wanted more details, just nodded as she wove her lie.

"I guess growing pot is pretty common out here. If I'd been smart I would have checked out the barn before I bought the place."

"But you are safe now, correct? The culprits arrested, the grow-op shut down."

"Yes, I'm in no danger. The cottage and the property are mine now." She didn't tell him about the crystal grid the order had installed, keeping out anyone who would wish her harm. She didn't want to lie to Wren, to have it sitting between them, but she couldn't see an alternative. She was attracted to him. She would be foolish to pretend otherwise, but telling him who she really was didn't seem possible. At least not at present.

As they approached the rail fence, Wren climbed over first and held out his hand. She took it to steady herself, and when she landed on the other side of the property he held fast to her hand, giving it a quick squeeze before starting the final leg back to the cottage. Bear repeated his earlier manoeuver with the fence, wiggling through the opening at the bottom.

The terrain was so much easier to cover than the overgrown forest they just come through, but Wren still held her hand. If she hadn't been so focused on the warmth of his flesh against hers and her questions about her false memory, she would have detected the intruders earlier. As it was Bear noticed them first, his hackles raised as he lowered his head, his gaze focused on the cottage.

CHAPTER FORTY-NINE

It was the white Range Rover she spotted first, the type of vehicle the order favored. Bear remained at her side but had raised his head, sniffing the air. Then without a sound, he trotted towards the cottage, his tail wagging. Someone from the order was waiting for her at the cottage, and it had to be Vivienne. She hadn't had a chance to talk to her since her healing time, and she wanted to thank her for finding the scroll. Dropping Wren's hand, she took several steps, quickening her pace, her broken blisters momentarily forgotten, until her cottage came into view.

Lizzie stopped abruptly, her heart stuck in her throat.

A man and a woman stood on the porch facing the front door. The man was several inches taller than his companion, and he had his arm wrapped protectively around the woman's small waist. The woman leaned into him as if she didn't have the energy to stand on her own. She wore a thick grey sweater several sizes too big despite the warm day, and her curly hair, the color of copper, was pulled back in a haphazard ponytail.

As Bear approached the visitors, his plume of a tail waving a friendly greeting, the man and woman turned around.

In the time it took her to realize she was holding her breath and then exhale, Wren had come up beside her.

"Friends of yours?"

"In a manner of speaking." Lizzie squared her shoulders and marched towards the cottage. "More like ghosts from my past," Lizzie said as went to find out what Gideon and Madison were doing on her front porch.

About the Author

Lora was born in the small town of Fort Saskatchewan, Alberta; the middle child of five girls. In 2006, she and her eldest sister moved to a hobby farm in the remote Kootenay area of British Columbia and for five years had several country adventures which included raising chickens and goats, encounters with wildlife and wrangling the neighbour's horses. Currently she lives in BC's Fraser Valley in a household of women spanning two generations of family with a collection of cats and a teacup Chihuahua affectionately known as Mexican Kitty.

Connect with Lora:
Website: http://loradeeprose.com/
Facebook: https://www.facebook.com/pages/Lora-Deeprose-Author/94913817417
Goodreads: https://www.goodreads.com/author/show/2895248.Lora_Deeprose

71533255R00227

Made in the USA
San Bernardino, CA
16 March 2018